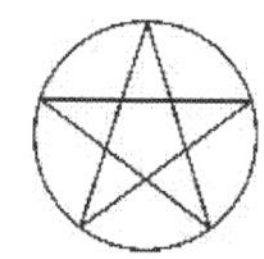

THE MISFIT MAGE AND HIS DARLING DEMON

MN Bennet

The Misfit Mage and His Darling Demon

Diabolic Romance Book Two

MN Bennet

Paperback ISBN: 979-8-9872532-9-8
Ebook ISBN: 979-8-9872532-8-1

Edited by Charlie Knight (CKnightWrites.com)
Cover art by Miblart (miblart.com)

www.mnbennet.com/

DEDICATION

To all the overthinkers of the world. I'm right there with you.

AUTHOR'S NOTE

Thank you so much for returning to read *The Misfit Mage and His Darling Demon*! I'm delighted to share more of Wally and Bez's journey in this wonderful world of magic. There's so much to enjoy about this Diabolic Romance, but I do want to offer a note on the content included in book two. If you've read book one, many of the warnings are similar. Lots of bad humor to love and steam to warm you up. That said, there are some elements I always prefer making readers aware of before diving into a book. For those interested, I've included a list of content warnings on the following page.

This book contains the following elements:

Foul language
Graphic violence and gore [descriptive]
Torture both mental and physical
Blood
Murder [some brutal]
There are several open door, descriptive sex scenes between adults
Depression and anxiety
Self-mutilation [magic based]
Cannibalism [magic based]

1

Walter

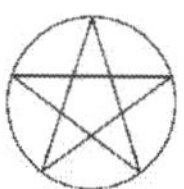

My entire body trembled in Bez's grasp, his chest pressed against mine, a hand firmly planted between my shoulder blades keeping me in place while his other hand rested delicately at the small of my back. I kept my thighs tightly wrapped around Bez's waist, my hands hooked at the joints of his wings. Even with my eyes squeezed shut, I could feel his smirk. It caused a tug in my own trembling cheeks.

Our minds, bodies, and emotions were very much our own, yet something primal coursed through us. The Diabolic essence he'd shared with me created this synchronized spark.

That said, whatever joy he had in this moment didn't pass to me. I gritted my teeth, annoyed and uncomfortable. He moved too quickly, too aggressively—I could barely catch my breath.

"Bez…" I gasped. "You need to slow down."

"Relax. I'm almost there." Bez slid his hand further down, then gripped my butt.

"Don't you dare get any ideas."

"What? I've always wanted to join the mile high club."

Bez flapped his wings rapidly. I opened my eyes, squinting from the furious wind carried between the two of us in the night sky as he soared faster, which helped add to the scowl I gave.

"Fine." He huffed. "Just want to get a firm grip on—what is it you mortals call it, a slice of pie?"

"The expression is cake," I said, feigning frustration because his touch did excite me. "You know this."

He'd referred to my ass as cake multiple times. Attempting to introduce Bez to social media in an effort to catch him up with the millions of things he'd missed out on when trapped inside the orb was a huge mistake on my part.

"Ah, yes. Cake." His red eyes glimmered. "Such a lovely cake you've got. I must ensure my dessert is properly secured."

With that, Bez took a sharp turn, zigging and zagging through the sky. The jostle churned my stomach a hundred different ways as he seemed to follow the street patterns below—completely unnecessary considering we flew high above even the tallest Chicago buildings.

"Here." Bez descended.

I craned my neck, taking in the bright city lights so luminescent it was as if night couldn't pierce the busy streets. High beams from oncoming traffic caused a glare in my glasses, and the sound of every car raddled in my head, a nauseating cacophony of blasting music, honking horns, and accelerating mufflers.

Bez hovered above, outpacing the flow of traffic on the highway leading deeper into the city. He hated noisy cities—even when dimming his senses, any venue with too many people made him irritable. Yet, the second he got home today, he demanded we leave the house for some impromptu outing to Chicago. If I'd known he was going to fly me all the way there, I would've protested harder.

Bez landed in an alleyway downtown. My legs wobbled as he released me, so I kept my hands on his shoulders until I found my bearings. He didn't allow me a chance to rest or catch my breath, though, pulling me out onto a less crowded street near some secluded restaurant.

I took in the elegant stonework of several buildings and the prominent turquoise clock of the historic Marshall Field.

"Whoa. How in the…" The drive from Galena to Chicago was three hours, yet according to the time, we'd gotten here in under thirty minutes. Still, I would've preferred flying on my own, broom in hand, saturated with my mana to maintain a gentle breeze and at an appropriate speed. Not Mach whatever matched a jetliner, forcing me to hold on for dear life. "What are we doing downtown?"

"We're here for a night on the town—something to celebrate."

I quirked an eyebrow. "Celebrate what?"

"Our anniversary, of course," Bez said plainly as if it should've registered.

Our what? No, no, no.

"Six months today."

This wasn't our anniversary. Not possible. I'd never forget the date, any date—*I'm incredibly good at remembering specific details*, one of the few skills I had going for me. Though, I'd been totally engrossed by work lately, doing my best to make the most out of my freelance gigs because as grateful as I was to have Bez in my life, as much as I wanted to walk away from the Collective, the policies, the hypocrisy, I very much missed the repository. Cataloging fenced artifacts didn't come close to the sophistication or resources of working in the archives of the Magus Estate, but it offered a routine which I needed for some semblance of normalcy.

My head pounded, thoughts spiraling through a hundred different things. I'd done what I always did. I'd allowed myself to become so fixated by work that time simply vanished. No. Not possible; our six-month anniversary was nineteen days away. I glanced at my phone, checking the date because there was no way I'd screwed this up. And if we were getting technical, it *was* nineteen days, five hours, and thirty-two minutes away.

"This…" I bit my lip. "I think you're, um, well, maybe…you're incorrect because—"

"Look at that frazzled little face trying to piece it all together." One of Bez's tails playfully tickled my chin as he strutted past me toward the neighboring restaurant. It was in an elegant building, so he must've made reservations. "This is not our dating anniversary, the one you so desperately needed to put a label on…"

I frowned. I wasn't desperate. I simply preferred precise clarification. Plus, it was nice knowing for certain that Bez was, in fact, my boyfriend. A term he claimed to find juvenile, yet the few times I'd introduced him as such, his breathing had hitched momentarily—a funny response considering Bez didn't require the "rudimentary functions of mortals" as he put it with biting snark.

"No, no. This is our real anniversary," Bez explained. "A far more important date to commemorate. It's the six-month marker to when we first coupled."

My jaw nearly dropped before I pulled my face into a smile. He'd counted the days and knew the exact six months that'd passed since we first coupled? My ears burned. *Coupled.* Made it sound almost endearing like love making, but I recalled it as a very carnal experience much like most of our sex. Still, there was a tender passion to it, as there'd been every time since, and that meant something to Bez. Meant enough to plan something special. A surprise.

"Aw, that's really sweet."

"Yes, the sound of your begging moans as I railed you again and again were quite *sweet*. Almost as delectable as the menu options here, I'm sure."

"And your lack of tact takes away all the charm to your actions."

"If you'd like to see my charming actions in action, we can—"

A passerby gasped, followed by a second, and then a third. I turned to find a half dozen people standing outside this restaurant staring wide-eyed at Bez.

"Shit." I pressed my hands together, channeling mana between my palms and releasing a glamour to wipe away the shock these people had observed.

I'd spent so much time with him that the Diabolic features tearing through his host body hardly registered at this point. When we were in mixed company, I had to ensure he blended.

In order to create a potent and successful glamour, I had to envision and believe the illusion I casted upon others. The four curled ram horns protruding from his head vanished, no longer ruffling his shaggy black hair—orange roots removed. He could love the tacky neon color all day long, but my glamour, my rules. I washed away the beautiful pink of his sclera and shifted the crimson of his irises to a vibrant green. I'd glamoured his eyes in every human color under the sun and a few others bordering outside the box but enjoyed the pop of Bez with emerald eyes best.

He pulled his wings and tails inward, tucking them inside his body and wrapped within his essence, while I delicately stitched the holes of the gray suit jacket and matching slacks. No glamour for the holes—gods, he'd ripped through so many good clothes, I had to finally master a slew of sewing incantations just to avoid his need to buy new suits every day.

Once I'd fixed his suit, wrinkles and all because he'd most likely whine if he had to go in looking unpresentable, I laced a trace of Diabolic haze around the glamour cast in the air. Smoke swelled above us like a storm cloud, spreading along the street in a thick fog. Crimson flashed within, adding to the reminiscent lightning effect, but the haze lacked the thunderous sound. Lacked all sensation in fact, except visual which only Bez and I could see.

A basic glamour itself would be enough to fool any human who looked at my dashing boyfriend, but with Bez's essence coursing inside me, I preferred balancing it with my Pentacles of Power so I could practice each. Truthfully, I only had a fraction—a very tiny fraction—of the effect Bez had with his own abilities, but the potential remained, and I sought to cultivate it.

"You know, you could've cloaked yourself and saved me the hassle of wiping their minds."

"I only do this so you can improve, Wally."

"Uh-huh."

He claimed it was to help me learn all the ins and outs of casting his borrowed essence, but I suspected Bez was too lazy to care. If it weren't for me, he'd leave an obvious trail of magic everywhere he went, tasking the Collective to clean up after his antics, but that'd mean they'd catch us. Which I didn't want. Ever. Another reason we typically avoided bigger cities with more prominent mage influences.

"Besides, you've got to get your casting cardio in"—Bez strolled close behind me, hand on my lower back as he guided me toward the door—"but not the mortal cardio. We'll find other exquisite ways to workout later. Thinking perhaps we replay a bit of what makes this an anniversary worth celebrating."

I rolled my eyes, perhaps playing a little hard to get. In truth, if Bez even suggested dragging me into the bathroom between courses, I wasn't sure I'd say no. He'd been gone the last two weeks, securing freelance work for me, and I admit I'd wanted to jump his bones the minute he walked through the door. Instead, he rushed me into getting ready for a surprise.

"Bez, this place is something. Something very nice." I grimaced, lingering by the street corner where the valet greeted others. It was more than nice. The ambiance exuded opulence in a way I hadn't experienced since attending family events.

Bez had planned this evening for me. I didn't want to burst his bubble, his efforts, his consideration, but…

"Not to complain because the gesture is great. It's just…why are we dining here? I mean, I love the surprise. Absolutely think it's, you know, sweet—please don't interrupt. I just don't understand why you wanted to surprise me here. In the city. Chicago. A major transient hub for the Collective. Which you know because we discussed it when taking on work in Galena"—a few hours from Chicago and outside major Collective influence—"which, by the way, has plenty of fancy restaurants that I've mentioned multiple times. Repeatedly. Some with really fascinating stories. One with a cool historical tour beforehand. Seems like that could be…hmm…more discreet?"

Bez stared, slowly blinking and smoldering. Gods. His lashes were so full and perfect, always accentuating his eyes no matter what color I gave them.

"And I know what you're going to say," I added before he could use some snarky wit to charm his way out of my concerns. "Who needs discretion when I have you subtly glamouring the details away?"

I lightly saturated mana to move in sync with my steps, surmounting the glamour around the street, allowing it to follow our path inside and wipe away any magical mishaps others might observe.

"But nothing this deep into Collective territory is subtle." I swatted away his tail. "Any sign, even someone sensing my spark of mana in the air, could reveal our presence."

Another reason I used Diabolic essence in tandem with my casting. Since Bez's magic couldn't be detected, it helped cloak mine.

"Well?"

"Sorry." Bez yawned, stretching his sharp jaw in the most exaggerated sense. "I assumed this would be one of your hour-long lectures rehashing precautions."

"I wouldn't rehash them if you took them seriously." Or listened. I knew he was tuning me out this very second.

"That tiny town you picked has much to admire, a lack of mages at the top of the list, but it doesn't have what I wish to offer. Something that'll whet your appetite." Bez looped his arm through mine, escorting us past the restaurant.

"Wait, where are we going? Don't you have reservations?"

"No. Why would you think that? I didn't bring you here to eat." Bez chuckled. "Doubt any dining experience could match my expertise in the kitchen."

I scrunched my face, hoping he didn't plan on cooking for me. Bez had many talents, but his taste in food wasn't one of them. My stomach churned, half anxious about where he was leading us, half remembering his kitchen concoctions, the most recent being a cookie dessert pizza topped with pickled peppers, sauteed mushrooms, and spicy cool whip.

"The last six months have been less than amazing. There have been fun times, it's been calm, but not nearly as many sights and adventures or travels as we intended upon when we took our leave from Seattle."

True. Bez wanted to show me the world, yet the Collective wanted to show us their reach and prove that no matter where we went, *justice* would find us.

"You deserve all the joy there is in unraveling the mysteries of the world. Instead, you've been working nonstop handling artifacts procured outside of mage hands. You've done wondrous work, helping decipher lost or arcane facts, rarities some never fathomed, cultivating loyal clients, yet that's all you've had time for—work."

Bez batted his long lashes, and I found myself lost in them and the softness of his voice. No sarcastic lull, only kind praise.

"I like working. I like routine," I said.

"Perhaps, but you put yourself through longer hours of laborious research now than when working in that awful repository. And as far as routine, we haven't even had that. These freelance gigs send me all over retrieving baubles; you spend as much time searching for a new place for us to maintain a low profile as you do meeting the absurd demands of clientele."

The demands weren't absurd. Some simply expected perfection, and considering what they paid and the relics they acquired, it wasn't a big ask. Plus, they were still less demanding than most of the archivist practitioners I'd worked for at the Magus Estate.

"In fact, you've been buried in that Fae artifact for weeks, when you should be experiencing it," Bez said.

"It's more of a Fae relic stolen by witches and modified into a tool that's now an ancient artifact I haven't quite figured out yet. The only thing I do know is, like most Fae items, it lacks even an ounce of their magic within."

"My point is, I promised adventures unlike any other. Promised to show you this whole world and hidden majesties you've never seen."

Golden lights spelling Chicago on an orange sign filled the entire street with luminous light. The Chicago Theatre. Its letters twinkled above the billboard displaying a performance by Regular Rhapsody.

"What are you planning?" I asked, curious and perplexed.

"A performance unlike any other." Bez withdrew a pair of tickets from his blazer and ushered us inside. "Prepare to witness a show you'll never forget. One of the greatest mysteries the Mythic world has to offer."

"At a Regular Rhapsody concert? I'm honored, I guess." I half smiled, biting back a giggle. "Not the celebration I anticipated but certainly a surprise all the same."

"You're mocking Regular Rhapsody?" Bez tsked. "Their velvety melody is obviously above the caliber of your simple mortal ears."

Oops. I'd best keep my mouth shut.

Music. One of the few mortal things Bez adored beyond reproach. The range of voices, the unique melodies of every instrument, and the combinations they all created. He enjoyed all music from classical and pop to rock, country, rap, all the way to the oldies—it didn't matter. But he had a major soft spot for Regular Rhapsody, a band that mixed orchestra with techno and had lyrics somewhere between screamo metal and bubbly pop. It seemed Bez's ears had the same eclectic tastes for music as his tongue did for food. He'd discovered this band two months ago and played their music on a loop, insisting I'd learn to love their bizarre combination. I hadn't.

I frowned. I bet that was why he encouraged my choice in moving to Galena. There were certainly other places. How long had he been planning this special date night? One that also served his interests.

"They're merely the opening act."

"Huh?"

Bez ignored my question, escorting us through the lobby. Before I could attempt asking for clarification, he swatted at people in our path with his tails and left me busy glamouring away the incident. No posted signs indicated another performer tonight, and I didn't see any hidden glyphs revealing the band had connections to magic; there were plenty of mages and Mythics who used their abilities to acquire celebrity status.

Inside the theater, a sea of red filled the huge auditorium where thousands took their seats, and Bez led us to our row close to the stage and centered in the crowd. I focused on my glamour, ensuring none of his features were glimpsed, then felt the lightest tug of his essence.

He'd buried my mana beneath his Diabolic haze, obscuring himself so I wouldn't have to cast during this concert. Kind of sweet. Not sure how much I wanted to see Regular Rhapsody, but I found myself curious about how this tied to a Mythic performance unlike any other.

I tried listening to the introduction as the curtain rose, the kind words to the packed audience, and even the lyrics of the opening song. However, I found myself lost in Bez's smile as he hummed along. He'd planned this evening to celebrate us, our relationship, and offer me a special night to remember, but I'd probably only carry the happiness this date brought him.

"Pay attention, Wally." Bez nodded to the stage as a pink mist seeped around the band.

A woman entered the stage. Her magenta skin stood out against the soft, bubblegum pink magical vapors trailing ahead of her. A silver crown sat atop her head, and her ears were elongated like a rabbit's, covered in feathers as vibrant as a peacock's.

She crouched, taking long, flowing steps with a dancer's grace. The lightest movement of her arms caused a ripple in the smoke like she moved through water. I studied each sway of her body, eyes wide and unblinking, yet she flickered in and out like a glitch on a screen. A rainbow of colors streamed off her hands, carrying the band's music and vocals higher and further and louder. The array of colors took on musical notes. A violet breve, a green minim, a flurry of indigo semibreve, then a single yellow quaver dancing from behind.

"What's going on?" I asked, a note twinkling close enough to touch.

"Fae Divinity."

My heart raced. I squeezed Bez's hand, he had it open like he'd prepared for my shock and waited. That explained it. Fae almost never revealed themselves. When they did, they beguiled everyone who laid eyes upon them in this world.

"How did you know about Fae Divinity? This is unreal. Impossible. No one knows what venue they'll choose. Not even the highest-ranked members of the Collective are privy to such secrets. And it's only—"

"Once a century, the Fae will pick a place to join in a performance, revealing themselves to mortals while putting on a show unlike any other." Bez rubbed his thumb against my tense palm. "I do, occasionally, listen when you ramble."

"But how—"

Musical notes popped across the theater, exploding with chaotic melodies which held the most harmonious sounds. Echoing screams, enchanting whispers, effervescent lullabies. And like that, the audience was enthralled. The true performance would now begin.

"You're not the only one capable of researching things for work, Wally." He winked, washing away the glamour of green and allowing his lovely crimson eyes to fully radiate. It wasn't as if anyone in the audience would notice now. Their awareness had shifted toward the magics of Fae, locked and lost in this event.

Bez had found a once-in-a-lifetime experience almost nobody ever witnessed and surprised me with it. Me. Walter talks-too-much Alden, misfit mage and a disgraced legacy

2

Beelzebub

Wally's entire face beamed, captivated by the beginning of the Fae interlude meant to entrance patrons as they witnessed their performance alongside the mortals in Regular Rhapsody. Wally leaned close, resting his head against my shoulder, eyes still watching the stage in awe. I breathed in the scent of the fruity shampoo he used on his curly, blond hair. It mixed with the delight oozing from his pores.

"Fae Divinity is the rarest of rare events," he said, hazel eyes refusing to blink because he had to view it all, know it all, experience it all. "They perform for the audience of unaware spectators, reveal mysteries of their realms—but supposedly different things to each person in attendance, sort of like a private show within the show that's already wrapped inside another show—and this causes those who experience it a subliminal memory of inspiration."

Wally yammered on about the Fae as if I had no knowledge on the topic, despite being the one who orchestrated our date night. With a bit of help from Mora, naturally. It was thanks to her extensive connections that Wally and I found such lucrative freelance work. When she approached me on the importance of celebrating anniversaries, she *claimed* this was the event of the century, one Wally would adore well into the next century. Yet I didn't see her clamoring to snag a pair for herself and Kell when procuring me these terrible seats.

I stared at the private balcony seating above as Wally continued his incessant rambling about theories behind the gyrating movements of the pink Fae he called dancing. It seemed the mortals had a better skill with it than these fairies.

I sighed.

Nothing about this event seemed all that fascinating. Truthfully, the so-called concord of the added Fae frequencies took away from the true instrumental harmony of Regular Rhapsody. Quite a disappointment. Clearly, when Mora praised the unique appeal, she must've meant for mortal spectators. At least Wally enjoyed himself.

"You see, they sow these seeds into audience members, then send them off to accomplish all sorts of amazing things," Wally continued, an excited tremble in his voice. "Big and small. It's like a ricochet of inspiring events because, again supposedly, those seeds of inspiration can spread to others who didn't see it, leaving them yearning to find their passions, and in turn passing that desire onto those they meet."

"So, it's like a disease?" I smirked.

"No. It's good." Wally's lips tightened into an unwanted grimace before a smile fully set in again—he couldn't be bothered during such a spectacle of the lone pink Fae dancing and singing and beguiling all. "Some people go on to become performers, too, others healers, artisans, philanthropists, protectors, or simply kinder people. It fuels their desires, which in turn, the Fae supposedly absorb and strengthen their magic off the sparks of fulfillment they've conjured. No one knows for sure—though, I did a thesis and have quite a few theories—but the enthrallment hits every single person in the audience and—"

"I am aware."

"Of course. Sorry." Wally's eyes almost flitted in my direction, yet he remained attached to the incoming Fae frolicking onto the stage, accompanying the first. They moved with the gentle finesse of ballerinas while another floated close to the rafters reciting sonnets of dead poets and mixing languages both known and unheard in this world.

I did find the appearance of the Fae strutting about the stage intriguing, each resembling a mortal form more dominantly than anything else, not what I'd anticipated. Many Mythic had mortal-esque features, bipedal in nature, some more animalistic and quadrupeds. Yet I'd always heard the Fae had a range of aesthetics almost as diverse as Diabolics, so perhaps they augmented their features to blend for whatever reason.

"It's a shame I'll forget this," Wally whispered. "I mean, I could take notes—but I suppose someone else would've thought of that, too. After all, it was the Fae who introduced glamouring to mages during the accords several millennia ago. They're quite secretive. More secretive than the Collective…"

Damn, he was going to explain the entire history of the Fae instead of simply enjoying the performance. I huffed, releasing my own resentment to make room for his joy. For Wally, discussing every aspect was part of the fun he'd have when recalling this memory. And he would recall it.

"You won't forget a thing," I said.

He snickered. "I wish."

"Walter, the Fae have power which compels all things of this world from the mortals to the Mythics, to the arcane magics and mysteries of nature."

"That's what I was saying. Weren't you listening?"

"I was." I moved in close to his neck, nuzzling the back of his ear with my nose and tickling his skin with soft breaths. "As I said, the Fae control all that comes from this world, not that which dwells in it. Their sway holds no bounds over the Diabolic."

"And since I have your essence…" He practically squealed. "That means I'll remember this."

"Just another benefit of having me inside you." I blew a kiss.

He rolled his eyes, playing hard to get poorly because as his eyes went back to the stage, his hand landed on my leg, quickly drifting up my thigh and resting there.

"No one remembers their encounters with the Fae. Even mere glimpses are wiped from one's mind. I should document it. No. Maybe. No one else has. Although that might draw their ire, and we already have the Collective breathing down our necks. That could be part of why there aren't documented encounters with the Fae. Well, none with their physical presence. Always with their relics, carrying a message they wish to share. I wouldn't want to anger the Fae, but what if others wanted to know about this? There could be some curious mage working on research who'd benefit."

"Maybe you should address all these questions after the performance." I kissed his cheek tenderly with reeled-back affection. I wanted to pull him in close and kiss his lips with fiery intensity, especially after two weeks away, procuring artifacts for his clients and running extra errands for Mora while she figured out where and when the damned Fae would appear.

I stifled my desires, though, because I wouldn't take away from this moment. After all, I was irresistible, and poor Wally would find himself so enamored by pleasing me, he'd miss the entirety of this simple show.

I wasn't certain why he or anyone else found the Fae so intriguing. They were simply secretive Mythics with a higher tier of magic that allowed them control over dimensions and to create meager temporal folds in reality. Basically, knockoff Diabolics—equally as murderous, from what I recalled.

"Look. He's handing out seeds of passion to everyone." Wally's legs bounced as he watched a violet-skinned Fae hovering through the audience. His butterfly wings fluttered, sprinkling glitter, while he carefully placed a shimmering seed atop the heads of each person he flew past. Their euphoric haze remained, and magic washed over them, radiating, then seeping into their skin.

"You never get this excited when I give you my seed—and I do so with far more passion than this fairy."

"This is sacred, ceremonial," he whispered, ears burning bright red. "Don't make it dirty."

"Ah," I said, leaning in close enough to graze my teeth along his earlobe. "Perhaps you're reminiscing your enthusiasm for my seed, after all."

"Shush. He's approaching. No funny business."

"But of course."

I averted my gaze when the Fae arrived; he floated before us, extending his golden-taloned hand and revealing a glowing green seed. Wally scooched closer, eyes wide and a smile filling his entire beautiful face. How he must've wondered what passion this seed would offer. I only hoped it didn't add to his already-driven compulsion for research. Gods, he had enough motivation and fulfillment there.

The violet Fae lingered, trepidation in his creased brow. He closed his hand, clutching it and the seed close to his chest, then flew away.

"Oh, no." Wally sighed. "Did I…did I do something wrong?"

Despair consumed him as he sank into his seat, casting his eyes downward as if he no longer saw himself worthy of witnessing the sparkle of the Fae performance.

"Get your glittering ass back over here and give us our stupid seeds of inspiration," I growled, "or so help me, you fairy fuck, I'll rip those wings off and stuff them so far down your throat you'll be—"

"Bez, stop. You'll cause a scene." Wally pressed his hand against my chest, his pulse thrumming almost as rapidly as my enraged heart.

"I'll cause a lot more if that tiny-pricked bastard doesn't get back here." I stood, adjusting my rolled sleeves, fully intent on plucking out a Fae's still-beating heart.

Several of the dawdling dancers froze on the stage. Music continued as one feathered Fae hummed in the band's ears, casting more waves of rainbow-hued notes into the air. I was a few seconds away from unleashing black flames to burn down this entire theater.

"It's okay." Wally squeezed my arm. "I'm honored just to be here, to hold onto this memory. I don't need inspiration or passion. I get both from you. Don't, you know, kill anyone."

"I'd never." I allowed his grip to pull me back into the seat. "Simply wished to have a word with them is all."

The rhythm of instruments slowed, softening. All Fae halted their movements, stiff but not frozen. Their gaze, no matter where they stood or hovered, peered upward toward a single balcony seat where a low chime rang. Glitter carried static through the auditorium, mixed with a screech. Bubbles blossomed, each exploding and releasing a foul note.

"This must be the Fae dialect," Wally said. "Their actual voice. It's beautiful."

It was ugly, a noise reminiscent of the beeping screeches Wally's lap computer would make when it turned a sickly blue and died merely at my *attempt* to use it.

A snow-white hand waved from the balcony. Gaudy, golden rings covered the long, slender fingers of this individual's hand, their arm covered in the sleeve of a fine red coat. Whoever sat there hidden away kept captive attention from the performers with that simple gesture.

The pink Fae who began the performance skipped along the air like she bounced from hidden clouds beneath her bare feet. Retrieving a seed from the Fae who'd denied Wally, she made her way toward us, dropping the glowing green seeds before turning on her heel and fluttering back to the stage.

The seed stopped short of landing, floating before my entranced mage as he watched tiny roots crack the shell, preparing to offer inspiration.

The roots of mine reached out, whispering high-pitched Fae tunes, and I snatched the seed with black and crimson tendrils, devouring it beneath my essence. All the magics carried inside the seed decayed to nothingness. I didn't desire inspiration, so I repurposed the power into fuel.

A snap of fingers boomed throughout the auditorium, and the snow-white hand retreated as the musical notes of the performance continued.

"Absolutely stunning." Wally didn't sit awestruck for long, though.

He traced tiny sigils of intricate incantations around the growing seed which sought to attach itself to him. Protective wards sprang to life, taking the shape of a cube no bigger than a six-sided die, and locked the seed inside.

"Stealing?" I tsked, shaking my head as disapprovingly as I could muster without breaking out into laughter. "Shame on you."

"I'm not stealing," he whispered, tucking the warded seed in his jacket pocket. "You can't expect me to pass on the opportunity to study unfiltered Fae magics."

"For shame, Walter," I teased. "I don't expect to hear you call out my so-called thievery after this."

"This isn't stealing, Bez. They gave me the seed for inspiration," he said, determined to justify himself. "I simply believe I'll find it more inspiring to study than to have it course through me."

"I wouldn't want anything other than me inside you anyway." I winked.

Wally blushed, returning his attention to the ongoing performance.

I continued enduring the banal show of Fae trying too hard to shoehorn in the unique styles of a dozen different Mythic arts, watering them down for mortal eyes, and butchering classical wonders with off-key melodies. All the while, Wally remained captivated. His hand bounced on my thigh, not in a desiring sense, but one craving to scribble notes. I could assuredly discern the gears of his mind whirled with a thousand different tests he'd planned on using in his study of Fae magic. Of course, this would all come after he'd properly preserved the seed, keeping the energy intact.

Without his repository, he lacked the true foundations to complete tasks as he once did. Perhaps that should be something I strive to obtain for him, yet it'd only become a hassle moving such an assortment of tools every couple of months. Hopefully, he'd remain content even if I couldn't offer him everything like I'd so boldly professed when dragging him from Seattle.

I remained lost in his lovely eyes until the performance ended. As the final bows set in, Fae vanished from the stage, and the audience returned to themselves, applauding for the illusion weaved into their memories, but none clapped as hard as Wally, who rose to his feet, unknowingly inviting others into an undeserved standing ovation.

Wally could barely contain himself as we exited, snorting at the mortals making sense of the lost time, those dazed by the inspiration that'd hit them come morning, and the subtle waves of glittering Fae hands as they veiled themselves behind the fabric of this realm.

"This was the most amazing night ever." He strutted beside me, arm wrapped around my waist, squeezing and holding me close. "So what's next?"

"Next?" I asked, lingering by the exit, indulging in the soft movement of fingers which lightly strummed, tugging at the fabric of my shirt tucked into my slacks. "What more could this city possibly have to offer you?"

"No dinner plans, nightcap somewhere, sightseeing perhaps?"

"Have you not had your fill of excitement, my love?

He let out an exasperated sigh. "Suppose you're right. Not sure anything could top that." He smiled, hand sliding until he gripped the front of my belt and pulled me toward an unoccupied wall neighboring the front doors. "Well, almost nothing."

Stepping in close, my chest warmed, heat spreading throughout my body as Wally trailed his knuckles under my shirt, running them along my abdomen.

"We should probably get home," he whispered. "I'd like to show you how much I appreciate just how thoughtful you can be."

"Why wait until we get home?" I leaned in, kissing Wally.

His sweet lips tasted of strawberries, always the most delicious fruity flavors from his lip balms. I kept myself reserved during the performance, but now I wished for nothing more than to have him, hold him, unleash all my pent-up desire. The kiss, which began gentle, turned assertive, biting, all-consuming.

Wally rubbed my sides, running his hands up to my ribcage, then hesitated. They initially went to my back, prepared to reel me in closer. His leg had lifted, thigh rubbing against mine. But he stopped himself, stopped me by shifting his hands to my front, pushing away just enough to separate our lips.

"PDA, Bez." He nodded to mortal bystanders gawking, clearly jealous.

"No worries, my shy beauty. Not a soul will see or hear the pleasures I intend to elicit from you." I unveiled my wings, releasing a gust of black wind carrying a fast-acting haze to completely cloak our presence. "Shall we continue?"

"Bez. I'm not letting you fuck me against the wall of a crowded lobby." Wally giggled, grabbing my hand and pulling us toward the exit.

"Prude."

"Watch it." He tightened his grip, interlocking his fingers between mine. "As flattering as a Diabolic haze in The Chicago Theatre is, I was thinking something a bit more secluded."

I wanted him now, but I'd respect his need for privacy. "I'll have us home in fifteen."

"I hope not." He rested his head on my shoulder, his tongue teasing my ear and warm breath sending a quiver down my spine. "I wanted to revisit your proposition on the mile-high club. Not sure I could handle joining the club if you went *too* fast."

"Are you screwing with me?"

"Never." He kissed my neck. "Well, there will be screwing, but I was hoping you'd be the one doing it."

I placed my hand on the small of his back and guided him to the door where it'd take everything not to mount him the second the crisp air of the night hit.

A collection of pink butterflies materialized at the entryway of the door, forming the pink Fae who'd led the performance and delivered our trivial seeds of inspiration. Her stance appeared playful, her smile sincere, but her eyes were wide and locked onto Wally.

I stepped ahead of him, flexing my muscles and nearly tearing the cheap fabric of this suit—I wasn't sure how much longer this host body would hold all my glory.

"What do you want, fairy?" I clamped my jaw.

"Walter Alden, the mage wanted by the Collective, attending our performance," she said with a dismissive shake of her head. "This evening, you were gifted inspiration, coveted magic kept secret, and somehow managed to walk away with it almost entirely unnoticed. The baron wishes for an accounting of these observations."

"Your baron can go fuck himself." Coating my hand in essence, I manifested outstretched black claws and lunged forward, prepared to gut her.

She vanished.

In the seconds it took to plant my arm where her heart should've been, a flurry of butterflies fluttered in her place, reappearing behind Wally.

"The baron only wishes for words with the mage." She snapped her fingers, and Wally exploded into a million silvery specks of glitter, each fading to nothingness before a single fleck hit the floor.

In an instant, this Fae had abducted Wally.

I roared, furiously flapping my wings as the pink Fae transformed into her gathering of butterflies. Summoning a massive whirlwind, I whipped about all the feeble mortals in this lobby, focusing the wind on pulling these colorful insects into my grasp.

She'd either rematerialize, or I'd spend the night ripping the wings off each and every one of her tiny bug decoys until she returned my mage.

Snatching one of the butterflies, it crumpled like an autumn leaf in my hand, burning with pink fire and leaving only embers in my palm. Every single butterfly followed suit, leaving a pink inferno swirling around the wind I'd conjured.

I dropped to my knees, tightening the tether connecting me to Wally and feeling only the faintest snag of his presence.

No. I had to find him

3

Walter

I took my glasses off, brushing the glitter off the lenses only to smudge them since, of course, the glitter had faded on its own. It'd been months since I'd teleported through Fae magic, but I recalled the sensation quite well. So much so my breathing hitched when memories of time spent tucked inside the Dimensional Atrium exploring before returning to long hours hidden inside the repository of the Magus Estate.

I shook away the memories. No time. I'd been taken somewhere by the pink Fae who appeared from a swarm of butterflies. An actual kaleidoscope of butterflies, which would be fascinating to study. Did she tame the insects through something similar to a familiar bond like mages? Were they mere puppets conjured through Fae resurrection and repurpose of nature? Or were the butterflies simply an illusion meant to hide or distract from her actual teleportation movements?

"Stop," I said. "You need to figure out where you are."

I took a deep, quieting breath. Where had I ended up?

"Ah!" I shouted. I was floating above the empty auditorium and nearly plummeted to the ground when I fell back.

Ow.

No. Not nearly. Not at all. My butt thudded against something hard, and my hands remained flat on a surface level holding me upright. I tapped my knuckles, knocking on the invisible flooring.

At least the Fae hadn't taken me far. I could hear Bez roaring beyond the auditorium, yet he felt so distant.

Scrambling to my feet, I swallowed my anxiety and rushed across the unseen floor. "I'm not going to fall. I'm not going to fall. I'm not going to fall."

The chant did little to assuage the growing fear I would suddenly come across an invisible hole in the invisible floor and fall from a very visible height. Knowing my luck, I would flail about, worried I'd break a bone, and land squarely on my head.

Ow.

I backstepped, rubbing a hand on my bruised face. Dammit. I hit a wall halfway toward the theater exits. Invisible like the floor. It seemed I'd been teleported into a box of some type. Or a cube. Gods. Was this some type of ironic justice because I'd stolen the Fae seed, encasing it in an enchanted cube of protective incantations? Well, not *stolen* stolen. They'd freely given me the seed and never once explained its purpose. It was mere happenstance that I knew the actual intent. They couldn't really expect to hold me accountable for something they had no idea whether or not I knew was actually wrong.

It wasn't wrong. It wasn't stealing. That was just Bez teasing me.

I fidgeted. Bez. He continued roaring outside, followed by explosive sounds and loud clanks as the building shook.

I reached into my pocket, retrieving the Fae seed. The green hue held such an inviting allure meant for study. So many secrets. So many unknown answers. Unknown questions, too. There were things I likely hadn't even pondered to ask myself about the mystery of the Fae until this very moment. I wanted to know it all. But more than that, I wanted to reach Bez.

"I'm sorry for the misunderstanding," I said. "I didn't realize I wasn't allowed a souvenir. I'm just a simple guy who doesn't know things. Any things. Anything really."

"You are far from simple, Walter Alden," a deep voice said, carrying a light echo.

Appearing at the opposite end of the theater sat a ghostly complected Fae wearing a bright red suit, which added to his stark white skin. Golden rings clinked against the railing of the balcony where he sat, strumming his elongated fingers. His bright white teeth held a shine in the dim theater as his smile widened, filling his entire face. Quite literally. His mouth stretched ear to ear. I tensed when he tilted his large head, one more than twice the size of his thin shoulders, studying me.

"I have to go," I said, fighting back a squeak but unable to keep from shivering.

Huge black eyes, bigger than my clenched fists, stared at me. Through me. Into me. White swirled hypnotically, then zigged and zagged like a game of Snake.

I held out my trembling hands, extending the encased seed to return. *Shit.* I should've removed the enchantment before offering it back. Not that the Fae didn't already realize what I'd done.

"The Fae Divinity is an exquisite event held only once a century in this realm," he said, hopping off the balcony and onto the invisible floor. Each step he took cast a ripple, revealing the fine hardwood floors holding us in the air. "It is a rare honor to host this event, one I treated with cavalier disregard as I've held the honor of hosting a half-dozen times."

Everything quieted.

I turned, searching for the raging roars of Bez, but found the auditorium faded beneath us, replaced by the wooden floor. The theater walls vanished behind stone-crafted walls. This place resembled the foyer of the Magus Estate more and more with each breath. It wasn't, though. The rocks used held more glimmer, seeped with magics perhaps, but much of the estate had been fashioned to be considered inviting to the Fae since so much of Collective resources and power stemmed from cultivating a strong relationship with the Fae.

A panoply, a full suit of silver plate armor, stood perched on its own next to the door without a stand to keep it upright. The chest piece had a noticeable dent. It looked out of place with no second suit on the opposite side. I shook my head. This was no time to note the poor placement in décor when I should be finding a way out of here.

I raced to the door, reaching for the handle. Locked. Duh. Maybe an incantation could force it open. Not sure what would be appropriate since everything here had a strange hum to the deeper layers of magic; everything felt off, warped slightly. Even my connection with Bez strained.

"Consider me shocked when I discovered Walter Alden was in attendance." The Fae stood inches from my face, his mouth ready to devour my head in a single bite.

I fell back onto the floor, dropping the seed and clambering to distance myself from him.

He knelt and retrieved the encased seed. His nails punctured my incantations, disrupting and destroying the protective wards instantaneously.

"It's no wonder you made such a delightfully intricate incantation to hold our gift to the mortals." He blinked, but only a thin translucent eyelid coated his giant black orbs. A nictitating membrane like some animals have.

"Like dogs and penguins and camels and…" I bit my lip, stifling the mutterings.

"You seem frightened. Nothing like the Walter Alden discussed at Court."

"You know me?" I gulped.

"Who hasn't heard of the warrior Walter Alden, the mage who tamed the devil Beelzebub himself? Tempered the Diabolic's murderous spirit and spared the Collective."

"Excuse me?"

"Had I known such an esteemed guest would greet our modest affair, I'd have put true effort into this evening's performance. Instead, I offered baubles unworthy of someone such as your station." He shattered the seed between his fingers, waving the wafting magical energy away.

"Wait… You're not mad at me?"

"What?" He gripped his blazer, feigning offense. Or perhaps actually offended I made the suggestion. His expressions were difficult to gauge. "I am honored to meet your acquaintance."

"Sorry. What?" I tried to wrap my head around what he'd said.

He extended a hand, offering to assist. I forced a smile and accepted, nervous I'd offend otherwise.

The Fae stepped back, straightening his blazer. "Apologies. I was so lost in awe, I didn't properly introduce myself. I am Baron Novus—" His tongue clicked, and a sharp ringing hit my ears, making me cringe before he cleared his throat. "Hmm, I'm unable to find the mortal sound which translates. Simply Novus will do."

"Nice to meet you, Baron Novus." I lowered my tense shoulders. "I'm simply Wally."

"To think a devil and one so feared came to my Fae Divinity. It'll be the talk at Court."

"Bez isn't as frightening as people think," I said, wondering how many Fae he'd slaughtered searching for me and if he'd kill

Baron Novus for this misunderstanding. "They just don't know him. Speaking of not knowing Bez, it'd probably be a good idea if we—"

"Not him," Baron Novus interjected, flicking one of his long fingers back and forth. "You, Walter Alden, the misfit mage who brought a city to the precipice of defeat and then abandoned them to their own devices, leaving them frightened of recourse. Of your might. Your control. Your Diabolic pet."

"I'm sorry, what?" I raised my eyebrows.

"The entire Court has watched with curiosity. Mages scrambling with uncertainties on how to handle you. Calculating unknown quantities of the carnage or kindness you will unleash based solely upon your whims. Will disturbing you lead to their downfall? Will leaving you untended allow you to amass an army to lay siege upon the Collective? Will the Mythics hear the rallying cry after you emptied Collective coffers? All questions many chancellors and magi have behind closed doors."

So much of what happened—from Ian's intentions and my mother's plot to Bez's assault on the Collective, all the way to my attempt at undoing it all—had spiraled into a messy web of half-truths, rumors, misconceptions, and apparently flat-out fallacies.

I figured the Collective was wary of us. Not us. Bez. Worried what his ire would bring down on them if they searched too fervently. But I never suspected they avoided us outright. Here I spent the last six months frightened, terrified one misstep would expose us, lecturing Bez on reeling in his antics and dodging anything and everything that might lead the Collective our way.

"Your incantations are truly marvelous, by the way," Baron Novus said. "Elegant and layered with such sophistication."

"Uh, thank you." I shrugged. "I studied a lot."

"The craftsmanship, prodigy level."

"No, not even." My ears burned.

"I must ask, how did you know the precise incantation to encase Fae magic without crumpling the raw Mythic residue in the process?" He stepped in close again, his huge eyes staring down at me.

"I-I-I, well, you see, I'm flustered." I bit my lip. I didn't mean to say that.

"Why? Have I done something?"

"No. Not at all. Absolutely not. It's a lot to take in. You grabbing me, Bez is probably worried—in fact, I'm worried about the other Fae alone with Bez—and then there's all these nice compliments…but I just need a minute to collect my thoughts. And check on Bez. And again, your Fae." I swallowed the lump in my throat. I hoped they weren't all dead.

"Oh, everyone's fine. Mitah informs me Beelzebub's tantrum has been contained within the empty halls of The Chicago Theatre. I suppose we'll have to reimburse them, but he has slain no Fae, all safely tucked behind a veil, and it seems all our mortal guests left frightened but unharmed. I'm certain the Collective will clean up any traces that leak out into the world."

"Okay. That doesn't change my concern for Bez. We're…" I didn't want to say connected, which he probably knew already—who didn't? Still, our bond had a wonky faded sensation here in this weird Fae-adjacent plane, and I couldn't fathom how Bez felt.

"I completely understand. You worry for your paramour." Baron Novus snapped his fingers, and the room swirled round and round until black fire filled my vision.

He'd definitely understated Bez's reaction. The entire auditorium was engulfed in flames. Seats were either burning or torn to shreds. The floorboards of the stage had been ripped apart.

Dread struck me. My concern for Bez mixed with his anxiety about my absence. Even so, I pressed a hand to my heart, comforted by the fully bloomed connection of our bond no longer disrupted by Fae temporal magics.

"Now, if you please, I do so wish to continue our conversation," Baron Novus said, unfazed by the destruction surrounding us.

"I need to find—"

Bez. He appeared in front of me in an instant, his blurry form taking shape as his speed came to a halt.

"Wally! You're safe." He grabbed my arms, his sharp claws gently squeezing me.

"Yeah, this is one huge misunderstanding. A colossal level of social confusion… I'm fumbling for words, but I'm safe."

"At a loss for words?" Bez furrowed his brow. "Hardly sounds safe to me."

"Just in shock." I eyed the devastation. "Big reaction."

"No reaction is big enough for your absence." Bez craned his neck, glaring at Baron Novus. "And you must be the one who sought to steal from me."

"I'm not a possession, Bez."

"I didn't say that."

"You kind of did."

Bez snarled, dragging his claws along the backs of burning seats. Those same claws which held me so tenderly shredded the metal backs. He lunged forward, swiping at Baron Novus.

"Wait," I shouted, no command in my voice but a plea for his patience.

After six months of living with Bez's essence circulating inside me, I'd learned enough not to accidentally invoke commands upon him. It was something I'd never do, but I didn't want him to slaughter the Fae over some confusion on appropriate customs.

Baron Novus vanished into thin air.

"I have exhibited the utmost patience, Walter," Baron Novus said from above us. "I didn't disturb you during the performance, allowing you to enjoy our modest show, and I've given leniency for your untampered Diabolic, but I now wish to continue our conversation."

"I'm going to fucking gut you," Bez shouted, flying into the air.

His swipe missed a second time, and Baron Novus appeared on the stage now.

Bez cursed, zipping toward him in a blur.

I channeled essence, stirring it through my body and mixing it with my mana. Not nearly enough to keep up with Bez or hold my own against him, but hopefully enough to make a point. I raced after him, putting everything I had into each blurred step. My body moved so quickly, my eyes couldn't keep up with it.

"Stop." I reached out, snatching Bez by the wrist and averting his claws from stabbing…well, the air because Baron Novus had vanished yet again. "Please, Bez. Relax."

"I can't. You were gone. In danger. These fucking fairies abducted you. Took you from me, and there wasn't anything I could do." His eyes watered until the crimson of his irises burned bright, and rage replaced the sadness in his gaze.

I pressed my forehead against his. "I'm fine. Honestly."

"You are now." One of Bez's tails coiled around my waist and pulled me closer. "I still have to kill them. The audacity—"

"Audacity?" Baron Novus snorted. "I am a Royale of the Fae Court. Your audacious threats would be met with a swift end should your bluster be anything more than a tantrum."

"We've talked about this." I pressed a hand to Bez's fast-beating heart, attempting and failing to soothe him. If he didn't stop, he risked the Fae Court descending upon us. "Killing can't be the first option every single time."

"You were abducted. It is the only option."

"Again, a mis—"

"I'd hardly call it an abduction," Baron Novus chimed in with the absolute worst timing. "If I sought to abduct Walter, I'd have taken him to a Fae realm, not a simple pocket portal for quiet discussion."

"And what is it you wished to discuss with Walter?" Bez bared his teeth.

"My intent was to understand how he created such a precise incantation for the gifted seed," Baron Novus said. "Though I must admit, I became a bit enamored being in the presence of one so grand."

"Enamored?" The word held disgust falling off Bez's tongue.

"Walter, please explain your process."

"Process?" I asked. "For the incantations. I-I don't know. It's sort of second nature, I guess. I'm used to identifying the specific hums of magical frequencies in a variety of different Mythic artifacts from when I worked in the repository."

Though, back then, I required a wand to place incantations, it was only thanks to Bez I finally learned how to stop overthinking every single step.

"Yes, but Fae frequencies tend to shift seamlessly, making our magic difficult to pinpoint and intangible for those brazen enough to try."

"Oh, well, you see, I used to study what I could in the Dimensional Atrium," I said, biting back the urge to explain how it was a gifted region for mage use from the Fae since, as a Fae and member of their Court, he probably already knew that much. "I even wrote reports on how the frequencies never quite matched the hum of relics gifted from Fae, which also rarely held Mythic residue. I suppose they did, but never anything stemming from Fae magics, so they were impossible to analyze. And technically speaking, we weren't supposed to analyze anything in the Atrium either, but it was mostly harmless musings."

Baron Novus clapped his hands, the smile filling his face returned. "Remarkable. To think a mage would hold such in-depth comprehension of our magics after seeing only a single layer of it. I am rarely astounded, but consider me charmed."

"If you want his fucking autograph, next time, just ask." Bez snarled. "Your curiosity has been sated, now begone before my little mage's pleas for mercy fade, and I rip off your oversized, empty head."

"I myself have only encountered Diabolics and their leash holders on select occasions," Baron Novus said. "But I was always under the impression that those with bound Diabolics kept a tighter hold on their behavior. You must be truly formidable, Walter, to allow your devil such slack."

I waved my hands back and forth, straining to grin and feeling my blood boil from the offense Bez took from the comment. As he should. Baron Novus might've meant well with his honesty, but the blunt tactlessness of it was going to get him murdered. "He's not on a leash."

"Yes. If one of us were to don a leash in this relationship, it'd certainly be *my* Walter."

My face scrunched as the smirk on Bez's face, and the snark in his voice left me frazzled.

"Hmm. Mortal mating practices, I presume." Baron Novus withdrew a card from his breast pocket and blew a breath carrying a cacophony of echoing whispers.

Releasing it from his fingertips, the card whirled, dancing delicately on a breeze as soft words continued murmuring, all the while golden letters became engraved upon the card. It landed at my feet, written in Sylvan symbols—the Fae language—that burned brightly on the vanilla card.

"I've heard you take on freelance work and wished to extend an offer to a potential career opportunity."

I picked up the card. Though the letters seemed aflame, the card was icy to the touch. "Really? What kind of work?"

"It would require extensive hours, remote opportunities," Baron Novus said. "But some of my possessions would not be suitable for travel, so you'd need to work here."

"In The Chicago Theatre?" I asked.

Baron Novus' wide mouth formed a thin smile, made exceptionally thin by his lack of lips. "No, no."

He flicked his wrist, wiggling his elongated fingers with whimsy. Golden rings clinked together, and glitter funneled from his palm, directed by the melody of seemingly random noises his jewelry made. Fascinating how the Fae used a tune of any kind to harness or control their vast magics.

"You would work in my villa." Baron Novus held his arms out, beckoning, flaunting the silhouette of a home's entryway behind him. "I have many precious gems that need proper examination. Your expertise in the field would be most fortunate, and I'd be honored if you handled my belongings with half the care you've shown to the many artifacts you've studied for the Collective. I would love to hear your assessment of them."

"Thanks, but no thanks," Bez said. "Walter has his hands and mouth full assessing my precious gems. They require all his attention at the moment."

My face burned. Bez looked half a second away from whipping his dick out and marking his territory.

"Hmm. Such crude euphemisms, devil," Baron Novus said, adding a high-pitched chime at the end.

"You should leave before my graceless nature matches your dancing fairies, and I butcher you like your leading Fae butchered this evening's performance."

"Consider the offer, Walter Alden," Baron Novus said as he vanished, his voice still carrying around the destroyed auditorium. "Perhaps after you've had a stern talking to with your Diabolic, you can make a sensible decision."

Bez's glare fell onto me. "Oh, yes, Walter. We should have a stern talking."

“Awkward introductions aside, this seems like a great opportunity.” I clutched the card, giving Bez a weak smile. “Maybe even a funny anecdote for the future.”

“Most certainly. And so long as that anecdote doesn’t involve fairies, share the story with whomever you wish.” Bez snatched the card away, ripping it to pieces and tossing the scraps into his black flames.

4

Beelzebub

The anniversary of our intimacy should've ended with me taking Walter home and bedding him, getting my dick wet, and plowing him throughout the night. Instead, it was ruined by the Fae. What should've been a night of Walter rambling about the joyful experience he had observing the Fae and sharing all his annoying theories turned into a discussion on the grand opportunity he'd been given, reasons we should consider it, and how inconsiderate I'd acted by taking the offer from him. What he considered an overreaction to my misunderstanding pissed me off more than the damn Fae who'd snatched him away to begin with.

Unable to sleep, I stayed awake on the couch watching angry wives drink and scream and scheme, babbling about the import of their lives. Their pettiness delighted me, and I took a bit of satisfaction that their loud voices on high volume gave Walter a restless night, too.

I glared at the glint of the golden letters on the card. Destroying it didn't work. It reappeared to Walter upon our return home, refusing disposal until Walter alone officially accepted or rejected the offer. Tricky Fae magics. So, I did the sensible thing and kept it within my reach on the coffee table, out of his grasp.

"Did you seriously have to watch that all night?" he asked, groggy and surly. "Maybe we can have a real conversation about the offer today. You know, instead of you shooting me down every time I attempt to bring it up."

"I have never once shot you." Tempting as that was, given his attitude.

He huffed and walked from the bedroom through the three-foot length of space he dared call a hallway that led directly to our kitchen-dining room combo in this open-floored humble home.

I wanted something more spacious since we would remain stuck in this tiny town for the foreseeable future thanks to the freelance work we'd gained through Mora's connections, but Walter claimed this fit our budget. He glamoured the renters into overlooking a background check, forgoing deposits, and accepting a month-to-month cash payment lease when he could've easily used that charmed magic to sweet talk us into something more accommodating. But oh no, he put his foot down and demanded a low profile.

So if he got to make grand declarations on what we could and couldn't do, then so could I, which was why I made it clear he wouldn't accept the Fae's offer.

"There's no coffee?" he asked with aggravation in his gravelly voice. The first cup would remove the gravel, but I was certain the spite would remain.

I slurped the rest of my cup. "Nope. Fresh out."

"Real mature."

"Perhaps your fairy friend has coffee." Perhaps he had better coffee, too. We were all out of sugar. Coffee was only ever good when made with sweet and bitter in equal measures.

"I don't understand why you're being so difficult about this." He went to make a new pot. "I know things got off on the wrong foot—"

"There is no correct foot for abduction."

"How many times do I have to explain? It wasn't exactly an abduction, per se. In fact, it's common practice for the Fae to see something or someone they like and snatch them from our realm. It's just how they do things. Had I been less surprised by being grabbed for a friendly conversation, I would've remembered that fact."

"I don't care about the semantics behind Fae customs where they declare abduction a form of conversation or courtship."

"Courtship?" Walter scoffed. "Please tell me this isn't some misplaced jealousy."

I scowled. I wasn't jealous. Walter was mine, and I was his, and I held zero concern of another lesser, far more inadequate lover attempting anything to come between us. That said, I didn't like the pheromones wafting from that Fae as he studied Walter. I didn't trust the Fae.

"The so-called job offer is nothing more than a ploy." I pointed to the television when Sandra came back onto the screen. "Television, freeze. Freeze, I said." I grumbled and retrieved the clicker to freeze the screen as Sandra's face went blurry mid-image. "Take Sandra, for instance. She has offered her best friend an opportunity to go into a business venture with her, some pyramid tactic meant to deceive simpler mortals, but in truth, Sandra only wishes to lure Monique into a false sense of security so she can uncover her secrets and exploit them because Monique…well, that's a much longer story, but she is a wicked siren—actually a harpy I think, great glamour to keep the mortals unaware—not the point, which is Sandra is luring—"

"Are you seriously using daytime television to teach me some lesson on manipulation?" Walter huffed.

"The point," I continued, "is this offer is a trap."

"If he meant to harm me, he could've done so immediately. He could've killed me, killed you. Simply not returned me to our plane of reality when I asked. Why do all that?"

"It's called the long con, Walter. I can go back to season seven's origins if you wish to see when Sandra's machinations began."

"This is a great opportunity to take my work and my abilities to the next level. Practitioner level. You said you wanted more of that for me."

"I do. Not with someone who clearly has no interest in you, though." I stared, considering carefully, but Walter needed this bubble of delusion popped. "He's only interested in you because of me. This con is meant to harm me."

"Of course, because it couldn't possibly be about me." Walter sighed, his heart thumping hard and blood coursing faster. In part, the fury probably came as an extension of my own, but the sadness weighing heavy on him—that was all him. Sorrow I'd etched by being what he considered as unreasonable.

"I'm glad you enjoyed the performance," I said, upset I'd hurt him and upset I'd allowed some Fae to drive us into conflict through his manipulative ego-stroking. "I'm glad you can take pride in the attention others have noted of your talented work. You are talented, the most studious mage I have ever met. But I am uncomfortable with you taking this offer."

"Because you don't trust I can take care of myself. Because you think I'll just walk directly into an obvious trap."

"No."

"Yes, even though it's been my judgment, my caution that's kept our profile low the last six months, my decisions that have led to zero traps—don't you dare bring up the gremlin faux pas—so why can't you trust my judgment now?"

"I do trust you and your choices." I clenched my teeth, swallowing the rage I had and the guilt from Wally's sadness. "I don't trust the Fae. They are shifty. Imbued with greater magic than any other Mythics, more pompous than mages, as cunning as Diabolics, and far too many unknown factors for my liking. There are few things in this realm I lack insight on—"

"Oh, please." Wally poured a cup of freshly brewed coffee, the gravel in his voice fading simply from the first inhale. "You can't even figure out how Instagram works. Clearly, you lack insight on more than you realize."

"Algorithms are dumb," I snapped before composing myself.

"Speaking of insight and bizarre introductions, we didn't exactly get off on the right foot."

True. It was my left that kicked him down the stairs and pinned him to the floor of the Magus Estate. I smirked. We did have unique circumstances, and I was certain he tried to rationalize our connection, our outcome, into the factors he played in his head when planning for things. Like risks. Which this was.

"I trust your judgment," I said. "Always have. Always will. I simply wish you would trust mine."

"Fine." Wally sulked, dragging his slippers with each step back to the bedroom.

"Do you wish to talk more?"

"Nope. I need to get back to freelance gigs. Lots of super fun work to get through."

I sat in silence, keeping the screen frozen on Sandra's face and listening to the intensive notes Wally scribbled, providing highly detailed backgrounds on items that would, in turn, be pedaled for far higher sums than we'd be compensated given the amount of effort he put into all his labors.

I wanted him happy, wanted him to treasure his work like he once had, but I refused to budge on this Fae nonsense. Obvious trap.

My telephone buzzed, and I ignored it. Few had my phone number, yet unknown mortals found it all the time, wishing to discuss my expired warranty or someone warning me of tax evasion that the IRS sought, which required I send them currency immediately through something called a money order. Fuck the mortal government. They could fight me over their pennies.

The incessant thing persisted. I huffed, contemplating disturbing Wally, as only he knew how to use the magics of the apps to block unwanted callers. It'd be easier to just break the damned thing, but Wally was already mad at me, and I'd already gone through a half-dozen telephones. Apparently, this thing cost a lot, which was absurd for a fruit, one made of metal or not.

It wasn't some unknown caller—it was worse.

Mora. And she sought to video call me from the glow of the screen request.

I dragged my finger along the wiggling answer prompt four times before the FaceTime thing activated.

"Bezzy," she said as she moved about Mercury's Marketplace. Snippets of shop signs revealed themselves during her strut through the street.

"Why do you insist on calling me every time you are out and about?"

"I'm a busy person. Not all of us can sit at home most days relying on our mortal partner to do the heavy career lifting."

I growled and went to hit the red end button.

"I'm teasing." She lifted the phone to greet me with a coy smile, always something wicked hidden in her eyes even when *playing*.

"What do you want, Mora?"

"Checking in. How'd the evening go? Was Wally in awe? Was he captivated? Was he ever so grateful he decided to relive the event which created such a lovely anniversary?"

"I'm not telling you the details of our evening. I'm not one to kiss and tell."

"You've answered your phone while in the throes of passion twice; surely you can tell me how your date went. I'm curious."

I furrowed my brow. No, she wasn't. Mora rarely showed an interest in the play-by-play of my romance. She wanted to fish for details on the Fae Divinity.

"It was interesting," I said. "Fluttering Fae, bewitched mortals, Wally got a job offer, the flight was relaxing, no Collective presence, I stopped for—"

"A job offer?" Mora interjected, as suspected. "Quite exciting. Doing what exactly?"

What was she up to?

"Nothing." I shrugged. "He declined, preferring the flexibility of working with your illustrious clientele."

"I'd hardly call them illustrious; irksome, entitled, incompetent, annoying… But I digress." Mora moved the camera of her telephone to her soft smile, positioning herself somewhere secluded where the sun didn't hit. "This sounds like a wonderful opportunity for Wally. One he shouldn't pass on."

"That's what you said about selling those petrified gremlins, and I'm still cleaning slime off my suits from that botched venture."

"Nothing ventured, nothing gained, Bezzy."

"We have plenty of other ventures to explore. We'll gain through those." I clicked the red button. "Goodbye, Mora."

"Wait."

I clicked the red button again. Dammit. "Telephone off."

"Listen to me." She moved closer, like making direct eye contact would somehow hold my attention.

"Off telephone." These things were so much easier to handle when they had hook switches to slam.

"Diabolics have been going missing as of late," Mora said, all the playful banter lost from her voice. "Mostly younger demons, but enough for the news to travel."

"What the fuck do I care about missing Diabolics?" I pushed the red button again but somehow pulled up photos I'd taken, or the ones taken by my pocket most days.

"Rumor has it, a group of Fae was seen in Bael's realm wrangling lesser demons," she said her devil's name with contempt. This must be serious since Mora despised all things in relation to her Hell dimension nearly as much as I did my own. "Everyone knows Bael's a boring, lazy ole devil who leaves his doors open for his demons to come and go as we wish, but how'd Fae find their way through? Under his nose? Undetected?"

"Okay. The Fae is controlling demons to jump realms. You suspect the one running last night's performance?"

I knew he was foul. If he dabbled in Diabolic bonds, then chances were, his only intent of grabbing Wally was to determine the strength in our bond, how to fracture it, and possibly claim a devil for himself. Undoubtedly. I'd learned all too well that fools who didn't fear devils sought to control them in one form or another. The arrogance.

"Why not just kill him and leave me out of your plots?" I asked.

"It's not that simple."

"Dear Mora, don't tell me you're concerning yourself with the lives of whichever demons were pathetic enough to end up bound to some snooty Fae nobleman?" I snickered. "Fine. Being ever the gracious friend, I'll kill him and his little Fae entourage on your behalf."

Wally couldn't fault me for that. After all, he trusted Mora's judgment for work, so obviously, this was a rational, well-thought plan.

"It's more than that," Mora said because it could never be simple. "No one can contain more than one demon's essence in them without succumbing to illness and death. More to the point, no demon, commanded or not, can walk through a barrier leading into a Hell realm, especially bringing someone not of a Diabolic nature through. Bael might leave the door open, but it's still too intense for Mythics or mortals to cross the dimensional threshold."

I sat in contemplation, watching the inquisitive playfulness cross Mora's face once more, returning true to form.

"How's this Fae getting himself and a horde of fairies through? What's he planning? And Bezzy, the question I'm most curious about is if he's found ways for Mythics to cross open doors to Hell, how long before he'll find a way to unlock closed Hell realms?"

My chest tightened, mind jumping in a thousand directions. I dropped the phone as Mora prattled on about hypothetical questions I didn't fucking care about. She knew it, too. She'd struck a chord with one already.

What would happen if some Fae entered Beelzebub's realm? The true Beelzebub. Could they enter it? Would they find an enraged devil who awaited a chance to leap out of his realm to retrieve his missing essence? Essence I stole. Would they find a collection of reigning demon lords ruling in the devil's stead? Demons I abandoned. Would it be a mere abyss of ruin indicating a devil's demise?

Any of those would expose my false identity, revealing I'd taken on the guise of Beelzebub to ensure I never needed to fear threats from anyone. This could compromise my safety. Wally's safety. The Collective didn't like us skirting their rules, but they avoided us as much as we avoided them. Safer all around. They didn't want a wrathful devil to contend with, but if they knew I was nothing but a phony, feeble demon, they'd hunt Wally and me to the ends of the world. This one or any other we escaped into.

"Bez. Bez. Bezzy," Mora called out, her voice becoming shriller with each shout of my name. "Are you even listening to me?"

I retrieved my phone, glaring at her.

"Why Wally?" A ridiculous question. It was because of me. This Fae likely sought the essence of a devil to assist in his scheme for tearing through dimensional realms. He'd end up sorely disappointed if harnessing my essence was a required ingredient to unlocking closed doorways.

"I'd have sent Kell—tried to, in fact, but Baron Novus is extremely picky in the lesser beings he works with. Extensive research, consideration, long waits that can last the better part of a century just for him to reject someone for a position. But rumor has it, the noble has some hard-on for Walter Alden. Apparently, a lot of Fae do since your little mage is all the buzz among their Court right now. Their equivalent of fifteen minutes of socialite fame or whatever." Mora shrugged. "Point is, Wally is in."

"No." I clamped my jaw.

"You should be proud. I'd be honored if the Fae looked at Kell in such a way."

"Before or after you ripped out someone's eyes?"

"Never. Anyone is welcome to admire Kell's beauty. It's their tongues I take when their mouths overstep with flattery." Mora grinned, mischievous as always. "Let Wally take the job. He can snoop about and discreetly find intel. Once we know how it's done and if he's shared this knowledge with others, then we can kill him. Heck, I'll even let you have the honor, Bezzy."

If I did nothing, I'd ensure Wally's safety from this sinister Fae. But I'd risk an arrogant Mythic learning how to navigate the realms of Diabolics, something that shouldn't be possible, which could unravel my secrets.

Fuck.

"I should've known your interest in my anniversary had a nefarious plot behind it."

"That's unfair," Mora said with a dramatic, whiny lilt. "I love love and wish you many more celebrations. In fact, I've heard about—"

I hit the red button, and it obeyed the swipe of my finger, hanging up on Mora. I had no time for her if I was meant to make a decision, either of which could endanger Wally and myself.

All knew me as the devil Beelzebub, and I couldn't afford some pompous Fae to uncover or unlock anything that indicated otherwise.

I closed my eyes and lay back on the couch. Unraveling my essence, I sent my mind to traverse in an astral sense, mentally plucking at the strings connecting realms while keeping part of my essence anchored to my physical form. The Fae weren't the only beings capable of traveling through the blackness of space between time and reality, though I had no intention of actually tearing dimensional walls apart. I merely sought to observe the barren roads leading to otherworldly doorways. Ignoring the rhythms of other lesser worlds, Fae realities, and countless possibilities, I searched for tethers that led to locked doors of infinite Hell realms until I found the one I wanted—Beelzebub's Hell. It remained sealed, far off and mostly forgotten as I hoped it always would.

When I first arrived in the mortal realm, I regularly checked for the possibility of his Hell opening again. It took years to learn he'd never be able to open his door, given the piece of him I'd escaped with. Whether out of paranoia or curiosity, I continued to check for the better part of a century. The paranoia was that Beelzebub or one of his many subjects would drag me back and carve out the devil essence coiled amongst my own. The curiosity from a guilty conscience, not for the billions of demons I trapped for eternity, but for the one who'd shown me kindness.

Eligos. A true knight of valor.

He'd made me believe the mortal realm was a place anyone could recreate themselves, being the champion they wanted, but I learned too soon upon my arrival here that mortals, mages, and Mythics only ever saw me as a heretic monstrosity. Suppose Eligos wasn't wrong in his many speeches on demons being whoever they wanted because I did recreate myself as a champion no one would oppose.

I tsked, dragging my essence back into my body on this plane. I didn't have time to reminisce about old, dead fools. Eligos dug his grave when he helped lead the charge in a foolish coup to conquer a devil.

If Mora's intel was accurate, then this Novus needed to be dealt with. I didn't care a bit about whatever demons he exploited, but I'd be damned if I allowed his hubris to destroy the life I'd created, especially since I finally had a life worth living with Wally.

5

Walter

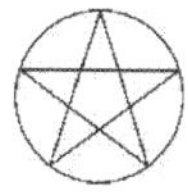

Was I pouting? Maybe. Was it justified? Probably.

"Definitely justified," I muttered as I continued the monotonous task of forming complex sigils at my workstation for a derelict Fae relic, not that anyone would know since it was imbued with so much witch magic only the original framework of the clock indicated Fae origins. I slowly unraveled crudely placed incantations that overloaded the structure and nearly disintegrated the gears. Not the kind of Fae craftsmanship I'd like to work on, not even close to the type of artifacts I could work with based on Baron Novus' offer.

The only thing I'd managed to fix from this clock was the cracked glass casing that surrounded the clock and would sit neatly on the base of the device. It needed sturdy symbols to absorb and store the magics within the clock itself without shattering.

Twirling the gears, I couldn't figure out why the second's hand continued moving faster while the hour's hand barely slugged along. Despite carefully disassembling it and removing the haphazard and lazily lain incantations by the owner, this anniversary clock still needed lots of attentive care.

I grumbled. Anniversary. One hell of an anniversary, too. Anniversary clocks were supposed to run for exactly one year from when they were wound.

I couldn't believe Bez unilaterally decided for us. For me. And yes, I'd made a few unilateral decisions, but that was regarding avoiding Collective mages and Bez's general impulsivity.

Flashes of the flames destroying The Chicago Theatre hit, followed by Bez's frantic expression—something I hadn't seen since Ian stole Bez's essence and forced his obedience. Bez wasn't impulsive last night. He was protective.

I only wished he hadn't shut down when we talked last night. He'd refused to come to bed, claiming his essence was too wired. Total lie.

And this morning, the way he hurled around his trust in my judgment. The way he slipped in, "Always have. Always will." My mouth went dry, and I swallowed hard.

Gods, he even twisted my guilt trip and threw it back at me ten times stronger, sufficiently claiming it for himself. Dammit. He had more Alden family skills than I did.

A soft touch trailed along my neck, and I smiled. The gentle movement was like fingertips walking over my shoulder.

"Tony." I reached my hand out to offer my scorpion familiar an easy step onto the workstation, where his gaze rested.

He stayed planted on my shoulder instead.

Tony, which was short for Anthony, which was short for Antoninus, which was short for Titus Aelius Hadrianus Antoninus Augustus Pius, most commonly known as Antoninus Pius, the most peaceful emperor of Rome. A fitting name for Tony since he was kind and docile, also an emperor in his own right. And like

Antoninus, Tony wasn't magical but navigated the world between Mythics and mages quite well.

The actual Antoninus kept Rome out of conflict better than any other emperor and even expanded relations with many Mythic creatures, despite the mage council of the time disliking such things as the most powerful mages declaring themselves gods of the era. To think, their legacy still stood from the pantheons born through their arrogance.

Tony pinched my cheek.

"Ow."

He jabbed his tail in the direction of my incomplete sigils.

"I *am* working," I said. "Just a bit distracted."

He scurried down my arm, his feet clicking along my workstation, seeping mana I'd shared with him into the sigils to help complete these tasks. Sunlight from the window shined against his black exoskeleton. Tony always knew when my mind wandered too much and I risked falling behind schedule. Without the threat of angry archivist practitioners regularly scolding my lackluster work ethic, I struggled to maintain such rigorous deadlines.

"Thank you," I said.

Our connection had strengthened as the familiar bond grew. I wasn't certain how much he understood, especially since I only grasped about a fraction of his intentions, but we did have a solid understanding of one another. He'd even gotten really good at helping me decipher things. Some of my knowledge might have passed over to him through our connection. A shame our bond wasn't close enough for him to communicate with me psychically. According to the Pentacles of Power, that was the most advanced skill in the familiar bond.

Tony hissed, and I straightened my posture because he hated when I slouched for long hours in the chair.

"I thought you said that thing wasn't supposed to do that," Bez said, strolling into my office space completely carefree.

Oh. Tony's hiss was about Bez, not my hunched posture. Most emperor scorpions only hissed during their adolescence, but Tony regularly vocalized himself whenever Bez came around. Perhaps the familiar bond added to his reasoning as an added form of communication. It was peculiar, but I figured Tony was a little jealous of the attention Bez got from me. I slumped over my desk, continuing my work so my familiar wouldn't have to worry about that right now.

"Maybe he's as annoyed with you as I am." I scribbled incantation symbols, allowing Tony to saturate them so I wouldn't have to slow down.

"About that." Bez squatted next to me, his tails twitching behind him, clearly attempting to draw my attention.

I kept my eyes on my work.

"Wally."

"I'm busy." I couldn't do masterful guilt trips like Bez, but I had years of observing passive-aggressive productivity thanks to my family.

"I wish to discuss the offer you received."

I snorted. "Think of another thing to add to the list of reasons I can't accept it or just want to point out once again how it's not really about me, but you?"

"I would like us to reconsider it." He placed the card in front of me. "Make an official decision."

"Reconsider it?" I sighed. "You want me to *officially* decline the offer, don't you?"

I'd stormed into my office, hoping to avoid this, maybe get some time or perspective to come up with a way to convince Bez why this could work. Would work. Tearing this card apart felt like squandering a once-in-a-lifetime opportunity, destroying a winning lottery ticket, giving up a dream job I didn't even consider daydreaming about because it was too big, too important, too special for someone like me to ever land.

"I would like you to accept, but—"

"Excuse me?" My pulse pounded against my throat, whether from my excitement or Bez's nerves or both. "Why? What are you getting at?"

"It's come to my attention that this is a potentially viable and necessary opportunity…"

I smiled. Bez used a lot of words to skirt around him saying he'd had a change of heart, that he might've overreacted, or—dare I say—maybe that he was wrong.

"This is no laughing matter." Bez stared at my smiling face. "We need to discuss the risks—"

"Absolutely." I grabbed his tie and pulled him closer.

His balance wobbled, but he caught himself against the arm of the chair. I pressed my lips against his, ready to have any conversation on the seriousness of taking this job, but mostly I wanted to stop being grouchy, maybe a little petty, and show him how much I appreciated him. What he did for me before and after the show. Hell, getting us tickets to the show alone.

"Something I have to work on, maybe we have to work on, is learning to pause arguments to enjoy celebrations." My lips met his softly, tongue searching for his and the way he'd respond with an aggressive, leading kiss. He didn't, though. Instead, I guided this kiss, lust taking hold. "I shouldn't have gone to bed a jerk."

"Wally, about that, before we commence with much-needed pleasures, I have to explain—"

"The only thing I want you to explain"—I stood, tugging his tie and watching him stand, towering above me—"is what you plan on doing with me."

I kissed his neck, nuzzling him; my hands rested on his shoulders as I led him backward toward the door.

"Actually, no explanations." I unfastened his belt, continuing to direct him into the bedroom for some well-overdue acts of affection. "I'd rather you surprise me."

Carefully, I shuffled around my piles of paperwork for jobs, stacks of half-read books for personal inquiries, and the single map Bez had on unicorn migrations. My research wasn't nearly as tidy as his, but at least I'd bought my materials, unlike Bez who, as he'd put it, 'pilfered' the map from Mora's collection. One we now knew was completely outdated.

Bez complained my messy system would spread to the entire hovel if he hadn't insisted otherwise, so to prove him wrong, I made sure to keep the chaos in the bedroom. If I had my external organization strewn about the office, I'd never get actual work done.

"First, allow me to explain," Bez said, groaning as I ran my fingers under his waistband and got a full grip on his growing erection. "Wall—"

I kissed him again, this time with my teeth biting his lip. "You're talking a lot. Usually, you're the one telling me to keep conversation to a minimum since I have this habit of sometimes kind of a little bit getting sort of chatty in the middle of sex."

Bez had planted his hands on my shoulders, bracing some distance from my lips reaching his. Dammit. I'd done it again. Gotten too talkative. He wanted to talk. Maybe apologize. Or explain all the stipulations he'd demand if I were to accept this job. We'd have that talk, of course. But I didn't want a conversation souring the mood, or more accurately, I didn't want my own insecurities souring such a lovely gesture Bez had done.

"We'll discuss it all," I said, unable to quiet my mind. "But I'd much rather save the chitchat."

With that, I pushed Bez back onto the bed and dropped to my knees. There was only foreplay that'd stop my rambles or Bez's, it seemed.

"Wait, this isn't…" Bez ran his fingers through my hair, a firm grip pulling my head back right as I licked the tip of his cock. He growled from the gentle massage of my tongue, and instead of tugging me away, he pushed me further onto his cock.

My eyes watered, and I gagged, taking in the entirety of his shaft so quickly. Still, I relaxed my jaw and planted my hands on Bez's sides, moving with the subtle thrust of his hips.

My throat constricted as his cock throbbed inside my mouth. Slowly, I worked my way up and down. I couldn't get a full breath through my nose, but I didn't want to stop, to slow down, because the warmth coming off Bez made my skin tingle and my body vibrate.

"I need…" Bez let out a feral snarl. "Walter, I need you to accept the job so we can learn this Fae's secrets and kill him."

I choked on Bez's cock and his words.

What?

I pulled back, wiping spit from my chin. "What?"

"I thought that'd finally ruin the moment." Bez grimaced, pulling his boxer briefs over his fully erect dick, the bulge pointed upward on an angle.

"You can't just kill a Fae." I stood up, ready to storm out of the room but waited, waited for an explanation as Bez pulled his pants up and fastened his belt. "Honestly, as worried as I am for Novus, not sure you can kill him, considering last night's performance."

Okay, that was rude, but Bez hadn't landed a single blow on the baron, and that said something, given his speed and strength.

"Bah. Annoying Fae parlor tricks." Bez waved a hand. "The next time our paths cross, I won't be caught unaware of his shifting temporal frequencies."

I turned to leave, but Bez snatched me by the wrist.

"Wait. There's much I need to explain." His voice was soft, pleading. "There is a chance this Fae is using Diabolic bonds to dabble in dimensional travels, tearing through thresholds which shouldn't be possible."

Bez pulled me onto the bed, and I sat on the end next to him as he explained the difficulties of navigating in or out of Hell—any Hell—how anything non-Diabolic would burn eternally, lost in the cracks of the dimensional folds. A part of me wanted to comment or question if this helped stem the origins of fire and brimstone, but I kept quiet, putting a pin in most of my curiosities.

Mora had informed him of Baron Novus' intentions and his intrigue with me since many Fae supposedly found my actions fascinating. But I wondered if Novus actually did or if that was simply a façade to mask his true interest in Bez. Who was I kidding? Of course it was. I was a joke. The fact I even allowed myself to buy into the flattery of my supposed talents, this offer.

Bez was right. "It was a trap all along."

"I suspect," Bez said, his expression soft and not holding any of the smugness I deserved.

"Surprised you're not gonna mock me for always being so gullible."

"Seeing the best in others and hoping they recognize the value you possess does not make you gullible." Bez patted my thigh, hand resting on my shaky knee until I'd stopped tapping.

"What happens if you find proof the Fae baron is actually doing this, stealing Diabolics and trying to get into Hell realms?"

"If *we* find proof," Bez corrected.

We. He wanted me to be a part of this. My chest swelled, flattered he trusted me enough to take part in this, and then tightened, frightened of what it meant.

"So, what happens to him?" I asked again.

"I won't lie to you, Wally." Bez's eyes flitted, avoiding direct contact or finishing his response, it seemed.

"You're gonna kill him."

"No." Bez rocked his head side to side; his shaggy hair swayed between the roots of his curled ram horns. "Maybe just unalive him."

"We just talked about not impulsively killing people."

"*Just* implies it only recently happened, and we know your lectures have been long-standing." Bez rolled his eyes. "And to be clear, it won't be impulsive. I'm already putting much thought into exactly how to kill him."

"Could we maybe look for another way?" I bit my lip. "I can get pretty crafty when dealing with dangerous threats."

"I prefer it when you get murderer-y with those threats."

I frowned, making a face because his expression shifted to the same minxy smirk as the night I'd ended Ian's life. Ian. The misfit mage who sought to reveal magic to the world, topple the Collective, and kill Bez and me. Killing him wasn't something I regretted. It was a decision I made with ease. I suppose the only regret I had there was I didn't have any regret, which made me an awful person.

"Killing a Fae—that's big. They have the Collective wrapped around their fingers; they basically run the Mythic Council…"

"Through whispers only." Bez scoffed.

"Which is a pretty big deal that so many different Mythics heed their mostly silent advice."

"Blah, blah, blah-bidy, blah. And I suppose you think his nobility makes him a more difficult target."

"Well, yes." Standing, I moved closer between Bez's spread legs. "If the Fae Court is anything like the Collective regiments, then working outside sanctioned authority would likely cost him all his standing. Remember a certain chancellor whose coup cost her all title and casting privileges?"

A not-so-subtle reminder I could handle tough decisions. After all, I'd exposed Chancellor Alden to the regiment leaders, and from the one email I'd received from Al, our mother's treachery apparently landed her a one-way ticket to the Collective's most secure penitentiary.

"I just don't want to do something we can't walk back from," I said, fighting back the urge to add I couldn't kill with such a clear conscience as Bez and how sometimes the way he killed with such a nonchalant attitude frightened me. Worse. Sometimes it excited me, knowing no one and nothing would stand between us because he'd always protect me no matter the danger.

"Fine. I'll let you concoct whatever it is you wish, but if it doesn't completely remove him as a threat from you, me, and I suppose others—since a pompous Fae with a skeleton key able to bounce to and from any Hell realm would be a danger to all—then I'll be left with no choice other than to more permanently remove him as a threat."

"It doesn't sound less murderous when you say it that way."

"It's not meant to," he said, his smile gone. Bez kissed my chest directly over my fast-beating heart. "Know that I shall respect your rules. No impulsive decisions. No unaliving without purpose. Cross my heart, not my tails."

I squinted at his three gray tails, which had stretched long and straightened from one another, all lying at different ends of the bedroom.

I kissed Bez. A light peck, waiting for him to reciprocate. He remained hesitant. Reserved. I kissed him again, a bit more assertively, and straddled his waist as I did.

He pulled away, taking a wispy breath in sync with mine. "I expected you to be less enthused once I explained the situation."

"You're treating me like an equal, not just some little mage you have to protect. I find that very enthusing. Enthusiastic? No. Point is this is what I like to see."

"I've always considered you my equal, Wally." Bez ran his hand up my stomach, resting it on my chest over my heart. "In truth, you are my better through and through."

Bez smiled so big it reached his glossy, crimson eyes. An expression of pure admiration.

Swept away by passion, I grabbed his hand and kissed his knuckles one by one, unable to stop. His fingers had a sweet flavor like he'd dipped them in syrup. Knowing Bez, that was exactly what he'd done. Essence coursed through me, through him, too, extending to his fingers that I continued kissing. They shifted into claws. I licked them, running my tongue down his palm and reaching his wrist, where I planted tender kisses as he caressed my face.

"I'm glad to be treated as an equal. Flattered you sometimes see me as your better." I slid a hand beneath his horns, grabbing his ruffled hair, and pulled him into an all-consuming kiss, parting only for air and a need, desire, to tell him. "We'll have to put a pin in that since it's not true. I'm no better than you, Bez." I kissed him, unable to break away for too long. "But right now…"

Bez smirked. Dammit. I'd done it again. Talking, talking, talking.

Too late, might as well say it. "You know what I'd like from you?"

"Name it." He stroked my cheek.

"I don't want to be an equal right now. But someone solely for serving your needs."

"My worthless Walter."

"Not a nickname I'd approve of under any other circumstances." I grinned nervously, aroused and buzzing in anticipation for his touch. "I don't know. Maybe it's just me, but it feels like it's been forever since we, you know, and I feel like I'm rambling more, or maybe we just have more going on, or maybe I've forgotten how to—"

Bez threw me off him, shoving me face-first onto the bed. I gasped as he stripped off my pants and tore through yet another shirt. At least I learned an incantation to mend the stitching. I shuddered as his lips worked their way down my back and further.

His tongue was aggressive and delicate all at once as he slid my underwear off.

I moaned. Bez slowly worked his way up my back again, lightly kissing the nape of my neck before biting. I quivered, then reached out with my hands to find his.

Bez leaned away, retrieving a bottle and pouring lube on his palm. I could see his arm moving back and forth in the corner of my eye as he stroked himself hard. He smacked his wet dick on my bare ass.

I arched, moving closer to him, craving him, wanting him inside.

His clawed hand wrapped around my throat, pulling me into a further arch than comfortable as he worked his way into me. I stifled a groan. Once he'd gotten the tip in, he pressed his chest against my back, holding me tight by the neck and pushing us both forward onto the mattress.

With all his weight pressing down on me, he allowed gravity and gentle thrusts to do the work. After he'd buried himself all the way inside me, I moaned, but Bez slapped his other hand over my mouth, silencing me.

"I can't wait to hear you beg, but first, I have other plans."

He moved faster, harder, keeping a tight grip on my mouth and throat, leaving me delirious and letting out muffled gasps and grunts, lost in the ecstasy of him. The only noise aside from my own was Bez's satisfied growl as he pounded away, and our skin slapped against each other until I couldn't contain myself. My body warmed, tense and twitching in his embrace as I climaxed.

6

Beelzebub

I'd barely fully undressed by the time I came. After rolling onto his back, Wally pulled me in close, and I kissed him again and again, seduced by his panting. He craved air and me, only able to choose one, he chose me. This continued for a time until I released his lips from mine, and he rested his head on my shoulder.

Already aroused, I wrapped my thighs around one of his, letting my semi-hard bulge rub against his leg.

Wally rolled on top of me in a blur, channeling essence. I wasn't sure when, but his assertiveness had blossomed tenfold since unlocking a few of my Diabolic abilities. His orange aura radiated against the sunlit bedroom. Crimson coursed from his core, feeding upon his magic at the singular act of harnessing Diabolic speed. Well, to a point. His movements were fast for a mortal but paled in comparison to what I'd used in the bedroom, the living room, private lounge of that club in Denver—honestly, wherever and whenever I could ravish him.

It was important I shared my demon essence with him, keeping us bonded, but it required a delicate balance. I made certain never to offer him so much the essence would devour him entirely as I sought to keep him safe, not in danger.

I sat up only for him to shove me back onto the bed, a hand pressed between my pecs.

He adjusted his glasses, staring down at me with a fiery passion. Leaning close, his breaths hit my ear. "Let's not allow conversation to interrupt this time."

I smirked. "You're the only one talking."

He shushed me by placing a finger over my lips, holding a subservient gaze that had all my attention and my body's attention, too.

Our lips locked in a passionate kiss. My tongue massaged his, and he panted, pulling back only long enough to bite my lower lip before shoving his tongue back into my mouth. Wally ran his hands up and down my biceps, finally reaching my clawed hands and interlocking our fingers. He guided my hands, craving them, desiring me to caress his supple flesh, all the while keeping us locked in powerful kisses directed by him.

Such a commanding lover whose kisses stirred my insides, sending a warmth through my chest further down.

He kissed my collarbone, trailing his way down my chest and stomach and sliding his tongue lower and lower, following the trail of warmth where my blood surged. The lightest graze of his teeth along my abs, tickling, taunting, tantalizing me with bites. It made me hard. Made me want to snatch his hair and jerk him up here so I could bite him. Taste him. Tease him.

He'd slipped to the end of the bed, kissing my hip bone.

I gently ran my fingers through his curls before grabbing a fistful of hair.

Wally ran his tongue along the length of my shaft as I clutched his hair, yet he controlled his own movements—for the moment.

He teased me with his tongue, demanding my authority. Gods, how I relished his submissive dominance. Always eager, always willing, always mine…

His mana radiated a delicate orange aura joyfully swirling through the room as my crimson essence captured and ravished his magic, adding to the humble dominion I'd created in this hovel. Not nearly as vast as the Diabolic voids I'd once had, but enough to stretch the length of the town. Given his new job might take him to and from Chicago, I should trickle my essence through the nearby city.

I groaned. The warmth of his mouth enveloped me, and I rolled my eyes back, taking in the blissful sensations.

Allowing him his fun, I added more power behind my grip, ignoring his muffled gulps. He would have it no other way, so I lay there, steadily pushing his head further until his nose reached the base. When his hands squeezed my thighs—not my hips or butt to maintain his grasp—I relented. A subtle cue we had when he couldn't handle it…when his throat needed a second to adjust. Allowing him a breath, he took several quick, heavy inhales. Only after he'd caught enough air did I push him back down, which he didn't resist.

The arch in his back lessened, and his muscles tensed, but he continued bobbing.

Finally, I pulled him off my dick and zipped behind him. I spun him around and flipped him onto his back before he realized what had happened.

"Relax, love." I grinned down at his head hanging over the edge of the bed.

I removed his glasses, already sliding off his upside-down face, and then slipped my cock into his warm mouth. Leaning forward, I kept his hips steady as I slowly sped my thrusts. I hadn't pushed the length of my shaft all the way in, allowing his throat a chance to adapt to this new position, but once his reflex stopped constricting and his gagging gulps turned into steady inhales, I lifted a leg onto the bed, arching over him and took a jackhammer position pounding into the back of his throat, the sudden slap of my skin against his face served the count of seconds passing to minutes.

I continued until I felt myself nearing, slowing my hips every few pumps to alter the rhythm enough to help deescalate my own pleasure in his tight throat; I stalled finishing so I could stroke him closer to completion.

His legs twitched as he came, and he moaned with the full length of my cock inside his mouth, making it impossible to hold back another second. I gripped the sides of his head, groaning as my cock vibrated; a euphoric explosion shot down his throat.

Gently, I rubbed his Adam's apple until he swallowed. "That's my little mage. Nutritious, delicious, and offers far more inspiration than any Fae seeds could."

"You're an ass," he said, spitting out my flaccid cock, clicking his jaw back and forth to remove the tension.

"As the mortals say, 'you are what you eat,' so I suppose you're to blame for my behavior." I winked, to which Wally responded by taking my fine silk shirt and using it like a common cum rag. "Dick."

"You are what you eat or whatever, right?" Wally chuckled—a cute, carefree laugh not holding the weight or burden of a ploy we still had to discuss. Instead, lost in the afterglow of sex, he tossed my ruined shirt at me, catching it on my left horn. "Damn. Was aiming for the other one."

"Shocker, Walter's aim being off."

"You're one to talk, considering…" Wally tipped his head, giving me the worst judgment face. "Sacramento."

"Don't you dare. That doesn't count." I huffed. "Too much tequila and not enough unicorn."

Wally put on his faded pink briefs. It'd taken time, but I'd managed to turn them into such a cute color and ripped apart the other pairs with insatiable teeth. For whatever reason, Wally deemed himself above wearing pink, but I loved him in such soft colors.

"No post-coital cuddles?" I plopped onto the bed as he finished dressing.

"I have to finish that clock, then I have some incantation spell pages to cloak, which will need to be shipped like two days ago. Also, there's that troll decoction I needed to create a comprehensive list of ingredients on, and I should probably…hmm…"

"Other work can wait."

"Yeah, I guess, um, I should contact, you know." Wally stretched his lips wide, fighting a frown but unable to smile.

"Contact that Fae lord?"

"The baron, yeah."

"Same thing." I rolled my eyes, retrieving the card I'd slipped off Wally's worktable. "You might need this."

"When'd you take that back?"

"I didn't take it back." I dangled the card in front of him, smiling as he jumped, unable to catch the card or my tail. "I simply retrieved it when you pushed me into the bedroom, demanding satisfaction only my dick could offer."

Wally squeezed my tail. His tight grip was unrelenting. I tossed the card to another tail. I could play this game all day.

"We need to finish our conversation before you move into accepting this Fae's proposition for a position."

"It sounds weird when you say it that way." Wally scrunched his face.

"Let us contact the noble, where you'll accept his offer on the contingency I remain present. He'll certainly not object, considering my presence may, in fact, be part of his objective. Also,

I made it clear last night, I do not abide well when lacking your company."

"Wait. So you don't trust me to handle this alone?"

"I do."

"Then why are you going with me?" Wally's brow creased into his pouty scowl. "And if, like you said, you're his objective in this mystery to traveling through Diabolic realms, then shouldn't you not be there? You know, not walking into a trap? If this is actually a trap and Mora hasn't simply gotten the details wrong."

I did trust Wally. I didn't trust this baron who was brazen enough to kidnap, bind, and possibly kill demons in great numbers. A group of mages or Mythics banding together to take down a single Diabolic threat, I could respect, but the gall of a single entity holding their own against my brethren, the ability it required—that was a danger unlike any other. I had limited experience with the Fae. Perhaps I'd underestimated their capabilities or overestimated Diabolic powers. Either way, I wouldn't send Wally into a wolf's den alone.

Wally continued staring while I was left smirking in silent contemplation. "I do trust you to handle this alone, which you'll be doing. You'll be alone with the Fae in his villa while I excuse myself to use the little Diabolic's room. You'll keep him busy and distracted—again, alone—and I'll search for clues."

"All the while remaining close by."

"Only if you insist, sweetheart."

Wally glowered. "Let's just get this started."

Wally muttered half-concocted theories on the complexities of the card for the better part of an hour. Turned out the damned thing required deciphering, which proved difficult—even by Wally's standards.

He said a few Fae phrases, and the card twinkled. As he continued, the shimmer fizzled out, and he grumbled.

"What's the problem this time?" I asked, standing over him while he sat in the center of his office floor with Mythic books surrounding him, each a codex on different linguistics.

"It's weird," he said.

"That much I gathered."

"I didn't realize this would be such a complicated read. The Sylvan symbols used are mostly elementary phrases anyone could learn. Even people with no understanding or knowledge of magic." He waved a hand at me, head buried in a book. "Hell, even you could grasp these terms."

"Screw you."

He completely disregarded my comment, lost in his research. "The problem is they're rearranged with what I thought were incorrect letters, but they're actually other languages. A few human and some mostly dead Mythic dialects." He laughed to himself over what I could only guess was some trivial nerd humor. "Guess he made the decryption as a test of sorts. Make sure he didn't make a hasty choice in offering me a position. That would be flattering if the position were genuine and not like a trap."

"The only one you better be flattered taking positions for is me."

"This is serious, Bez."

"I'm very serious."

"Oh, I think I got it." Wally scribbled some notes, copying the symbols from the card onto a piece of paper in a different arrangement. "Ready? This should theoretically bring him here or his villa."

"As long as he doesn't break my things."

"It shouldn't be phased with our reality." Wally stood with the paper in hand.

All the same, I coiled a tail around Wally's waist, claws drawn and essence stirring. I wouldn't take the trickery of the Fae lightly a second time around.

Wally began reciting the incantation, summoning this Novus Fae to us, where I'd do my best to play nice for Wally and Mora's sake. My own too. Only long enough to uncover his secrets, then I'd accidentally knock him off a high ledge, into a sharp stake, or into a boiling cauldron. I couldn't be faulted for clumsiness.

The paper in Wally's hand burned pink, crumpling to ashes. "Shit, I think—"

He exploded into glitter, lost from my grip as each sparkled before fading to nothingness.

I zipped about the office, searching for his scent, his presence, his anything. He couldn't vanish into thin air.

Not again.

The card remained, and I snatched it up, trying to mentally rearrange the slew of symbols Wally had rewritten on the now-burned paper. I couldn't recall. I hadn't paid attention and didn't know the first thing about the Fae alphabet.

I shouted, fighting back the panic of quick, wispy breaths. Was this panic mine or Wally's? It had to be mine. I couldn't sense any trickle of his being.

Not a trace. It was like he'd moved dimensional planes and teleported all at once while also closing the door behind so seamlessly it left this plane undisturbed.

I dove into the shadows of my void realm, hoping the ethereal sensation of running through the pocket world sparked some extra connection to our bond. Perhaps something bordering the walls of this plane would help me find Wally. Feel our bond. Sense his mana. Anything. The faintest tug of his link.

Nothing.

I soared throughout the town of Galena, veiled behind my Diabolic web, searching for signs, but I couldn't feel him anywhere.

I sprinted from across town back into our house in a fraction of a second. Once I emerged, I searched the room—every room—for dimensional tears, tiny fractures like at The Chicago Theatre.

Nothing.

My chest tightened with each failed lead; a heavy pressure like iron made of fear and guilt weighed heavy on me.

Raged seethed out in a maelstrom of black lightning, surging with a gust throughout the main living space. Electricity crackled, knocking kitchenware from the cupboards, and wind hurled furniture everywhere. My claws and tails slashed through everything in my path. None of it soothed my fury.

I stormed into Wally's office, tearing at the fibers of energy in the room, searching for any trail. Still nothing.

Antoninus, the most irritating and worthless scorpion that ever existed, hissed.

"I don't speak annoying fucking insect. But if you're warning me not to disturb Walter's belongings, I hate to break it to you"—I smashed a trinket meant to pass off to Mora for payment—"he's already gone."

Wait. Mora. She put me up to this. Risked Wally's neck, and now I have no way to help him. But she knew something. She must have. This was her lead, after all, and she found the Fae Divinity performance where no one else could.

I quelled my essence and went to retrieve my telephone, ignoring the clatter of the scorpion's claws and profane hisses. The tiny bug scuttled into the living room carrying the card used to steal Wally.

"You're trying to tell me something?" I knelt in front of the creature, waiting for a response when he dropped the card, pointed feet walking over one symbol in particular. The insect walked over this one sign three times over. "You want me to say this?"

Antoninus didn't respond. Of course not. Despite sharing knowledge from the wealth of Wally's mind, this tiny, insignificant creature lacked proper civility.

I read the phrase. He stepped onto another set of symbols, and I followed suit by speaking them aloud until I reached the third one.

The scorpion stung me.

I growled. “I don’t know how to say it.”

Antoninus pointed his stinger at a collection of books, which I’d have to root through since the tiny fucker couldn’t flip to the necessary passage.

“If we don’t find Wally, I’m going to eat you,” I said, flipping pages. “After I boil you in chocolate cheese.”

We worked together, me doing all the heavy lifting of identifying what this bug wished me to read and translate next. Either I mispronounced something or skipped over something because he kept hissing.

“Unless you’re going to tell me how to properly say it, shut the fuck up.” I huffed. “Just click your claws or something when I say a word correctly.”

The scorpion hissed.

I squinted, desperately attempting to decode these symbols and rescue Wally.

7

Walter

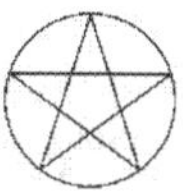

I stood barefoot on a stone floor. Not stone. Clay with a stone-like texture and an oddly polished finish. I swallowed hard. Golem flooring. Not flooring crafted from golem Mythics, but actual floor made out of golem hides. The luster added to alter the color and add a shine was proof enough of Fae manipulation. Nothing was ever just right for the Fae, so much so that they needed to augment and alter everything to fit their perfect desires.

Perfection. The sentiment sent a shudder through me, reminding me of every Alden trait I'd never fulfilled due to my imperfections in a family that never faltered.

I shook it away, shook away the need to study the floor, shook away every curious inkling that crept inside me. What I needed to do was figure out where I was, how I'd gotten here, and how to contact Bez. No. Escape. Because I already knew where I was and how I'd gotten here. The Fae summoning pulled me through into Baron Novus' villa. Somewhere tied to another plane, where I literally spoke the chant voluntarily, offering myself and my mana.

Bars surrounded me from every side, forming a circular shape around the pentagram traced in chalk along the stone—correction, clay—ceiling. As if the tips of the pentagram weren't far out of reach, they each extended far beyond the bars confining me. No chance I'd be able to knock off one of the altars silencing my magics. An archaic but completely effective way to diminish a mage's connection to the Pentacles of Power.

At each tip of the pentagram sat a totem, each representing a connection to magic from the Pentacles of Power. I couldn't believe how willingly I'd walked right into this trap. I should've caught on as I uttered the words. No, I should've known based on reading alone. I was so distracted translating, solving the puzzle, proving I knew what the fuck I was doing. I sighed. I had no idea what I was doing.

I couldn't write or speak incantations to will the bars to heed my call. I couldn't saturate the floor to strengthen my resolve. I couldn't glamour myself in a desperate attempt to cloak my presence. I couldn't summon elements to defend or destroy. Most of all, I couldn't contact Tony or even feel my familiar's presence.

Our link was as disjointed as my severed connection to Bez.

Bez.

He must be so worried.

I trembled, and the essence coursing through my body stirred. My veins blackened. I quelled the surge of Diabolic power radiating within me because there wasn't enough to be wasteful. We hadn't performed the offering in weeks, and if I burned through what remained, I'd be screwed. More screwed than I already was.

Still, this gave me an opportunity. Even if Novus knew I had essence, he didn't know how to smother the power, or perhaps he believed the bars did the trick. They were covered in incantations. Guess I'd have to test my luck eventually, but first, I needed to properly evaluate my situation.

"Walter." Novus floated into the room, literally hovering a foot above the ground as he entered through a glowing blue door that disappeared behind him. "Marvelous you could join me."

"What's going on?" I asked with a strained, cringy smile. Anything to appear as dumbfounded and simple as he assumed, and quite honestly, accurately assessed since I waltzed right into a caged trap.

His white skin held a glowing hue to it, the light traveling along his skin following a continuous pattern like blood flow. It highlighted the silver armor behind him, the same one from the foyer—exact dent on the chest piece. I doubted Novus lugged a full suit from his foyer to wherever the hell we were. A cellar? A dungeon? Did villas come standard with dungeons? Definitely a construction addon. The armor stood tall—not perched by anything at all—next to a bookshelf, far from my reach, and filled with many expensive collectibles from fresh gorgon eyes, a half-dozen harpy feathers, a petrified goblin egg, leather-bound tomes, and countless other baubles. Not baubles. Illegally obtained artifacts. This must be where he stored all his ill-gotten goods, including mages bound to Diabolics.

"Surely, we can end the pretense," Novus said, drawing my attention from the vast collection of rarities.

His face had changed. His entire head, in fact, was no longer twice the size as before, less rounded with more sculpted features for high cheekbones and a sloped nose. His smile still stretched long with thin lips, but the curl of his smile didn't quite reach his ears like before.

"Your face, it's changed."

"Ah, yes." He ran his elongated fingers along his cheeks, rubbing his chiseled chin. "During the Fae Divinity, we often attempt to augment into the human form. It helps establish better synchronizing with our audience. Walking in their shoes, so to speak. Their very tiny-footed shoes."

“Fascinating,” I said, faking enthusiasm. Well, not entirely, because I had no idea they differed from humans so much. “And you thought humans had such large heads?”

“So, we’re still placating? So be it.” He released an exaggerated exhale. “I drew inspiration for the performance from human infants, but I’d forgotten how much larger your newborn’s heads are compared to fully grown humans. We Fae are the opposite, born as vast as an exploding star. Only through temperance, wisdom, and age do we mature into a more confined adult. Whereas all the species in your realm are quite bizarre, growing larger and wider before wilting away over the course of a few seasons.”

“Few have the longevity of the Fae,” I said, grinding my teeth into a smile. “Not all worlds can harness time and space with such ease.”

“Quite the travesty, too. Why even bother with such ephemeral existences? I’ve taken longer naps than most beings on this plane live.”

I needed to keep him talking until I devised a plan of escape. How I’d accomplish such a feat was beyond my grasp, but I had Bez’s essence. Hopefully enough to escape this pentagram keeping me from accessing mana and magic.

“Why are you detaining me here?” I asked.

“Isn’t it obvious?”

Yes. Some attempt to use me as leverage against Bez, though killing Bez wasn’t his intention—otherwise, we wouldn’t be having this conversation.

“I can only assume this is because of the Collective,” I said, a weak lie, which hopefully he bought. Didn’t need to tip my entire hand yet.

“You think I’m here for some bounty?” Novus scoffed. “Do you believe me that pedestrian?”

"Then why have you taken me? Why make the phony offer? Why not simply take me from the Fae Divinity performance?" He'd already snatched me away that night, pulled me into another plane of existence which disrupted my connection to Bez much like now. How powerful was he? I scrunched my face. Strong enough to flaunt his abilities, give me fake flattery, and set up this trap.

"With so many eyes on me? No, Walter. As far as any Fae are concerned, I was merely an intrigued member of Court seeking to converse with a notable mage." He hovered toward the bookshelf, running his hand along the spines of several books.

Books to titles I knew—tomes stolen from archivist vaults across the world. The skill it'd require to break into a vault guarded by a Magus themself. Given how I'd been framed for such an incredible feat, it was difficult not to quake with curiosity and terror at the skill Baron Novus possessed.

"Besides, the best traps require bait and patience," Novus said, his grating smile unyielding. "I waited three centuries before acquiring my first demon. Surely, I could show some restraint when acquiring a devil."

"This is about Bez?"

"Naturally. Beelzebub is the only devil to dwell so long in the human realm, left unguarded and now vulnerable due to his romance."

I hated this. Hated being such a weakness for Bez. Literal kryptonite. His downfall. I had to escape. Stop Novus. Prove I could outmaneuver this trap.

"You're not the first to try and fail to control a devil," I said a bit smugly, goading him into talking, revealing his plans, and stalling for time to strategize.

"I do not seek to control the devil."

"Then what?"

"Diabolics are a brutal species, most thriving on violence and destruction, the very thing that birthed many of their Hells, gave creation to devils, and made way for legions of demons. Quite frankly, I'd rather have nothing to do with such disgusting entities."

Metal clinked behind Novus, and I looked past him, searching for what moved or fell. Nothing. Wait. Had the suit of armor's helmet turned? The slits in the visor were vacant yet positioned to stare directly at Novus. I shut my eyes tightly. No. It'd always faced that direction. I was seeing things. Still, the clinking continued.

"But they possess a glimmer of potential." Novus wiggled his fingers; the rings rattled, casting ripples of color matching sound waves of their contact. That was the clink I'd heard, had to be. "Like the Fae, they are the only other creatures in existence to master dimensional travel. To a degree. Demons, being base in nature and skill, can merely pass through barriers of any type, which is quite a feat considering the dimensional wavelengths can be excruciating on the body. Even the portals and pocket worlds the Fae have bestowed onto the Collective and Mythic Council are so diluted they may as well be two-dimensional. It is with Diabolic essence from demons that I've attained a higher form of travel than any others in the Fae Court. It has allowed me to venture further than any before."

"So you're kidnapping Diabolics to travel between dimensions, something the Fae can already do?" I studied the shelves as he spoke, rambling—no wonder Bez tuned me out. Did I always drone on and on like this?

"You speak on it as if you understand it."

I rolled my eyes, landing them back on the purplish-green harpy feathers.

"The Fae Court controls all travel, dictating who can travel where and when and how long." He waved a hand, disgruntled, while I did my best to tune him out and plan. "With the demons I've acquired, I've created my own separate dimensional wavelength, unique as it's mixed with Fae and Diabolic magics, each working in tandem to tear fabrics dividing worlds asunder. I will create my own form of transport for all those willing to pay."

The harpy feathers seemed like the best option for escape. They were arranged on a metallic stand, displayed as delicate, but quite the opposite since those quills could hack through their stand, the bookshelf, and just about everything on the shelves. Or in this room, including the bars.

I clenched my fists, digging my nails into my palms. Not sure I had enough Diabolic essence to wield telekinesis long enough to direct the feathers to shred these bars to pieces. Plus, I didn't know the defensive measure of the incantations on the bars. For all I knew, they'd been placed to block Diabolic abilities, but I wouldn't know until I tried.

I could try to impale Novus with the feathers. Oh, Bez would have a huge laugh if I went that route. All my scolding on murder and where did my mind go? I'd probably miss, given how Novus dodged Bez with ease.

"Thanks to you, Walter Alden, I shall obtain Beelzebub's essence. Devils, that is where the real power comes from. They can rip through the most potent veils of reality and illusion—no rituals, no loss in strength, no permission necessary. With it, I should be able to create a truly unique traveling port—one that ceases to decompose from the infinite friction of dimensions cutting off paths deemed dangerous. I'll be triumphant, capable of reigning higher than anyone in the Court."

Boy, would he be furious to learn Bez had only a tiny fraction of Diabolic devil essence coursing through him, not nearly enough to pave a path to his future, let alone tear through the walls of any Hell realm. I wouldn't let him learn his plot for some dimensional traveling monopoly was bound to fail because I'd get out of here before he harmed the demon bound to me.

The petrified goblin egg sat on the center shelf; its rigid bumps accentuated its off-white color and contrasted with the smooth, golden stand displaying it. These fossilized eggs were resilient and wouldn't break if I accidentally knocked it off the shelf when channeling telekinesis, which was good since the insides contained an acidic smog that'd melt someone's lungs with their first inhale.

Or! Or, or, or that acid mist could melt through the bars entirely. Also, probably me. A bad idea for sure, but the only one I had.

I'd have to hope I had enough essence to enact the plan and survive it. I trembled.

Screw it.

Reeling the essence from deep in my gut, I sent the energy to my hands and waved them at the harpy feathers. My fingertips tingled from the strain of Diabolic wisps oozing out of my pores, knocking things off the shelves. I didn't have much to waste but needed to throw enough around to hide my actual target.

The petrified egg rolled off the bookshelf and hit the clay floor with a loud thud. It didn't crack, not that I expected it to. Maybe the floor, though.

"Boorish behavior." Novus fumed, the lines in his furrowed brow deepened. "Such a juvenile attempt to thwart a trap. Though, it is good to see Diabolic essence coursing through you so strongly. All this would be for naught if you lacked a leash for your devil. After all, I'll need enough intact once I've extracted what's attached itself to you."

Extraction. The essence flowed through every part of my body. Attached to arteries, weaved through my muscular system, moving with blood flow, stitched throughout organs, and basically latched onto my nervous system. He couldn't seriously believe he had what it took to remove it, did he?

Harpy feathers fluttered, twirling in their descent. One by one, they stabbed the floor around the egg. I grimaced. All I needed was one to strike the egg. Just one. The tip of the quill landed atop the stone egg, sliding into the rocky shell like cutting through butter.

A hiss released from the egg, followed by a putrid yellow smoke, which immediately disintegrated the harpy feather allowing for a bigger airway of escape. The smog melted the bookshelves, ate away at the floor, and soon reached the bars.

I moved away to the corner of the cage, back pressed against the cold steel bars. I had to wait until enough of the bars in front of me had rotted away to slip between. Looked like the smog ate away the clay flooring a lot faster. I steadied my shaky legs, channeling essence and preparing to create a gust that'd hopefully be strong enough to carry me through the smog unscathed, past Novus, and out of the door leading beyond this dungeon.

Novus clapped, creating a cluster of gleaming lights which obeyed the rhythm of his applause. The glowing orbs moved into the yellow smog, absorbing it instead of disintegrating. As a shiny light swallowed the toxic air, the color dimmed and turned a dark gray before crumbling to ashes.

Dammit. He'd removed nearly all the smog in seconds, which meant there was no buffer to distract him with. He'd definitely catch me if I tried to move past him, and the bars still hadn't melted all the way through—not like the huge hole in the floor creeping closer to me each second.

A dark hole leading deeper into this dungeon wouldn't offer an escape from the villa.

Novus continued removing the smog.

Fuck it. I didn't have any other options, so it looked like I was improvising—more.

I conjured a black gust, knocking what remained of the smog, spinning and knotting it in windy waves around Novus. His flawless snow-white face bubbled and burned. He shouted, furious and pained, but I didn't stick around, jumping through the hole in the floor.

I landed in a dark corridor, hitting the stone floor hard. Glitter illuminated the rocks beneath me, but they followed the flow of my moving hands. Once I stood, the only sparkle came from the pressure of where my bare feet were planted. I wiggled my toes on the warm stone, then ran forward, searching for an end.

After several twists and turns through long stretches of doorless hallways, I paused to catch my breath.

Diabolic essence continued funneling through me, but I still couldn't feel Bez. However, I did feel the restoration of my mana. I muttered an incantation for illumination, lighting my path through these seemingly infinite hallways.

Walking ahead, I traced more incantations for defensive wards if anyone attacked, alerts on the presence of other magical signatures, and a highly complex set of symbols that should theoretically guide me to an exit, assuming a villa located on a different plane of existence had an exit.

"Walter Alden," Novus screamed, his voice a wailing screech at the far end of a corridor.

The piercing sound vibrated along the walls and floor, sending a glimmer rushing toward me. I raced ahead, cutting a corner just in time as sound waves barreled through a wall. Stone exploded, sending glittered dust and chunks of rock everywhere. The other side of the wall was brightly lit, so I ran through the debris, desperate for an exit that may not exist.

I entered a gigantic room and came to a stop, mesmerized by the vast collection of books, larger than anything displayed in the archives. Walls that stretched several stories high, shelves that floated and moved in a rotation similar to a conveyor belt. I could spend a lifetime researching in this room alone. So much information. Everywhere.

Novus tackled me, crashing into my back and sending us tumbling over one another as he clawed at my face and arms. The left side of his face sizzled and oozed pus; his teeth grew bigger and snapped shut, nearly biting my nose off.

I shoved him back by the shoulders, but he reached out, wrapping his long fingers around my throat.

Everything blurred.

My heart pounded.

I couldn't breathe.

A wall burst, and the immediate terror was replaced by relief when I saw black flames devouring everything in his path.

Bez.

I grimaced at the sight of so many books lost in the fire and rubble, but I couldn't fault him for rescuing me. How had he gotten here?

He cackled, sending torrents of flames throughout the library.

"Bez, stop." I fought against Novus' tightening grip. "H-help."

"Oh, that's right." He quelled his flames, then descended to the floor a few feet from where I struggled against Novus, eyes wide with rage, claws at the ready, and teeth bared in a way that meant he'd rip this fucking Baron to shreds.

Good.

8

Beelzebub

Immediate relief hit once I saw Wally, felt his presence, tasted his sweat in the air. Aside from a few cuts and scrapes, I didn't note any major sensations of pain from Wally and our strengthened bond, no longer hidden by the temporal folds of time and space. He struggled against the Fae that continued attempting to strangle him, conserving a massive amount of Diabolic essence. Clearly, I'd have to guide Wally better in understanding how much circulated through his being. Then again, the entire process was still new to me, too.

An elemental barrage proved most effective when navigating through this maze and tearing down the walls which stood between Wally and me, but now with many books ablaze, I could feel Walter's panic in his swelling chest. I huffed. Prioritizing the preservation of these dusty old tomes over his well-being. With a twist of my wrist and a curl of my claws, I simmered the flames I'd unleashed upon this library. Not that it seemed to matter; sparkling lights blossomed from the symbols etched onto the marble floor and cast radiating waves of rejuvenation and restoring damage to books and repairing the disarray in this library.

I prepared to lunge ahead, eviscerate the Fae who'd pinned Wally beneath him, but my worried little mage broke free from the tight grip on his neck, took a deep breath, and knocked an oozing clump of flesh off the rotting face of the Fae with a solid punch. Nice.

Wally turned, eyes wide and begging for assistance, so I paused. Keeping my feet firmly planted where I stood, I raised my shoulders and gave Wally a perplexed expression. "What do you want me to do? I can't just impulsively slaughter the man."

"This is not the time to make a point, Bez." Wally kicked the Fae in the chest, using the leverage to frantically crawl away. "Just do something!"

"But what if this is all one big Fae misunderstanding? I wouldn't want to overreact," I said, keeping a careful eye on the Fae's swiping hands, the erratic flow of magic, and the profane hollering of vengeance. Ugh, such an insufferable man. All that pompous dignity washed away the minute he suffered a minor blow.

Wally's breathing steadied, our waned airways no longer blocked.

"Are you serious right now?" Wally asked, skirting around a strike and running between aisles in some futile attempt to avoid the conflict.

"You made it very clear my nature defaults to murder, and I can't jump into this situation rashly. My instinct upon arriving here was kill first, ask questions later." I zipped past the Fae, shoulder-bumping him so he'd follow my blur when I reached Wally at the end of an aisle. "Yet you may have a point. I must contemplate these possibilities, Walter. Your lengthy lectures have left an invaluable impression on my heart."

The Fae bolted for Wally, splintering shelves through the harsh melodies carried in his seething exhales. This obnoxious and enraged Fae had yet to acknowledge my presence, though. Considering the burns on his face, I surmised Wally gave the man an acid bath which he sought recompense for. Good for him. Both of them, actually.

"Not sure who to root for," I said. "My lover or my potential soon-to-be BFF. Oh, the funny stories Novus and I shall share when out on the town. One day, we three will laugh and laugh about this awkward anecdote."

"Fuck you"—Wally ground his teeth—"Bez."

"Not here, Walter. Though, I'm flattered." I winked, which he missed, of course, due to desperately dodging Novus' flailing swipes intent on slashing my little mage to ribbons based on the augmented golden rings which now coated his fingers like an eagle's talons.

Claws slashed at Wally, tearing his shirt and nearly drawing blood. Crimson glimmered beneath his tattered shirt. Thankfully, our longstanding bond had increased the lengths my Diabolic essence extended in protective measures. It now guarded him from more than mere mortal wounds, reacting to his subconscious instinct.

The Fae snatched Wally by his curls and flung him into a shelf. I winced from our shared back pain.

No matter. Wally was in no immediate danger, having the evasive upper hand from the infuriated fairy. Thus, I waited. If things got risky, I'd kill the bastard. In the meantime, I was more than satisfied observing and making a point.

Dropping to the floor, I sat crisscrossed with my elbows on my knees.

Antoninus hissed, pinching my ear from his perched spot on my shoulder. Fucking bug got his claw caught on my earring.

"Begone, pest." I flicked a finger and sent the familiar hurling into a far-off bookshelf. Good riddance. His poor tutelage was the reason it took me so long to decode the damn card, making me nearly miss this delightful conflict.

His hiss sizzled out in the distance, and the angry clack of his claws grew faint. I stifled a snicker.

Wally traced incantations in the air. Their luminescence held the faintest orange hue, displaying how far his control over the Pentacles of Power had grown since most incantations cast only glowed a standard white. Thrown into the midst of conflict, Wally always flourished. He waved the incantations at Novus, caging the Fae, but not fast enough. Novus shattered into specks of glitter.

I shook my head. "Lazy technique, Walter."

"Shut up."

"Fine. You've obviously got this under control." I pretended to zip my lips.

The glitter formation of the Fae flickered erratically as it funneled through the air, looping about and discreetly gathering behind Wally. Novus reappeared, startling poor oblivious Wally, whose elevated blood pressure suggested the teleportation was instantaneous.

The movement was hardly instantaneous, in my opinion. Despite the shock on Wally's face. Nope. In fact, much slower and easier to track than at the theater. Perhaps with my emotions more in check, I was able to note his dimensional movements easier, or his fury prevented a proper stealthy shift between the atmospheres. Either way, killing him would be succinct as soon as Walter learned his lesson.

"Had I known I was in for such a show, I'd have brought a snack."

Wally ignored me as his desperation grew. Channeling currents of wind, he sent stacks of precious books flying at the angry fairy.

I sighed, perhaps feeling a pinch of guilt for my adorably misguided mage. "I can offer assistance, but I need you to say those magical little words."

"Help?"

"That's *one* word, Walter."

"Please!" Wally backed into a corner, whimpering and confused like an adorable puppy.

I crossed my arms, unyielding until he'd said the words. He knew them.

"I love you?"

"Bah." I flicked my tails, sending a small spark of black lightning coursing between them but offering Wally nothing. "As if I'd be swayed so easily by declarations of affection."

"Just kill him already!" Wally shouted.

"That seems rather dramatic." I stood tall and stretched my arms, playfully grinning. "But I suppose if you insist."

I ran at Novus, who'd finally acknowledged my presence and transformed into a glittering form, which he used to quickly conceal the presence of his Fae light beneath various layers of reality. Fascinating. He'd tucked himself behind the veil to hide his movements, whereas with Wally, he didn't bother with such things. It was only through deep examination and unblinking eyes I could seemingly slow reality and study these actions that happened in fractions of seconds.

He burst into a glittering discombobulated form. He unzipped the walls dividing planes of existence. He jumped into this world of light. Now, he moved around like a rat under a carpet, the subtle alterations in the air revealing him.

Unveiling my wings, I slowed my pace, making it easier to pivot my direction.

He froze, still hidden behind a veil. Fool thought he was safe so long as he remained incorporeal, but I ripped my way through his villa, studying the hidden plane he kept us on so nothing about the frequencies of teleportation would catch me off guard a second time.

Coating my hands in essence, I tore through the barrier dividing us and snatched a clump of glitter. Tendrils whipped from my wrist, lapping up the stray magic of the Fae's current form. He might've believed himself untouchable in this form, but with his Mythic residue divided a million times over as specks of twinkling dust, it was rather easy to eat.

He regathered his form, wheezing and backing away. Bloody and broken, with the rot on his face sinking even deeper.

"Wait, don't." Novus crawled on his belly like the insignificant worm he was. "You need me. Especially in this place. If you—"

SPLAT.

I smashed my heel through the back of his head. It caved in, splattering blood, chunks of bone, and gooey grey matter onto the floor.

"You talk too much," I said, grinding my foot into the marble flooring.

The squish beneath my shoe was divine, coupled with the fading melodies of the Fae's magics. It seemed this entire villa ran on horrid, pitchy tunes humming along like a locomotive, but now it all stilled, replaced by the spasming of a corpse and splash of pumping blood gushing from a formerly intact head.

"Gods." Wally cupped a hand over his mouth, his face sweaty and green. "Did you have to crush his head like that?"

I shook off the queasiness he sought to share with me, having nothing but joy in the messy muck at my feet.

"You practically begged me."

"Only because you were going to let him murder me to make a point."

"Nonsense." I scoffed. "I'd have drawn the line at light torture."

"Asshole. I can't believe you—"

"Saved your life? I know. I'm as shocked as you." I spun around, hand on my forehead to convey phony exhaustion, which Wally didn't buy. "Thankfully, I was able to decrypt the complex secrets hidden within that card and teleport to you."

Wally's anger faded, replaced by curiosity because of all his emotions, Wally's curious nature for answers about everything remained intact. "How'd you manage that?"

"I listen when you talk, obviously."

Antoninus skittered behind Wally, the scorpion quickly approaching with each step of his tiny, pointed feet. I used a tail to subtly chuck the scorpion across the library again. He'd simply take all the credit, insisting he'd been the reason for Wally's rescue when it was clearly my essence which activated the sigils, and I safely flew us through the dimensional barriers warded throughout this villa.

"What'd you learn during your visit?"

"Visit?" Wally twisted his lips, a musing gesture when searching for a way to express something. "That Baron Novus has a lot of illegal relics, access to lots of magics, and was planning on creating his own dimensional traveling port. Or I suppose he has but wanted your essence to add to it. Not sure why. Other than a devil's essence would be a thousand-fold stronger and fast track his agenda."

"So, nothing we didn't already know?"

"Next time I'm held against my will in a separate dimension by someone who wants to bleed me of essence and control my boyfriend, I'll be sure to direct the conversation to more revealing secrets."

"That'd be considerate, all I'm saying." I batted my lashes, watching Wally's face turn red from flustered aggravation. "Let us search this place."

"You know, I suspected he wanted to control you, but he didn't. Whatever he's doing with Diabolics doesn't involve a bond."

The foul stench of demon essence seeped into every wall of this villa expressed that much.

"There's more than bonds," I said. "Hell realms themselves use Diabolic essence from feeble demons to strengthen borders, enhance defenses, and make life generally more streamlined for everyone else living there. It's similar to the mortal working class, only devils shred demons and pour their discombobulated essence into the fabric of Hell."

"That's awful."

"Yes, terrible. Truly," I said. "I'm more curious about how the Fae managed to pull off something like this."

"A Fae," Wally said. "From what I gathered, in my completely unhelpful detainment, is that Novus didn't trust a lot of other Fae knowing his plans. Chances are this was a solo act."

"Perhaps." I sniffed the air. Mythic residue permeated the air almost hand and hand with the Diabolic essence coated throughout, but I couldn't discern if the magical residue came from visitors, captives, or his collection of trinkets. "Keep careful attention all the same. I don't desire being caught off guard by any Fae loyalists."

"We could start our search here." Wally rushed off, immediately heading to a podium where he'd clearly guessed correctly on a directory for this vast book room. "There could be useful information about how this villa works, how he's using Diabolics, a map to the place maybe. Seems huge from what I've seen so far."

"Please. I tore my way through the bulk of the villa. Simply a manor, smaller than the one you worked at when a part of the Collective." I conjured black flames between closely pressed palms. "I say we save ourselves the hassle and burn this entire place to the ground. No secrets to uncover or potential partners to exploit in a heap of ash and rubble floating between worlds."

"Absolutely not." Wally grabbed a book off a shelf, clutching it to his chest like he'd birthed a baby of words. "There are one-of-a-kind artifacts here. Tomes of knowledge that could benefit everyone. Secrets kept from the world. Things to—"

"Fine." I smothered the fire. "Explore, research, catalog, just stop talking about it."

Mora would be displeased if I destroyed the villa without uncovering Novus' methods anyway. Then again, fuck her. She'd conned me into a celebration that tossed us into this situation to begin with. She should be stuck here, unraveling secrets and listening to Wally's discoveries.

I sighed. This library alone would lead to a million new lessons and rambling discussions. I felt it in my bones.

"Let's save the library studies for another time." I waved a hand, telekinetically taking the stack of books Wally had already started piling up for his reading and moved them back to a shelf. Any shelf. I didn't care about the librarian's code of organization. "I want to find where he's keeping the demons. Even if he's funneling their essence throughout the villa, he has to keep their hearts and minds in one place."

"Unless he has a sign saying demon parts here, it could take some time," Wally said, retrieving the books to place on proper shelves, the gears turning in his maze of a mind. He was about to enter a tangent; I could feel it from the tension released from his muscles. "This place could be even bigger than we realize. Fae are known for spatial compressions, so there could be layers upon layers of the villa itself."

"Doubtful. This gaudy mansion seems to keep everything on display, probably easiest to remain undetected and streamlined by maintaining one reality."

Though, the frequency here was slightly off compared to most Fae traveling ports, completely different from what was used at the

Fae Divinity performance, which was already challenging to read. Best compared to stations on a radio, similar to the fact I didn't understand how those screeching sounds traveled through wires, simply that I could detect them. If Wally could see the threads of time and space laced in this library alone, he'd probably have a better system description. After he jizzed himself in utter delight and created an obscene amount of categorical research.

"Where should we start?" Wally asked.

"I'd say where he kept you. Chances are, he meant to carve my essence from you and lure me to that spot."

"I didn't see any Diabolics in that room."

"Can we just go?"

Wally led the way through the labyrinth, using an incantation to manifest a torch that lit our way through long-winding corridors.

"I think it was this way."

"You don't remember?"

"I wasn't exactly drawing a map as I ran for my life," he said with a note of a huffy snark. "Wait a second."

I mouthed one, two, three, four, and five before he continued. Definitely more than a second.

"This wasn't here last time." He walked toward a doorway, trailing his hand along the faded symbols lining the frame.

The door glowed blue, holding the faintest hue of a pocket portal.

"Then we've clearly gone the wrong way."

"No." He pointed to a hole above several yards ahead. "That's where I fell through unless there are a bunch of acid-made holes here."

"Let's hope not."

"You know what this means?"

"No." I stifled my annoyance because I had a good idea.

"It means even if you cut through a lot of the villa searching for me, there could've been entire rooms cloaked behind wards like these." Wally studied the symbols. "You were saying something about that being unlikely?"

I grumbled at his cocky tone.

"My best guess is all these protective wards shielding the villa and hiding pathways were linked to Novus' magical signature."

Funny. The Fae noble was as arrogant as the dead magus I never got to pluck from this earth. Abe had similar security measures, tying his magic and life force to everything in the repository. I loved when grandiose fools were slaughtered, and their treasures were easily taken.

I snatched Wally away from the doorway and wrapped him into a tight embrace, flying us through the hole back to where he'd arrived. If I left him to his own devices, he'd spend hours studying the door's symbols. Hell, we'd have never made it out of the library with Walteresque sleuthing.

Wally scrambled loose from my grip when we landed on what remained of the clay floor. I quickly noted the trap above meant to cut off all access to magic and mana for those bound within the confines of the pentagram. Eyeing the oddities which remained shelved in this room, I found myself impressed by how he'd managed to break free completely independently against a foe such as Novus, who had far more age and skill in casting.

I smiled. My brilliant, worrisome little mage didn't require a rescue. Had I not dropped in, I believe he'd have ended that damned fairy on his own. Wally was simply perfect.

"Oh no," Wally said, running his fingers along a melted bookshelf. "I think the smog I released destroyed some of the artifacts."

My fingertips tingled.

"Don't touch it." I swatted his hand with a tail. "Could still be caustic."

"Doubtful. Goblin smog has a very short half-life." He frowned, gesturing at a pile of liquified metal. "Potent stuff, though. Melted a full suit down."

"That's not nearly enough metal to make a suit of armor."

"Maybe some trickled down into the labyrinth." He shrugged. "It's not like it got up and walked away."

"Ooooo, gorgon eyes." I looked at the tasty pair displayed on a shelf. "Think they're still fresh?"

I reached out to pluck one of the succulent optic nerves out of the glass container and into my belly.

"No." Wally popped my hand. "We don't have time for your funny business."

"I was gonna eat them, not screw them." I pouted. "I reserve all the funny business for you."

He rolled his eyes and rested them on the nearby door where the aroma of magic permeated from behind, thick and intoxicating in the air.

"This way," I said, leading us through the door and down a long hallway toward an iron door where the bulk of power radiating inside this manner stemmed. "This is the central source of power."

Wally adjusted his glasses, scanning the symbols lining this door like they seemed to do for all here. "You sure?"

"Yes." I grabbed the handle, which wouldn't turn. "Looks like it's locked, but that's no problem."

I coated my hand in Diabolic claws because I didn't have all day for Wally to examine the locking mechanism when I could efficiently slash this door to pieces.

"Infidous metronome caustious," Wally said, followed by other mutterings.

The symbols lining the doors peeled off the wall, glowing and changing their arrangement. Clicks and clanks followed their new placement, and the door swung open.

"How'd you do that?" I asked.

"Same secret code as the invitation on the card he offered. Guess Novus didn't concern himself with changing his passwords."

"What a moron. He's just asking to be robbed."

"Says the guy whose password is 1-2-3-4," Wally said, mockery in his tone.

"What? It's so obvious no one would ever suspect it. Plus, I'm not worried about some mortal stealing my telephone." But I'd delight in chopping off the hands of one foolish enough to try.

This room oozed as a central hub where all mana and essence circulated, yet nothing in here indicated a prison for the demons Novus had acquired. Their Diabolic essence merely lingered stronger before moving elsewhere. Beneath the concrete floor, pipes creaked and trembled, funneling the magics like fuel to power this villa.

There was nothing noteworthy here aside from a large screen that filled the entire back wall and a control panel covered in Sylvan symbols. No exotic baubles on display here like in the room where Wally was detained. The single chair in front of the panel and screen was a good sign. Maybe this Novus fellow truly did work alone.

Wally traced his fingers along the operational controls because he always had to touch things. "This is like the helm."

"The what?"

"Of a ship."

"This is a house, Walter."

"Yes," he said, pointing to a blinking blob on the screen. "But it's moving through time and space. Well, not like time travel exactly—which would be cool but involves too many quantum entanglements. Even briefly rewinding it could create an astronomical effect that causes an entire dimension to fold in on itself. I actually peer-reviewed a dissertation that explored the concepts…" Wally looked at my perplexed and unamused face. "But I digress. My point is, this room the helm, courses the navigation of the villa—also a ship—through the different planes of reality. These are probably the controls, which'll take time to figure out, and there's gotta be a blueprint around here somewhere. With that, we might be able to find where the Diabolics are being held or harvested or other not fun things. Hmmm."

Fuck me. This place did have different layers, which meant it'd take forever to search. It would've been quicker to torch the whole damn villa.

"We'll be here for weeks," I said, shoulders slumping.

"Maybe months." Wally's hazel eyes twinkled with joy, darting about and soaking in all the gizmos and gadgets of this room.

"I suppose this is an upgrade to our humble abode."

"What?" Wally asked with a squeak, not of fright or confusion but one meant to hide his enthusiasm.

"It's far more efficient to make this our home, at least for the time being. It'd require too much mana and time traveling between planes."

"Can we just take his place?"

"Pillage and plunder."

"We're not pirates."

"Which is a shame, but I'm reminded of my favorite mortal expression that's kept your world moving forward." I planted my hands on my hips, puffing my chest and boasting. "To the victor go the spoils, one of the few mortal sentiments I can get behind. And we were victorious. Me mostly, but you had a small, supporting role, I suppose."

"It would allow me to make the most of my time." Wally bit his lower lip biting back a dozen side tangents, no doubt.

“Plus, I can finally give our old home the pyre it deserves. I will be burning something down today,” I said with a grin. “It’ll be far easier to torch than clean all the stuff I broke.”

“What?” Wally raised his eyebrows.

I skirted past him, examining the navigation system in search of a basic floorplan. “Where do you think the master bedroom is?”

“Can we rewind that conversation a tad…” Wally looped his fingers round and round.

“I’d like to christen it.” I ignored his befuddled question, using a tail to playfully tickle his chin. “Then again, we should properly lay claim to all the rooms in this massive home.”

“Okay, but what did you trash exactly because some of that stuff was client work, and then there’s my personal collection—”

“What do you say, Walter?” I wrapped a tail around his waist and yanked him close to me. “Shall we introduce your lovely moans of ecstasy to this room? Or would you rather continue asking questions you know I’m not going to answer?”

9

Walter

A week had gone by, and I'd barely gained any understanding of the navigation systems here at the helm of the villa. I'd tried spending time researching in the library or exploring the doorways, which might very well lead to an instructional manual, but *someone* insisted I stay here in this room unless otherwise escorted. The same *someone* only ever brought me to the kitchen or the bedroom he'd claimed and horribly trashed the artwork he deemed 'crass' or 'tasteless' among other less polite phrases.

"Any progress?" Speaking of the annoying someone… Bez came strutting into the helm, wet hair sticking to his small horns still exposed, and one of his tails patted down his muscular abs as he fiddled with something on his dress shirt.

Since arriving here, he'd begun absorbing the trace amounts of Mythic residue wafting around the residence, which helped stitch up his host body. We'd planned on getting him a new one, but I didn't like the idea of killing some poor person and taking their body, and

Bez's Diabolic features weren't a problem so long as the Collective didn't catch wind. With so much extra magic, it seemed he could repair the tears in his human suit and tuck away those features.

"I don't like the cleaning supplies here," he said, picking at lint. "I prefer the ones at our former residence."

"It's lint, Bez. It'll follow you to any plane."

"Only in the cheap machines. Clearly, that Fae had no respect for his wardrobe. Even I acquired acceptable utilities for us."

I smiled. I'd refused to pay an extra grand for the washer and dryer unit Bez wanted, and I told him no stealing, so for a solid six weeks, he stalked every Black Friday event across the tri-state area—yes, every store. Every tip. Every possible savings on 'fallible currency.' Then he dragged me to some sale two days early, six-hundred miles away, all so we could have a proper unit. Admittedly, they were a great washer and dryer, wonderful on water use, nice on the utilities, and it always made me happy to reminisce about the domestic bliss we shared.

Even if it was short-lived or an illusion. I enjoyed following Bez anywhere and everywhere.

"What?" he asked with a sour expression because gods forbid he endure the travesty of lint, which he wouldn't have to deal with if he changed the filter. "Have you made any progress on pinpointing the Diabolics?"

"Nope. I'd make more progress if you'd let me explore some."

"Absolutely not. Especially since I have to step out." Bez grabbed a stack of books I'd pulled from a short visit to the library.

"Hey. What're you doing with those?"

"Selling them," he said casually. "What? You said they held no intel on the villa, so they're useless to your studies."

"They hold ancient rites on countless Mythic practices, secrets seeped in spellcraft that could take decades to decipher, knowledge that's priceless."

"Not that priceless. I'm certain Mora will find a buyer real quick."

"W-what?" I jumped out of my chair. "No. You can't just sell them to anybody."

"We have bills to pay, and this junk isn't doing anyone any good sitting in storage."

"I'm the one who manages our day-to-day expenses, and we're fine."

"That Fae performance you insisted on attending was rather pricey," Bez muttered.

"I didn't even know about it until you took me."

"Well, it cost a small fortune, and I refuse to be indebted to Mora even if it was a ploy on her end." Bez swaggered across the room, eyeing up anything and everything he could pawn off. "I can't have her pleading I owe her favors if I ever decide to rip out her manipulative heart one day. It's undignified."

"So, you're just leaving?" And taking priceless items beyond either of their comprehension. I swear, Bez and Mora tossed artifacts about with no regard. I wondered if Kell dealt with this from Mora, too.

"Only long enough to send these off and return. I'll be back soon."

By "send them," he meant using the stealth incantation for the Hawk's Eye Traveling spell. Cloak their presence and ship them discreetly to Seattle, where Mora would, in turn, find a buyer and then wire us the payment—minus her exorbitant commission.

"And by soon, I mean very soon. Don't get any ideas about snooping around." Bez glared. "Now that the wards are down, I can feel your link with ease."

I folded my arms, not in a pouting way. A furious way. He'd stumbled onto that discovery when he went home to retrieve our clothes and knew I'd wandered around. Or so he said. Honestly, I think he just rolled the dice on that one and got lucky. Bez knew there was a ninety-percent likelihood I'd explore, so he happened to guess right.

He jabbed me in the forehead with a sharpened black nail, not his claws, but the glamoured almond nail shape he liked so much. "I mean it, Walter."

"Yeah, yeah." I brushed his hand away. "I heard you."

"Yes, but you had the gears-turning expression, which means you probably weren't listening."

"Yes. I'm listening." Mildly. Bez tended to think I overthought things and thus acted rashly, which was the opposite of overthinking, but I didn't have the time to have that argument with him because I wanted him gone, so I could explore.

Bez reached into his blazer's inside pocket and pulled out a dagger.

I quivered. Not just any blade. The Demon's Demise. I hadn't looked at that weapon since stabbing Ian in the chest and watching the life drain from his face. My stomach twisted. I didn't like thinking back on Ian. How much I hated him. How good it felt ending his life. The way he convulsed beneath my hips as I straddled him, the stillness of him as everything about Ian faded to nothingness and he died.

I snatched the dagger from Bez. "How'd you even fit that in your pocket?"

"Magnetism incantation. Works better than the refrigerator."

"What're you doing with it?" My stomach churned; I'd put this in a tightly sealed and enchanted box for a reason.

I couldn't very well leave it behind, but I couldn't risk it being used on Bez or me or Mora or anyone with Diabolic essence since it could easily carve it out. That was the only reason.

"We did keep it on the off chance we stumbled onto a menacing demon, and we might get our chance," Bez said, smirking.

"Huh?"

"This boat of a home seems quite empty, rats included, but there's a lot of essence and Mythic residue circulating throughout. I haven't investigated nearly as much as I'd prefer..."

He hadn't snooped because he wanted to keep an eye on me.

"It's unlikely to happen since chances are the chunks of essence floating about are merely used as fuel to keep this thing moving, but on the off chance a demon appears—gut it."

"You think that's necessary?"

"Absolutely. Never mince words with demons. Kill them and save the conversation for their eulogy. That's my motto."

"I should've tried that when you kicked me down the stairs." I grimaced.

"You did. And failed spectacularly." He puckered his lips. "Then I ravished you, which I wish I had some time for now, but alas, work calls."

I rolled my eyes, mainly because of how he'd repainted our history to suit his banter and his boasting over work. Bez hated work, calling it a classist system to oppress joy, yet he wanted all the fun things which cost money.

"You think I can hold my own against a demon?"

"Not a chance. You'll be dead in a minute. Less than if they realize you're screwing a devil. But since you're insistent on exploring without me at your side, we need proper measures in place."

I clenched the blade's hilt.

Tony clacked his claws, startling me.

"Ah, yes, Antoninus," Bez said the name mockingly. "If you toss him at a Diabolic foe, you might buy yourself a few more seconds."

"Rude." I bopped Bez on the chest, to which he merely snapped his teeth like biting the air, then grinned.

Tony hissed. And for good reason. I hadn't even realized Tony had gotten here when Bez nearly dropped a book on him during our *one* library visit since moving into the villa. Bez claimed he must have snuck into his slacks when he went through the portal to rescue me, but I suspected there was more to the story. I just didn't know the full story…yet.

"Just stay in here, keep the door locked, and be sure to run if something jumps out of the shadows." With that, Bez walked toward the white glowing seven-sided star sigil and vanished in a cloud of golden, sparkling specks.

The helm had the only exit on or off the villa's dimensional voyage, back to our plane of reality. Well, the only one we'd found. Bez was right. I needed to remain here. Not that anything had appeared or attacked us since arriving and dealing with the former Baron Novus, but it was doubtful an enemy would strike with a devil nearby.

I gulped. "I'm going to double-check the door."

Tony skittered toward the operation's panel, obviously dismissing my fear as paranoia. But it was like double-checking the stove, deadbolt, or light switch in another room—it never hurt to air on the side of caution, whereas it could be deadly to throw caution to the wind.

I reexamined the incantations I'd added as an extra locking mechanism on the entrance. The glow of the symbols held strong, and even a regiment chancellor would have difficulty breaking through. These wards would keep anyone from just walking into the helm. Excluding a Fae, of course, since they could simply move between dimensions and skirt the laws put into place. Or a Diabolic, who could do the same, and also use their essence to devour and destroy the incantations altogether.

Oh, gods. I was screwed.

Why'd Bez have to put that in my head? I hoped he'd return soon. Mainly because he'd planted horrible doubts about my death without him here, and also, I had nothing to research. I'd scoured the books I'd brought that didn't remotely assist in comprehending how the navigation system for the villa's helm worked, which didn't matter since he'd stolen them to pawn off to Mora.

Tony clicked his claws, directing them to the navigation panel. He was right. Sometimes the best way to learn a system was to explore it with a little hands-on instruction. Plus, it'd distract me at the very least.

I set the dagger down and joined in to investigate the control panel, doing my best to recall Sylvan symbols without a handy guidebook for linguistic references. Each letter of the alphabet acted as a button to push. Tony trailed alongside a set of seven repeatedly, careful not to tap them but pointing his stinger every time he crossed those particular letters.

"You're clearly better at memorizing the Fae language than I am," I said. "Alrighty, buddy. I'm gonna trust your judgment."

I pressed the first, second, and third symbols he'd shuffled past. When I reached for the fourth, Tony hissed.

"Oops." I followed his very clear order of directions.

Gears whirled. Followed by clanks and thunks and lots of twisting knots sounding below and above this room.

"Shit. Pretty sure we hit a few incorrect buttons."

A learning curve that hopefully didn't break anything.

I looked at the door, triple checking the ward held strong, which of course, it did.

"Maybe we shouldn't play with this," I said.

Tony ignored me, his thirst for answers bolder than mine, and continued trailing by different buttons.

"I just think…"

He clicked his claws as impatiently as Bez when enduring my overthinking anxiety.

"Let's just wait."

Tony hopped onto a button, then a second.

I reached out to scoop him up before he caused irreparable damage, but he reached a third, and the navigation course screen blipped away.

"Look what you did!" I backed away, tugging my curls.

What if this changed our course? What if it altered the dimensional frequency? What if Bez couldn't find us now? What if we were stuck on this villa floating between planes of existence forever?

The screen lit up, no longer a black hue with a green dot for a destination but a hundred gray screens indicating various cameras spread throughout the villa.

"Look what you did." I stepped closer, watching the mini screens flicker and switch views to other rooms. "Whoa."

Some were to rooms I didn't think Bez or I had stumbled onto, which meant the live feed worked through trans-dimensional recording. A totally intricate system beyond even what the Collective had access to. They'd often tried setting up security systems inside the Dimensional Atrium, but the technology receivers never responded outside the pocket realm.

"Tony, you're a brilliant mastermind." I extended a hand so he could climb up my shoulder. My palm brushed over a single letter, barely grazing it, yet the faint button glowed white and then blinked over and over.

The seven-sided star portal exit nearby joined in the flickering until the glowing doorway vanished altogether.

"No. What'd I do?" I took a deep breath. Several deep breaths. Several speedy, panicky deep breaths. "Shit."

BANG.

My heart hammered almost as loudly as the something that pounded against the door.

BANG.

It hit the door a second time.

"Shit."

BANG. BANG. BANG.

"Shit. Shit. Shit." I grabbed the Demon's Demise, holding it firmly, and desperate the door held strong. "Please don't be a demon."

Then again, would this Diabolic killing blade work on anything other than a Diabolic?

Tony hissed, stabbing his stinger at the air.

"Right," I said with a shiver. It was sharp. Stabby. Stabbing worked on just about any threat.

A harsh scraping replaced the pounding against the door.

I squeezed the hilt until my trembling body settled—mostly. I swallowed the terror bubbling inside me and cast saturation throughout the helm. As suspected, the incantations on this side began to falter. Whatever slashed at them from the other side had tremendous power, hacking away magic put in place without setting off any of the defensive recoil enchantments. Those wards were supposed to create a barrier to prevent interference and explosives to strike out when tampered with.

The handle fell to the floor.

The door creaked open.

A lump grew in my throat.

Six glowing purple eyes stared from the darkness of the corridor. Literal flames danced in the irises, eyes bigger than my fists.

"I'm not afraid of you," I said with a squeak, one that gave away the obvious lie.

The monstrous silhouette burned bright blue and lunged from the shadows.

10

Beelzebub

My breathing hitched, heart racing, and my muscles tensed. Full-blown physical distress struck all at once. I dropped the stack of incantations I'd nearly finished putting together to ship the books off, sinking into this dread. Our link remained strong, undisturbed by dimensional planes separating us, though a snag in the bond hit as the doorway leading back to the villa vanished.

Wally.

I ground my teeth.

Fuck, I couldn't leave Walter alone for five seconds without him finding a way to endanger himself. I bet he'd tinkered with the damn navigation system, touching things he shouldn't. There could've been a hundred different security protocols set in place, and knowing Walter, he'd triggered every single one.

I took a sharp inhale, steadying the budding fear, and exhaled Wally's emotions. I'd need my mind as my own if I intended to rescue him. The dimensional wavelengths dividing realms remained invisible to most, but I harnessed Diabolic essence, circulating it through my eyes. With clearer vision, I studied the various threads stringing together veils meant to keep worlds from falling in on each other.

I lacked the precision or expertise to tear holes through dimensional walls like the Fae, but I could also punch a path directly to Wally. I didn't need to be delicate in the patchwork, and I didn't bother stitching the road I paved by ripping through cosmic energy. Each step weighed heavy as I floated through the ether of space and time. A starry void with twinkling distractions. I ignored them and slashed shrouds along the original route to the villa. So long as the villa hadn't changed course or frequency, I could retrace the steps.

One. By. One. I tore luminescent barriers asunder.

With the cloaking wards down, it didn't take long to sniff out the direction of the villa. My connection to Wally served as an anchor, dragging me down to him. Dammit. If I sniffed out the drifting Fae residence, it would be easy enough for any Diabolic to find. Suppose the Fae could too, which probably meant one had. Sure, Wally believed Novus kept his work quiet, but there had to be another Fae he trusted, others as corrupt as him, as foolhardy to pick a war with the Diabolics by stealing our essence to fuel his endeavor.

War.

I shook my head and continued pressing forward.

That was the incorrect word. A one-sided slaughter was no war, and the second any devil, a true devil, discovered this, they'd lay waste to any and all involved. Hell, one might very well devour an entire Fae dimension as compensation. Might destroy our world as collateral. The only blessing about all-powerful god-kings was they often considered themselves above the trivialities of lower, lesser worlds with entities even more worthless than the muck under their feet—their demon subjects. If one deigned the actions Novus attempted as a threat, everyone and everything would pay the price. It wouldn't matter if someone learned my secret then; there wouldn't be a single soul left to exploit it.

I wheezed, nearly collapsing through a void of empty space. Something pressed down on my chest—Wally's chest—crushing my lungs. He must be fighting for his life this very second. I needed to move faster.

I reached the villa, barely noting the fine craftsmanship of the stone walls—that Wally would've gawked at given the opportunity—before landing on the terrace. Shattering the glass panel doors, I zipped inside and darted directly for Wally. The festering wound of fear had been replaced by bubbly excitement.

Had he turned the tables? Was I overreacting? No. This fleeting sensation had become weaved with anxiety. Wally needed me now!

It took only a few seconds to run through the upper floors and reach the wall adjoined to the corridor which led to the helm. No time to find an entrance, so I blasted a hole through the wall with black lightning.

Claw marks cut deep into the incantations lining the entryway, and the metal door was left ajar.

Blue flames lined three muscular necks; each fire carried a hint of purple at its core. Powerful paws pressed on Wally's chest, pinning him to the ground. Jaws lined with fanged teeth hung wide, slobbering toxic saliva all over Wally. He struggled beneath the grasp, locked in combat against a foe who'd easily overpowered him. A disgusting tongue reached out, lapping and licking Wally, tasting the flesh of his face, most likely before biting off his head.

The Diabolic killing blade lay just out of Wally's reach. His worthless familiar clicked his claws, protesting as Wally fought against the terrible beast that must've guarded this home despite the death of its master.

I conjured black flames, preparing to incinerate this foul creature and free my love.

"No. Wait. Stop. That tickles." Wally giggled. Actually, fucking giggled when entrenched in the throes of combat.

His confidence was commendable, but this beast would not heed his warning. I needed to eliminate the threat.

"Die, you damn dirty hound of Hell." I threw a fireball at the beast.

"Bez, no!" Wally waved a hand, redirecting the flame. All three heads of the monstrosity that'd attacked him turned their attention to the ball of fire bouncing around the helm.

"What are you doing, Walter?" I snapped.

"He's harmless."

"He is an attack hound." I pointed to the three-headed beast. "He is attacking you right now!"

"He's playing, Bez." He reached out, stroking the short, black fur. "He's a puppy."

"He's disgusting. The foulness of the saliva must carry a potent toxin that's fried your brain or perhaps locked you in an illusion."

"I think it's just what he ate. Not sure what kind of puppy chow someone feeds a growing Cerberus, but his breath is almost as rank as yours."

"How. Dare. You." After I'd literally ripped through worlds to rescue him, he had the audacity to say I had bad breath.

"It's only after you eat certain foods." Walter feigned an apologetic grin like I'd buy it. "It's not my fault you think raw liver and onions are an aphrodisiac."

"With chocolate peppermint." I crossed my arms. *Mint is in the name.*

Walter's hand grazed the flames as he pet the Mythic beast. They flickered brighter, leaving him unscathed, while the center head nuzzled his face. Revolting.

The left head turned his fiery eyes at me and growled. I glared and bared my teeth. I wouldn't be intimidated by some tiny monster.

"Bez, leave him alone. You're going to scare him."

"Good." I huffed.

With that, the attention of the Cerberus fell onto the black fireball, which continued bouncing around the room thanks to Walter's incompetent overpowered use of telekinesis. The three-headed puppy gave chase. I hoped it would catch the flames and burn itself in a pile of ashes.

Antoninus hissed as the beast crossed his path. Finally, something me and that annoying scorpion could agree on.

The three-headed monster ran back and forth, biting at the fireball and falling short.

"Careful, Weather," Wally shouted, brushing the fur that clung to his shirt with the adhesive of slobber.

I shuddered in revulsion.

"Oh, no." Wally's face tensed as the hound snapped the black flames with powerful jaws. "What do we do?"

"Grab marshmallows."

Antoninus' clawed clatter clearly held the same sentiment.

Then the most unconceivable thing happened, the little abomination swallowed my flames and belched. Smoke blew out of the left and right head while the center head yelped, mocking my Diabolic fire with a lopsided tongue hanging out of his mouth. Fiend.

But of course, Mythic beasts often exuded elemental dominance over one in particular, and this one thought itself a master of flames. Well, if he liked fire, perhaps I'd offer him some more.

"You want to play fetch, huh?" I conjured another black fireball, tightening the size to instill more heat and catastrophic destruction in a denser form. "Why don't you try catching this…"

"No." Wally wagged a finger. "Weather, sit."

"What are you doing?"

"He already destroyed the door," Wally said. "Put the fire away, Bez. You two can play later."

I smothered the flames, savoring the scorched sensation on my palm.

"What's with the name?" I asked.

"Weather? It just sort of came to me. Not sure if he's already been named yet, but I think he really likes it. Huh, Weather?" Wally patted the center head, which responded by joyfully barking.

"Weather? As in whether or not you should kill him before he kills us?"

"Don't be silly. Weather as in"—Wally pointed to the jovial, panting center head—"Sunny"—he pointed to the surly, snarling left head—"Stormy"—then he rested his hand on the gloomy right head—"and Cloudy"—which stared with glossy, flamed eyes and timidly lowered his head when Wally scratched his pointed ears.

"Sunny, Stormy, and Cloudy? You realize that makes no sense."

"Makes perfect sense." Wally frowned.

"It's only one beast. He doesn't require three names, no four names. Mortals and their obsession with titling everything in existence. So vexing."

"I know I've named his personas, but it helps kind of understand his alter egos. And they all tie together to his name, Weather." Wally's glee became a nauseating pit in my stomach. "Did you know that while a Cerberus has three heads, three dominant personalities, and three functioning brains, they work as a singular entity?"

Sunny plopped back, spreading his legs, and began licking his testicles while the right head, Stormy, attempted to bite his own wagging tail every time it batted his side.

"I wouldn't call his brains functioning," I muttered.

"It has to do with some consensus in their mind and nervous system," Wally said, ignoring me in favor of lectures and continuing to pet the Cerberus. "The personas act independently sometimes, but they are all the same little guy."

"Little? The beast is bigger than a Great Dane!"

"Actually, his size is more comparable to the Bernese Mountain Dog, which is..." Wally rambled, continuing to fawn over the Mythic beast. "...but for a Cerberus, he's basically only twelve to sixteen weeks old. Maybe a bit older if he's the runt. Hard to know for sure since I've only read about Cerberus' in textbooks, but the size charts seem very comparable especially given the expressive nature of his personas. Formative but still in the exploring phase. Plus, the size of his paws. You know, they're viciously loyal creatures and make wonderful guardians."

"You mean guards. Usually, guards to horrid underworlds filled with specters and foul spirits refusing to accept death and the beyond, lingering in an attempt to haunt the world."

"Aw, you listened when I talked about my report on *The Hades Complex*?"

"Whatever." I huffed and turned my head away. "How'd that thing even get up here?"

"Tony and I were researching the navigation system," he said, which was a fancy way to put 'touching things they shouldn't' if you ask me. "And I think we opened his kennel in the lower levels. Being so young, chances are he sniffed out the only source of life in the villa and found me. And Tony."

I glared at the bug, who didn't appear all that fond of the beast sniffing and yapping at him. But good riddance since he was equally culpable for this turn of events.

"You know, a Cerberus can sniff out anything, living or dead. He might be really helpful in tracking down the source of the missing Diabolics."

"Doubtful. Diabolic essence is unlike any other substance in this world or any other. We're far too complex for his nose. All three of them."

Wally returned to the beast that rolled on his back, exposing his stomach for affection.

"So, he just obeys you?"

"Not really. He's still just a puppy, but I did learn he's gone through some obedience training—if you can call it that." Wally went over to the navigation screen, which had been replaced by images of all the rooms. Not images—recordings. "Turns out the pink Fae—really need a name for her—was in charge of disciplining Weather."

Wally hit a few buttons, zooming in on one screen and rewinding it. The timestamped symbols zipped by as the screen rewound. The screen stopped on an image of the pink Fae from the performance who abducted Wally and vanished into a flurry of butterflies, holding a metallic whip in front of a cage where the Cerberus sat.

Weather's—ugh, I hated that name—left head growled at the image as the right head whimpered. The image alone conveyed the malice in the Fae's face, the rage in one Cerberus head, fear in another, and a desire to please through kindness in the central leading head.

"Guess she has access here, so you were absolutely right about keeping an eye out for others," Wally said. "Not sure if she'll show up again, but we should be ready for anything since she knows about the villa."

Good. I'd hoped to cross paths with her again so I could gut her for taking Wally in the first place.

"How'd you learn all this?"

"After Weather greeted us, Tony and I went back to studying the cameras, then he obviously got a little rambunctious again."

"A little?" There was nothing little about that three-headed hound except his brains.

"There's surveillance all over the place. Other than Weather, there hasn't been anything on the live feed recently." Wally side-eyed me. "But it doesn't help that half the cameras went dark after *someone* arrived."

"Your life was at stake, Walter. I didn't have time to knock."

"You didn't exactly rush to my aid either."

"I'm going to be the mature one here and not lower myself into a petty argument of who did or didn't do what."

Wally's brow furrowed, his lips twisted, but he remained speechless, lacking a proper comeback that didn't result in him being immature.

"I hate you," he muttered, returning to the system controls.

"And I love you, in spite of your childish ways, Walter."

He glowered.

11

Walter

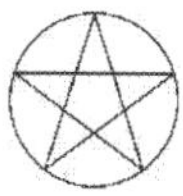

I woke up snuggled in a warm blanket and cushy bed, unsure how I'd ended up here, but gladly sank into the cozy feeling. The last thing I remembered was searching for texts to help explore and control the villa in the library. Well, attempting anyway. It'd been a pretty exhausting last few days, between all the attention Weather sought, to the way Bez scolded Weather every time he tried to play, sniff, or begged for a piece of Bez's inedible dishes. Tony also added to the flames of chaos—sometimes literal between Bez and Weather—by trying to sting the puppy every time I turned my head.

I never considered myself the nurturing type, so kids weren't high on my list of priorities. But having to wrangle the three of them while acting as the only productive person here and having almost no time to myself was a strong reminder. Tending to a familiar, Mythic beast, and Diabolic was exhausting enough.

Still, I'd made serious progress in understanding this ship. It was, in fact, classified as a vessel, not a house, in the schematics I'd found in the library. I shivered, wrapping myself tighter in the blanket, thinking back to Novus' caved-in skull.

Thankfully, Bez had disposed of the body, which I hadn't asked for details on other than to ensure it didn't lead back to the Fae, so either he burned the corpse to ash or tossed it into the vacuum of dimensional space. Either way, the library's self-preservation wards did wonders for cleaning up the blood stains and removing the stench of death. I liked the automatic cleaning and organizing enchantments in this library; I just wished I knew how to enact the catalog commands when researching.

It took time to decipher the text, but I'd managed that, too. Not that I comprehended the translation since it followed the Sylvan alphabet yet used some coded styling in the manual breakdown. It didn't matter. Soon, I would unravel every single part of the ship, from how to work the control system for navigation, to figuring out where and how the Diabolics were stored, all the way to the biggest bonus of learning where each portal doorway in here led and what they held. I could spend forever here, learning everything, charting a course wherever, whenever to take us anywhere in the world and beyond with the push of a few buttons.

The curtains leading to the balcony were drawn open, letting bright starlight shine inside the bedroom. Since the villa skirted between planes, remaining on the edges of cosmic space with one half and orbiting our world with the other half, the light of this hidden world held a similar effect to the aurora borealis. Twinkling colors poured inside. They sparkled against the furniture set up outside the walk-in closet, the adjoined dressers—which were only adjoined because Bez dragged a second one from another room and slammed them together—and the ivory bedframe posts. Bare cream walls caught the colors and reflected them back at me, stinging my eyes.

I brushed sleep dust from my eyes and grabbed my glasses placed on the nearby nightstand. Bez must've brought me to bed.

He could be sweet when he wasn't being obnoxious. Speaking of obnoxious, the first thing my clear vision landed on was the one portrait Bez hadn't removed and tucked away elsewhere. A self-portrait of Baron Novus, which remained on full display with the added touches Bez had made. He'd punched a hole through the head and wall to match the actual Novus whose head he'd kicked in.

"Wakey, wakey, dry eggs and plain ole bakey." Bez paraded into the bedroom, crystal tray in hand while using a tail to shoo Weather from trudging in behind him.

Not that I liked Bez's disregard for the puppy most of the time, but I couldn't handle being plopped on by a nearly two-hundred-pound Cerberus while half asleep for the third time. If not for Bez's essence, I'd probably have broken something or, at the very least, have a mild concussion from the eager tackles.

"You made me breakfast?" I asked skeptically, mostly reserved for the normal-looking dish presented on the tray Bez placed on my lap.

Scrambled eggs and bacon with a glass of water and orange juice.

"Yes, a difficult task since your palate is lacking, but I worked on keeping all the flavor out of it. No sugars, salts, or sides to make this a truly spectacular dish."

He wasn't kidding about the lack of seasonings. I took a bite of the dry, unsalted eggs. Did he even add milk? Complain one time about not wanting dairy in a dish, and he took it off the menu forever. A scoop of vanilla ice cream on top of broccoli was in no way the same as broccoli and cheddar. I swear, the only ingredient he added to these eggs was passive aggressiveness. At least the bacon was perfectly crunchy and plenty salty to compensate.

"Not that I don't love the gesture, but why the gesture?"

"No reason." Bez checked his phone, something he never did—ever. He'd sooner hurl it into the void of time and space before responding to notifications. "Just want you to know I value your work. I know you've put a lot of effort into learning how this villa functions."

"Yeah," I said, tearing a piece of bacon. "Pretty sure in a few more weeks, I'll know this whole place inside and out."

All I needed was a single manual, one lead that would connect to others, and soon I'd know how every gear, floorboard, and symbol in this massive place worked.

"Don't worry," I said. "Finding the Diabolic essence is still high on my list of priorities."

Weather hadn't been all that helpful in that regard. Then again, it'd only been a few days, and he didn't exactly know what I was requesting.

"I hate to say it, but it could take months on our own," Bez said. "I don't even know where to begin, and usually, you're better with research but…"

"But what?" I asked.

"But maybe it's time to call in reinforcements?"

"We don't have reinforcements. I can't think of one mage that'd help me unravel the mysteries of an illegally obtained Fae home, which also has a lot of illegally acquired artifacts." My stomach twisted in knots—I didn't really have friends to call on, no one from the Collective who'd really missed me since I took off. Maybe my siblings cared…maybe. But I was certain, Collective priorities would overtake any family loyalty if I showed them the plethora of items in the former baron's possession.

"I wasn't thinking of mages," Bez said. "More like…"

His phone rang, which he ignored.

I quirked an eyebrow. "How do you even have service here?"

We were literally hovering between worlds.

"I don't even know what Wi-Fi stands for," he said, dragging a finger over the red end button and clicking the green accept. "Why would you suspect I know how it works?"

Seriously, one hell of a service provider. Probably a Collective conglomerate that I should look into, but still, impressive reception.

"Bezzy, can you hear me?" A muffled voice called out, but only one person called Bez Bezzy.

"Dammit. I hung the telephone up."

"You hit accept." I chuckled.

He was more obstinate in learning how modern tech worked than my late grandmother, both favoring that the best advancements came during the 50s and everything after that was downhill.

"Where are you?" Mora asked. "This place is a maze."

"Wait, what?" I sprang up, nearly knocking the tray off my lap. "How'd she get here?"

"I might've told her if she wanted answers on this Diabolic kerfuffle, then she needed to help." He sighed. "She wasn't supposed to just waltz in until after I talked with you. Leave it to Mora to just invite herself in."

"You know I can hear you, right?" Mora asked loudly.

Geez, when had Bez hit the speakerphone?

"It's not like you own this place," Mora added. "It's not in your name or anything, so it's as much mine as anyone else's."

"Hang up on her," Bez grumbled and tossed me his phone. "I better go find her before she snoops around for the deed and tries to evict us."

"You're kidding?" I half-grinned until Bez's very serious expression remained unchanged. "You are kidding, right?"

"It wouldn't be the first time. I should tell you the story of how she had me kicked out of *my* first-class suite on a boat. And all so she'd have an extra room for her luggage."

"That's rude," I said, hanging up the phone.

"It's fine. I threw an iceberg in her path, so in the end, I won."

"Wait, what?" I practically jumped off the bed.

"Better find Mora before she causes havoc." With that, Bez zipped away in a blur leaving the door wide open, allowing Weather to bulldoze his way inside.

"Wait," I said to them both—Bez for bolting away and Weather for bolting onto the bed, tackling me.

Sunny licked my face while Cloudy nuzzled my neck, and Stormy glared, definitely annoyed to be dragged along for the ride.

Bez couldn't be referring to what I thought he was referring to, right? I considered it, then rolled Weather off me and climbed out of bed.

"We're finishing this conversation on shipwrecks and icebergs," I shouted, half expecting him to dart back for a last word and disappear again. But he didn't. "Okay then, guess I'm going to explore on my own." I patted my thigh, coaxing Weather to follow me. "Might find our way to the kitchen. Maybe I'll give Weather one of your juicy sirloins." I muttered the rest, "since we all know you didn't feed him this morning while making breakfast."

No response. Well, not from Bez anyway. Weather barked—a yappy squeak from Cloudy, who had the biggest appetite of the three.

I shuffled over to Tony's tank, carefully keeping my steps close together since Weather had a tendency of nudging me with each of his heads when walking underfoot. Tony immediately crawled up my arm and settled on my shoulder. Usually, Tony's a big fan of making his own way around, but since Weather tended to thud about and his paws were awfully big, I figured Tony wanted to avoid dodging the pup stomping about.

"I can't believe Bez invited Mora here," I said with a clear edge of aggravation based on Sunny's cocked head of surprise. "Sorry. It's just he really doesn't think I can handle anything, does he?"

I knew way more than Mora on all things unknown, based on the fact I'd properly upsold nearly half the trinkets she didn't realize were treasures. She didn't bother doing research—not even on her clientele, I'd wager. How was she supposed to help figure out the schematics behind the villa?

Tony clicked his claws, possibly supporting me or a show of dominance toward Weather since he trudged close behind, practically stepping on my heels as Sunny rubbed his head against my leg, looking for pets.

"It doesn't matter. We're going to have a breakthrough today," I said loudly, half-expecting an eavesdropping Bez to make a quippy comment before vanishing in a blur again. Guess he had actually gone in search of Mora. "We're going to figure out how everything in this mystery Fae house-ship thing works. In fact, we're going to figure it out right now. Before Bez finds Mora."

Who probably wasn't even here to assist but pilfer whatever wasn't welded to the floor.

Sunny cheerily joined in with a yappy bark of agreement while Stormy growled in support. Definitely support and not annoyance by being dragged along for the ride.

I confidently walked down the hallway, some swagger in my steps—maybe channeling a bit of Bez's boastful strut. The slashed iron door was open when we arrived. I couldn't remove Weather's claw marks, but I had managed to fix the incantations that secured the helm. Was it Bez or Mora who broke the wards to enter?

"Oooo, pretty," a high-pitched voice said.

Feminine for sure, but nothing like Mora's lilt.

I opened my mouth to speak, ask if this was Mora, but hesitated. Anxiety tangled knots in my chest. If I was wrong, I'd announce myself.

"Could be the pink Fae." I bit my lip since my need to mutter every waking thought won out. But her voice, the Fae who'd grabbed me, was on the deeper side when declaring Baron Novus sought an audience with me and whisked me back into the auditorium, albeit one plane off from reality.

Sunny and Cloudy had curious eyes when sniffing at the doorway, no fright in their expression like from the surveillance footage I'd seen of their interactions with the pink Fae. Stormy didn't snarl nearly as much either.

Maybe it was just Mora.

I stepped inside the helm and spotted a Black woman in a camel tan jumpsuit, which accentuated her deep brown complexion. Had Mora possessed a new host body? It was hard to know since Mora kept all her Diabolic features hidden, including her eyes.

"Mora?" I asked with raised brows.

"Nope. She's around here somewhere. Probably." The woman shrugged. She held a screwdriver that she forcefully wedged into the screws of the navigation controls.

"Hey," I shouted. "You can't touch that."

A pile of various fasteners lined the control panel. She didn't know the first thing she was doing. Without proper schematics, there was no way to know for sure it wouldn't break something. Yes, pushing a few buttons was one thing, but taking out all the screws, nuts, and bolts was a completely different thing. Besides, the screw tops didn't match any known type of screwdriver tips, from flat-heads, Philips Head, and spanners to Pozidriv, Torx, Hex, or even specialty tips like for computers or jewelers.

She completely ignored my request, continuing to fiddle with things she shouldn't.

"I said you can't touch that." I added as much authority to my voice as possible. "You'll break something."

"I wonder if this design incorporates so many other Mythic phrases to confuse non-Fae from deciphering the Sylvan alphabet," she said, disregarding my presence again as she took a panel cover off and chucked it onto the floor. "Or maybe it's meant to deceive fellow Fae who might not be permitted here."

I rushed over to the discarded panel, frustration mixing with panic in my churning stomach. She'd definitely forced the screws out; the metal holes were dented and practically chiseled. Gods, she'd break the entire helm if given half a chance.

"I'm not going to ask again." I stood, fire building in my chest. Quite literally, perhaps, as my mana raged, coursing alongside the Diabolic essence in me, each capable of swaying the elements with great effect. "Step away from my navigation system before you break something."

She leaned forward, stretching the full length of her body onto the panel toward the navigation screen. The wiggle of her hips knocked over a small stack of screws. They clinked against the floor like pennies, bouncing or rolling and disappearing somewhere in the room. Weather chased the sound of one, sniffing around to investigate.

"Oops. I'll get those after I test a hypothesis."

Or Weather would get them and eat them. Cerberus' had stomachs and digestive tracts that could literally devour souls; he'd have no problem eating a few loose screws. Speaking of loose screws, I needed to deal with whoever this woman was.

"I said stop." I summoned fire with my right hand, tracing a protective incantation with my left.

She turned. Several locs draped the left half of her face. They were long, reaching her waist—well, the high-placed belt tying her outfit together above her waist. The lime and forest green tips hung at her golden belt buckle; the greens went about halfway until her hair went black all the way to her roots.

"You didn't, technically speaking." She giggled.

"Excuse me?"

"You suggested I shouldn't be messing around because I could damage something. But I'm not. I'm performing a diagnostic."

"You can't just perform a diagnostic on something you have no understanding of," I snapped. "Stop touching things that don't belong to you!"

"It doesn't exactly belong to you either, now does it, Wally?" She smirked, wicked and wild all at once.

Shit. Was she another Fae? Novus had talked about them augmenting their features to resemble humans, but even so, those I'd observed had several obvious Mythic features or something distinctly non-human. She didn't look any bit out of the ordinary, so what was she? A mage, perhaps? I gulped. Worse. What if she was one of the missing Diabolics in the villa? No. They'd been discombobulated, or Bez suggested as much based on how their essence was scattered throughout the villa.

I released the flame, favoring saturation over elements, and poured my mana into the floor, filling the room with my magic, searching for hers. It was easy enough to detect but pure and radiating throughout her, as opposed to mages who drew on the residue of magic in the atmosphere.

"W-who are you?"

"I see you've met Kell," Mora said behind me.

I fumbled with the incantations, nearly dropping them when the sudden arrival of her voice startled me. Especially since my saturation hadn't remotely noted her presence.

Damn difficult to detect Diabolic essence.

It didn't prevent me from noticing Bez's sudden arrival, but that had to do with the tug of the tether linking us.

I blinked a few times, taking in Kell, the witch who'd waltzed right into the helm and began tinkering with things, potentially undoing days of careful observations I'd made.

I turned, taking in Mora's appearance from the bubblegum pink headband that kept her chestnut locks pushed back, to the click of her matching stilettos tapping while she eyed the incantations stacked in my palm, all the way to her jeweled accessories, each highlighting attention to the strapless, skintight magenta dress that held the ensemble together. A very short cut, too, revealing a tattoo covering her entire right thigh. A black and white portrait of a man, several colorful flowers, and animals.

Had Mora gotten these tattoos? Could Diabolic flesh be tattooed, or was this a glamour similar to what Bez did with his piercings? Maybe the tattoos came from the former tenant in the body she possessed. In which case, why hadn't she simply glamoured them away? I shook my head, pushing random curiosities out.

"Such hostile mana permeating. I do hope you two are playing nice," Mora said with a flick of her wrist, jingling her bracelets. Telekinetically, she waved over a dozen suitcases into the navigation room. Bez wasn't kidding about her moving in. Who needed that many clothes ever?

I anxiously grinned at Bez, who looked annoyed, either by the fact I'd cast hostile magic—as a warning, to be fair—or by the way Mora had just invited herself here. Personally, I was more annoyed by Kell, who couldn't keep her hands off things she didn't understand the first thing about.

"Of course we are." Kell wrapped an arm around my neck in what I could only assume was a friendly hug, but it felt more like she meant to strangle the life out of me. "We're on the verge of being besties, babe. I can feel it."

Tony hissed, then crawled down the back of my shirt. My face burned from flustered rage, between Tony wriggling along my back, Bez's stifled snickers, and Kell bopping her hip against mine as she forced me into a side hug.

"In fact"—her chokehold grew tighter, and she whirled around on her heel, dragging me with her toward the panel—"I was just about to show him how to take this hot ride out for a test drive."

"Wait, what?" I widened my eyes and scrambled loose from her unwanted embrace. "You can't just throw this thing into drive. It's not a car, and we're certainly not on a road. We're floating between realities on a clear and designated pathway, one seemingly carved out by Fae and Diabolic magics, meaning it's illegal and uncharted."

"Not uncharted," Mora said, side-eyeing Bez. "Bezzy just happened to kill the only person who knew the route."

"Walter made me. I wanted to be friends with the baron."

"Liar." My cheeks puffed in protest. Nope. Not the point or the argument that needed my attention. I turned back to Kell. "The slightest deviation off course could kill us, throw us into an endless loop of quantum entanglement, leak magical radiation—which I suspect might work as an additional fuel source—and that'd basically have all kinds of catastrophic effects. The villa could explode—again, we die—or the radiation could hit the atmosphere and have horrid ramifications on an ecosystem introducing magics the Collective or Mythic Council can't quell. We're talking exposures, higher rates of magic indoctrination, potential long-term effects I can only imagine—"

"Geez, you're such a worry wart," Kell said, tapping buttons she shouldn't fucking touch. "You always such an overthinking buzzkill about every little thing?"

"Yes," Bez blurted.

"No." I glared at him. "I'm just obviously the only one here taking precautions into account. Let's at least wait until we've read over the manual,"—something we should all do several times over for proper clarity—"made a list of the dos and don'ts, done diagnostic tests on all the systems, and fixed whatever you've broken with all your tinkering. Anything before you just type in coordinates you couldn't possibly understand."

"Or, and hear me out, Wally," Kell said with an annoyingly cocky grin. "We could skip all the bullshit and dive right in."

"No, because…" I bit my lip, not bothering to finish because Kell had already gone back to ignoring me. So frustrating.

"Let's see what I've got in my handy dandy hat of tricks." She materialized a big black hat with a long-pointed tip and a wide brim.

Seriously? I let out a deep sigh. A witch's hat was as cliché as someone could get.

The air turned thick, causing uncomfortable humidity because of her sorcery—essentially the witch equivalent to incantations. All their magic drawn from the Four Corners had a different name than the Pentacles of Power mages channeled, but the specific uses remained similar between Mythic witches and human mages.

A moderately complex spell of sorcery to conjure the hat. Not all that proficient since she had to utilize nature's blessing in tandem, which manipulated the atmosphere around us, creating this gelatinous air that made my skin sticky and my lenses fog.

Sorcery came from the southern corner of fire and like fire, the spells used offered balance through creation or destruction.

Nature's blessing stemmed from the northern corner, basically serving as a catch-all that mixed elemental control, saturation, and familiar bonds.

She shouldn't need to harness both when summoning a silly hat.

"Where did I put that lever?" She held the hat upside-down and rifled through it, digging her arms all the way in up to her shoulders.

Oh. I widened my eyes. She'd added a small temporal fold into the stitching, probably repurposing carbon dioxide or other odorless gasses to cloak her items in a nearby storage facility housed by the earth itself. That was really sophisticated.

Okay. Admittedly, she had *some* skill for someone so impulsive and chaotic.

"There it is." She withdrew a long, metal lever and tossed her hat on. "Now, I don't have nearly as much experience driving stick as you, or so I hear." She batted her eyes in Bez's direction, making me blush. "Wanna show me the ropes of steering this bad boy?"

I grabbed the lever she offered, intent on snatching it away. Instead, she dragged me along and jabbed the lever into the navigation system.

I couldn't decide who I hated most in this situation. Kell for jumping in and ignoring all my hard work, Mora for bringing her flighty witch wife, or Bez for inviting them to begin with when I was so close to figuring out the correct course of action.

Electricity crackled on the dismantled panel; I screamed; Kell cackled; lights flickered in and out; the lever trembled in our grasp.

"Hold tight, everybody," she shouted. "This is gonna be one hell of a ride."

Everything vibrated, and the helm turned fuzzy.

12

Beelzebub

"No, no, no!" Wally frantically waved his hands, trying to catch countless books that flew off shelves in the library. "You need to stop this right now."

He'd remained pouty since Mora and Kell showed up, spending all his time in the library determined to make a major discovery on the missing Diabolics. Given how Kell waltzed into the villa and started up the control panel before he had a chance to finish studying, I sort of understood. Wally did love understanding all the ins and outs before making a careless move, making him a terrible pairing for Kell, who lacked self-control when anything caught her interest. She was a dog with a bone, worse than the three-headed mongrel Wally finally locked out of the library after he ate a half-dozen books.

And Walter had the nerve to say my tastebuds were terrible.

Books flipped open, pages rippling as some were torn loose from their spines after the extra speedy flight that sent them hurling off one shelf and crashing into another. Wally scrambled to catch a few, protect their pristine covers, and shield them from colliding into each other in the interstate-level traffic Kell had created. A whirlwind of chocolates, earthy, woody aromas permeated throughout from the musky pages. Wally couldn't keep up with it all, probably couldn't fathom the hundreds flying about, but he did have his eyes on the one who conjured this mess.

Kell sprinted up the side of a bookcase abandoning the wards she'd attempted chiseling away. Like the minxy cat she was, Kell used a mix of sorcery in her boots and telekinesis lent to her from Mora's essence coursing inside her. Gracefully, she landed on top of the bookcase and sprang to a nearby one hovering in the opposite direction.

"I absolutely one-hundred percent draw the line at dismantling the library." Wally pursued her, distrustful his protests would make her yield—they wouldn't; she wouldn't.

I huffed. Why'd Mora have to bring Kell of all the witches in the world?

"I'm going to streamline the system," Kell said.

"You don't even know how the system works," Wally accurately stated since she'd spent the last few days recalibrating the navigation system after our swift ascent between realms fizzled out somewhere in Alaska, of all fucking places.

Our windows offered a clear view of snowy mountains—which Wally immediately knew the name of, Mount something, showcasing his completely useless trivia trick—but the villa and our presence remained tucked behind the veil. Whether inside or outside, like the villa itself, we were intangible to the mortal realm unless using the official Fae portal exit. Even as a demon who could tear through layers of dimensional fabric, I couldn't find the hidden strings which kept the villa divided from everything else. Novus certainly had created a complex system.

"I know I can make the library more functional," Kell said, continuing to tinker with the tops of the bookcases. "You just have to trust me, Wally."

"I don't have to do anything!" He snapped his fingers, calling a broom forth.

"Neither does Kell," Mora sighed. "I literally only brought her to assist in disassembling whatever device is being used to hide and detain the demons here."

Gods. Was Walter really going to chase Kell throughout this entire library?

"I'm going to update the cataloging system," Kell said, hopping onto another bookcase every time Wally's pursuit closed in. "There were some clear design oversights when constructing this place."

Kell had always possessed nimble dexterity; it was what kept her alive every time she drew the ire of covens or the wrath of the Mythic Council. Nice to see she hadn't lost her edge after such a long relationship with Mora. Truthfully, I always figured Kell needed an indomitable force for protection against the mighty enemies her curiosities had cultivated. Hence why she'd cozied up to the most cunning demon in the mortal world.

Still, as spry as she remained, Wally continued giving her chase, refusing to let up. I smirked, observing the few close calls between the two of them. My heart pattered with joy from the bubbling rage swelling in his chest.

"Don't you think there should be a one-click step when searching for a book?" Kell asked, weaving around the chains Wally thrust at her with an incantation.

Not a super strong set, but it was impressive as always how much magic he could harness when too preoccupied to overthink his casting limitations.

"You were saying how you wished this library had a Nexus Grimoire like the repository," I said in some desperate hope to soothe Wally's sour mood.

From what I recalled during my time spent in the repository at the Magus Estate, the Nexus Grimoire served as a catchall for every book chronicled within the magical and tech-based link. Sort of like a supernatural database, much like the Googly app on my telephone.

“Shut up, Bez. You’re not helping.” Wally seethed, possibly feeling the tug of our tether as I tightened our proximity in an effort to assuage his rage. It didn’t work.

“Goddess.” Kell beamed; her round cheeks rose high as she shot me a full-faced grin. “That’s exactly what I was thinking, Bez. A Nexus Grimoire but better. Are you in my head? I promise those salacious thoughts are completely hypothetical.”

She puckered her lips, preparing to blow a kiss until Wally closed in on her, forcing an impromptu somersault escape on Kell’s part.

I rolled my eyes. I could only read her thoughts when casting nightmares in her mind, to lift the floorboards of secrets kept, which I only ever did once. Had to ensure she wasn’t using my wicked demon friend for something sinister and selfish. Lesser beings often had nefarious tendencies.

“You think someone can just make a Nexus Grimoire all willy-nilly?” Wally paused, catching his breath.

The rage hadn’t settled. In fact, it grew with each inhale because while he stopped chasing Kell, she dismantled more wards.

“Whoopsie.” Kell jumped off the bookcase that she’d inadvertently removed the hovering sigils, too, which sent it crashing into another bookcase. “It’s a learning curve. One that’d be easier without interference.”

“You clearly have no idea the amount of labor and tireless effort that goes into properly cataloging an extensive collection and setting it up to maintain structural integrity with a Nexus Grimoire,” Wally said, biting his lip and hopefully the tangent he’d prepared to spout off.

He'd assisted with an update to the Nexus Grimoire in the Magus Estate once before, linking new books added to the repository. It involved tedious tasks of properly documenting the texts, altering the formatting from one book to another, and a hundred other things I hoped he didn't plan on listing off. Kell certainly wouldn't listen to it all.

"Mortals and Mythics." Mora strutted away toward the entrance. "They're so adorably dim."

"Walter is the furthest thing from dim. He's a genius," I said, joining her because, at this point, Wally would simply have to exhaust himself before seeing reason. Whenever the levee that made up Wally's compassion, consideration, and compliance to all things broke, his anger became impossible to settle.

It was entertaining to see he didn't reserve these moody outbursts solely for me.

Wally lunged ahead, releasing his hands from the broomstick in an attempt to grab Kell, who hopped onto the tip of his broom, shifting the trajectory. Then she bounced back off, blasting a light breeze from nature's blessing to send him whirling through the air until his face turned green.

"A genius of the learned sense," I added, clamping my jaw as the sensation of bile rolling up my throat hit with what was surely a fraction of what poor, ridiculous Wally endured. "Research, decoding, preservation of things, history mostly."

"Obviously," Mora said with a lilt of irksome sarcasm. She'd always considered Kell the cleverest lower being the world had seen; it must have bothered her I found a smarter mortal. "As adorable as watching Kell and Wally hit it off on the wrong foot or fist or magical spell, I was hoping once we'd settled in, we could actually explore and make progress on this Fae contraption trapping Diabolics."

"I suppose. The sooner we find the demons, the sooner you and Kell can leave."

Mora averted her gaze, her lips twisted into silent musings. I figured she had other plans, something that bolstered her swift action of coming to assist hands-on, which she rarely did, but I had no intention of surrendering the villa or treasure troves hidden inside it. Wally would appreciate them far more. And with a traveling, cloaked residence, I could finally show Wally the world as promised without constantly skirting around Collective territory.

"Kell…play nice, my love." Mora sauntered out of the library.

I followed her out into the foyer, which diverged into several paths, each leading to different wings of this villa, from the main house to the catacombs of pocket worlds below where the former host kept troves of treasures.

"I've already explored the upper levels of the villa with Walter," I said, ushering her in the opposite direction toward a spiral staircase that led to the labyrinth. "However, the maze below seems to stretch endlessly with pocket portals storing all kinds of baubles."

"I highly doubt a Fae royal would keep cheap trinkets. Even what they hold sentimental usually comes at a high price tag." Mora eyed every portrait on the walls—likely appraising them—as we reached the staircase. "Has Wally checked the value of these oddities?"

"No." Mainly since I didn't want him jumping through doorways that could lead anywhere or everywhere. "He's mostly kept his attention fixated on understanding how the villa functions and where the Diabolics are kept. Not that we've made any headway."

"I see." Mora studied the lanterns that illuminated our path, lighting the dark stone corridor with each step and dimming the path behind. "Perhaps he can be a bit more inviting toward Kell. She's only trying to help, even if her impulses are a tad inconvenient at times."

"The last impulse led to carrying us to the middle of nowhere before the traveling mechanism—which Kell still doesn't understand—broke down." I scoffed. "Suppose the only benefit to being in this damned cold state is that it's off the Collective's radar."

"The mages have their hooks in Anchorage and the pipelines, but true—they don't have a vested interest in this area." Mora lightly strummed her fingers against the damp wall as we walked further. "It could've been worse. Better middle of nowhere snowy mountains than floating through literal nothingness between dimensional walls on an automated course destination set by the former host."

She had a mild point. Who knew where the dead Fae had charted next.

"Hmm." Mora pressed a hand against the wall; heat radiated from her essence, attempting to search the faint energy as if I hadn't already attempted such things. "I get what you mean now about the disturbance in their essence. It feels like it's layered everywhere throughout the villa, but I can't see it anywhere. No void webs, no trail, no spark of individuality. Just a faint, foul stench."

"We're already difficult enough to track. If Fae magics find a way to amplify our cloaked presence, I don't see that going well."

"Could be quite profitable," Mora said.

"How could you possibly need more currency? You take an exorbitant amount in your finder's fee. I can't even fathom the absurd prices of your other services."

"You should see what I charge my enemies." She smirked. "And it's not about money. I have more than I can count, enough to roll around in bed with Kell, and no need to add to my income revenue."

"Bah." I waved a dismissive hand. If she tried turning this into another discussion on why immortals should focus on their investment portfolios, I'd strangle her. She only ever used currency as a way to distract or confuse me.

"To answer your question, Bezzy, it's about power and prestige."

I stifled a laugh. "I always forget your obsession with status and authority."

Power was the only thing Mora had to work for in the mortal realm, likely a humbling experience for a former king of Bael's Hell. One of several thousand, but still a fraction of a hair above the millions of other demon lords or the billions of Diabolic peasantry, good for nothing but eternal servitude.

"What can I say"—Mora twirled past me, curtsying—"you can take the demon out of the monarchy, but not the monarch out of the demon."

"Before you go recounting the number of kings and queens you've been inside or had inside you, answer my original query."

Her lips curled into a minxy yet reserved smile, her eyes distant, looking at nothing but memories. Mora had a certain expression when reliving her long list of lost lovers, one I'd been privy to observing too many times. Those lesser beings incapable of eternity lived on forever every time her mind wandered, even if only for fractions of seconds at a time.

"I'm always looking for ways to cultivate relations with our brethren, and I can think of quite a few demons that'd offer their souls or a thousand others for the peace of mind that comes with a full-proof cloak from fellow Diabolics, especially from their devils. Who knows? Maybe this tech can be applied to Mythics, mortals, or all of the above."

I didn't like the idea of that one bit. There'd already been a few demons circling like vultures since my reemergence, my bond with Wally convinced foes I'd lost my footing as an all-powerful Diabolic deity. If they actually managed a blitz attack, it could prove irritating, constantly watching, waiting, and wondering what old rivalry with some worthless demon I'd sparked merely by living my best life.

"Could benefit you, too." Mora stepped in close, shoulder-bumping me. "Beelzebub of history drew quite a lot of attention. Perhaps the Bez of the future seeks a more reclusive romance, one without prying eyes."

I glared.

She'd kept an ear close to the ground on whispers of demons daring enough to challenge a devil with a mortal attachment, something she herself had always remained vigilant about. Suppose I never figured it that difficult given how Mora handled herself when linked to lovers, but the minute I bound myself to Wally, that theory vanished. Considering Mora's observations since I left Seattle, I probably have her watchful eye to blame for this entire situation. Her extra attention on demon threats likely led to her discovery of missing Diabolics, the Fae involvement, and this fancy dimension-defying villa. The question was, what purpose did she have in acquiring it? Mora never revealed her hand, so asking outright would only result in skirting the truth, given how carefully she weaved half-truths and intricate lies.

"So, you're only interested in the cloaking magics? Or is there more to this technology?"

In most cases, if I desired the truth from Mora, I had to follow the web she weaved in hopes of finding the answers I sought.

"I told you," Mora said. "I don't want this type of travel to become so easily accessible. Mythics and mortals have no business gallivanting around the Hell realms. And there's no profit in expanding tourism in Hell."

"Their perception is so limited; they wouldn't even register half the sensations."

"Exactly. Who was that fool that inaccurately chronicled his short stint? Damien, Donnie, Derek…"

"Dante?" I asked, playing confused with Mora, who knew the name but wanted to tiptoe the conversation in a distracting direction.

"He never even went." Mora let out an exasperated sigh. "Drank too much wine with satyrs, listened too intently to sirens, and lost himself in a delusional, drunken stupor. But could you imagine if someone did go to a Hell realm uninvited? I know of few as lenient toward interlopers as Bael."

I could imagine it. Had imagined it for some time, in fact. The terror of someone finding a loophole into Beelzebub's Hell.

"Speaking of Diabolics," Mora said. "How about we split up, cover more ground?"

So she could sleuth about undisturbed, evaluating anything and everything? *Yeah, right.*

"Sounds like a plan." I nodded.

Mora vanished in a blur, and I followed suit, listening intently to the light patter of her shoes and the swish of her body darting down long stretches, then cutting quick corners. While I couldn't observe her in action, I heightened my senses, absorbing the slightest vibration, which created a full scene of events.

It helped Wally's pursuit of Kell had lessened. It didn't help that Kell wiggled her hips, taunting him as she ripped apart incantations from the library. I cracked my neck, savoring the released tension carried in Wally's shoulders, and focused on Mora.

The slightest brush of her fingertips on items big and small, the soft murmur of a satisfied hmm, the lingering steps as she paused to examine something closely. There must be a thousand things in this villa she wanted, yet she didn't grab a thing. Not even pocketing a small trinket, which I'd already done with the less gaudy jewels in the baron's collection.

Silence would strike for the briefest of seconds when she leapt through a portal before reemerging and continuing her search.

Mora really did want to resolve the missing Diabolics above all else, it seemed.

Thanks to Wally's investigations, I knew the contents of several rooms and had sleuthed through the pocket portals the cameras didn't cover. But I played along, zipping about, leaving no stone unturned. We wouldn't find any Diabolics.

Something about their disappearance didn't add up. They were ever-present in the air yet simultaneously hidden. I could almost feel their claws at my throat, hear their wails in my ears, but nothing concrete. Nothing tangible. Only the rot of their decay as their essence remained unattended to, incapable of recovery.

I hopped through a glowing golden portal into a room that held nothing more than gorgon artwork; the tether connecting to Wally remained strong. Petrified stone statues posed in blissful, heroic, or entertained positions—none the wiser they were about to be immortalized for someone's private collection. Powerful mana oozed from one in particular, not that it'd do him or anyone any good. Once locked in stone, only a gorgon themselves had the magic necessary to undo the effects. Still, no point telling Wally about these befuddled fools. He'd likely task himself with the duty of undoing the petrification.

After an hour or so of searching, I leaned against a wall semi-studying Mora's movements as she continued her futile scrutinous search. Across from me stood an unlit portal. The symbols were properly stacked around the doorway, spelling out the secret code Novus used to get in or out of the villa, inside the helm, and for every other doorway…all except for this particular door. Why?

"I've never felt more incompetent in my life." Mora pouted. "This place has everything except for Diabolics."

"We could still burn it down."

Mora frowned until her eyes rested on the doorframe symbols. "Why's this closed off?"

"Busted, maybe." I shrugged.

"Or…" She fiddled with the symbols, rearranging them into odd patterns. Incorrect patterns, too.

It seemed Mora's mind processed them the same way mine had when reading the Sylvan alphabet. When I first studied the letters, they reminded me of Hell's and the way Beelzebub would create barriers to and from his various dwellings throughout the realm, which was probably why my brain worded them out of sequence. Mora didn't have Wally's insufferable familiar to hiss and scold her for placing them incorrectly like he had when I attempted to open the portal to the villa and rescue Wally. She'd be at this for ages until she wore herself out.

A luminescent black door activated.

"Well, well, what do we have here?" Mora's smile carried a bright shadow from the reflection of the watery portal.

"How'd you do that?"

"It seems Novus tied this particular door to only open for someone who understood how a Diabolic codex works, which implies he was not only abducting demons to harvest essence and power his ship but that he was perhaps allied with some." Mora stepped toward the rippling door. "Fascinating."

More like dangerous.

"Shall we?" She extended a hand.

Screw it. I grabbed her hand and stepped through.

Upon arriving, the first thing I did was check the snag of the tether linking Wally and myself. My heart hitched the same as it always did when nearby, so this hidden dwelling didn't take us too far or block our connection. Good.

The strain in my muscles hit far stronger than the minimal exertion of running around these lower levels. No, this hit with a full-blown wave of exhaustion as the receptors harnessing magic constricted, yet mana and essence coursed through my body undiminished.

I chuckled to myself at how Wally had finally tuckered himself out. The humorous pondering piqued Mora's interest, but her gaze quickly landed on something far more terrifying.

This place was the engine by all appearances of twisting gears and loud machines. Literal darkness covered the walls keeping it within and divided from the rest of the home. Placed upon a railing stood a mantle securing six Diabolic orbs, each containing a demon and their essence. Wires were wrapped around the tiny orbs, trailing down their stands, and connecting to a hub that fueled everything.

"Hmm." Mora walked the ramp, trailing her fingers along the railing leading to the six tiny orbs no bigger than a marble.

Guess I shouldn't have complained so much about my time spent inside the orb Remington trapped me within. "Didn't realize I had such spacious accommodations."

"These are made to house a demon, not a devil."

I tsked. "As if anything could truly contain a devil."

"You still have a piece of one."

"Always will." *Unfortunately.*

I ground my teeth, ignoring the reminder of the tiniest bit of Beelzebub's essence intertwined with my own. The two seamlessly synced, an eternal connection to the devil I'd sealed away with every demon of his making.

"Clearly, these things were designed with some structural integrity." Mora smacked her forehead with an ah-ha moment. "No wonder we couldn't track the essence. These orbs make it utterly impossible to detect anything."

I raised my brows. "What would you know of it?"

"Not much. Only that they're hard to pin down." She shrugged the words off like a random musing, but in all our time together, I couldn't recall her having any prior knowledge of Diabolic orbs until I ended up locked away inside one for the better half of a century.

Did that mean Mora looked for me when I was imprisoned? I shook away the curiosity, the confusion that came with gauging Mora's intentions. She didn't look that hard since all my days were spent in the same boring repository.

Mora stepped in close, studying the swirling, discombobulated essence of each orb. "I suspected it'd require more Diabolic essence to safely usher a Mythic to and from a Hell realm."

I joined her, running my fingers along the mantle housing these six troublesome Diabolics that could potentially open Beelzebub's realm with the right mix of Fae magic, a bit of devil essence, and the wrong hands.

"Well, I'll be damned all over again." She nodded past the railing.

Deeper in the lower reaches of the engine room spanned hundreds of other orbs, and each contained a demon. And those demons were powering this place.

"Fuck." This was becoming an even bigger headache.

13

Walter

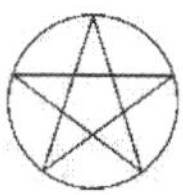

I was still exhausted after unsuccessfully chasing Kell through the library when Bez dragged me through the lower labyrinth, demanding I help decipher the construction of this bizarre room. Thankfully, Kell hadn't been invited, which made sense, considering it held hundreds of unique orbs. None of which were the same make or model based on the six displayed on an upper railing. Each distinct orb was much smaller than Bez's but slightly different in size and shape from one another. Two had a wide oval shape, whereas one looked like an upside-down egg held in place by the wires attached. The others were all perfectly rounded, yet at a glance, different in size, like a penny next to a dime.

"This is how Novus was shielding himself and the villa when jumping into a Hell realm?" I asked, studying the discombobulated essence within each glass container.

"You tell us," Mora said, arms folded as she walked the railing. "You're the only person either of us knows who's actually examined a Diabolic orb."

True. I'd studied the orb containing Bez on countless occasions, curiously determining if he possessed awareness, even if his fractured essence seemed mostly lacking sentience. Turned out he was very aware.

"Time to put your expertise to use," Bez said.

Expertise was a stretch.

I eyed the six orbs, wondering if they were all as aware as Bez during his time contained in the repository.

I swallowed hard.

The subtle shift of broken energy inside the orbs cast shadows, dancing against the light of this engine room, revealing the faintest tracings of the symbols etched onto the glass. I'd never realized the symbols which held Bez were of Fae origin. Like the Sylvan letters lining the doorframe to the tarlike portal leading into this room, they were spelled out in what seemed to be utter gibberish. Not that my understanding of the Fae language was anywhere near proficient, but it was still intriguing they combined a dialect with Diabolics.

"Similar to how they use codes and riddles and so much more by entangling it with other Mythic languages, even a few humans," I muttered. "It's like the Sylvan alphabet has an almost symbiotic effect with magic, creating powerful incantations, wards, seals, enchantments, and a million other things all dependent—"

"You weren't kidding about the history lesson." Mora sighed.

"Told you," Bez replied. "It's the price of acquiring his insights; you have to take all the rambling, too. Just plug your ears, grit your teeth, and think of something happy until he finishes."

I rolled my eyes.

The most fascinating part of all this was how the Fae constructed something specifically designed to contain Diabolics, seemingly with Diabolic assistance. "Or at the very least a study of their culture, which begs to question, how far back the Fae have been observing the Diabolics since these orbs go back—" I bit my lip, ignoring the agitated thump of Bez's tails smacking against the grated metal floor.

Truthfully, I didn't have an inkling of how far back these orbs went. Fifty years at the very least since Magus Remington used one to store Bez, but the finish on his orb never held any ancient remnants of mana seeped over centuries like much of what we kept stored in the repository.

"Eventually, even Walter tires of his tangents. Should only be a few hours of mutterings until he blurts something of value."

"Be a lot faster if you stopped talking about me like I wasn't right here."

"Ah, yes." Bez pointed the tip of his tail at my crinkled forehead. "He also gets cranky when interrupted during his studies. If you observe the number of lines currently on his forehead, I'd say this is a level two on the scale of seven for Walter's rage implosions."

Seriously? I ignored Bez and Mora and returned to observing the orbs. I wanted to hold them, closely inspect the sigils, but until I deciphered how the wires worked, I didn't want to touch them and risk disrupting the flow of energy.

"Can I help?" Kell shouted, barging through the portal; a smile already plastered on her face and grabby hands at the ready before the glowing black glob of dimensional travel faded away.

"I thought you wanted to finish working on the library construction?" Mora asked.

Construction? More like destruction. Half the books ended up flung off the shelves thanks to her new cataloging system, and since she'd fucked up the framework of the original design, whatever protective warding of rejuvenation was put in place to keep the texts in mint condition had also broken.

"Yes, a curious musing which I plan to return to, but this is business," Kell said. "Important. Takes priority over everything.

Besides, you know I know engine systems like the back of my hand. I'll learn how this baby works in…"

"Back of her hand?" I ground my teeth. "Bet she doesn't even know how many fingers are on her damn hand."

"Someone's still testy, I see." Bez stood next to me, invading my space and blocking my light.

"No." I pointed to the orbs and his shadow. "Do you mind?"

"Quite testy," he snickered. "Please bring all that rage to the bedroom this evening. I can think of a hundred ways to release all that pent-up frustration."

"Shut up."

"Yes, sir." Bez mimicked zipping his lips, remaining far too close to focus.

"Do you mind?"

He grinned, finally stepping away, then smacked my butt.

I jumped. Wide-eyed shock replaced my furrowed brow.

"I love you and all your crafting ways," Mora said, leading Kell back to the portal, "but Diabolic orbs are quite fragile and—"

"And she's worried you'll break them all in some haphazard improvement and call it a renovation," I blurted a bit louder than intended.

"That's not fair," Kell protested. "The library was mostly your fault."

"Excuse me?" My blood boiled.

Kell turned her attention to Mora. "Plus, isn't he the only one here who actually broke a Diabolic orb?"

"Yes," Bez and Mora said in unison.

"Not true," I snapped.

I simply failed to stop it from breaking—something Bez should have shown a bit more gratitude for instead of rewriting history.

"He's also the only one here who's examined these artifacts," Mora said. "We need his expertise."

"And we don't need hundreds of demons running rampant around the villa because of your tinkering," Bez said.

"What if I'm extra careful with them?" Kell pleaded.

"No," we all said.

Kell scowled, dragging her feet as she left. Honestly, given all the unfamiliar equipment here, Kell would make the better choice for examining—assuming she could investigate without touching things—since I had no idea how the wires drew energy from the orbs to power the villa. After all, the purpose of the orbed artifacts was to completely cut off the energy from everything. It kept Bez discombobulated and unable to cast, interact, or even fully feel, but somehow Baron Novus combined Fae magic to Diabolic essence with technology and superseded the basic design of Diabolic orbs.

Bez continued flicking his tails, as careless about fragile artifacts as Kell.

"Careful," I said as one of his tails moved over the furthest orb, causing the essence inside to stir.

"Wait. Do that again." I pointed to Bez's tail. "The demon reacted."

He swung a tail over the orbs, each recoiling from his presence.

"They are aware," I said. "And they don't like your essence. It's like they're trying to back away from it. From you."

"Likely in awe of the devil essence radiating from him," Mora said.

Right. Bez wasn't a devil, but he'd taken part of Beelzebub's essence into himself before abandoning the realm and subsequently sealing it off entirely.

"Not that any of that matters," Bez said.

"It all matters when trying to untangle and understand how this works," I said. "Which could take weeks. Months. Years."

Bez groaned.

"They're aware," I said. "Don't you feel bad for them?"

"I *feel* annoyed by the headache they've given me," Bez said. "It'd be easiest for all of us if we simply snuffed them out."

"Don't be impetuous, Bezzy," Mora said. "Not every demon is an enemy."

"Plus, removing them from the equation of how this villa functions could very likely cause it to break down, explode, implode, cease to exist, or a hundred other things. All of which I'd rather not be here to experience," I muttered aloud, jotting some notes on the symbols for further study.

Between chasing Kell through the library, studying unknown Diabolic-Fae technology, running laps with Weather around the villa, and keeping Tony entertained since his jealousy hadn't dissipated, all I wanted to do was pass out. The shower I took did absolutely nothing to wake me after so much research. I returned to my bedroom, sighing at the stack of books I'd piled around the bed. This was supposed to make research comfy and isolated, but now they all stood in my way of sprawling out onto the bed.

I sulked, adjusting my glasses. It was fine. I didn't need to *sleep* sleep anyway. Just a quick power nap, then I'd figure out how the secret engine room worked, hopefully before Kell broke something else during her not-so-helpful renovations. I crawled onto the bed and sank deep into the mattress between the stack of books.

Sunny barked, climbing onto the bed and inviting himself next to me, much to Tony's snapping-clawed protest. Tony was much lighter and quieter than Weather, which I preferred, but the way Sunny rubbed his head on my chest, his snout pressed against my sternum and released heavy huffs that turned into happy breaths was soothing. Cloudy adjusted his paw so the heavy-footed Cerberus didn't put all his weight on my bladder. I knew it was Cloudy because he was the most considerate of the three. Sunny only considered cuddles and playing, Stormy only wanted food, exercise, and to be left the hell alone, and Cloudy wanted to make sure he wasn't, quite literally, overstepping.

I scratched Cloudy's ear, letting him nuzzle against my hip while petting Sunny to lull him into sleep. Tony remained perched atop my head, digging his claws into my curls and nestling.

"Bedtime, guys." I yawned. "Just a real quick nap."

…

Someone jostled me. I sprang up, eyes wide and alert, studying the room.

"Wakey, wakey, got something far better than eggs and bakey." Bez nudged me.

I looked around the room. No Tony knocked onto a pillow from the movement of my head, no Weather disturbed by me lunging upright. "Where are—"

"Being besties in the playroom." Bez had a full smile practically reaching his eyes as he ran his hands along my sides, easing me back onto the bed.

"Our place doesn't have a playroom." I couldn't help but smile back because I loved calling this villa home, even if it wasn't. I loved having a place with Bez.

"Mora's shoe room is quite entertaining to the hellhound. All three of them are enthralled by the textures."

"You didn't."

"I most certainly did. Besides, Antoninus enjoys scuttling through her luggage in whatever hidey holes he finds." Bez slinked onto the bed, laying his head on my crotch, his hands rubbing up my thighs. "All rested up?"

"How long was I asleep?"

"Mortal standards? Not nearly long enough." Bez tugged at my pants. "By my standards, far too long."

"I was just napping."

"Said pretty princess Sleeping Beauty." He used his teeth to unloop my belt.

"Aw, you called me pretty." I chuckled, running my fingers through his shaggy hair, which smelled of the same berry-blended shampoo I used. It was still slightly damp, the black and orange glistening. "I am actually tired, though."

Bez's tongue grazed my hip bone as he unfastened my belt with eager hands. "How tired?"

"Hmm." I practically growled as his lips met my lower abdomen, lightly kissing my skin.

Bez continued the gentle pecks, working his way back up my stomach and slowly lifting my shirt with his hands. While he teased my skin, he used his tails to carefully remove the books from the bed—no heavy thuds from tossing them but light taps as he stacked them on the floor. I giggled. So sweet. So considerate.

The sensual touch of his fingers came with a slight pulse, a delicate tingle of static that hit like a jolt of caffeine, sending a rush of adrenaline coursing. I thrusted my hips, then unfastened my pants as his lips kissed my chest.

"Well?" he asked, lips close enough to lick.

I kissed him, rough and impatient. With one hand gripping Bez's hair, I guided the tilt of his head, leading his tongue with mine as I unzipped my pants with my other hand.

"I'd say you're wide awake now." Bez broke our kiss, snickering. When he went to press his lips back against mine, I pushed his head away, further down where I wanted his lips.

Without a second of hesitation, Bez yanked my pants to my knees and wrapped his mouth around the tip of my cock. He teased me, rotating his tongue and piercing around the head, pulling away every time my hips bucked, keeping only the head in his mouth. I groaned, feral and excited, relenting to his need for patience. No, not patience. Playing. When I shuddered, vibrating from the sensation of his practiced tongue hitting every nerve in the best way, he swallowed the entirety of my hard cock.

"Show off." I bit my knuckle, doing everything not to cum and, of course, not to talk.

I wasn't nearly as endowed as him, but I had a nice size. It was humbling when he reached the base in one swift motion without the slightest hint of a gag reflex. Bez hummed, something that made his throat constrict, adding to the pleasure.

He stopped right as I thought I'd explode, stripping my pants off entirely, and met my lips with his. I kissed him, taking unsteady breaths as the erupting sensation settled.

"I love how the sounds of your orgasm taste." Bez buried his tongue in my mouth, his hand stroking my slick cock until I couldn't contain it, until I moaned, and Bez swallowed every noise with a more vigorous kiss. I convulsed, cumming on us both. My body warmed as I shivered from the ecstasy. His hand continued working, jerking every pearl out of me. His lips didn't relent, tongue dancing along mine.

"I, uh, need a second." I took wispy breaths, breaking away from his full lips so I could take a moment for my body to settle.

"Take as much time as you require." Bez had an eager glint in his eyes.

I lay back, and Bez rolled me onto my stomach. His nails trailed down my back as he reached my ass, slapping a cheek before spreading them both.

"I can keep myself more than occupied." He licked me with his tongue, a light flick, a delicate slather, just barely entering me, teasing and tasting, before he pulled away and spit onto my hole.

The anticipation of his pause made me quiver. I wanted to tense, but my muscles were puddy for him to play with.

He returned. Such a warm and wet feeling, and it sent a subtle tingle through my body, adding to the sharpness of every sensation. I squeezed the sheets, buried my head in the pillow, and basked in the pleasure. Bez took his time; the speed of each lick guided my moans that escaped the plush pillow and added to the eager arch of my back. As he continued, the comforting feeling spread throughout my entire body, a serene, electrical bliss firing off in every nerve, lighting me up on a cellular level.

"I'd say someone's quite ready." At some point, Bez's hand found its way back onto my cock, gently stroking until I throbbed. I stifled a throaty grunt, holding onto the perfect touch. He rolled me onto my back again, a tail wrapped around each of my ankles as he pulled them above his head. He propped my calves onto his shoulders, lubed me up, and thrust into me.

I gasped at the quick, suddenness when he buried himself all the way inside me. I turned my head, searching for something to muffle my voice.

"Relax." Bez released my legs, guiding them to wrap around his hips, moving in closer in a quick motion and pressing his forehead against mine. "Relax."

I took a slow breath. Bez didn't move. He waited, allowing me a moment to adjust as I took in his full shaft. I cupped my hands at the sides of his face, running my fingertips through the short hairs above his nape and pulling him into a kiss. A kiss that instructed him I was ready and wanted him. Needed him.

His thrusts started out slow. There was a patience to them; each slap of his skin against mine held a surge of fiery desire. It hit me like a wave, the craving linked through our bond. An unyielding need.

"I'm ready."

His eyes glowed, the reds a dark crimson and the veins along his face shifting to a faint black. "You sure?"

I leaned forward, he moved in to meet me, kiss me, and then everything blurred. Pure pleasure as he pounded faster and harder, hands caressing me with gentleness despite each rough thrust pushing me deeper into the mattress. I lost myself, lost track of time. Bez growled, pumping into me again and again. Faster. Harder. Aggression bloomed between us. I bit down on his shoulder, burying my shouts.

Bez's wings sprang out, widespread, and wrapped around us. Feathers tickled my skin, then squeezed our bodies into a tight cocoon of sex. He rolled me on top, laying his wings flat on the bed, his hands on my hips guiding—no, directing—my thrusts. My entire body warmed, euphoric. I came. Again. Unable to hold back. It didn't stop Bez. He continued, seeking more, always more. I obeyed his hands, moving my body to meet his satisfaction. Desiring above all else in this moment to feel his release, his pleasure.

I pressed my hands on his shoulders, pinning him as I led the pace, the control, all while watching his face scrunch, his eyes dilate, and his mouth twist. Bez rolled back on top of me, wings retracted, arms wrapped under mine, pulling me close with a strong hug as he buried himself in me, unrelenting. I whimpered, panting in sync with every swift thrust. I dug my nails into his back, running them down his shoulder blades after he shoved his cock all the way in. He grunted, cock twitching. Bez kissed my neck, licking the skin and lightly biting as he came.

Bez rested on top of me, his chest sticky against mine, our hearts beating in the same rhythm. His body synced to mine so naturally, Bez felt like an extension of my very being most days. We sat in silence for a few minutes, my eyes searching the room and seeing some of the books in the corner. Books that'd help me solve how the Diabolic essence was used in this villa.

"So, you really don't care about all those demons trapped inside those orbs?" I ruffled his shaggy hair.

"Is this really the conversation you wish to have after sex?"

"There aren't any demons you like?" I asked, dodging his avoidance tactic and bulldozing directly toward a bit of honesty. If I allowed Bez to lead the conversation, he'd skirt the truth with crass humor, deflect with flirting, and I'd end up face down ass up in a matter of minutes. "Not one Diabolic?"

"Nope." Bez kissed my collarbone, light pecks trailing up my neck. "Hate 'em all."

"Aside from Mora, of course."

"I don't like Mora. I simply know it's wisest not to cross her." He slid his hands around my waist, already trying to get frisky to avoid conversation.

"If you don't like Mora and very much believe in killing Diabolics as a priority, why not kill her?"

"You're insatiable, Walter. You always want me to kill away a problem."

I grabbed one of his curled horns and jerked his head back, getting a clear look at his wicked smirk. "I'm being serious, Bez."

He released my waist. "Mora was the only demon to offer me aid in the mortal realm."

"Really?" I asked.

"Yes. And had I met another before her upon my arrival, I doubt I'd be as fortunate now." Bez nuzzled my neck, nibbling.

"No hickeys," I protested.

"But I must mark my claim," he said, sucking on my skin wrapped in his teeth.

"I'm trying to have a serious conversation."

"Fine. I'm trying to have serious sexcapades, but fine." Bez huffed. "I keep Mora around because she basically saved my life and sort of helped me navigate this world for a quarter century before I ventured on solo explorations. At the end of the day, I don't kill her because I feel indebted. Suppose I always will."

Bez's crimson eyes glossed over. He closed them as his lashes became wet with tears. I kissed his eyelids, silently waiting for him to continue. If he chose to continue.

"She could've snuffed me out the moment our paths crossed. Chances are it would've been a bigger payoff for her."

"I know you can die, but you're so cavalier about anyone being bold enough to challenge a devil. Do you really think she could've, you know?"

"I was so feeble, incompetent, and naïve when I arrived in the mortal realm, holding no notion on how to harness my Diabolic demon abilities, let alone the fragmented devil essence circulating inside. If Mora wanted, she could've easily overpowered my essence when we first crossed paths—shredded it and added to her own power. A demon like Morax, acquiring the power of a devil, even a tiny fraction… Oh she could have made an even bigger name for herself than she already has."

"But she helped you instead?" I asked, truly engrossed by every word. "How so?"

"I can show you if you're curious." Bez trailed his fingers up my stomach. "We both know you love to snoop."

"Huh?"

"You know, diving into my memories."

"Unfair. That's unintentional." I'd only fallen into his past three times while we slept. It was mostly his fault, too.

I couldn't control what his subconscious thought and I certainly wasn't the one demanding spooning as we slept. Cuddling was all Bez, all the time, and after a whole day of saturating things, sometimes I'd inadvertently latch onto his past.

The first time I learned the truth about him, about Beelzebub. The other two times, I caught snippets of Hell and the actions of demon lords I couldn't forget. Even their blurred forms in those foggy memories were haunting. The scent of blood, the anguish in

Bez's voice, the horrors of demon corpses. It wasn't surprising he held no regard for his fellow demons, but I wished there was someone, something good he had from his long time in Hell.

He walked his index and middle fingers up my chest like a pair of legs, his sharp nails delicately touching my skin. "With my permission and guidance, I may be able to steer where and what we see."

"Really?" I buzzed, practically jumping up with excitement. The only thing keeping me mostly still was the weight of Bez's body, pinning me under him. "Show me. Please."

"It'll require some intense, synchronized saturation." Bez wrapped his arms around my back, pulling me into a tighter embrace. His hips pushed between my thighs, and the length of his shaft rested beneath mine, pulsating.

"I don't think your dick actually has to be inside me to share memories."

"Since when did you become an expert in the Pentacles of Power?" Bez joked. "I assure you, in order to divulge such memories, it's important to be completely in sync."

"Maybe, but it doesn't require cock warming."

"I'm not certain what mortal concept that is, but it sounds truly delight—"

"Liar." I glowered. "I've seen your browser history."

Bez grinned; his cheeks went a bit flushed, but not in an embarrassed way. Nothing ever embarrassed him when it came to his curiosities around sexual explorations, one of the handfuls of things he'd masterfully learned how to look up online. That and murdering people in MMORPGs, which I considered slightly therapeutic and better than actually murdering them. Though, I hadn't told him how I hacked his characters with upgrades to make his slaughter fests successful. He didn't understand the first thing about grinding for levels, and he certainly didn't have the patience for it when he destroyed a Nintendo Switch over a few busted poke balls and a shiny Eevee.

He stared at my unyielding expression, giving me puppy dog eyes like that'd work. "Fine. Can't blame a devil for trying."

Bez interlocked his fingers of my left hand, pressing both to his heart. He channeled the mana from his tattered host body, which I quickly synced to. In a matter of moments, his head fell onto my shoulder, the weight of his unconscious body pressed down on me, and each breath I took drew me further into a drowsy state.

14

Beelzebub

Fuck, fuck, fuckity, fuck.

The gray overcast sky was a familiar horror to the woods I'd spent my first winter hiding within, the lush blankets of snow now seeped and stained with blood. I'd hoped to pick up at a later part of this memory, somewhere in the nearby cabin or the following day back in town.

It wasn't that I didn't trust Wally with the truth. Of all the people in all the worlds, in any and every time, he was the singular being I trusted with all things. I just hated the idea of Wally seeing such weakness. My vulnerability. My inability. I wanted him to see my strength, my perseverance, my insurmountable power, so he'd know I could and would always protect him from threats.

"Gods, are those corpses?" Wally stared at the black flames lapping up a stacked pile of bodies, burning so perfectly the fire only ate away the flesh, bone, and remnants of magic, avoiding the forest altogether.

The sweet, steaky aroma tickled my nose, teasing me with the savory smell carried in this memory. Wally's face turned queasy, likely finding the scent putrid, and missing the delectable flavor of candylike mana in the air, dancing on our tongues like snowflakes. Another reason I didn't want the memory to pick up here since this particular part involved an acquired taste.

I fought a smile, soaking in the scene of detached limbs and organs strewn about. Some we'd toss into the fire to add as kindling, others Mora would retrieve for a meal or potion or future barter.

Wally's eyes widened as he studied a particular favorite corpse of the mage who led the charge for this battalion of vanguards. His body dangled from a tree, his head bashed into the trunk—completely embedding his skull through the bark, which required a powerful and precise telekinetic strike that knocked the fool into the tree, slamming his head through the thick trunk without disturbing a single branch or shaking loose the snow. Picturesque. Captivating. Artistically etched into my mind for all of time.

"How many people did you kill?"

"Me?" I smirked. "None."

"Uh-huh, sure."

I snickered, allowing him to believe I had a hand in this fine craftsmanship that belonged to Mora. She always slaughtered with such finesse, messy and careful and artistic all at once.

"Where are we?" he asked.

"Outside some Puritan settlement, well within Collective territory."

"Why here?"

"You wanted to see how I met Mora." I pointed beyond the black flames where she stood wearing the host body of an older blonde. Abigail Steward, a judge's wife and personal favorite of mine. Of all the hosts Mora had throughout the centuries, I always enjoyed Abigail best, perhaps because of how unassuming she acted as the matriarch of a God-fearing town, the motherly dotting she displayed for everyone, or how Abigail's seven children treated me like a sibling when I arrived guised as a cousin none had met before. They were such a happy family, unaware their mother had been replaced by a demon pulling the strings to influence a town of hypocrites.

"You needn't fear," Mora cooed, daintily stepping around stray pieces of flesh and blood splatter, hiking the edges of her dress up to keep it clean from stains. "There are such few Diabolics here in the colonies, most finding this endeavor unfruitful, but I'm always searching for a new venture."

Wally followed Mora's gaze, tilting his head curiously as she spoke at us, through us, to the figure guiding this memory. He turned, taking in my appearance in this memory. His eyes stared at the four horns atop my head, barely distracting from the disheveled mess of knotted, straggly hair. Then Wally's eyes fell to the slow healing burns on my light gray skin. The freshly charred, ragged clothes indicated these scars hadn't come from Hell, where I'd escaped, but from mages who sought to rid themselves of such a fearsome beast.

There were gashes sliced along my muscles from enchanted weaponry meant to hack me to pieces since the mages quickly learned a Diabolic with no host couldn't be bled dry so easily. I tsked. Muscles. Like I had much in that slender form, barely competent and lacking understanding of how to heal the Diabolic essence circulating through me. My wings were widespread because I'd considered flying away when the demon presented herself, slaughtering the foes who meant to detain and destroy me.

Wally's expression softened, not with sadness but polite curiosity in a way he would use when gently prodding for answers to things he wanted to know. "This is you."

"Yes," I said, fighting the urge to fidget like my past self, whose bare feet bounced back and forth in the crunching snow. "That's who I was."

Was.

Because that weakling didn't represent a single shred of who I'd become. I let that nothing wash away along with the blood of mages centuries in their graves. This weak, unwanted thing wasn't me. He wasn't Beelzebub. He wasn't Bez. He wasn't the persona I'd carefully crafted of the god-king toying with a mortal world out of boredom and curious fancies.

"You're a demon." My former self so astutely surmised after looking Mora over. I rolled my eyes at his baffled expression.

"And you're a devil," Mora replied, curtsying. "A pleasure to meet your acquaintance, Lord Beelzebub."

I hadn't replied to her assumption, hadn't corrected or denied it. Back then, I'd believed I was playing her, but in truth, Mora always knew more than the hand she revealed.

"I was honored to hear that a devil of such high esteem had come to grace us with his presence." Mora stepped through Wally's body, a ghost of the past rippling by as he remained silent and fully observant. "Then shocked to learn how disgracefully these mages treated you." She twisted her face in disgust and spit. "Collective trash. Apologies your visit has been met with such crass actions."

"I'm used to it." My past self shivered, not from the cold I couldn't feel without a host but from the acknowledgment my entire existence had been met with caustic hate from devils, demons, mages, Mythics, and mortals.

"I must ask, Lord Beelzebub." Mora continued subtly closing the distance between herself and the scrawny demon radiating devil essence. "Why run from these mages instead of ending them where they stood?"

"I..." My past self swallowed hard, struggling to find the right words.

"I see. So much time in Hell must've left you disoriented, confused on how to navigate the mortal plane in all its simplicity."

Mora had a glint in her eyes, one I hadn't noticed then, only registering the carefully crafted compassionate expression she gave. "If you like, I can offer my guidance until you understand this world better."

"So, Mora was the first person to acknowledge you as Beelzebub?" Wally asked, ignoring her small talk to garner trust from a frightened feeble demon pretending to be brave. Always pretending.

"Yep, and thanks to her, soon other demons caught wind of me. They sensed the same devil essence Mora would, in turn, help cultivate. In time, I made a name for myself that spread like wildfire." I smirked. "It helped that I set actual flames to feed the legend."

"Wait, then why was the Collective attacking you now?" Wally asked.

"Did you not see my appearance?" I gestured to my scrawny form and obvious features, such as the three tails that twitched nervously the entire time speaking with Mora.

"Yes, you're not possessing a host, which I know isn't a requirement for Diabolics, but I always thought you preferred it for the sensations."

"I do."

"I just don't understand why the Collective would strike if you hadn't done anything wrong. Harmed anyone. Did you harm anyone?" He bit his lip, face reddening and entire body warming with guilt from the blurted question.

"No, I didn't. They attacked me, hunted me, because they saw a vile demon, a Diabolic, that didn't fit into the Collective philosophy or the accords they'd put in place for Mythics."

"Sorry. Sometimes I forget—or am willfully unwilling to accept—that the Collective is just cruel to be cruel most days."

"In defense of the current Collective," I said, playfully batting my lashes and nudging his shoulder with mine to lighten the mood.

"I did spend the better part of the next century slaughtering mages whenever the whim struck."

"But not when you arrived," Wally said, conviction in his voice and a lack of remorse for the bodies he watched Mora telekinetically throw into the fire. "What'd you do when you first arrived here?"

"Damn, Walter." I pointed to the conversation between the former Mora and my past self playing out right in front of us. "I thought you wanted to know how I met Mora, why that—"

"All I want—all I've ever wanted—is to know more about you. All of you. All the parts you're willing to share." He stepped in close, delicately running his fingers along the hairs of my forearms, sending a delightful shiver through my body, then he cupped my hands into his. "No judgment. No reservations. I love you, Bez. I love everything about you. Even the things I hate—and to be clear, glorifying carnage and casually killing people are not high on my list of favorite things. But the Bez who lived in Hell had somber eyes; the Bez in this memory has a soft, curious expression. I want to know what he desired when he came to our world. What dream did the Collective take from him? From you?"

I practically choked, trying to form words. Gods, he was insufferable, always making me feel…seen. I hated how it made my insides warm and fuzzy. But I also couldn't imagine my life without those sensations anymore.

"Back when I first arrived, I wanted to be a champion for anyone in need," I said with a laugh because it was funny. It was pathetic and worthless and met with fear and disdain. Not only from the mages who didn't like pushback against their authority but also from the Mythics who found my essence rotten and the mortals who believed me the literal Satan due to their tiny, glamoured, and simplistic existences.

"You wanted to help others? Why?"

"Because I was deluded." I ground my teeth, unable to find the words for my obsession with true heroism or the guilt I carried for escaping Hell, leaving behind so many I despised, but wondering how many others like myself clawed at the locked walls, desperate for a reprieve I'd denied them.

I took solace in the fact that the knight who sparked such ideals in me had already lost his life before I abandoned my Hell. It would be far more gutting to know he suffered behind those closed doors for all eternity due to my cowardice.

Eligos, the dead fool, painted the mortal realm with such grandeur as one of the few demons offered leave from Beelzebub's domain. Beelzebub found the errant knight exhausting, how he had always returned to Hell explaining the nobility of honor and valor and compassion and generosity and too many virtues. Eligos proved anyone could achieve anything if they believed enough. He fought harder, stayed true to himself for eons, and even in the coup that killed him, he protected the demons around him.

Eligos…

The knighted demon in all his glory appeared in the memory, flickering in and out much like the forest itself, shifting to the walls of a castle I once had the displeasure of calling home. A place where I cleaned and served and obeyed for what should've been all of time, taking small comforts in his visits, his tales, his journey for change.

"What's going on?" Wally asked, watching the shifting memory.

I snarled, exhaling the frustration. Reminiscing of Eligos made me weak. His image. His belief. His kindness.

"It's nothing. I'm just not focused." I shrugged away the fleeting thoughts. "Thinking of one thing sort of spiraled into another thing, and all this dredging up the past is making my memories mix and get muddled."

Wally stared at the flickering knight so intently, the image of Eligos remained in the snowy forest near Mora and my past self, completely out of place with the memory.

"This whole thing is your fault," I teased. "I'm starting to think your whole overthinking behavior is contagious."

"I know him." Wally pointed to Eligos.

"You may've glimpsed Eligos during one of your saturated visits to my past," I said nonchalantly. "He's no one special. Just some demon from Hell. My Hell. But again, nothing—"

"No." Wally trembled, panic in his voice. "I've seen him here in the villa."

Wally reeled all his mana back into himself, retracting every ounce of saturation and snapping us into an abrupt awakening. The room was fogged over, perhaps a fleeting sensation from the weather in the memory or Wally's lethargic state after jolting awake.

"What's wrong?" I asked.

"I've seen that exact suit of armor three times now."

"Wait. What are you talking about?"

He sprang from the bed, tossing his clothes on, speaking in jumbled half-uttered thoughts, and rushing out of the room before he'd even squeezed his hips into his skinny jeans.

I sighed. Clearly, showing him my past had broken his curious little brain.

His feet pattered, swiftly rushing through the living quarters toward the helm. I took my time dressing, listening intently to his mutterings from afar. Once I'd slipped on my gray blazer and donned a scarlet pocket square, I zipped out of the room and closed in on my adorable but often frantic mage.

He burst into the helm, lost in his dazed inquisitive thoughts, not acknowledging my presence or Mora and Kell, who sat in the lone chair by the navigation panel.

Kell straddled Mora's lap as the demon caressed her wife's waist and kissed her neck. Heat and lust wafted off each of them, yet Kell's eyes lingered on some broken mechanism to an unnecessary project she was forced to abandon for romance. It sat disassembled on the control panel near the locked box holding the Demon's Demise that I wanted Wally to keep at the ready if need be.

Wally brushed past the pair, ignoring the giggle Mora's tongue elicited from Kell.

"Of course, now you're all in," Mora teased, her lips moving up to meet Kell's, but her gaze shifted to me. "Kell's always enjoyed an audience, but your mortal never struck me as a voyeur, Bezzy."

"Finally, something about him I like." Kell kissed Mora, grabbing ahold of her demon's hair and controlling the tilt of Mora's head as their lips enveloped each other with passion.

Kell thrusted her hips, rocking the chair that Mora kept from tipping over with a steady flux of telekinesis.

"Walter's not here for the show. Don't you have a room for this?"

"Three, in fact." Mora moaned as Kell continued.

Admittedly, Mora and Kell were always a fun pair to play with, but neither were Wally's type, and I no longer held the interest of burying my cock in whoever I stumbled upon. Plus, I had even less interest in sharing Wally with other partners.

"Why is he here?" Kell tore herself from Mora's lips, one hand resting on Mora's shoulder, the other instinctively venturing lower. "The command protocols still aren't functioning, so if you're trying to move us somewhere, it'll—"

"Where's the footage?" Wally asked aloud, but only to himself based on the inflections of his voice. "Gotta find the dungeon place thingy. No. No cameras there. But where else…"

I rushed past Mora and Kell in a blur; a powerful air current was carried by my swoosh, which spun their lover's chair round and round.

Wally's eyes flitted about, studying the hundreds of security videos he'd pulled up.

"Foyer works. Date was…" He bit his lip, puzzling together something in his maze of a mind.

"What are you doing?" I asked, placing a hand under his chin and turning his attention to me. It seemed the only way to steal his focus and get a proper answer.

"I've seen that armor before. In the baron's villa."

"You've seen a suit of armor," I corrected him. "We've seen a few dozen while investigating."

Novus had a vast collection of mortal armor and artillery spanning centuries back from across the globe.

"No. That exact suit." Wally returned to the control panel, zooming in on a camera positioned in a foyer.

He rolled the footage back.

"You think you saw it," I said. "Knight armor can be easy to confuse."

"No," he snapped. "This was the exact same suit this Eligos demon wore. I know how to distinguish minute details. That suit of armor came from tenth-century England."

Wally was right about the century. I recalled Eligos' particular fondness for that suit, having earned it on a pilgrimage in the mortal plane. He regaled many about his journeys as a knight errant.

"See." Wally paused the footage.

I found myself more fixated on the framed image of his frantic expression on camera—the same expression he had now—from the night of the Fae Divinity, backstepping from a looming shadow that must've been Novus.

"Look." He pointed to the suit of armor positioned behind him. "It's exactly the same."

I shook my head in disbelief. "They are similar."

"They're identical." Wally pointed. "Everything down to the dent, which should've struck me as odd considering the pristine condition Baron Novus kept everything else in his collection. Fixing damage like that would be easy, even without magic, so long as you know what you're doing."

I thought back to the many memories of Hell I kept buried, to Eligos, his nobility, his honor, his tales which offered a small reprieve from the constant torment of my existence. He'd earned it by slaying some Mythic beast—*a dragon, I think, which is as cliché as it can get*—and saving a village of mortals. That dent. The singular scuff he'd received from the slow-moving beast because he'd deflected a blow meant to kill a child.

He had been particularly proud of the suit's durability and the war wound it obtained, even as others mocked his sluggishness and need to prioritize a finite, worthless mortal life. It hadn't bothered him at all, though, and I loved how no one's opinions ever deterred his desires, his tales during meetings among the hierarchy of demon lords.

I swallowed the lump in my throat, the memories best left buried. None of them mattered. "Eligos is dead. Saw it myself."

The former reigning devil smashed Eligos and so many demons to pieces, shattering their forms and scattering their broken essence among the thousands of other defeated demons. A rebellion for the ages, one that Eligos would've told a thousand times over, except he had died.

"Diabolics don't die, not like others. You said that." Wally tugged at his hair, yanking away the confusion festering in his overworked brain, so he could come to a sound conclusion. "He could've been brought back or survived the attack or…"

I'd seen Wally get this way when unraveling a secret layered in lies and mysteries. Usually, he had great insight, fantastic instincts, and a knack for the puzzles people created. Hell, locked in a room with Mora, he'd likely learn all her secrets over a single cocktail.

But he was wrong about Eligos. I couldn't explain the similarities. Perhaps, I'd seen it around the villa, substituted it for my repressed memories of a fallen friend, a demon I regretted the death of.

"Even if Eligos had survived, which, to be clear, he didn't," I said. "He couldn't get through a closed doorway."

"Precisely." Mora smacked Kell's ass to draw our attention.

"Babe, he seems serious," Kell said, slipping off Mora's lap and straightening her skirt.

"More like overthinking it. Beelzebub's Hell is completely sealed off," Mora said, indicating she too kept a watchful eye on the world I'd abandoned, ensuring that particular Hell never opened again. "No way in or out."

"Unless," Wally interjected, continuing his wild theories, "Novus had been left to his own devices, which—oh yeah, he was—potentially figuring out a way through this locked realm in some nefarious plot. For all we know, Eligos is—"

"I never considered the former baron nefarious so much as narcissistic," a hauntingly chivalrous and familiar voice said. "Vapid, callow, arrogant by any man's measure. Certainly. Nefarious. Not even sure the Fae truly know the meaning, despite millennia of observation."

I quaked at the sight of his full suit on display, moving gracefully with his aligned essence and demon form navigating from within. Eligos didn't possess hosts, favoring the armor for the limited mortal shape. Well, the Eligos I knew. This couldn't be him.

Still, those golden eyes peering through the slit of the helmet were uncanny.

"As for Beelzebub's sealed Hell," Eligos said, nodding his helmet at me. "Getting him here was the first step in undoing that travesty."

Fucking Eligos. How was he here? How had he survived? What did he want with me? Why was he trying to free Beelzebub?

"How did you escape?" The words left my lips like I'd become the frightened, whimpering demon all over again.

"You weren't the only one to cross through the portal before it sealed away," he said, which meant he'd been in the mortal realm for centuries. "Though, the state of near-death you left my essence in, it took a while to regain my bearings."

The state I left him in? My heart thumped loudly in my eardrums; the room whirled.

"So many tried to flee before you sealed everyone away and everything for all of time, but the triumphant devil did all in his power to keep a single one from crossing through. Seemed only my tattered broken being managed to skirt past unnoticed. That and the devil himself."

Eligos wasn't the only one to escape our Hell. I had, too.

Armor clinked; Eligos' blurred steps rattled against the floor.

"I've waited far too long for this hedonistic traitor." Eligos unsheathed his blade. "The mortal realm has left you weakened, Beelzebub."

What? He thought I was actually Beelzebub? The devil essence circulating deceived most, but couldn't he see the layers of demon essence feeding upon it? Couldn't he see the demon who listened to his tales a million times over? As someone who served the actual Beelzebub for eons, shouldn't Eligos have seen right through my deceit and known I wasn't him?

I reached out to my right, intending to stop his sword hand, but only grabbed air. His glove clasping the hilt rang from my left. Eligos held his bloody sword, and the room swirled.

I choked, struggling to stand upright. Wally screamed. Had he been harmed, too? Was that why I found myself struck with such fatigue? I tried calling out, but my throat burned. Blood soaked through my clothes. My legs wobbled, and I toppled over.

15

Walter

He decapitated Bez. I watched his head spin around, flopping onto the ground, crimson eyes rolling back as his body collapsed. My entire being trembled, terrified, petrified, locked in place. The demon in the suit of armor cut off Bez's head. I grabbed my throat, inspecting an injury that didn't exist because the essence circulating between Bez and me didn't match or inflict the injuries he sustained back onto me. I wouldn't feel the pain Bez endured, not unless he…he died.

Dead. Gone. Bez just had his head hacked off.

I clenched my fists, trying to contain my shaky muscles. Bez wasn't dead. It took a lot more than that to kill a Diabolic; it required destroying his essence on a cellular level. Or killing a mortal they linked to, like me.

I pushed away the thoughts. I needed to focus on the now. Help. Stop this armored demon knight from actually killing Bez.

"You're the one who captured Beelzebub's heart." The knight's voice echoed not simply from inside the helmet but stirring around the helm.

Did he have a Diabolic shroud up or essence casting a void realm? Was that how he moved throughout the villa unnoticed? No. Bez would've detected it, right?

"You may prove useful, mortal." Eligos made a fist with his free hand and snatched me into the air with telekinesis.

I kicked my legs in a futile attempt to wriggle free, but it was like being dragged by a powerful tide.

Suddenly, my body rocked back and forth midair, frozen and locked in place. Eligos' telekinesis pulled me, yet something stalled his hold. Not something but someone.

Mora.

She strutted toward the knight in shining armor, arm extended and power holding him at bay.

"Lopping off Bezzy's head." She smiled. "Gotta be honest, I'm going to have to remember that one the next time he runs his mouth at one of my parties."

"Morax, correct?" Eligos ground his boots into the floor, shifting his stance.

"The one and only." She curtsied yet kept one arm firmly aimed at me, telekinesis fully intact.

"They call you a king in Bael's charade of a realm, yet the Morax I know was no king, merely an undistinguished noble."

"You've been reading too much mortal fiction." Her joyful expression almost hid the crinkle in her forehead from the strain of overpowering his grasp. "Let this be a reminder of your place. Knights kneel to kings."

Mora lifted her other arm, spinning the air above and slamming a tremendous force of energy down onto Eligos. I gasped, the telekinesis from each of them releasing me. I fell onto my back with a heavy thud, not nearly as hard as Eligos, who resisted every inch. His armor cracked, compressed, and black tendrils laced with golden hues throughout whipped between the openings of the suit, stitching the blemishes together like they fixed a host body.

"Quite powerful. I'd always heard Morax was a demon of cunning, never that she possessed a warrior's spirit."

"Cute." Mora strained, forcing Eligos further into the floor—literally cracking it to pieces in order to push him onto his hands and knees. "I usually kiss my fans before killing them. But I'll make an exception this once since you're rather irritat—"

Kell screamed.

Blood gushed.

Mora panted, barely holding a sword already embedded in her chest.

She stood in front of Kell on the opposite side of the room, saving her witch.

When had Eligos thrown it? How? Telekinesis? A tendril? Some other Diabolic ability?

He'd zipped forward in the few seconds when Mora's hold waned, speeding toward her in a haze. My eyes barely registered the movement, even with essence coursing through my body and months of studying Bez's playful darting about.

"You're as vulnerable as Beelzebub, it seems." Eligos grabbed the hilt of his weapon, twisting it. "But I have no need of a petty, vile demon such as yourself."

Diabolic energy raged between the two of them. Tendrils laced in gold and emerald clashed, destroying everything in the helm. A large gust of black wind carried Kell away, hurling her at the exit.

Exit. I needed to escape. With Bez. With Kell. Mora knew that. I struggled to breathe between the realization that I was facing a demon, Bez was lying decapitated, and the oxygen was being siphoned by the whirlwind Eligos and Mora each summoned, dragging one another into close combat my eyes couldn't analyze.

"Even before visiting Bael's realm with that arrogant clown, Novus"—Eligos continued slowly driving his blade further into Mora's chest—"who traipsed about believing he could master our essence, I'd seen the lackluster conviction of your world."

"So trite, right?" Mora jested, brow furrowed, heels broken, and feet dug into the floor to keep her stance. "I've heard of you, too. The tragic demon knight who deluded himself into thinking his foolhardy valor meant a damn thing. How quickly the world forgot you."

The world, maybe… But this demon Eligos meant something to Bez. I felt it in his memory and the helm, the anxiety in his body's tremble, the patter of his quickening heartbeat, the shocked expression unable to mask mixed emotions.

"The problem with you, Morax, is even the best warriors in Bael's realm couldn't hold their own against the lowliest of Beelzebub's." Eligos whipped behind Mora, attempting to impale her through the back.

"You talk too much." Mora caught the tip of the sword with her palm, slicing her own hand to hold the weapon at bay. Black lightning surged from each of them, clinking against the metal but deflecting from the natural conductor. Eligos protected his weapon. His armor. He had a weakness, too.

"The Morax I know is all talk, a con artist with an aristocratic flair and a heart only for herself. It's nice to see there is some fight in you." Eligos' golden eyes shimmered behind his visor, squinting with rage, the kind of disgusted hate I'd seen at far too many family dinners. "Still, as one affiliated with such a corrupt devil, you're unworthy of the universe I'm creating."

Mora clenched her hand, cracking the blade.

Symbols of high-tier incantations formed from the gaps in Eligos' armor, latching onto the wind that whirled around the pair. Explosions of fire and smog and barriers burst throughout the helm, a cacophony that forced me to press my hands to my ears and squeeze my eyes shut.

One. Two. Three.

The entire villa rumbled. Exploded. I opened my eyes, wheezing and barely able to see through the thick smoke.

Mora stood, feet barely touching the floor as she appeared unconscious, pinned against a wall with blades pressed through her chest, neck, stomach, thigh, and right hand. Eligos had more weapons. Where? How? Must've been the incantations he used to summon them.

Mora roared, tendrils whipping about erratically as Diabolic essence flourished. Her brown eyes burned a bright emerald and fully bloodshot, the whites replaced by a faded lime green.

Eligos revealed a small dagger summoned by an incantation. Upon closer inspection, those sigils were Fae, which meant even without possessing a Fae, he must've fed on a lot of Mythic residue belonging to them. In one fluid motion, Eligos drove the dagger upward, stabbing Mora through her throat and into her skull. She gurgled, body convulsing, and tendrils slowly retreating inside her host body. Her eyes rolled back, and her essence stopped stirring.

All the smoke drifted to the opposite side of the room, funneling into a tiny, condensed ball of gray mist floating above Kell's palm. Her sorcery was skillful, but she didn't seriously believe she could fight a demon, did she? One that defeated Bez and Mora? My chest tightened as each inhale became harder. I needed a plan, needed to help, needed to run. I scanned the helm, searching for anything of use, and my gaze rested on the control panel littered with Kell's projects and a box Bez had gifted me.

"You put your hands on my wife." Kell hurled the ball of smoke, which burst wide when Eligos attempted flitting past it. The smog transformed from a gas to a sticky liquid that held the demon knight in place. As he struggled to get loose, the substance clung to every piece of his armor and hardened to stone. "Now, you die."

Incantations from sorcery floated around Kell; flames conjured by nature's blessing circled her feet; she muttered something that summoned silhouettes of apparitions behind her—the power of evocation, allowing her to commune with the spiritual guidance of deceased witches.

"*Get your damn demon-killing blade to stab this bastard.*" Kell glared at me, her words echoing in my head through a telepathic link that came from psychic perception. "*Once I rip every single piece of scrap metal off him, gut whatever foul thing reveals itself, and I'll burn him with flames guided by a hundred generations of witches.*"

Kell harnessed the Four Corners of witchcraft masterfully and simultaneously: sorcery, nature's blessing, evocation, and psychic perception, all while maintaining a strong unflinching stance. I couldn't even stop the quake in my legs or the panic in my chest.

"Now," she snapped, throwing fiery sigils at Eligos.

I leapt to my feet and darted to the control panel. Something cracked, and rocks were flung in my direction. I spun around, dodging them, and grabbed the box holding Demon's Demise before crashing onto the floor.

"I always found witches tiresome." Eligos stood behind Kell. "I see why the mortals preferred burning you lot from their realm."

He balled a fist, and the protective flames surrounding Kell turned black and burned bright. She screamed, engulfed by a tornado of fire.

"Kell!" I shouted.

In an instant, Eligos appeared in front of me, drawing his sword. "You should be worried about yourself, misfit mage."

I tried to open the box, saturating mana in the air to create a barrier. Not fast enough. Eligos swung his sword. I was going to die. Bez was going to die. Mora and Kell were going to die.

A black fireball smashed against Eligos' armored head, burning his helmet until tendrils sprang from the visor and smothered the fire. He halted his strike, the tip of his sword pressed against my stomach. We both turned our attention to Kell's burning body, collapsed on the floor.

Tony was perched on the Cerberus' back, guiding Weather into the room. Sunny held my work grimoire in his mouth. It was filled with all the incantations I'd learned over the years. Cloudy licked the black flames burning Kell's scorched flesh and swallowed big gulps of fire. Stormy, in turn, belched the black fire and snarled. Tony used an incantation he took out of the grimoire and guided the flaming projectile at Eligos. They worked in tandem to distract Eligos, who unfortunately deflected the flames with ease, now aware of their presence. No. His posture shifted in the most minute manner, indicating he planned to zip across the room and kill my familiar and Mythic beast.

Not happening. I pried open the box and lunged at Eligos, mustering all the Diabolic essence coursing inside my body to match his speed. I jabbed the demon blade through the open slit of the knight's visor.

Eligos shrieked, thrashing about and punching me in the stomach so hard it knocked all the air out of my lungs. I choked, breathless and shaking on the floor. The blade clinked nearby. Eligos' armor rattled as he attempted to mend an injury his essence couldn't.

Demon's Demise made it impossible for Diabolics to instantly recover since it repelled their essence from wounds it inflicted.

I forced myself up and retrieved the blade, intent on stabbing every weak point in this suit of armor, but a barrage of black elements whirled around Eligos. He wailed, still incapable of stitching the injury to his face. Rocks and fire carried by wind protected him and blocked the only exit on or off the villa.

Fuck.

I raced toward Bez, grabbed his head, and ran out of the helm deeper into the villa with Weather and Tony at my side.

We needed to escape, survive, and find a way to kill this demon later.

16

Beelzebub

My head throbbed, jostling about as I swam deep in the depths of my mind, searching for all the essence I'd lost. The devil essence radiated brighter in this void of complete blackness, making it more tangible, almost alive with a will since I'd lost so much of my demon essence.

Where had it gone?

My eyes flitted, catching glimpses of a corridor and then a bright green light. I sank deeper into my mind, searching for the energy to wake up. I needed to wake up. Protect Wally.

"Shush," Wally said with heavy, exhausted breaths. "We have to be very quiet."

Weather whimpered, Sunny based on the joyful inflection soured by sadness. When had the dog shown up?

Wally's breathing didn't weigh on me, didn't register, but I could sense the pain in his winded breaths. Why couldn't I feel his pain? I ached all over yet couldn't form a fist to express my fury.

Eligos attacked me.

Then what?

It was darkness. Diabolic essence boomed, noisy, screaming, blood, but all too far away.

"Bez." Wally sobbed. "Bez, why aren't you waking up?"

I attempted to call out, but my throat… I floated in this darkness, unable to speak. Had I lost my voice? Was it some spell? Where had my essence gone?

The blackness of devilish essence whispered, calling me deeper into the nothingness of my mind, and Wally's voice became a hollow whisper. As I fell further away, pieces of my will drifted, remaining far from the infinite depths, and a power I never should've taken radiated.

Beelzebub's power. The true strength of a devil offering me the voice I needed. Strength. An escape from this nothingness. But with my demon essence waning, lacking, lost—would I be able to harness and control such power, or would it control me?

It seemed I'd be lost in darkness no matter what I chose.

Crimson splashed in the black sea surrounding me. Oil and blood raged and swam further.

"Why isn't this working?" Wally said, gritting his teeth.

I clamped my jaw in protest to the painful grind of his molars. I felt it. Felt him. Whatever he'd done was working. I swam through the sludge toward the trickling crimson blobs. Reaching out with a hand, I pressed clawed fingers and popped the bubble.

Wally shouted, and flashes of him appeared. With his teeth ground, stifling the urge to shout, black tendrils laced with my crimson aura whipped erratically. They smacked his face, slicing his cheek and cutting his arms, but he kept resisting their protests.

Holding the Demon's Demise with both hands, he cut into his tender stomach, swirling the tip of the blade and yanking out essence. My essence. Why was he carving out our bond?

I backed away from the crimson, unwilling to watch further. I'd failed him, and now he literally wanted to sever all ties between us.

"Wake the fuck up, Bez!" Wally shouted. "I need you. I need to know you're okay."

The crimson whirled around me, tearing apart the blackness and pushing the devil essence back into the subconscious where it belonged. Dormant and obedient to my will.

Wally… *What are you doing?*

I flexed my muscles, still incapable of talking to him but unable to ignore the pain he endured. What began as a searing burn against my phantom body became a slight discomfort. The more I felt my flesh return, the less I felt the connection to Wally, to the man I loved.

I ascended further, unveiling my wings to surge upward and be released from the prison of my sleeping mind.

"It isn't enough essence," Wally said through wispy breaths. "Must've wasted too much, or Bez really is… No. NO! Tony, hand me the grimoire. There's gotta be an incantation I can use. Something to help him heal his…his missing body."

Something slammed. The grimoire, perhaps.

"If I weren't so weak, I would've grabbed his body, reattached his head, but now all that essence is gone, and Bez is…"

That was what happened. That fucking prick Eligos decapitated me. *Dammit.*

I huffed, continuing my flight toward Wally's voice. His need to ramble guided me, and I loved him even more for being my chatty beacon of light. Although, he had a point. He'd lost my body, and it'd take forever to fully recover my lost essence now. I wasn't even sure where to draw on enough energy to restore it swiftly. One thing at a time.

I collided with a hard ceiling, blocking my escape from this infinite slumber. Not fucking happening. I slashed the barrier, one made of bone, easily defeating it with my claws. Ripping my way through, I lunged forward in a huge explosive rage.

Blood and bone and meat splattered this tiny dark storage room where Wally hid from Eligos. I panted, taking in his frazzled expression, the blood soaked into his shirt, the chunk of grey matter dangling in his blond curls.

"Where the hell are we?" I asked, approaching him to remove the bit of brain in his hair.

"You're…you're…you're…" Wally bit his lip.

"Yes, yes, I'm alive, and I'm infuriated. I'm going to slaughter that f—"

"You're tiny!"

"Excuse me?"

Wally pointed at me.

"I'm what?" I scrunched my face and turned to find the disassembled remains of my former host body. Well, the part of the body my essence instinctively coiled within after some asshole chopped off my head.

My head. The crater of where I'd erupted lay in pieces after I broke free of a host and reformed my essence into a fully-fleshed demon body. Bone and blood were splattered at my feet. My busted jaw looked rather large. An oozing, bulged eye hung from the socket and stared at me with a glossy stillness, reflecting my image in the iris no longer possessing my crimson touch.

I looked more or less true to form with all four curled horns atop my head, three tails lively as ever, and claws sharper than any blade. My gray skin looked a little flushed, but I was soaked in blood and covered in meaty chunks after escaping a fatality.

Wait. Wait.

"Wait a second."

"I didn't say anything," Walter rudely interrupted my train of thought.

I furrowed my brow, closely inspecting my proportions in comparison to the head I'd broken out of. The busted eye was almost at my height level. The eye, hanging from a head lying on the floor, was almost as big as me. "Goddamn motherfucking piece of bullshit biscuit twat licking cock guzzling cuck."

I bit back a roar and turned to look up at Wally. I had to look up to him because with all the essence circulating inside me, there was only enough to fully form me in my natural demon body as a pint-sized version.

"That was unnecessarily vulgar."

"You're unnecessary." I pointed an accusatory clawed finger at him, then huffed, pouting, but releasing my misguided rage because I needed to conserve it, cultivate it, and send it all back at Eligos a hundred-fold. I took a calming breath, brushed my sticky, ratty hair back, and flew up so I met Wally at proper eye level, which meant having him stare up at me.

"What happened to you?" he asked.

"With my host body in shambles, I had to take on my true form."

"But you're so small."

"Yes, well, it's not like I'm rolling in essence right now." I ground my teeth, glaring at Wally and resting my gaze on his bleeding stomach. Shallow slices that he made to hack out the essence I'd given him, injuries he inflicted while knowing full well that without my essence, it'd take him much longer to heal. My expression softened. "Thank you. If you hadn't provided me with essence, it might've taken me several days, possibly weeks, for me to fully self-actualize and awaken."

"It was all I could think to do." Wally's shoulders shook as he cried, tears smearing his bloody face. Such a beautiful face should only be covered in the blood of foes, never his own. "I'm so sorry. I froze. I froze, and Kell and Mora… They were…they were…killed."

I amplified my senses, attempting to analyze the various layers throughout the villa, but in my weakened state, it was difficult to make out the subtle distinctions. It was hauntingly silent. However Eligos moved about this place, he knew not to leave a trace of his presence. One thing I did detect was a shroud of essence newly weaved throughout the labyrinth below. Its stink wafting a foul odor of agony.

Mora. What had Eligos done to her? Wally suspected death. Given her struggle to cloak her scent, he might not have been far off, but she dwelled out there somewhere.

"She's fine," I said dismissively to Wally's anguish because I couldn't allow sadness to overcome me. Mora never died. She'd never die. She was the one constant I had in this long eternity. And I hated it. Hated her and her annoying mischief. I ground my teeth. She'd live to kill another day, I believed… I knew it.

"I saw her impaled."

"You also saw me decapitated, and I'm right as rain." More like rain droplets, not the tsunami of strength I usually represented.

"Kell was burned alive," Walter blurted, clutching his shaky thighs. "If she dies, then Mora, no matter how powerful Diabolics are… She'll die."

"Whatever, Kell's fine. Mora's essence is still floundering about." Because she tried to lay claim to my villa. Mine and Walter's. I'd remember that and deal with it after I dealt with Eligos. "Basically, if Mora's alive, Kell's alive. Unless, of course, Mora severed their link to save herself, but considering she finally found someone who can tolerate her obnoxious behavior past the one-year marker, I doubt that."

"Bez." Wally crawled toward me, picturesque on his knees and covered in blood while looking up at me, which was unfortunate since we didn't have time for such fun things. "Kell was set on fire. Actual fire. I mean, Weather ate some of the flames, but there was so much fire. Charred skin. The smell was awful, and she screamed so loud."

"Wally, she's a witch." I grinned. "She's used to being set on fire. It's how witches witch it up."

"How can you make jokes?"

"Would you rather I sat here and cried all day? No. I need to be productive. I need to find a way to amplify the recovery of my essence, restore some of my power, then locate Eligos, murder him—after I torture him—"

"You're six fucking inches tall," Wally shouted before covering his mouth to silence an outburst that'd already escaped. Thankfully, Eligos wasn't lingering nearby. "How are you going to stop him?"

"First of all, I'm seven inches and three-quarters. Let's just put that on the record."

Wally laughed, an outlandish, unhinged laughter where he clutched his injured stomach, cradling his ribs as he toppled over, unable to contain himself.

"Is something funny, Walter?"

"No, not at all." He wheezed, then snapped his fingers, calling the three-headed hound over. While he petted Sunny's head, Wally buried his face into Weather's stomach, cackling. Stormy nipped his ankle, forcing Wally to stop with the nonsensical over-affection. Sunny and Cloudy were displeased but hid it when Stormy snapped his powerful jaws at them. Good for Stormy. Fuck all this holly jolly garbage of joy. "It's just, um, haaa! I've never seen you so desperate for precise measurements."

"Wow." I landed on the ground, brushing away curdling blood off my chest. "You think now is the best time to joke about my size?"

"No." His lips tightened as he fought back laughter and forced himself not to smile. "We're all going to die, and all I can do is make dick jokes?"

His eyes welled up, his smile grew again, then instantly fell into a frown, lips trembling. This was too much for Wally. His chest swelled and deflated, taking rapid, wispy breaths. I'd failed him, dragged him into this situation, left him to fend for his life—our lives, and now I needed to remind him that the devil Beelzebub was a terrifying force no foe could defeat.

I hated seeing him so lost in his frantic mind. I grabbed his clammy, shaky hand, lightly caressing it, which didn't soothe him. Well, there was only one solution to snap him back to the reality of the situation and think more rationally. I squeezed his palm, spun around, and threw him over my shoulder.

"Gods." He gasped. The sudden shock of being slammed onto his back reeled some sense into his glossy hazel eyes.

Antoninus clacked his slightly more formidable claws now that I'd lost a bit of my stature, but I snarled to remind the familiar I would crack open that shell and wear it to battle. A battle I needed to contend with soon, given Eligos had the edge after he got the drop on Mora and myself. Mostly Mora. She should've predicted this nonsense.

"How'd you do that?" Wally asked, somewhat composed at this point. "I must be a hundred times your weight."

"Please. You'll always be a feather in my delicate grip."

"But you're six…you're so small."

"Walter, I know this is hard to hear, especially coming from someone such as myself, a true stallion below the belt, but it's never the size that matters. It's how you use what you got."

He half-smiled, the kind that showed he was too flustered or annoyed to give me the satisfaction of a fully happy expression, but one lost in my words, allowing the rest of the world to fall away. I yanked his curls and pushed him until he sat upright. All the panic had passed. Good.

"There will be plenty of time for more jokes, Wally," I said. "First things first, I'm going to need you to enchant me something to wear. I must face my enemies with the dignity of a fine suit, and unfortunately, I've lost the remaining Mythic residue I had stored up, so I can't enchant a proper ensemble."

"Of course." Wally weaved together glittering enchantments. "What are you planning?"

"Kill a demon, save my villa, and take my boyfriend on a lovely date to forget his recent woes." I smirked, reminding Wally that no matter what, I remained confident, even if it wasn't true.

I'd allowed myself to be caught off guard, let my memories of Eligos hinder my reaction, and now I'd lost almost all my strength. He was one of the strongest demons in Hell, one even Beelzebub tolerated due to his power, and now I had to face him, kill him, all while wishing to ask if he remembered me.

If he knew I wasn't Beelzebub, not truly, would this situation play out differently? I didn't think so. Eligos was a Diabolic of honor. If he knew the pathetic know-nothing demon he'd championed, rooted for, and offered advice had guised himself as a devil to intimidate enemies and slaughtered thousands over the centuries, his principles would resign death for my actions.

That was fine. I could exploit his rigid beliefs and kill him first. He wouldn't be the first demon I'd ended—certainly wouldn't be the last.

17

Walter

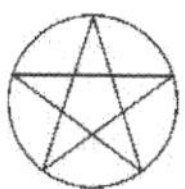

Bez adjusted the red tie I'd materialized with an incantation to properly fit it with the dark blue suit I'd created. "We're going to have to move soon. Can't risk Eligos sensing your magic at work."

He was extra surly and less appreciative for the outfit. I couldn't decide if that had to do with his pint-sized rage, the fact he'd had his head chopped off, or the fact that Mora might actually be dead. He acted like he didn't care, willfully shrugged off her fate, but I saw how his eyes darted about scanning the essence laced throughout the villa. I'd seen him do that every time we moved somewhere new, searching for potential threats, unwilling to share his concerns, and I always remained quiet—because if he knew I knew, it'd make him even more worried than he usually pretended he wasn't. Bez was complicated. Lovely, sweet, and caring too.

"Are you listening to me, Walter?" Bez snapped his tiny fingers. "Move."

"Right." I grabbed Tony, placing him on my shoulder, and offered Bez my other shoulder. He scoffed, flying at eye level as we exited the pocket portal storage room and entered the labyrinth of the lower levels again. This seemed the best place to hide. With all the essence funneled throughout the villa, even Eligos must've struggled to navigate his way through this maze. Maybe that was wishful thinking.

Sunny barked.

"Silence, hound!" Bez snapped.

Cloudy whimpered. Stormy growled.

"Don't think for a second because of my current stature, I won't muzzle you, you grumpy fuck." Bez pointed at Stormy. I was about to intervene until Sunny licked Bez from head to toe, completely slobbering all over him.

"Disgusting!" Bez fumed, arguing with Weather about proper dog etiquette, which didn't sound like a real thing, nothing I'd researched anyway, which could make for an interesting study.

Tony's claws clacked as he cheered for their fight.

"Stop that." I gave him a look, then paused.

His powerful joy of a potential battle between Bez and Weather came in crystal clear. I felt the entirety of his emotions, the words trickling just beneath the waves of his feelings. I smiled. Despite everything, despite always failing and requiring others, I continued to show some tiny bit of progress. Our familiar bond had grown, probably more to do with the fact Tony was the best familiar a mage could ask for, but still—I was one small step toward mastering the familiar bond from the Pentacles of Power.

I tilted my head, letting my hair bounce against Tony's shell.

"Mush, beast." Bez sat on Sunny's head, holding his ears and directing Weather to run through the labyrinth.

"Wait up." I followed, meeting them at a glowing sky-blue door that led to another storage room filled mostly with paintings.

We stepped inside, and I wondered why Bez picked this place. Maybe he didn't realize the lack of importance of this room. Before everything fell apart, I did my best to study the surveillance and memorize the layout of the villa since Bez didn't want me exploring alone and hadn't bothered searching until Mora arrived.

"If I'm going to end Eligos, I'll need to restore some of my essence," Bez said, sitting crisscrossed on Sunny's head. "Normally, I'd soak in the natural energy from the environment, but there isn't much of that here in the villa, being all disconnected from reality and blah, blah."

"What about the artifacts? There are thousands of magical items in the baron's home."

"Former home." Bez folded his arms and had a cocky little expression. "And the trace amounts of Mythic residue in those isn't much help. Better than nothing, I suppose, but I'd prefer drawing upon an organic source."

I sat next to Weather, petting Cloudy and rubbing Sunny's chin, all while avoiding Stormy, who wanted no affection whatsoever. "Do you want to talk about Eligos? I know he—"

"I want to talk about how to quickly kill him." Bez glared. "Not too quickly. I'd like to break that armor of his, make him cry, then he can die."

Bez hid it—poorly—but Eligos meant something to him. We both knew that much, yet he pretended all the same, so I let him. If untangling these feelings burdened him, distracted him, it might cost him when confronting the demon knight. I had to do my part to ensure Bez survived this.

"Oh, the armor," I said, mind replaying the battle between Mora, resisting a shudder as blood and burns surfaced. "He shielded it, protected it. I think he's possessing it, if that's possible."

"Anything's possible with Diabolics. Even surviving death and escaping closed portals, it seems." Bez's angry eyes didn't waver.

"I do need to figure out how he managed that. He thinks I'm Beelzebub—which I am, in a sense—but that means he hasn't been in Hell, our Hell, since I fled with the devil's heart. It's a good sign, indicating that damn dead Fae hasn't figured out how to open closed dimensions but doesn't explain a bit about how Eligos got here."

Bez needed magic, something to restore his essence, and if the artifacts wouldn't help, maybe he could use other forms. "Like mana."

"What?" Bez and Sunny cocked their heads in unison.

"Sorry, thinking aloud. But I think I can help you." I gestured to myself. "When expelling my mana, you can draw upon the residue it emits."

"One—and I say this in the sweetest way possible—you have a lackluster amount of mana. Two, the moment you cast, especially for a long period of time, Eligos will immediately detect our location."

"What about a host body?" I asked. "I could offer—"

"Absolutely not." Bez slapped a hand on Sunny's head, then scratched the Cerberus' forehead, soothing the pup after the brief startle. "Can't risk it."

"Yeah, since possession tends to kill the original host." I sighed, realizing how terrible my plan was.

"Yes and no. Not always, but I have this tendency of"—he ran his little thumb along his thin neck and rolled his tongue out, playing dead—"offing people because I'm bad at sharing my space. Mortal bodies are so cramped, the collision of consciousness tends to lead to me pushing them out."

"Collision of consciousness?"

"It's a whole thing, requiring a very delicate touch not to kill a host. Plus, possession without overwhelming a host body with all of my essence involves a lot of finesse. There's this ratio factor involved: how much flows in the veins, circulating throughout the body, versus how much radiates on the surface level, sort of like a shroud." He hopped off Sunny's head and paced the room. "It's basically impossible and a wasted effort when it's much simpler to just kick out the former tenant before securing a body."

Weather followed Bez back and forth.

Admittedly, little Bez was adorable and such a delightful distraction during this horrible event. All his mannerisms remained the same, the swagger in his hips as he strutted, the slight hunch in his shoulders when he flew about, escaping Weather's shuffle behind him, and the wicked grin on his little minxy face as ideas of revenge crossed his mind. He looked like a perfect doll replica of himself.

"Well, there's less of you, so you wouldn't need as much space, so maybe?" I hesitantly suggested.

"No." He folded his arms. "I love being inside you, it's my favorite activity, but possession is so invasive."

"We don't exactly have a lot of options," I said, thinking over everything in the villa, where we could go, what lay dormant in all the various pocket portals, but my thoughts kept going back to the helm.

Images of Kell's burning body. Mora riddled with blades. Bez's head spinning in the air as his body collapsed. I grimaced.

Mora and Kell were out there somewhere, dying, suffering, and in agony. And me? I sat there, unable to even formulate a simple plan, unable to remotely offer help. At least they both put up a fight against the demon knight. Hell, even Tony and Weather fought back while I froze. I hated how no matter what I did, it was never enough.

Bez flicked my forehead with a solid thunk. "Get out of your own busy brain. I need it."

"Huh?"

"You're overthinking. Overthinking Walter is only useful when researching. We're in survival mode. I need impulsive Wally.

Angry Wally." He growled. "Show me your rage!"

"I-I-I don't know if I have any rage."

"You do. It's spectacular and calculating and able to weave masterful constructs."

I nodded. *Think. Think, dammit.*

Bez descended to the floor, clutching his chest.

"What's the matter?"

He ignored me, eyes darting about. Had he sensed Diabolic essence? Was it Mora? I held my breath. Was it Eligos?

Bez convulsed, falling to his knees. "Well, well. Might have a plan after all."

"What's going on?" I offered my hand to steady him, assist him up, but he remained on the floor, taking deep breaths and searching for something with each inhale.

"My essence is calling out to me." He craned his neck, eyes looking past the portal and deeper into the villa. "I can feel it reeling me back, offering a chance to reunite before it fades." He chuckled. "Surprised Eligos didn't destroy my body."

"The baron needed a devil's essence for something. Maybe Eligos needs it, too."

"I'll be sure to ask him after I reclaim my essence."

"Reclaim it?" I asked. "What does that mean?"

Bez collapsed onto the ground, eyes closed, and body as still as a corpse. I trembled. I needed to do something. Even if Bez reclaimed his lost essence, and that was a big if since I had no idea how or what he was doing, he'd still need magic to replenish his energy. Possession was out of the question since I was the only mage here, the only living being here.

Tony hissed, stinger pointing at Weather tugging at the fabric covering a stack of portraits.

"Don't even make that suggestion." I furrowed my brow.

Tony hissed again, jabbing his stinger at his cruel idea. I looked to see Sunny licking a painting while Stormy gnawed on the exquisite frame. Maybe Tony simply wanted to make sure I didn't allow Weather to trash more expensive things. I pulled the pup away, cringing at the missing paint on Medusa's face. Wow. An actual self-portrait of the original gorgon. That was probably priceless, and now basically ruined in all of five seconds, thanks to a hungry Cerberus.

"Wait a second, that's it," I said, gears clicking together to finally figure out something useful. "Tony, you're a literal genius."

We weren't the only living people in the villa. There were those gorgon statues Tony and I had seen on the surveillance footage. I hadn't mentioned them to Bez because he would've probably whined about me making a project out of restoring them, a mostly impossible task without gorgon magic.

"Or access to gorgon magic." I pointed to my scorpion familiar, who helped me piece together the idea. "Which we have. There are the fresh gorgon eyes, fully intact thanks to Baron Novus' obsession with collecting oddities and preserving all forms of Mythic magic."

I picked Bez up, cradling him in my arms, and rushed to the portal door. Weather scampered underfoot, stepping on mine, and I paused.

I kneeled down to look all three of them in the eyes. "You have to stay here, Weather. It's important, and I can't risk endangering you any more than I already have."

Sunny licked my face, playfully offering his protection, while Cloudy whimpered because I was making him stay, and Stormy bit the air, fire around his neck flaring up. Possibly his way of offering support or telling me to hurry up the goodbye—Stormy was hard to read.

"Tony, I need you to watch out for him." I watched Tony scuttle away, ignoring my request. "He's young and needs your guidance. I trust you."

I set Bez down and crawled over to Tony, who hid between a stack of paintings propped against the wall.

"I trust you because you trusted me, saved me, and I know you think I'm looking for another familiar. But I need you to know you'll always be the first animal I bonded with. I'll carry you with me always because you're precious and perfect and powerful. I love you, Tony. I love Weather, too. I hope you can accept that."

Tony skittered out and crawled toward Weather, where Cloudy had already slipped one of Bez's dress shoes off, chomping down on it. My scorpion perched on top of my grimoire and raised his claws until Weather moved next to him and sat.

"You two stay here—stay safe." I grabbed Bez and darted for the portal. "I'm going to fix this."

I raced through the labyrinth corridors, following the halls that led to the dungeon the baron held me captive in. The gorgon eyes were there. Once I got them, I could double back to the golden portal with the statues. I grimaced. It was pretty unethical to offer someone up to be Bez's host, knowing they'd die. Then again, they were living an eternal frozen life, which they wouldn't technically be freed from unless someone—such as myself—released them.

Whatever. It had to happen, and I could overthink the moral implications of how I was a terrible fucking person later.

I cut the corner and nearly knocked into someone, skirting around a haze of pink and blood splatters before tumbling onto the floor, holding Bez closely.

The pink Fae— the one from the Fae Divinity performance, the one who kidnapped me, the one who cruelly mistreated Weather—stood covered in blood, her clothes shredded, hunks of her flesh torn out. She faced away from me, likely dazed, perhaps fed upon by Eligos.

I gulped. "You're the Fae who grabbed me."

Eligos must've been incredibly fast because even Bez struggled to apprehend her given that butterfly teleportation she utilized.

"Fae?" She twisted her head, hair draped over her face as she turned to me. "Where is the Fae?"

"Huh?"

She approached, moving her hair, revealing her eyes that matched Bez's in crimson irises and pink where the whites should be. She stared at her hand, the one with visible black veins of Diabolic essence circulating through her.

"Right. I am a Fae now." She laughed, loud and erratic, her entire body shaking. I shuddered. "I never wanted to possess a Fae, just taste one. They always smelled so delectable, like sugary acid mixed with glittering blood and so much meat. Never got the chance, though. Trick. Tricked by the pretty Fae. He promised me the world, then gave me nothing but a tiny marble."

Was she talking about Baron Novus? If he captured her, how was she here? *Marble.* The orbs. Was Eligos unleashing other demons? There were hundreds of them. If he released them all, it wouldn't matter if Bez returned to full strength—they'd eviscerate us.

The demon possessing the pink Fae lifted her arm close to her mouth and bit down. She tore a huge chunk of flesh out of her wrist, nearly severing the hand entirely before tendrils reached out and properly reattached the limb.

"Still tastes a little sweet." She licked her bloody lips. "Shame my essence has almost soured the seasoning."

I kicked my feet against the ground, backing away without breaking eye contact. One blink, and she'd likely vanish in a blur. Her gaze tightened.

"Tell me, mage"—she bit off two of her fingers, allowing black tendrils to replace them—"what do you taste like?"

18

Beelzebub

My consciousness floated between the ether of realities like a phantom in search of my essence. I tracked it back to the engine room, where all the Diabolics were stored. Fuck. Drifting through the portal, I arrived to find the headless body of my former mortal host body. So frustrating after all the work I did to get that cheap piece of thread roomy enough to contain me in all my glory. Now it sat, slowly dying, and I couldn't interact with anything in this incorporeal state.

The only thing keeping blood flowing and the muscles from stiffening was my potent essence coursing through the veins, though all the Diabolic features had faded. Perhaps they'd retreated inward to conserve the life of this host. I didn't have a lot of experience losing my head. Lost an arm once, that was annoying trying to retrieve, but this was an entire fucking body. How was I going to get this back to the rest of me? When I lost my arm, I still had control over the receptors, but that proved pretty useless because it turned out that walking with fingers wasn't all that simple. Still, I had fully functioning limbs all attached, minus the head. If I focused, I might be able to steer it.

Metal clinked. I saw Eligos at the end of the railing, surrounded by unconscious Fae. Their magic was palpable in the air, despite the stillness of their bodies and shallow breaths. Great. What was he up to? He grabbed one of the five orbs powering the dimensional travel. Wait—weren't there supposed to be six?

Eligos squeezed the orb, breaking it open but holding the wildly whipping essence to keep it from flying throughout the room.

"Calm yourself," he said. "I mean to offer you freedom, yet you need to obey my guidance."

Arrogant asshole.

He held the essence over the head of a feathered Fae, lying completely unaware of the essence spilling into his mouth, nose, ears, and eyes. The essence poured from Eligos' grip like yolk slowly seeping from an eggshell. The body convulsed, the former person screaming as a demon burrowed their way into a new home and made it more accommodating without the presence of a Fae roomie. I'd deal with a second demon once I regained my strength; with these demons distracted, now was my chance to get it back.

I called out to my lost essence, attempting to bring back some of the composure in my limp limbs, but struggled to access full autonomy over my essence still circulating within the dead host body. Ugh. If I hadn't killed the former tenant, I might've been able to sway the anatomy better. Well, unlikely. Mortals didn't move too well without their heads. Still, I struggled to control my former body. Former limbs. Guide them to obey my essence's will, tugging on the ghostly strings like a puppeteer in the shadows.

The only way I could interact with the body was as a specter, whispering from the ether between reality, practically dipping my toes into the dream world. It didn't help Wally's soothing voice reeled me away from this objective, speaking sweet words and offering support. Why was he trying to comfort me?

My body jostled in his grip. Were we moving? What the actual fuck was he doing? I ignored it. If I allowed myself in the moment, I'd lose the weak hold I had over my lost essence. I trusted Wally. Whatever was going on, he had a reason and would handle it. This was my only opportunity to reclaim my lost essence before it fully faded from my grasp.

I stared at the body, willing it to move, demanding it in this astral form to heed my call and obey. Fingers wiggled. I focused again, and then… Nothing.

"Move, you piece of garbage!" I kicked the air, wishing I could kick myself. I'd kick my own ass, given half the chance.

The fingers tightened, and a fist formed.

"Yes." I snarled. "You got this, you beautiful bastard. Now, carefully lift yourself up."

My headless body wobbled, grabbing the railing and pulling itself upright. I turned back to Eligos, who continued helping ease the demon into the reality of their newfound freedom.

"One foot at a time," I instructed. "Make your way, quietly, through the portal, and then we'll meet up halfway."

I waited for my bumbling body to slowly approach the exit, knowing I'd have to move quickly once it'd escaped into the labyrinth. My chest tightened, reeling me away. Why was Walter hugging me so tightly? I shook it off. *Damn, I know I'm cute, but can't he tell I'm too busy for cuddles?*

"Devils truly are wickedly marvelous." Eligos appeared in front of my body, armor fuzzy as his body settled from the blurred movement. "I knew obtaining one, obtaining Beelzebub, would be all this vessel required to run eternally through any and all worlds."

I scoffed. He'd be quite disappointed when he figured out he'd been conned with second-rate demon essence and a small lump sum of devil essence.

He swung a fist. Oh, hell no. I commanded a counter, body obedient in the heat of the moment, and braced the strike with two raised arms. Eligos' metal knuckles tore through my skin.

Reeling back a fist, my body followed suit and swung. I wouldn't go down this time. I wouldn't let my shock distract me. I didn't care who Eligos was once upon a time; all he was now was a threat to my life, my future, my love—Wally.

The two of us clashed back and forth. Whether from exhaustion, lack of control, or fading essence, my body struggled to land as many blows as Eligos.

"This isn't like your world, Beelzebub." Eligos punched my side, breaking several ribs, then whipped behind it and kicked my body in the back, knocking it to my knees. "You have no claim here. Without your domain of Hell, you obviously lack your full fury. For centuries I cultivated the perfect plan, biding my time, waiting for a weakness to present itself." He kicked my body again and again, forcing it to yield beneath his heel as he stomped over and over, bloodying his boot.

"Bez," Wally's voice called out, "I won't leave you. Not ever."

What? I considered returning to Wally, getting an explanation behind the cryptic words yet comforting tone. No. I needed to return with a win. Needed Wally to be safe.

"When that feeble magus captured you, I wanted to strike then, tear the Collective asunder, but that damned Fae claimed it'd incite a war." Eligos continued kicking, breaking bones, unleashing lifetimes of rage unto the wrong foe. "It didn't matter. You laid waste to the mages and their city anyway, all with the help of your murderous psychopath misfit mage. That despicable filth, undeserving of all the world gave him and other mortals."

"What?" I roared, fuming with fury. He had the audacity to speak ill of Wally, speak lies on his name, paint a phony legend over the kindness Wally wanted to give the world.

My body sprang back in a blur, fully synchronized with my will, unfazed by Eligos' attacks. Now, that fucking knight would die.

The two of us sparred, his moves still too quick to counter, so I didn't waste the effort. I was Beelzebub's personal punching bag for eons; I could handle a few hits from an ignoble knight. Eligos swung a fist, and I finally managed to grab ahold of his arm, pinning it between my bicep and battered torso.

Now would be a great time for a headbutt. I sighed. I missed having a head. Missed having a fully functional body. No matter. I blocked his other arm, willing my body to squeeze the armor until it cracked. Eligos focused his essence on restoring his precious suit, and I used that fraction of a second to punch him in the head, knocking his helmet clean off his shoulders. But Eligos had already retracted his head to hide deep within the confines of his armor for protection. Gah—we looked like fucking fools, two headless demons dueling it out.

And over what? He wanted to punish Beelzebub for leaving Hell? Newsflash, he was trapped, rotting away, and I needed to make sure it stayed that way.

I commanded my body, having it keep a firm hold on Eligos' arm I'd pinned, then made the body flip over the knight, tearing his arm off in the process. He bellowed, furious shouting from within the suit as his body thundered inside the metal, and tendrils whipped chaotically, searching for the lost limb.

"Sucks losing a piece of yourself, doesn't it?" I cackled, instructing my body to lift the arm, and beat Eligos with his own armored limb.

Again. Again. Again. I pummeled him. Metal clanked, cracking against each other. Once I created a solid chink in the back of his suit, I'd punch a hole through it and rip him out. No hesitation. No sympathy. No reminiscing. I seethed with rage, unleashing all my hate, my power, and my will to survive. I'd tear him to pieces, reclaim the villa, kiss Wally, find Mora—yell at her for being so unprepared, and maybe hug her—then…

I gasped, feeling my tether to my former host body snap.

A lance protruded through my stomach, impaling me like a fucking shish kabob. The feathered Fae lifted it high, holding my flailing body no longer answering my willpower, my orders.

"Thank you, brother." Eligos struggled to his feet, retrieving his lost arm and reattaching it. "I knew the honor among demons was always stronger than the fear of devils. We are bonded now, family in belief and convictions."

"Ha, whatever," the demon dressed as a feathered Fae said with a laugh. "I always wanted to gut Lilith, the vile old shrew. Guess killing this second-rate devil is a close consolation. Who is he exactly? I don't recognize the essence."

"Beelzebub, and his essence is altered from bonding with a mortal mage. Weakened most likely," Eligos explained inaccurately. "And we can't kill him. We must harness the essence, cultivate it, and with it—we'll be able to lay claim to all Hells, raise armies of our brethren seeking freedom, and kill devils undeserving of their titles or realms."

"Even Lilith?" the feathered demon asked, lowering my limp body.

"Every devil." Eligos grabbed the lance from the demon, who didn't resist, and then he dragged my body to the edge of the railing.

With a wave of his hand, Eligos telekinetically removed all the wires that had been attached to the six orbs and rewired them to the lance. My body thrashed, anguished, and suffering. Even without the link to the rest of my essence, the suffering and pain were clear.

"What are you doing?" the demon asked, which I wanted to know too, holding tight to every snapping thread that kept my mind here.

"I've connected Beelzebub's devil essence to the ship," Eligos said. "Once I've retrieved all his essence, I'll be able to tear through time and space and use this vessel to attack other devils with the strength of one. Armies of Diabolics will rally behind us as we usher in a new era, one without devils."

"Oh." The feathered demon had a flabbergasted expression, either not understanding Eligos' impassioned drive or not caring, as few demons bothered with such irrational sentiment. "So where is the rest of the devil at? A head can't be that hard to find."

"I'm less concerned with his missing head, more so with the fiendish mage who fled with it," Eligos said. "I've sent another to retrieve the mage—alive."

"Boring."

"Necessary. If the mortal dies, so will Beelzebub."

The feathered demon's sapphire irises shimmered, and the sky-blue of the sclera around them widened with delight. "A dead devil?"

"No. We need him intact." Eligos patted the demon's shoulder. "Remember, in order to achieve the impossible, we must…"

His voice fell away, the engine room fell away, the smug smile of the feathered demon fell away, and I sprang forward, back inside my feeble body and still lacking the necessary essence required to finish this fight.

The scent of mana filled the room, and potent Mythic residue permeated beside me.

A set of golden eyes were on the floor.

"Aw, fresh gorgon eyes." I smiled, searching for Wally to tease him they'd taste best scrambled with a side of bacon.

But he was nowhere to be found. I sniffed the air. Sweat, blood, fear, and pain wafted from his recent arrival here, though his stay was brief. What had happened to him? Why'd he ditch my ragdoll body? And what the hell was he going to do with a random ass pair of gorgon eyes?

I turned around, taking in the room of statues filled with perfectly petrified potential host bodies. Hmm, it appeared Wally had stumbled onto these on his own despite the fact I hadn't shared the details because I didn't want him distracted by side projects.

My lips curled into a wicked grin, delighted by the bounty presented by Wally. The fastest way to recover a modicum of my strength was through possession, feeding deeply on the mana from a strong host. The villa wasn't exactly rolling around in a wide selection, and these statues could only be released through gorgon magic. Or the magic that still resided inside a fresh set of delicious eyes.

Guess I'd have to pass on the tasty treat. I had to figure out which one of these fools would make for the most suitable threads to find and kill Eligos in.

19

Walter

I cut a corner in the labyrinth where it forked into different pathways and finished my glamoured incantation, sending a false glowing version of me running onward. Desperately, I took deep breaths, not concerned about how easily obvious the distraction was. I didn't need to fool the demon, simply offer her another trail to follow. With any luck, she'd get lost stalking the mana I cast as a homing beacon to lead her into the twisting tunneled depths of this maze.

My legs wobbled. I braced myself closer to the wall. Even with all the adrenaline coursing through me, exhaustion had finally caught up. The bruises on my back and chest throbbed. The shallow cuts along my stomach burned, a searing reminder of the essence I'd cut out of myself. All this running made it impossible to catch my breath, and now I wanted to pass out and sleep away the pain. I squinted, lights in the tunnels making my vision blur.

Using the tip of the blade of the Demon's Demise, I scratched out the glyphs on the nearest lantern. Their damn proximity sensors made them light up when someone was close, and I needed this hidden corner dark and unassuming. I clutched the hilt, knowing I had to prepare for an inevitable conflict.

"I need…" I bit my lip, biting back the need to process. It was bad enough that every movement I made down here echoed through long corridors. I didn't need to offer up a sound description of my objective to the demon trying to devour me.

She was relentless. Nothing I did shook her from my scent. I barely managed to get the gorgon eyes before she appeared from thin air, demanding a taste of my flesh.

I needed to get back to Bez. Leaving him was the right option since I couldn't allow the demon to grab him. And I certainly couldn't fend her off with an unconscious Bez in my hands. He was unconscious, right? He'd be fine. Wake up soon. It still left me with sinking guilt that he'd assume I abandoned him. I only hoped he realized what I was doing by leaving him with the statues. Would he even know they were petrified? Would he know the first thing about smashing the pair of eyes onto a petrified person to undo the spell? I hated not having Bez's essence, lacking the faintest sense of our connection, which left me bare and hollowed out.

"Little mage, come out, come out," the demon's voice boomed from the end of the hall. She dragged her bare feet along the stone flooring, moving sluggishly despite the fact that she could bolt ahead in an instant.

I couldn't determine if her slow pace came from the chunks of meat she'd ripped out of her own host body before tiring of the flavor, her still adapting to her newfound freedom after being bound in an orb for who knew how long, or if this was her way of toying with prey.

She walked past me, sniffing the air as she contemplated which path to take. Lanterns illuminated her bloody back as she faced away, studying the labyrinth. I inched sideways, bit by bit, to hide further in the darkness, too frightened to blink on the chance she'd vanish.

She pointed to each path over and over like she was playing eeny meeny miny moe, then stopped and licked the wall of the path I'd sent my glamour.

Take the bait. Follow the trace trail of mana.

"Found you," she said from the opposite side of me, hidden by the shadows.

No hesitation. Not again. I swung the Demon's Demise, slashing her neckline, and backed away as tendrils sprang out defensively. She screeched, furious and making the stone walls rumble. I had to get a deeper cut. Stab her. Twist the blade.

"Disrespectful." Her rage had settled, and she sounded eerily composed, standing behind me.

When had she moved again? *Damn. So fast.*

I tried to whirl around, tracing an incantation in the air to create a barrier between us, but her hands slapped my back, knocking me flat on my face.

Before I had a chance to react, she'd flung me into a wall and kicked me until I rolled over. In a flash, the demon straddled my waist, seeping glittery Fae blood onto my already bloody shirt. She wrapped her hands around my throat, squeezing down. My face burned. I struggled, futile and incapable of loosening her grasp. Slowly, she slid further up, pressing the full weight of her body onto my chest as she cackled and tightened her stranglehold.

"Eligos said no killing the mage, but that was only to the one with Beelzebub's essence." She licked my cheek. "Not sure how many of you little misfits are roaming these halls, but there's not a trace of Diabolic essence inside you."

She released one of her hands, still choking me. My eyes teared up, and the room went fuzzy; everything faded except this demon's pink hand, which turned a sheen metallic black as she curled her essence over her fingers and transformed the limb into a sharpened blade.

"Well, no essence inside you yet." She sneered. "I'm going to have too much fun rummaging through your organs, picking the prettiest one to remember you by, and eating all the others."

I wriggled, attempting to knock her grip off, but she didn't budge. Every breath became a chore of survival, impossible and useless against such a tremendous Diabolic force.

"Don't worry. It's been so long since I've carved up a little magey treat, I'll probably end up killing you by the second incision. Hope you don't mind if I practice on your corpse."

She punched her clawed hand down, ready to impale my chest. Something cracked, and white light burst between us.

"Well, well, well," the demon cooed. "When did you muster that barrier?"

I'd pulled off the incantation? When? Instinct? Maybe I could do this.

The light shimmering between her blade-formed essence and my shirt popped, transforming into lightning that coiled up her arm, spreading across her body like the lights of a city illuminating all darkness, and pulsed. She leapt off me, zipping back and forth in an effort to shake loose from the magic, but the electricity clamped down onto her and sent continuous jolts that seared her flesh.

I gasped, sucking in all the air my lungs would hold again and again until the fuzzy dots lining my vision faded.

The demon grabbed the lightning with her bare hands, wrapping it round and round until tendrils writhed from the gaping holes she'd made by biting off chunks of her host body. Black essence with crimson hues whipped at the elemental strike, fizzling out the electrical attack. "Nasty, hateful witch bitch."

"Witch?" I asked, slack-jawed.

"Eh. I've been called worse," Kell said, static crackling at her fingertips.

Kell. Kell was here. Alive. It wasn't my attempt at incantations but her successful magic that stopped the demon from killing me.

The lanterns lit with each confident step she took, but her stance was shaky, and her breathing wheezed along the stone walls. She wore her witch's hat and a flared-cut black dress with white stitching. It hung off her shoulders. I winced, pained to see the discolored, twisted skin revealing a fresh burn across her left shoulder. The long sleeves of the dress covered what must've been many other burns along her arms. But veins across Kell's face and thighs glowed green, and essence circulated beneath her skin, moving like tranquil waves and adding an emerald hue to her brown complexion while subtly shrinking and healing the scars all over her body. Did that mean Mora had given her more essence? Were they both okay? Would they be okay?

"Stop daydreaming, Wally." Kell moved her leg back, shifting her weight as she summoned an array of protective sigils. "I can't do this on my own."

"Right." I dragged myself up, saturating the corridor, adding my mana to Kell's magic.

With a wave of her hand, Kell sent a half dozen sigils at the demon. What I considered protective were laced with explosive elements: fire, ice, and lightning. It didn't matter; the demon darted about this confined space, leaping from the floor to the ceiling, dodging the first two bursts. Kell flicked her wrist, changing the trajectory of the remaining sigils. But the demon scaled the wall, moving along the sides and racing in circles closer to Kell.

In a blur, the demon collided with a barrier of light cast by sorcery. Despite the witch's proficiency, a single strike shattered half the sigils keeping Kell shielded.

I slammed my hands onto the floor, rattling the ground like ruffling a carpet. It sent ripples similar to the tide of a lake, raising the stones one by one before they lowered back in place. Each disruption increased the momentum and added to my already strong saturation in play. This wasn't like a lake, more like an ocean of continuously stacked force surging closer. When it finally reached the demon, I threw all my mana into the strike, propelling the floor upward, twisting elemental control over the stonework to smash the demon between the floor and ceiling.

The lack of mobility in this space worked at a disadvantage against her too. Rocks burst, and dust swept through the corridor.

"Rude," the demon said.

Her voice sent a shiver down my spine, a spine fully in her grasp as she stood behind me. Again.

I spun away, adding wind to my escape, hoping the extra speed would allow me to distance myself. It didn't. She lunged forward, swiping her claws. Her strikes were deflected, met with resistance from Kell's sigils working faster to keep up with the demon's attacks. Each blow she attempted was aimed at my tendons, arteries, my most vulnerable points—somehow, Kell kept up with it, magic at the ready.

Grabbing the Demon's Demise, I planned to slice her clawed hand off the next time she attempted to gut me. Instead, the demon skirted around, now ahead of me again. Despite the slow shift in my direction, I managed to turn aside, stopping right as my back collided with the wall.

"You're becoming tiresome," she said, facing Kell.

"Back at you."

The demon didn't bother acknowledging me. Why would she? I couldn't do a damn thing against her. Even when I had Diabolic essence, I choked. Now, I had almost no magic at my disposal, no ability to keep up, and posed no threat whatsoever.

"You smell delectable. Perhaps a bit undercooked for my tastes. Witches are best when well done, I always say. No worries, though. I can fix that." Black flames formed in the demon's palm, swirling and burning brighter. She hurled the fire at Kell, who cast a barrier to block the swelling fire. Not a barrier, telekinesis. I could see the glowing green veins meant to heal her body receding the longer she stopped the Diabolic flames from engulfing her.

"Stop it!" I shouted, springing off the wall with all the rage in the world, stabbing the dagger into the demon's back.

She wailed and whirled around. Too fast. Her clawed swipe slashed my shoulder. I flinched, stifling a scream. It was only a flesh wound. A graze compared to what she intended to do to me, to Kell, if I let up for a second. I pressed forward, casting a glamour as I moved in to stab her a second time. She blocked my left hand holding the blade.

"Wrong hand." I stabbed her thigh with my right. "Can't believe that glamour worked on you. Guess you weren't kidding about being rusty."

The skin on her face cracked, tearing open from the infuriated scream she released. So much angry power that it tore her host body apart. In one swift, blurred motion, she knocked the dagger out of my grip, snatched a fistful of hair, and slammed my head into a stone wall. My glasses cracked, snapping in half, and blood ran down my face.

Black flames funneled forward, and the demon extended her hands, holding her own conjured element at bay. Kell and this demon remained in a locked stance, each using essence to try and burn the other one alive.

I tensed, flashes of Kell's charred body playing over in my mind again. The horrid screams she let out. My cowardly inability to do anything to help her. All I'd done was run. I couldn't let this happen again.

Not happening. I refused to remain idle during another demon attack. I wouldn't fail Kell a second time.

Ignoring the throbbing of my head and the pain in my muscles, I crawled to my discarded dagger and swiped the Achilles tendon, dropping the demon to her knees as her essence struggled to repair the damage. Bleeding her wouldn't work; I needed precise strikes to slow her recovery and prevent mobility.

"I should thank you." I swung the dagger. "After all, it was you aiming for my vitals that inspired the tactic."

I sliced the supraspinatus and infraspinatus tendons in her right shoulder. Her arm dropped, essence whipped about erratically, incapable of healing the injury but slashing at me when I moved in close. I couldn't stop. Not yet.

Black flames barreled closer to us, halted only by the demon's left arm casting the willpower to control them.

I ground my teeth and fought through the searing cuts caused by the defensive tendrils. I stabbed her left shoulder, missing vital spots. It didn't matter; I'd make it work. I buried the blade deep and twisted it until her left arm drooped.

Fire engulfed her, swirling close to me, but a gush of wind knocked me back.

Kell stepped in closer, brow furrowed and hands trembling as she controlled the demon's fire to burn the demon herself. "We have to eradicate every ounce of essence or she'll kill us."

I nodded. If I used my own fire, it'd only feed her essence, and without a connection to Bez's Diabolic abilities, I lacked telekinesis, so I summoned wind and circled it around the black flames, fueling them and turning their blaze into an inferno that Kell kept condensed through sigils, fixated on burning the demon to cinders.

She screamed so loudly it echoed through the entire hallway, shattering stone and cracking the walls apart.

I created incantations, settling the crumbling corridor.

Finally, it stopped. She stopped. Kell wobbled, planting her hands on her shaky knees, allowing the black fire to fizzle out as only charred remnants remained. Then, after a few deep breaths,

Kell waltzed over, a strut in her step, and kicked the embers, scattering ashes of the dead demon.

"I'll be damned if I get set on fire a fourth time."

"Fourth?" I quirked a brow.

"Yeah." Kell forced a smile. "Witch hunters back in the day, then my angry coven over a slight miscommunication about the use of dark magic—still peeved about that one, but I always say let bygones be bygones, which is probably easiest when you're bi and they're gone—and now that asshat of a demon. I'd like to think this is all just some unfortunate circumstances, but I'm starting to think it's a me thing, and that's not cool. It's hot. Literally. Flames. Alicia Keys playing in the background of my life soundtrack."

"Wait," I interjected because Kell rambled more than anyone I'd ever met. "Witch hunters?"

The last known recording of active witch hunters was around eighteen sixty-four, which would make Kell very old. Subjectively. Bez was old, old by human standards. Still, Kell must've been a century at least, older than most witches, especially for someone who looked thirty at best. Then again, there were unaccounted cases past the Collectives documents of witch hunter movements. The unofficial, totally unsanctioned witch hunters that came from the infiltration regiment of the Collective, which I'd found links going as far up to the nineteen eighties, but nothing concrete. It wasn't like I had access to those confidential files working as an acolyte in the repository. Still, I did pretty good piecing together rumors and theories and suspicions with only—

Kell stared wide-eyed at me.

"What?"

"Processing what you're saying." She waved her hand up and down. "The muttering's like listening to a bad ham radio."

"Oh. Was I talking aloud? Sorry. Bez says I sometimes do that a bit. A lot. Too much. Probably."

"No, no. I get it. We creatives need to share our wisdom with the masses somehow, right? How else would they learn?" Kell winked. "But we gotta fix your glasses. I don't look a day over twenty-five."

I smiled, heart racing and face burning. Kell was actually pretty amazing company. "I'm… I'm so sorry I didn't stop him, Eligos, I mean. What he did was awful, and I should've tried harder."

"It's nothing." She pushed herself back and lay against the wall. "Though you'd think by the third round, with essence added this time around, it'd get easier."

"What are you even doing here?" I asked between heavy breaths, my entire body puddy on the floor.

"Saving your ass, obvi." Kell snickered.

"No, I mean…" I swallowed hard. What did I mean?

"Mora dropped me someplace private to heal up, and I was zonked out on magic, pain pills, essence, and then I heard someone screaming murder," Kell said, pointing an accusatory finger at me. "So, being the benevolent witch I am, I hopped my happy ass out of bed and saved the damsel."

I glowered, then sighed. I was a damsel, incapable of handling anything remotely at this level, and the only reason I managed anything against the demon possessing the pink Fae was all thanks to Kell's timely intervention. Moving forward, securing the villa, removing Eligos and any other demons he brought, I'd do better. I had to.

"Okay," I said, changing the subject, perhaps burying my ineptitude. "But how are you standing right now?"

"Do I look like I'm standing?" She lazily gestured to herself, clearly too exhausted for flair.

"You know what I mean. You were on fire and…"

"And Mora's essence works miracles." Kell chagrined. "Though she didn't have much to work with, so I might've cast a bit of wicked sorcery to amplify the reserves I've got."

"Dark magic?"

Kell scoffed. "No such thing. It's only considered dark because it works around the rules and doesn't ask for Nature's blessing. And to be clear, she doesn't want to offer her permission for every little spell a witch casts."

"Nature?"

"Yeah." Kell's expression shifted into something happy, excited, and the undertones in her complexion lit from the green essence working its way through her. "She's primordial, chaos, and everlasting. Rules around the Four Corners are the construct of covens, not the goddess of all."

Witches abided and served only one deity—Nature herself. Kell had a point, too. If Nature didn't want witches casting so-called dark magic, she wouldn't make it readily available to them or continuously provide them full access to their Four Corners after accessing 'bad' magics. No, the only thing that stripped witches of their magic was their coven binding them, their Mythic Council imprisoning them, or the Collective discreetly killing them to save face with rules and regulations.

Kell clapped her hands; the loud pop echoed in the crumbling corridor. Thankfully, my incantations still held because I was just starting to like Kell, and given her knack for destroying things and making my life difficult, I highly doubted our friendship would survive being buried beneath rubble. Mainly because we'd die or I'd kill her.

"Oopsie daisy." She grinned. "I say we drag our butts back to the little hidey hole I was in and rest up until Mora and Bez handle this. Honestly, that knight might've got a drop on your baddie boyfriend. But challenging a devil? That's absurd."

Devil. Kell didn't know the truth about Bez. I guess that was a secret Mora kept safe for Bez from everyone. Even so, Bez was too weakened to do this on his own.

"No." I quaked, legs fighting me every inch I pushed off the ground. "Bez is out there. I have to help him. I have to stop that demon knight."

"Hun." Kell sucked her teeth. "I think you're out of your league. I think we both are. Let them handle the Diabolic drama."

"No. I refuse to accept that." I extended a hand to Kell. She didn't have to help me, didn't have to come with me, but I wouldn't abandon her here in the darkness of the labyrinth. "I'm going to prove I can do better."

"To who?" she asked.

Myself.

20

Beelzebub

I brushed away bits of crumbled stone clinging to the clothing and skin of this host, picking at the eggshell-sized rock like some tragic gargoyle waking up. Taking a deep breath, I exhaled the last remnants of the former mage whose body I possessed. He put up less resistance than the previous body I'd seized, grateful for the reprieve of the solitude in stone that filled the last six centuries of monotonous memories. I shuddered, pushing those dull, repetitive recollections summing up his existence away. He had a nice build and a similar facial structure, which helped hasten my composite to look like something resembling myself faster. My mortal aesthetic, at least.

Stretching side to side, I tried to loosen up this stiff shell of flesh and blood and bone and muscle. I didn't have nearly enough essence to feel stuffed inside, but I hated breaking new bodies in. I'd finally gotten everything about the last one just the way I liked it.

Feasting on the stale mana locked inside this mage's body, I replenished my essence a bit and leapt through the golden portal of this storage room, returning to the labyrinth of the villa. I immediately went to work enhancing my senses to search for Wally. I couldn't risk Eligos or the demons he'd swayed to find Wally first. Having lost our bond, I tensed at every trace of Wally in this maze. His scent filled every hall, sweat and blood and lost mana, all in equal measures, each thick and palpable in the air. I swallowed hard. Had he been harmed? Was a demon stalking him down here?

Diabolic essence continued seeping from every pore of the villa, making it impossible to tell if it came from the encased demons powering the dimensional traveling Fae ship or if it belonged to those Eligos had released from their orbs.

I darted through long, stretched halls, barreling ahead until I found a more concrete trace of Wally's presence. I needed to hear his heartbeat, see him take a breath, feel his warm body. He might've fled back into a pocket portal. No. Wally was smarter than that, which was why his scent filled every route down here. Knowing he couldn't hide, he led whoever stalked him down too many false trails to follow.

"Don't you look lovely," Mora said, braced at a corner, one hand balled into a fist and at the ready.

No. Not ready. She trembled, subtle, frightened, but unwilling to show it, to relent to any enemy that might've presented themselves.

Mora dragged a bloody hand along the wall, using it to steady her tattered body. She was riddled with stab wounds that hadn't healed. Her essence served as a thin thread stitched across her flesh, holding the blood and organs from spilling out entirely. Wally said Kell had been set on fire, but Mora didn't have a single scorch mark, which meant she prioritized healing those injuries, likely for Kell's sake more than herself.

I smiled at her. My heartbeat surged, a quick, uncontrollable feeling I almost confused for sentiment. It wasn't. I had a new host body—one with a heart irregularity, practically knocking on death's door before he ended up petrified by gorgon magic. That was the reason behind the excited thump in my chest. *The only reason.*

Settling these sensations, I curled my lips into a minxy grin and properly addressed Mora. "Dashing as always, which is more than I can say for you."

"I've had better days," she said, her voice gravelly.

"Roadkill's had better days." I pointed to the blood nearly oozing out of her. "Seriously, you look like shit."

"Charming as ever," she groaned. "Now that we're finished with the pleasantries, help me find that damned knight so I can kill him."

"He's not alone," I said. "Also, given your condition, bet you're revisiting the idea of marketing such powerful cloaks to Diabolics."

"On the contrary, it saved me a dance with some feathered fuck skittering about, so I'd say the cloak has potential." She wiggled her fingers, almost casting shadows out of her instinctual need to add panache to her tales.

So the demon that impaled my former body back in the engine room had already made his way into the labyrinth. The endless passages would only keep Wally safe for so long. I had to get to him.

"I have to find Walter."

"He's fine." She waved a dismissive hand.

"How would you know?"

"He's with Kell." Mora pressed her back against the wall, propping herself upright, even though her legs shook, ready to buckle any second. "I told her not to leave the room I'd sealed for her until she'd completely healed and I'd dealt with this demon debacle. But does she listen? I knew she'd wander off, so I've been tracking her."

Tracking her. Of course. That was why Mora looked so rough. Between the injuries she'd sustained and then pouring what little essence she had to offer into Kell, all while maintaining a tight link on their bond, I was surprised she managed to move at all. I ground my teeth. If I were stronger like her, I would've ensured Wally had part of me with him, enough to know he was okay. All I had was Mora's word, and I wanted to trust her.

"The two had a brief scare, but Kell's emotions have settled. Her thoughts express Wally's fine, too." Mora pushed off the wall, ready to collapse two steps in. "I need to change."

"You and me both." I joked, pointing to the outdated commoner rags of my current host.

"I mean bodies."

"Ah, so upstairs then?"

She nodded, dragging herself forward, fumbling. I swooped beside her in a blur. Resting my arm on her back, I cradled her as I lifted her up by her legs and pulled Mora into a tight embrace. She needed to conserve her strength, and we needed to move quickly.

"So chivalrous, Bezzy." She rested her head on my chest.

"No choice. You're moving so slow your age is finally showing itself, you old hag."

She chuckled and closed her eyes, resting.

I didn't want to abandon Wally down here. But he had Kell, his annoying familiar, and a hound literally bred to guard the doors of the afterlife. He'd be fine, and if I intended on ending Eligos and his demon entourage, it would help to have Mora, the craftiest demon ever, at my side.

With all the speed I could muster, I raced out of the labyrinth, upstairs onto the ground floor of the villa, then to the second floor, and into one of the guest rooms Mora had quartered off for her stay.

Breaking free of my grasp, Mora wandered to the middle of the room and stood silently, unmoving, with her eyes closed. The seconds ticked, and my very limited patience gave way.

"What are you doing?"

"Offering Catherine a farewell. Not that she can hear me since that damn knight in shining armor killed her." Mora sighed. "I'd been with her for twelve years. I'll miss our conversations."

"Yes, yes, quite tragic." I rolled my eyes. "But perhaps we can wrap this up and go kill Eligos?"

"Catherine was a beautiful soul, and her art was entrancing. You'd have loved it," Mora continued, practically ready to whip out a eulogy. "Now, I'll never experience her heart put on display again."

"Looks pretty displayed to me." I pointed to the gaping hole in her chest.

"Don't be so cavalier."

Mora had a way with hosts, always finding those desperately disinterested in engaging with the monotony of the world yet eager to indulge in the few loves they had. Mostly creative types, but Mora had found a few warriors tired of battle, philosophers who sought to sink into the deep recesses of their minds to find whatever theory of meaning they believed would change the world, and scientists who delighted at the chance to extend their research over the centuries.

They all remained safely tucked away in her wardrobe, a personal host to fit any occasion when she deemed appropriate. It sounded exhausting and tedious to keep up with their needs.

Once Mora finished her vigil to her lost host body, she strutted over to her luggage and withdrew a wrapped scroll.

"What's that?"

"It's where I keep my spares," she answered, slowly untying the magical strings.

"Guess we're just alerting Eligos of our location." I crossed my arms.

"Let him show up. I'm going to eviscerate him." The lace glimmered around her fingers as she wrapped it like twine. Each thin string radiated with magic, and the single wrapped piece of parchment she unraveled held a potency that screamed Fae magic.

"What's with the Fae pocket portal?"

"Easier than toting about all those coffins."

"Yes, but why not use Diabolic essence, carry them in a void world? That'd be simpler."

"I don't know, on the off chance my essence is shattered by a surprise assault, and I needed to ensure the magical seal didn't become undone, exposing their bodies to harm and leaving me more vulnerable."

"Touché."

She peeled off a single glyph on the parchment etched alongside hundreds of others. The ink fluttered from her finger, falling like a spiraling feather onto the floor, then expanded into a full-sized white coffin.

"It's surprising you found a Fae willing to help you."

"Please." She unlatched the locks and removed a few warded sigils. "How do you think I caught wind of Novus' scheming? I have connections everywhere. Though, I should've vetted the dead baron's affiliation with demons more thoroughly. Alas, live and learn."

Agreed. We would live and learn—right after we slaughtered Eligos and his demons.

Mora sauntered toward me, dug a nail into the back of her neck, and tore into the flesh. "Help a girl out?"

"Can't you just rip through it yourself?"

"I'd like to offer Catherine a modicum of respect." She glared.

"Fine." Channeling essence into my mortal fingertip, I created a sharp claw and dragged it down Mora's back, carving through the layers of flesh so she could hop out and leave the corpse mostly intact. Guess she really had fought hard for her life against Eligos since Mora rarely intertwined so deeply in a host body, such as seeping her essence into them on a cellular level like myself. By maintaining proper balance between her consciousness and a host body, it allowed her to leave without harming them, but also made for a more difficult possession. Her essence consumed Catherine during a collision of consciousnesses where Mora had to ultimately choose herself.

Instinctively, I faced away from her as she escaped and entered the room in her true form. The coffin creaked open, and the host gasped, their voice hoarse from years of sleep.

"Such a gentleman, Bezzy," Mora said with a deep baritone that she added a soft lilt to lighten. Her hand grazed my shoulder blades, indicating she'd possessed the new body seamlessly.

There were few things in the world that bothered Mora, but she preferred not to be seen in her demon form, something she lived with too long on Bael's Court as a reigning king in Hell.

"Whatever." I flexed, shrugging off her hand. "Who'd you pick?"

I turned, and Mora twirled as she adjusted her blazer, smiling with four large, fanged upper eyeteeth.

"Maurice." I nodded approvingly. "I always liked him."

"He's the only one durable enough to handle a few lucky shots from that annoying demon knight." Mora fidgeted in the itchy suit.

I smirked.

Maurice had terrible taste in fabrics and a weird mix of fashion sense, from stuffy and traditional to audacious and conventionally difficult to walk in. Guess it made some sense, given he was a vampire of nearly a thousand years who'd never adapted to the changes in the centuries, refusing to blend even though organizations like the Mythic Council demanded it. He'd agreed to Mora's arrangement with the stipulation that when she wore his flesh, she not put him in what he considered garish attire. He'd tired of life yet feared the unknowingness that came with death. Mora offered him a chance for the solitude of sleep, exploration of the world, and the quiet disconnect that came with observing change without interacting. Not sure why that worked on him—must have been a personality thing—but she always found individuals eager and willing to give themselves to a demon.

"Come along." Mora snapped her fingers. "We have a demon to slaughter."

"Demons," I corrected. "Remember, Eligos is working with others now that he's cracking open those orbs."

"Right." She planted her hands on her hips and pouted. "This is ridiculous. I say we just—"

She froze, eyes wide and panic-stricken. The bright blue of her host's irises turned emerald, and the veins on her face bulged and changed black. Her nose crinkled. There was such an exertion of her essence rising to the surface of her host. She avoided that almost always, given it could lead to a collision of consciousnesses.

"What?"

Coyly smiling, she ran her fingers through her hair, settling the Diabolic features that rooted into the vampire, superseding and deepening the possession in a way Mora never liked.

"It's nothing," she said. "Kell's being approached by a demon. Blah, blah—I know, once again, she's not paying attention to her surroundings."

What? My heart pounded. I grabbed my chest, almost confusing the sensation for Wally's fear, then remembered I had no connection to him. None. He was lost out there, in danger, and I had no clue. "Is Walter okay?"

"I guess." Mora waved a hand. "I don't know. Kell's lost in one of her daydreams, something about rearranging the stonework of the labyrinth to make it more accessible or whatever? Nothing on Wally in her immediate thoughts."

“Where is he?” I bolted in front of her and squeezed her arms. “Tell me.”

“He’s fine. They’re both fine. Aside from the fact neither one of them has any idea a demon is stalking their every step.” She flexed her biceps, resisting my grip and doing well to break my hold—another sign my essence was still waning despite the bit I’d replenished. “I’ve told Kell a thousand times to use the essence to track threats. She never fucking listens.”

“I don’t have time for your rants or your games. Let’s go.”

“I guess we’re just going with the improvised plan of picking off threats as they come instead of constructing a real course of action.”

“Wally. Now.” I growled, tails thrashing just enough to slice through her less valuable belongings.

“I’m teasing, relax.” She batted her long lashes. “But it is nice to see how close you two have grown.”

“Stop talking and fucking move.”

“Sheesh. Boys, so emotional.” Mora rolled her eyes, then zipped out of the room.

I followed quickly, desperate to find and protect Wally.

21

Walter

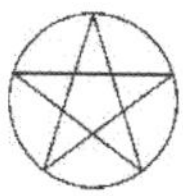

I traced my fingertips along the shallow cuts of my forearm, stitching the skin with a simple yet effective incantation. All those years spent helping Sarai study for the practitioner exam when she applied for the panacea regiment had finally paid off. These were basic at best, but at least it'd stop the bleeding. I winced, tugging at my shirt. Some of the blood had dried, making the fabric stick to my skin. It was like pulling off the world's worst band-aid. More like plucking since the tattered strings of my shirt didn't relent until the last second.

All I could think about was Bez. I had to hurry up so I could return to him, help him. I also needed to figure out how the dimensional travel worked, which meant returning to the helm or engine room was my best bet. Placing an incantation below my ribcage, I flinched. Before doing anything else, I needed to mend these injuries. Otherwise, it wouldn't matter whether I solved the demon's objective. Between my pale skin, the dried blood, the fresh cuts, and all the woozy blood loss, my complexion had gone full-blown ghostly. Trying not to clench my shaky stomach, I channeled mana into my core, drawing symbols with my fingers that'd begun to go numb.

"You should invert that one." Kell pointed to the incantations lining my stomach. "Oh, and overlap those two, then add an iron rejuvenating symbol."

Kell continued making suggestions while tinkering with the symbols she'd created with sorcery. Stacking basic spells to amplify their power did help make more advanced magics without having to exert nearly as much mana, but the way Kell put hers together—it was like jamming mismatched puzzle pieces together on top of a very wobbly Jenga game.

I swallowed hard, taking her advice and rearranging some of my symbols.

"I'd rip the protective restrictions on that one." She pointed to the incantation stamped furthest on my side. "It'll speed up the healing, minimize scarring, and offers a lovely buzz to mellow you out."

"I'd rather not be high on magic right now," I said, weaving another healing incantation.

"I would." Sapphire irises glimmered in front of me. The powder blue replacing the whites of the eyes made their shimmer all the brighter.

I snapped the incantation in half, changing it into faulty repulsion sigils, and slapped them onto the feathered Fae's chest. The demon possessing the body shuddered, then cackled. His elongated tongue lapped at his beaked mouth as he leaned closer, preparing to bite me.

Blood spattered, splashing my face.

The demon wailed, writhing with a hand punched through his chest. A heart pumped locked in a clenched fist belonging to a man who leaned out from behind the demon he'd impaled with a smirk on his face.

Bez. This was Bez. I smiled, studying the new face that hadn't quite adopted Bez's facial structure through a composite yet, but those crimson eyes illuminated by the pink replaced the whites of his eyes perfectly. Naturally, the first thing he prioritized changing was the hair of his body to a shaggy black with glamoured neon orange roots. He'd successfully possessed a new body meaning he had understood my cryptic clues after I abandoned him to lead the other demon away.

"You bastard." The sapphire-eyed demon gurgled, holding his essence in as glittery blood spilled over the feathers on his torso.

"Fair's fair. You stabbed me in the back first, asshole." Bez winked at me. "I missed you."

Stabbed him in the back? My body tightened. When did that happen?

"Are you okay?"

"Always." He blew a kiss, ignoring my concerns in favor of bravado.

"Good. I was worried, but…"

"I love you too, Walter. With all my heart"—he yanked his hand from the demon's chest and playfully tossed the heart at me—"and his."

The bloody organ hit my chest and then thudded on the floor, making a squishing sound, pumping blood and attempting to beat.

"Gross. Seriously, Bez?" I shuddered. "Why?"

"Wow. Romantic gesture completely lost on you." Bez grabbed the demon by the head and pulled him in close to make eye contact. "Can you believe how ungrateful my boyfriend is?"

"I'm going to…going to kill—"

"No sense in talking to you." Bez dashed toward the wall, slamming the demon's head against the stonework until my incantations holding that portion up shattered, and rocks collapsed onto the demon.

"Excessive much?" I muttered.

"Anything for you." Bez appeared in front of me in the blink of an eye, hands already pressing me against the wall, his mouth finding mine.

His touch was soft, considerate of the injuries I'd sustained. His lips were passionate and sweet but different somehow. Everything about this had a slightly unique feel. It had to be the lack of the composite taking full effect. His shoulders weren't as broad, and he wasn't as muscular—both made wrapping my arms around him that much easier. He was shorter too, which worked to my benefit since I didn't have to extend my neck as much to reach his lips. His lips that were thinner, not that I could talk.

"Okay." I pushed Bez off. "This isn't the time for kissing. We're not in an eighty's horror flick."

"I don't know what that means, but I'm just delighted to see you in one piece."

"I'm happy to see you too. And happy you restored some of your essence, even if…you know." I stared at Bez. Though the face was different, the expressions were true to form. So much of this body didn't quite fit him yet, but hopefully, he'd find himself in the flesh again. I knew that was important to him, feeling comfortable in his own skin—well, in the skin he acquired through possession.

Bez grinned, running his fingers along my abdomen. "You'll be pleased to know, while my composite hasn't changed much yet, this mage is pleasantly endowed—you know, since you're clearly a size queen."

"I am not." My ears burned. "This isn't the time for jokes."

"Who's joking? I'll gladly whip my dick out for you this second."

"Bez," I whined.

"Fine." He brushed my hair. "It's just so hard when you look so adorable."

"No, Bez." I pointed to the shifting rubble.

"You're going to pay for that." The feathered demon stood, shaking off rock and dirt.

"Learn to read the room, dickhead." Bez zipped behind the demon.

He wrapped his hands over the shoulders of the demon whose body began to blur, locking him in place. The demon wriggled in Bez's grip. Black drops pooled out of the pores of Bez's hands, taking form and changing to sheen metallic bladelike claws. Good—he'd not only gotten a full body back but a solid amount of essence restored too.

"You'll pay for this," the demon snarled. "Cheap devil like you has no idea who you're screwing with."

A vampire zipped in front of the demon that resisted Bez's grip, fangs glimmering against the light of the labyrinth lanterns. Definitely a vampire, not a ghoul—I'd studied the difference enough that I'd never have to listen to Bez mock me about it again. I almost died that night in the Magus Estate—once from him—and his takeaway was I didn't know the difference between vampires and ghouls.

"Should we fear you because you're Lilith's kid?" The vampire grabbed the feathered demon's head, yanking it back. "I recognize the essence this close. Foul and pretentious. Though aren't all the demons in Lilith's Hell her babies? Children she loves with all her heart, so long as they heed her warnings about not wandering into the wilderness of other worlds."

"Mora," Kell whispered, staring at the vampire. "Love the host you picked. Always fun."

The vampire—Mora—turned back, pointing a finger at Kell. "I have a scolding prepared for you, but first." She returned to the feathered demon, desperately trying to break Bez and Mora's hold over him.

"I had the misfortune of accompanying Bael to a banquet hosted by your mommy, Lilith," Mora said, disdain pouring off her tongue in equal measure to the blood flowing out of the demon's mouth. "She talked down to all those in attendance from lesser Hells, as she so eloquently put it, and made it quite clear nothing outside her world mattered. Not even her demons who abandoned it."

"You don't know her," the demon begged. "She'll…she'll do anything for her children, her progeny, her essence incarnate, even—"

"I'm tired of your voice. It's obnoxious and whiny." Bez dug his claws deep into the demon's flesh, shredding meat and bone, spilling blood everywhere.

Mora's fingers grew long and sharp, blackened with essence, and she tore into the demon's stomach. Bez's grip remained strong as black essence continued pooling out of him, forming into sharp spikes that stabbed into the demon.

The demon wailed, expelling his own essence to fight back, but waves of black flew from Mora and Bez simultaneously, lapping round and round. A sapphire hue laced in the black held a vibrance, sizzling and crackling against the darkness surrounding the three of them, then the blue flickered in and out like an erratic pulse. I gulped from the essence merging around the three demons, making it impossible to distinguish a single one in the tarlike blob filling the corridor.

Bones crunched, blood splattered, chunks of meat broke loose and spilled onto the floor like ground beef. I gagged.

Bez and Mora's essence intertwined, suffocating the sapphire light with emerald and crimson hues casting a brightening pulse after each muffled scream from the demon fully encased by Diabolic essence.

Kell took off her witch's hat, probably needing something to block the view like me. Instead, she rifled through the insides and pulled out a phone to snap a photo.

"Why?" I cocked my head.

"I never realized the awesome Christmas vibes those two give off." Kell tossed her phone into the hat and put it back on. "I'm gonna use this for my next holiday card."

"Why do I even ask?" I questioned aloud, shaking my head with silent judgment.

"This is how Diabolics contend with conflict," Mora said, adjusting the flounced frill of her dress shirt. The ensemble looked like something out of the twelfth-century Renaissance except for the tacky not-so-fashionable updates Mora must've added because they didn't have bell-bottom styled pantaloons during that period. Yeesh. I bit my lip to keep from commenting. She usually had better taste in her outfits.

"Get rid of the judgy face, Walter." Bez pointed a claw.

"I'm not judging her clothes," I blurted.

Mora frowned and planted her hand on a popped hip. "I fucking hate Maurice's wardrobe."

"I think you look dazzling, babe." Kell practically swooped toward Mora and kissed her. The two locked lips like we weren't being stalked and hunted by demons. Why was everyone kissing to say hello?

We're in literal life-or-death danger.

"I meant the judgy face on how we dealt with that demon," Bez said, zipping in front of me in a blur so quickly it snapped the air around my body before my eyes registered the movement.

I released a breath of relief, grateful to see his essence continuing to grow stronger again.

"Devouring demons is just how things work for Diabolics in Hells and other realms. Plus, with his shattered essence coursing through us, it's quite the pick me up."

"I see." I half-smiled, which Bez took as an invitation, running his knuckles along my tattered shirt as the essence coating his hand retreated inward.

His fingertips tugged at the bloody fabric, running his thumb over the dried flecks of blood while squinting at the fresh, soaked stains. Then, without any permission whatsoever, he yanked my shirt up, examining my stomach in front of Mora and Kell. "Those incantations are solid, stellar, in fact."

"That was all me, pure genius." Kell broke away from Mora's lips just in time to humble brag.

"Shut up." Mora snatched the back of Kell's neck, locking eyes with her. "I'm scolding you."

They returned to their kiss.

I tilted my head. "Are they like having a telepathic argument while making out?"

"Ignore them. That's what I usually do." Bez waved a dismissive hand. "As I was saying, those incantations are solid, but you'll need my essence if you want to fully recover."

"No."

The way I so urgently rejected the offer visibly upset Bez, making his eyes soften with sadness he quickly hid behind a furrowed brow and pouty scowl.

"I don't think you understand the severity of your situation, Walter."

"I do," I explained. "You need all of your strength right now, and splitting any of it will put everyone at risk."

"Bah. I'm not worried about everyone; I'm worried about you."

"I can wait. I'm safest with you at your strongest." I cupped my hands over his, hoping the gentle touch showed how much I cared and that my words conveyed this was the right option. "I'll gladly let you share your essence after we've dealt with Eligos and the other demons."

Besides, the demon possessing the pink Fae was sent to find the mage linked to Bez, connected to a devil. The feathered demon lunged for me, completely ignoring Kell. I wouldn't allow myself to compromise Bez, so if Eligos wanted to use me as a ploy, control Bez or trap him—I refused to make myself a pawn.

"Speaking of Eligos…I'd like to know where he is." Mora took Kell's hat and began rifling through it.

"Agreed," I said. "But we should probably take this conversation somewhere safer."

"It's as good as any place," she said.

"Especially since we have our shrouds up," Bez added. "It doesn't cloak from fellow Diabolics—not that any of that matters on this weird ship—but it'll alert us the second one steps into the territory we've claimed."

Right. I couldn't see their shrouds of shadows without essence. There was so much demon energy and their abilities I wouldn't be able to detect now.

Mora pulled out a laptop, floating it toward Kell, who immediately went to work typing on the midair keyboard.

"What are you doing?" I asked.

"Having her pull up the security."

"Not doubting Kell's ability to get into the system, but that could take hours, days even since—"

"Oh, I already hacked the system forever ago." The light from the laptop highlighted her mischievous grin.

When had she done that? I sulked. The day she arrived, likely. Not only was she screwing with the navigation system, moving us through dimensional space seemingly without forethought, but she was already setting up her own private viewing of the villa so Mora could definitely sleuth without prying eyes like Bez or mine.

"Weird," Kell said. "He's just standing in the helm, not doing anything."

We all squeezed in close, studying the screen. Eligos stood in full view of the camera, unmoving, golden eyes locked on the control panel. Three Fae with blackened veins lining their skin were behind him.

"Maybe Kell's tinkering saved us." I chuckled. "Looks like Eligos doesn't know how to work the system anymore."

"My system is flawless." Kell huffed.

"Or he can't access the necessary functions since releasing other demons," Mora said. "Lacking their essence might mean he can no longer power the engines."

"It looked like he'd replaced their loss by tossing my body and essence in their absence."

Wait. Bez had found his body in the engine room? That must've been when he got stabbed in the back.

"That's unlikely. Eligos is probably just a fool who doesn't understand the streamlined framework I made," Kell said. "With devil essence, he could probably keep the ship running ten times over, even if he only has a fraction."

"Right," Mora said, dragging the word out and eyeing me and Bez. "Still, we should take this opportunity to—"

"Attack him in the helm." Bez snarled, extending the claws on his raised hands, practically buzzing at the idea of fighting Eligos head-on.

"No," Mora said. "This is clearly an obvious trap to lure us into the helm."

Thank goodness for one levelheaded demon.

"I say we use Wally as bait to lure him out of the helm and then murder him."

"Hey, you're sounding less levelheaded now."

"What? He immediately went to grab you after decapitating Bezzy. I say we use that to our advantage."

"You're not wrong," I said.

"Yes, she is," Bez snapped.

"Not about Eligos being after me. But she is wrong about what we should do. You both are."

I studied Eligos' obvious stance meant to lure us there. He'd taken careful precautions to observe us the entire time since arriving in the villa. That type of analytical behavior indicated he probably already knew Kell had messed with the control panel; he might've also realized we had access to the security system or had some way of locating him. What he didn't plan for, what I suspect, anyway—was us gaining access to the engine room. The locking mechanism on the doorway was different from the others, and once we'd examined the engine and orbs containing demons, he made his assault, revealing himself that day.

"Walter, care to share with the class?" Bez stared at my lips because I was muttering. Oops.

"Right. We need to go to the engine room. Eligos won't suspect that or, at the very least, won't like it one bit," I explained. "We can retrieve Bez's body, more essence for our side, secure and fortify the room, and have Kell hack the system to sync the engine room with the helm, which will give us access to all the controls in the villa. Portals, travel, defenses, and basically turn this entire place against Eligos and his demons."

"That sounds incredibly complicated," Kell said with a wide-eyed confused expression. "And like it'll require a lot of improvising on my part."

"So that's a no?" I gulped.

"No," she said firmly. "It's a hell yes. I love this plan."

"I don't like it," Mora said.

"I like it even more now." Bez grinned. "If Walter's maze of a brain has deduced this to be the best course of action, I support it. Let's get going."

He wrapped his arms around my waist, pressing his chest against my back and lifting my feet off the ground.

"Wait," Mora said as Bez zipped past her. "Shouldn't we discuss…"

Her echoed voice faded once Bez whipped through the labyrinth, moving so quickly everything blurred.

"No time," Bez shouted. "Move your ass!"

I didn't realize how hard it was to breathe when he moved at that speed. Since meeting him, I'd always had a piece of his essence inside me, something helping me grasp the complexities of Diabolic power even when I lacked any understanding of how it worked. When Bez stopped in front of the sealed portal, I finally exhaled.

"Oh, no time to stop and talk?" Mora arrived, gracefully releasing Kell, who fluttered beside her in a telekinetic hold. "Guess since I'm the only one who understands how to open the door, we have all the time in the world."

"Shut up." Bez rearranged symbols lining the doorframe while I closely watched, completely incapable of making sense for a single phrase.

It all looked like gibberish slapped together. All the same, the portal glowed a luminescent black, rippling like water.

"Damn. Guess you do pay attention sometimes." Mora scoffed. "Well? Let's go then."

She grabbed Kell's hand and stepped through the portal. Bez and I quickly followed. The blackness ran like water across my skin, warm and soothing, carrying us to the pocket dimension containing the sealed-off engine room. But in an instant, everything turned white, so harsh against my eyes that I had to squeeze them shut. I shivered as the warmth turned icy.

Landing in the engine room, I brushed away the white flakes of Fae magic like brushing snow from my face. I turned to see Kell and a plain metallic wall with absolutely no sign of Bez or Mora. Not just that. No signs of symbols to open the doorway. It was one way.

"Shit." I panicked. "What happened? Where are—"

"I know, Bez looks rough," Kell said, not even glancing back at the missing fucking portal.

"What?" I followed her gaze and saw Bez's former bloody, headless body propped up by a lance impaled through his stomach connected to hundreds of wires.

I struggled to breathe. Six shattered orbs lay on the railing under the corpse's dangling feet.

"We have to find a way out of here." I pointed to the space where the portal should've been.

"No worries. It's probably just a glitch," Kell said, unfazed as she trotted onto the railing toward Bez's former body. "I can hack the system no matter what's up; the plan is very much still a go."

My chest tightened. This was a trap. It had to be. I led us directly into it, thinking I knew the first thing about outsmarting a demon.

22

Beelzebub

"What the actual fuck just happened?" I dragged my claws along the stonework wall where the portal should be in full effect, but nothing appeared.

One second I was stepping through the portal, Wally's hand in mine, and then everything burned, shoving me back into the labyrinth. I could tear this wall down, but it wouldn't lead to Wally. The engine room was in the villa, technically speaking, merely a dimensional layer or two apart, but the entire room was sealed off to limit access. I seethed with rage, ready to obliterate every piece of this fucking fairy hellhole until I found my Wally.

"Calm yourself, Bezzy." Mora traced her fingertips over the symbols lining the doorframe. "Something's missing."

"Yeah, the fucking portal."

"No. Look, Bez." She ground her teeth, snapping a fang in the process. "You just assembled these. What's missing?"

I followed her hand, searching for an inconsistency. But in truth, I wasn't paying attention when I threw them together. I sort of winged it, trying to impress Wally and show Mora up because I could be as clever as the two of them. The symbols looked right, then the door opened so quickly I couldn't help but boast. This was probably all my fault. My impulsive arrogance had once again endangered Wally.

"Wait." I reached for one of the symbols wedged between a stack in the most bizarre fashion, some archaic mortal language shoved between Sylvan and Diabolic letters. "This wasn't here before."

"And these two are missing." Mora pointed to gaps toward the lowest reaches of the wall.

"My doing, I'm afraid," Eligos' hollow voice echoed from his suit and through the corridor. "Limited the parameters to allow only those without Diabolic essence to cross through."

His glowing golden eyes stared from the darkness; every lantern dimmed despite his nearby presence.

I growled, summoning a coat of sheen black essence to line my forearms and shins. It expanded and hardened over the flesh of my body. Flesh that didn't have enough essence to create a full-body buffer. This conjured essence would lower the protection lining my body overall, but so long as I kept up with his movements, these shields would withstand any strike he attempted, from his armored attacks to the many blades he wielded.

"I'm going to kill you." I glared.

"Before or after I take out your king?" Eligos chuckled, his laughter rattled inside his suit.

Blurred figures whipped past me, snatching Mora and dragging her deeper into the labyrinth. Claws clashed, slashing through rock and flesh.

"In the mortal game of chess, kings are most valuable, yet the weakest pieces," Eligos said. "I hold no value toward Morax, but you do. And her weakness will be easy to exploit in order to hurt you."

"I'll kill you, then your damn demon lackeys—if Mora doesn't finish them first."

"Is that before or after I obtain your misfit mage and slaughter that insufferable witch?"

I froze. Did he mean to collect them himself? If so, he might attempt to skirt past me, the fearsome devil, and leap into the portal. I wouldn't drop my guard for a second, refusing to give him any opportunity to flee. Or had he already sent another demon to procure him? How many demons had he released? I heightened my senses, listening to the chaotic battle between Mora and the demons that'd snatched her away, attempting to discern how many—

Eligos appeared in front of me in a flash, hovering, fist raised, and a moment from punching right through my head.

I deflected his assault. Barely.

"Not happening a second time, asshole."

"For a god, you're lacking in a skilled move set." Eligos wiggled the fingers of his other hand before balling them into a fist.

Dammit. Of course I'd fallen right into an obvious trap.

I spun around, kicking his chest with the heel of my foot—which throbbed between his armor and essence and my current lack of either—then I used the blow to propel my knee upward and knock his three blades onto the ground before they gutted me.

Metal clinked against stone undisturbed. He didn't bother retrieving his lost weapons, which meant I wasted three seconds savoring a futile victory. I zipped up the wall, scanning the terrain in the process, and kicked off the ceiling to rocket at him, weaving between sharpened spears.

"I'm so sick of you, Eligos." I punched his helmet, cracking it slightly until the glow of essence restored it.

"You know my name, shocking." I could feel his hateful smirk over a shitty pun as black lightning formed around his armor, propelling toward me.

Gods. I evaded, continuing in a fight I didn't have the energy or conviction for. I hated him for hating me, but he only hated me because he believed me to be someone we both hated. Ugh. What was I thinking? Or overthinking. Snapping back to attention, I dodged a blow and leapt away. My thoughts were as absurdly convoluted as Walter's.

Wally. I needed to end this fast, rescue him.

I hated admitting it, but in my condition, facing off against someone of Eligos' level could drag out for hours, days even.

There was one thing that'd draw all this to a close.

Relaxing my muscles, I pulled my essence back into my core, circulating throughout my body but showing I meant no hostility.

"You intend to use Beelzebub's devil essence to break down doors to sealed Hells—all Hells, really—and rally demons to wage wars against every devil in existence."

"Those who once lived, those still reigning, and any others that conceive themselves into existence," Eligos said with a bravado I recognized from years of pining over the magnificent demon who sought change. "The devils will be no more."

We'd only spoken a handful of times in Hell, each a life-changing experience that I clung to, using as inspiration to change into the person I strived to become, the one who walked through the wake of destruction during the coup meant to bring down Beelzebub. Unfortunately, I used that chance to express my eternal cowardice and ran from the battle, abandoning a dying realm. I saw Eligos as a friend, an idol, a role model, and I failed him every single step on the journey to find myself. Only I hadn't found myself. I'd found comfort in a lie. A lie I needed to confess, hopeful it'd put an end to all of this. Not for my sake, but for Wally's. For Mora and Kell, too. I ground my teeth. That was a lie. I frantically desired to ensure Wally was safe above all else and would give anything, even my life, to know he walked away from this unharmed.

"Your plan won't work." I crumpled inward, shamefully averting my gaze. "I'm not Beelzebub. I'm not the devil you hate, the one you seek vengeance against. I'm merely a lowly demon. A pathetic demon too frightened to raise arms during the coup, one who slinked across the battlefield and snatched a piece of devil essence then fled to the mortal realm."

I awaited his reaction. His entire body stilled within the confines of his suit of armor, not a single sound. Those golden irises and the pale-yellow sclera of his eyes vanished in the darkness of his visor. Enhancing my senses, I searched for the faintest trace of Eligos stirring, reacting, doubting, or sinking into the truth of the matter. Nothing. His essence was pure silence, his armor immobile.

Perhaps now he'd see reason. He'd understand this fight was futile, and I wasn't his enemy.

Mora wailed, then snarled. She slammed one of the demons through a wall or the ground. It was difficult to discern this far away. The other demons had dragged her down several corridors, cornering her at a dead end of some locked chamber, only for them to meet theirs. With the silence from Eligos, the emptiness of the labyrinth and villa alike, every movement of Mora's battle came in crisp.

A demon struggled to claw their way out of the rubble when suddenly Mora's talons impaled them, making them gurgle. Her essence rumbled beneath her flesh, erupting from her pores in an effort to devour the first, but before she could, something hacked at her back.

Her boots swished and dug into the gravel of debris as she repositioned herself to strike the second demon, impaling them and redirecting her essence. A third presence struck her, forcing her to retreat, pivot, and knock that foe down in an attempt to devour one of them before the others recovered. This continued for some time, Mora gaining the drop on a demon, bringing them to the brink of death, and another interfering before she slaughtered any demon.

Her emerald essence radiated so powerfully, I could see the color in the clash of combat, taste her aura on my tongue, feel the fatigue in her battle.

I balled my fists.

Mora was better than this, but between the essence she lost fighting off Eligos, the massive amount she poured into Kell, and that incessant need of hers to prioritize a host body. I caught wind of it four moves back when she halted an attack and pivoted to scale the ceiling and return from a different vantage.

Those demons already had her outnumbered, the element of surprise, and the second they realized how to exploit her fancies, they'd overwhelm Mora. I couldn't allow that to happen. This needed to end.

"Eligos," I shouted. "You don't remember me, but I remember you. A demon of virtue, one who prides himself on all the deeds of a true knight. I also know you can spot a lie when you see it. You know what I've said to be the truth. I am not Beelzebub. Claiming my essence will not be enough to open his closed world. Take some small solace in knowing the devil Beelzebub can never harm anyone again."

There was no relief in this confession, not like when I told Wally. Every truth I shared with him allowed me to swim away from that pit of despair I'd spent eons drowning in. But with Eligos, divulging this carried a shame to it. He'd despise me, find the actions repulsive, yet he'd have to concede. Everything he did was to strike down a devil for his crimes against our demon brethren. His nobility wouldn't allow him to punish me for another's crimes.

Eligos laughed, a slow chuckle that reverberated in his suit of armor, each dragged-out syllable of laughter dinged against metal. I raised my eyebrows. Soon, it changed into a steady flow revealing the hilarity Eligos found for my confession, one that quickly enveloped the stone hall with an unhinged cackle creating a cacophony of clinks and rumbles.

"You think I didn't know?" Eligos wheezed between each word, incapable of stifling his amusement. "The imposter devil who fooled the world, many worlds, in fact."

Eligos barely composed himself, plodding forward and bracing himself against a wall.

"What?" I took a step back. "But when you acknowledged me as the devil, called me by his name, and laid the blame for his crimes at my feet… You were pretending?"

"Lying." Eligos snorted. "It's called lying. Sort of the same way you lied about being Beelzebub for centuries. I kept my cards close, a necessary precaution to determine the full extent of your power and that of the misfit mage you keep. After all, he wrought havoc down upon his Collective, tearing their system and balance asunder."

I widened my eyes. My revelation meant nothing; it paled in comparison to his.

"Turned out he was even less of a threat than your demon king or her witch."

He knew nothing of Wally. Not a damn thing.

"When I arrived in the mortal realm, my essence was in shambles after Beelzebub shattered it—the true devil. I laid in a state of decay, stuck between a cumbersome recovery and a slow death for the better part of a decade. I had no strength, no will, and certainly no desire to devour lesser beings to reclaim my destroyed essence."

My mind spiraled in perplexed thoughts, unraveling the enigma of Eligos' words. When did he find out? Had he overheard Wally and me discussing my demon secret? No. We often carefully skirted the words aloud, Walter's desire to respect my privacy.

"I finally found my will to restore myself when whispers of a barbarous devil emerged." Gloved fingers dug into rock, and the piercing scrape dragged my attention back. "A sadist who swept across the New World, slaughtering mages who defied his reign, chasing Mythics to devour, and flaying mortals who attempted to settle."

I'd been very loud and hostile in my early years after Mora's tutelage. She offered me the tools for survival and allowed me to choose whichever path I sought. In finding my footing, I learned all too quickly that no one wanted a kind demon, so I became a cruel devil. It was the best way to evoke a name for myself, create fear, force respect, and refuse to silently exist as some unknown weakling like I had for so long in Hell. I carried that name across the continents, exploring every crevice of the world and leaving a trail of mayhem in my wake.

"You knew this entire time?" I croaked, swallowing the pitchy fear in my voice. "For centuries? Why wait? Why attack me now?"

"As the former baron would say, patience is its own reward. It was my hubris and hasty plans that led to my downfall against Beelzebub. After such a massacre, I swore I'd never lose to a devil again. With the life and blood and essence of a phony devil, I won't have to worry about that."

Eligos lunged ahead, snatching me by the collar, and dragging me into a void of his making, a hidden layer of Diabolic essence circulating throughout the villa, allowing him fast travel anywhere and everywhere unseen.

This was unlike any demon-void world I'd entered before, with the pitch blackness illuminated by trickling comets in the background of this secret shadowed space. The flaming rocks burned in an array of luminescent colors, a rainbow of fiery destruction using Fae magics that further amplified his cloaking. No wonder I couldn't detect Eligos' presence when I arrived or pinpoint anything in the villa. He used the exact magics the baron used.

A fist rocked against my jaw, cracking the bone before disappearing into the darkness of the void. Light shimmered against the armored suit, where the helmet lay abandoned next to the empty suit. Here, in a world of Eligos' making, he favored skirting the shadowed walls of his reality in his own skin, which would make him even faster.

I gripped my jaw and wiggled it back and forth until the throbbing passed, and the healing began. Quickly, I manifested my essence, circulating it around my forearms and shins once again in preparation for his next assault.

A flurry of strikes hit me from every direction. By the time I'd memorized the pattern, Eligos had vanished back into the darkness once again. I reprioritized my essence to healing since guarding seemed utterly impossible in his world. Next thing I knew, something whipped me dead center in my back, breaking a vertebra. A heavy foot collided with the back of my knee to further assist in knocking me down. Then balled-up tendrils hit me in the stomach before lifting up and uppercutting my jaw. I spun through the air, all my bearings lost, my jaw refractured, and seeing only stars. Granted, the stars of Fae magic, but those blows really had left me dazed.

I had to escape. Eligos had the advantage in this void realm. He already possessed more combat skills. Add to that the fact his essence flowed strongly while mine still waned. My exposed secret offered no reprieve from this battle, only a revelation the valiant knight made a goal to bring me down all the same—since he saw me as nothing more than a devious demon playing the role of a devil.

Truthfully, was I anything more than that?

Exhaling a deep breath, I released my fear. I couldn't allow him to win. Whatever he had planned for me, for the fragment of devil essence I carried, I had to prevent.

23

Walter

I was practically hyperventilating as I approached Bez's headless former host, which twitched from the electricity circulating through the wires attached to the large golden lance impaled through the stomach. I stared through the holes of the metal-grated floor of the railing, cautiously searching for anything in the darkness. Meanwhile, Kell lay on the railing, sprawled out on her stomach, kicking her feet back and forth behind her while casually typing away at her laptop.

"You realize this is a trap, don't you?" I asked.

"No." Her fingers strummed with a steady ticking along the keyboard. "It could be a trap, I suppose. It could also be a coincidence."

"Oh, definitely." I scoffed. "The portal just coincidentally sealed right after we stepped through, separating us from Bez and Mora."

"They'll be fine. We're perfectly fine. They're probably trying to open it from their end right now." Kell snickered. "Without the slightest clue in what they're doing. Eons of wisdom between the two of them, and they wouldn't know how to flip a light switch here."

"Nope." I shook my head. "This is a trap. We're trapped here while Bez and Mora are out there, likely being attacked by who knows how many demons. We're going to be attacked next. Captured or killed or—"

"Stop catastrophizing."

"I'm not catastrophizing," I snapped, mostly due to the fact I was unaware of the term, and that pissed me off more than Kell's nonchalance.

"Point is, you're manifesting a lot of negativity preparing for all these unknown outcomes, and it's clogging the air and bad for my pores—you know, the ones recovering after being set on actual fire. I get it, keep your expectations low and assume the worst will happen. Mora does the same thing. Really says a lot about your personality, though, Wally."

"This isn't paranoia for the sake of paranoia. We know Eligos has been running this place or helping at the very least. We know he's after us. We know he knows"—*or thinks*—"Bez shares his essence with me. We also know there are other demons working with him. What we don't know is how many there are, where they are, or if they're here plotting right this second."

"That's a long way of saying you have no idea what's going on."

I furrowed my brow.

"Focus less on what you don't know and more on what you do know," Kell said, still playfully kicking her feet back and forth, not a care in the world.

"Well, maybe if you planned more for the unexpected, you wouldn't get set on fire so much."

"Rude," Kell said, twisting her lips into a soured expression. "If I let all the unknowns of a situation, of the world, control me, I wouldn't accomplish anything. But in the few minutes since you started spiraling, I've already gotten into the systems, taken a looksee, and achieved step one of what I can control. What have you done?"

I huffed, releasing my frustration and some of my fear. She had a point. If I dwelled on all the potential and very likely horrors, I'd stand here frozen, incapable of doing a damn thing to help.

"Here's what I do know: this place is running on magical fumes." Kell jabbed her screen, pointing to a bunch of codes, numbers, letters, and symbols I couldn't make the slightest sense of. "Despite connecting Bez's body—well, his old body—to the network, the ship isn't funneling essence from him, which means there are bound to be outages since a bunch of Diabolics have been released from their orbs."

She pointed to the shattered glass from the six orbs stationed at the edge of the railing that were littered about, catching the light of blood dripping through the grates of the metal walkway. The blood was glittery and must've belonged to the Faes Eligos used as host offerings to the Diabolics he'd released.

"Hence, why I choose to believe it's a coincidence until I have more info to formulate a sound plan. Right now, I can fix glitches."

The click, tick, and clatter of Kell's typing created a rhythmic echo in the near-silent engine room. A few machines hummed, but nothing with the roaring bustle like my last visit, meaning the dimensional capabilities had lost functionality or, at the very least, were limited.

"So, instead of trying to predict every possible outcome, why don't you prioritize what you can control?"

Right. I peered over the edge, taking in the hundreds of orbs still placed on pillared mantles in large groups, positioned throughout the lower end of the engine room. None of them were shattered, at least from what I could glimpse. Which meant Eligos probably just released the six demons up here on the railing that were trapped inside those Diabolic orbs.

"It doesn't look like any of the orbs below have been disturbed, which makes sense considering they're the only thing keeping the basic life support and magic of the ship intact, so I guess we don't have to worry about him releasing more."

"Doubtful," Kell said. "Only half the pillars are wired into the systems. I mean, they're all connected, but according to the diagnostics, they're not doing much of anything. My guess? The knight in tacky armor lacked enough host bodies to free the others, so he's just keeping the others on ice. Figurative ice. Do you think the orbs have a temperature? I wonder if I could find out."

"Focus." I said it to Kell but honestly needed to take my own advice and figure out what was going on and how I could help. Could I help?

"Heh-heh-heh." An unsettling, deep laughter rained from above, accompanied by a wheezing exhale.

I looked up, unable to see anything other than the starry black temporal void that kept the engine room contained within the villa yet separated by dimensional magics.

"Kell," I whispered, panicky and not-at-all paranoid. "I was fucking right."

"Yeah, yeah, untwist your panties, Wally." Kell hopped up. "*Of course there's a demon here, but I had to wait for him to reveal himself before making a move.*"

"*There might be others,*" I thought, replying through the telepathic link Kell had created.

"*No. Six shattered orbs. We killed one; Bez and Mora killed a second.*" Kell clamped her jaw. "*And from the brief glimpse I caught before losing contact, Mora's dealing with three others.*"

"*What?*"

"*That makes five, meaning this one is the final demon that asshole knight released.*"

"You should've said something," I snapped, unable to stifle the words into a thought because if I'd known, I could've planned for it.

"*While you were spiraling, all woe is me? Couldn't risk tipping the demon off.*"

She's using psychic perception right now; she could've easily told me without alerting the demon.

"*Believe it or not, my magic is a finite source,*" Kell thought, proving even my internal musings linked to her active telepathy. "*And I'm using a lot to keep from passing out every minute.*"

I reached for my sheathed dagger since it was the only thing I had which stood any chance of harming Diabolic essence.

"*Keep it concealed. It's best not to tip our hand until we know what we're up against,*" Kell thought, and I felt the snap as the link between us went silent.

That meant she wouldn't be able to call on the Four Corners. I wondered if she'd lost access to any of the others, prioritizing her magic and essence to heal her substantial wounds, injuries I'd made light of because she shrugged off everything she'd endured playing it cool. I had to do better.

She stared at the ceiling before moving her gaze toward the empty white wall where we entered.

Maybe she'd figured out a way to open the portal.

"If you need me to stall"—I swallowed the lump of insecurity tightening my throat—"I can buy you time to hack the doors."

"Unless you can buy me an hour, I think we're going to have to move to plan B." She nodded to the white wall. "The shroud is solid, almost impossible to see, but it's there."

Shit. If Kell could barely register the presence with Mora's essence coursing through her, what was I going to do? I couldn't see anything out of the ordinary.

"Heh-heh-heh." The taunting laughter came from the other side of the engine room.

I whipped around, saturating the railing walkway, desperately hoping I'd be able to conjure a strong enough barrier to withstand a blitz attack.

"I thought you said the demon was over there."

"He was." Kell shifted her stance. "He's fast. Faster than the other one."

"Heh-heh-heh."

The Diabolic shroud vanished, revealing a behemoth of a demon perched at the end of the railing with his spikelike feet wedged into the metal grates. My stomach churned, not at his features, but at the mess of blood and literal guts he adorned across his sunshine yellow skin. All he was missing was the cheery smile to add to his sadistic appearance. This demon didn't possess a Fae—not really. It was more like he wore the body as an accessory. Limp, bloody arms dangled around his trunk-sized neck like a scarf. Glittery flesh stretched in long meaty strands across the broad, muscular torso of the demon, and the legs swung in front of the demon's waist like an apron. He reached on either side of the railing, gripping the bars with each of his six flexed arms, slowly approaching Kell and me.

The way he treated his host body, the fact he didn't need to coil deep within the core to restore discombobulated essence like Bez required after his near fifty-year stint trapped inside a Diabolic orb meant the six demons Eligos released probably hadn't spent as much time locked away. He wasn't the only demon to carelessly wreck a host body either. The first demon I'd encountered literally chomped away at the flesh as opposed to using it to restore herself. This proved they didn't require host bodies and added to the question of why Eligos didn't reserve those Fae bodies for other demons like those locked on the lower platforms positioned on the pillars. Did he think the six locked away were in worse condition? Did he believe he could challenge a devil, even a weakened one, with only six demons? I eyed the other orbs below. Was there something wrong with those demons? Were they too weak? Or were they uncontrollable in some way?

"Would rather be eating that cowardly demon king," the demon said with his voice carrying two tones: one deep and breathy, the other had a lighter lilt like my own. The rattling combination made every muscle in my body tense, too anxious to saturate my terrain.

"What did you say?" Kell perked up.

His words came from the gaping Fae's mouth, whose face was stretched across the demon's bulbous head like a warped, bloody beanie that covered the Diabolic's eyes. I shivered at how he'd ripped through the Mythic he possessed. This was because he rushed to create a composite. Bez had explained composites took time and required organic shifts, constrained by the confines of the host; instead, this demon forced and pushed the limits of the body well beyond measure until he'd snapped nearly all the elasticity of the flesh.

"Heh-heh-heh." The laughter came from his actual mouth, a twisted swirl of jagged teeth. "Was supposed to catch the mage with devil essence. Beat him. Contain the devil." He snarled, mouth widening as he sucked in a vortex of air. "No devil essence here. No essence in the mage at all."

He sniffed out my lack of essence as quickly as the demon possessing the pink Fae. Not sure if that put a bigger or smaller target on my head. On the one hand, without Bez's essence, they had no use for me, so the demons wouldn't prioritize abducting me. On the other hand, without Bez's essence, they had no reason to keep me around and would probably just—

"Guess I get to eat the little misfit mage now." He released another breathy chuckle.

Yep. That answered my question. I was fucked. We both were.

"Be a dear, Wally." Kell took off her witch's hat, handing it to me.

I did as she asked, watching her run her fingers along her shaved hair, amplifying the glow of green veins on her hands but lessening their potency around the burns on her scalp. Kell redirected the flow of essence, ushering it from prioritizing healing to what I assumed was preparation for an assault on this demon. Would she add it to her spells or simply reveal some Diabolic level strength and speed? It was mesmerizing to witness how much control Kell had over the essence Mora shared with her.

"One of these days, I'm going to have to sit down and actually clean this thing out." She rummaged through her hat, ignoring the demon slowly encroaching on us, and tossing items out from cosmetics, a decorative pillow, all the way to a collection of scrolls possibly containing ancient spells. None of it caught her eye. "Oh, hey, little guy. I forgot you were in there. Sorry, Trix."

Kell pulled out a fluffy white rabbit and kissed his scrunched nose, then dropped him back into the hat, continuing her search.

"Did you just pull a rabbit out of your hat?" I asked, eyeing the demon who took deceptively deliberate steps.

"Magicians aren't the only ones with fun stuff up their sleeves." Kell winked, unphased by the frightening presence, while I wanted to collapse in a puddle of dread as the demon's shadow loomed over us.

He was toying with us, given he could've been on top of us in a second flat. He wanted to savor this. Or had orders to stall—not sure how that'd benefit Eligos other than keeping us as half-dead hostages to use against Bez and Mora. I hoped whatever Kell wanted to retrieve would shield us from his attack.

"There it is." Kell dug her arms in deep and fished out a large gun.

I think that's a gun.

Military-grade based on the size, but the Collective never made it much of a priority to learn about human weaponry, aside from neutralizing barrels, clips, triggers, and ammunition through single casted low-level incantations.

This one had a huge sawed-off short barrel with a rounded clip and a hot pink grip that Kell playfully slapped against her palm, carelessly waving the gun back and forth.

"Is that some type of modified super shotgun?" I asked, searching for the faintest traces of magic tucked within the weapon but finding nothing.

"Goddess, no." She bit her thumb. Blood pooled, quickly replaced by black essence holding a green glint. "It's a grenade launcher."

"Why?" I asked, baffled.

"It's for the modern girl with modern problems." Kell posed. "Remember what I said about magicians and their sleeves?"

"Heh-heh-heh." The demon clutched his bloody stomach with two of his arms, his body shaking as he stifled a laugh.

It didn't matter that Kell wielded military-grade artillery, I highly doubted she'd get a clear shot on a demon moving at blurring speeds.

She shook her hand loose, blowing on the pooled blood on her thumb. A toothpick fell from the loose, frayed sleeve of her dress, and she eyed it, then me. Right. Magician's sleeve was code for something. She had a plan. I just didn't understand a single part of it, and considering this was Kell, I couldn't be certain she knew a single part of it either. She planned on shooting the demon with a grenade launcher—a literal fucking grenade launcher—and wanted me to stab it with a toothpick opposed to my actual dagger?

I knelt to retrieve her secret after-dinner weapon and sighed. I was going to die, either at the hand of this demon, a misfire by chaotic Kell, or an untimely demise by whatever she'd spelled on the toothpick. The magic radiated off it in waves, unlike her actual weapon.

"Get ready." She smeared her bloody thumb on the side of the grenade launcher, willing the essence to obey her, and guided it with her hand toward the barrel.

"What're you doing?" I asked wide-eyed.

"In case he tries dodging."

The demon extended all six of his arms, letting out a deranged cackle. "Please. I have no fear of anything mortal or magical you throw at me. Hit me with your best shot."

"Sure thing, Pat." Kell fired a grenade.

It let out a loud pop, whooshed ahead, and hit the demon's chest. Kell grinned when it bounced off and immediately burst into a huge explosion of black fire.

The demon belted out a deep, pained roar and an anguished shriek. His two voices screamed in a disharmonious melody cracking the actual air in the engine room. Black static popped, making each inhale hot and dry as the atmosphere changed.

I understood. Kell didn't only use the essence to ensure it'd move fast enough to catch the demon if he fled but to augment the explosive power with something that'd burn up his essence.

"Anytime, Wally." Kell whistled.

Right. I picked up the toothpick, completely unsure what to do until the bristles tickled my palm. Seriously? Kell used size distortion to warp a broom into a pocket-sized tool. That was such an advanced spell. Geez—I really needed to step up my game. I squinted, then scratched off a sigil. When the broom expanded to full size, I straddled it and waited for Kell to hop on before zipping away from the black flames engulfing the railing.

"Not that I don't like your surprisingly well-thought-out plan, but we don't exactly have a lot of flying room." I whipped a sharp turn once we reached the ceiling and flew along the top of the engine room, keeping an eye on the flaming demon.

"All I need is a bit of distance." Kell wrapped an arm around my stomach and waved her other, aiming the grenade launcher.

"We're gonna die." I squeezed the broomstick tightly, steadying the turbulence caused by frantic mana casting.

"Maybe, but that's half the fun." She popped off another two rounds, propelling grenades directly at the demon still ablaze with black flames.

He vanished, refusing to allow another explosive shot to hit him. I jerked the broom handle, flinging us around to scan the room. The demon's screams raged from one end of the engine room all the way to the opposite side as he used his six hands to smother the traces of fire that clung to him despite zipping back and forth.

"It won't work now that he's aware."

"Wait for it," Kell whispered.

A second fiery eruption hit the demon in the back, swallowing him in black fire.

"I'm willing the essence to track him, target him." Kell giggled. "Way better than heat seekers. He can outrun my fraction of essence, but this small space doesn't give him a lot of options."

Wow. She'd accounted for everything.

By the time the demon had gathered his bearings and zoomed away from the fire, the other grenade gave him chase, forcing him to move at blurring speeds to avoid a third strike. Chunks of scorched flesh fell to the floor, discarded remnants of the Fae body the demon wore. A trail of glittery blood, black flames, and sizzling essence zigged and zagged throughout the engine room in every direction. It didn't matter. The explosion caught him, lopping off one of his arms and throwing it into the air. It flopped onto the ground, lifeless and severed.

I squinted, having trouble seeing without my glasses, but it looked like a straight cut, much cleaner than I expected from a grenade.

"We're not trapped in here with some dull demon," Kell said, aiming her grenade launcher. "He's trapped in here with a wicked witch and a misfit mage."

I surged with mana, absorbing the confidence radiating from Kell. Saturating the dry air, I laced it with magic which offered more mobility and control during flight as well as making it easier on our breathing.

Kell popped two more shots. "Gotta reload."

I muttered incantations, preparing a barrier and counterattack if the demon attempted to chase after us. But I wouldn't let that happen. I continued flying circles around the engine room, tracking the freshest paths of carnage made by the demon as he avoided Kell's last two grenades.

Another explosion hit, far to my right, farther than I realized he'd moved. I stared at the fire burning his chest, centered and controlled by telekinesis the demon cast. It charred his skin, but he kept the flames contained with his remaining five hands, working tirelessly to condense the fire, intensifying the heat into a tight ball.

Shit. I knew what he was going to do, and I wouldn't let him use the same trick Kell used on the first demon we encountered.

I flew away, racing in erratic patterns, ignoring Kell's profanities as she tried to reload. As expected, the demon contained the explosion and hurled it at us, steering the shot with telekinesis. This wouldn't end until he found a target. While I believed in the barrier I'd created, I didn't want to chance it with such an amplified Diabolic attack. At my best, I could probably only withstand a few physical strikes from a demon before my barrier cracked.

Whipping back around, I allowed the ball of fire to close in.

"If you're expecting me to stop that, I hate to break it to you, but—"

"Hold tight, Kell." I slammed all my mana into the broom, shifting our trajectory and sending us plummeting toward the floor.

"Dammit." Kell squeezed my ribs tightly as her grenade launcher flung from her grasp. A heavy clunk of her weapon hitting the metal grates of the railing pulled my focus.

We could double back for it. But first, I needed to lose this targeted strike. I flew furiously, following the splattered trail left behind by the demon, and turned onto the freshest trails until I reached him.

His mouth widened, teeth stretching out of his massive mouth like outstretched hands seeking to snatch Kell and me into his gullet. One of the teeth stabbed my shoulder, another cut my forearm, and black tendrils seeped through the cracks in his jagged teeth, latching onto my arm that held the broom steady. I trembled desperately, wanting to run, but I maintained my hold, waiting until the last second.

When the sizzle of the fiery grenade's eruption he'd condensed closed in, still following us, I retrieved the Demon's Demise, using the dagger to hack at the tendrils and then propelled us straight up to the ceiling. The fireball landed in the demon's wide-opened mouth.

Essence exploded, raining across the engine room.

Limbs flailed through the air, tattered and ripped apart with ragged tears.

The scream the demon bellowed became faint and disjointed, like bits of his vocal cords attempted to carry sound but were scattered among the muck of his broken remains in every direction.

I did it. I fucking did it. I helped, and I stopped a demon.

Kell hugged me, resting her head on my back as I slowed down.

"Woo," she boasted, hiding the wispy breaths of exhaustion she took. "We did it."

Right.

A bright yellow arm cut through the smoke holding a grenade. Wait—the fifth one never exploded. I'd been so fixated on the demon catching the fourth one mid-explosion, I'd overlooked the fifth one. But how was he moving his arm? His body was riddled with injuries, torn to bits, and… This arm. This was the first one he'd lost; I recognized the perfectly clean cut.

"Fuck." I pivoted as the thumb holding the grenade released. "He sliced off his arm intentionally."

He'd accounted for the overwhelming force of Kell's weapon, made it seem like he'd lost a limb, and planned to use it to turn the grenade against us one way or another.

I channeled all my mana, knowing there was no way to outrun the grenade inches from us, and amplified the barrier hoping it'd hold.

A blast raddled my eardrums, sending a painful piercing through my entire body.

Fire flooded my vision.

I spun in circles, and Kell's grip faded. Not happening again. Fighting through the carnage, I wrapped my arms around her, squeezing her close and safely within the confines of my barrier. I had no clue how I did it, how I found her amidst the fire and smoke, but I couldn't let anything happen to her, to me.

We nosedived in a spiral, crashing hard onto the ground.

I gasped as my back slammed and spasmed, releasing Kell before I flipped and rolled over a few times, thudding against a pillar.

My vision was hazy, but Kell was fine. As fine as someone could be after barely escaping an explosion.

Glass shattered.

A dozen or more orbs lay in broken bits surrounding me as chaotic essence lashed around me.

No. I couldn't stand, couldn't move. I couldn't even catch my breath. How was I going to survive a whole horde of demons?

24

Beelzebub

This fight was endless and impossible. Nothing I attempted broke through the layers of essence dividing us from the villa. Every effort I made to counter, block, or flat-out attack Eligos failed. He tossed me around like a fucking ragdoll, pummeling me before vanishing back into the shadows.

"You possess essence from the most potent Hell, yet received tutelage from a second-rate demon proclaiming herself a king," Eligos said with a mix of arrogance and contempt.

Mora had learned early on during our training even without accessing the devil essence in my possession, my own demon essence quickly overpowered her. It turned out I was a natural for violence from so much time spent observing the battles and deaths, all meant to provide Beelzebub with an ounce of entertainment. To say the skills went a bit to my head was an understatement, but each successful strike Eligos landed reminded me that the demons from my Hell battled on a level unlike any other Diabolics.

Eligos fought with such finesse; there was beauty in the blurring blows breaking my bones, ripping my flesh, bruising my muscles, all in an effort to force my depleted essence to heal the injuries or lose a second host in a day. These attacks were tactical—just strong enough to force instinct over strategy but not enough to provoke my essence to lash out chaotically. I shook away the blossoming admiration I had for his fighting style and dropped to my knees again.

Everything stilled. The trickling rainbow comets. The slithering shadows. The subtle patter of Eligos. He didn't know what to make of it, that much I was certain of. I'd gathered after the first hundred attacks that he planned to drag this out at a crawling pace, something vindictive and petulant. Not at all like the knight I had once respected.

I closed my eyes, stopped my breathing, and turned off every single sensation except for my hearing, which I amplified with everything I had. My joints locked in place, hands laying defenseless on my thighs, neck tilted, showing the exhaustion I feigned, all so I could stall his next attack and find him.

He knew I was faking. Otherwise, he would've struck already. No. He worried I had something planned, something he couldn't quite make sense of, so like a sneaky serpent, he hid and bided his time, believing he had all the time in the world. But he didn't. Soon he'd be dead.

"Taunting me, perhaps," Eligos whispered from afar, slightly to the right facing forward about six meters. I tightened my attention, pinpointing the slightest slither of his multitude of limbs seeping in and out of shadows. "I learned long ago not to arrogantly attack you. Play your game; I can wait for you to reveal your move."

I forced a cough, spitting blood I'd held down to add to feigned defeat and also relieve the thick burn in my throat. Blood dribbled down my chin. "That so?"

"Oh, yes." His voice echoed behind me, four and a half meters more centered than before. "I stalked you for the better part of a year, deducing the strength of the devil, believing my rebellion had left him wounded in the mortal realm, completely unaware you were a fake."

"When was that?" I licked my lips, savoring the taste of iron before letting the flavor fade so I could follow the near-silent drifting of Eligos moving to my left—now five meters exactly.

"It doesn't matter. What matters is my shortsightedness allowed me to fall into the clutches of a curious Fae seeking answers to questions I'd never once pondered."

"Bested by the baron?" I snickered. "He wasn't even that strong."

"His best years were behind him, having sunk most of his magic and power and influence into the creation of this villa." There was a gentleness in Eligos' voice, a hint of awe for Novus.

"Mad I killed your boyfriend?" I waited for the physical reaction it provoked… Nothing.

"Saved me the time," Eligos replied, no biting back rage or resentment, no hidden feelings whatsoever. Novus' death wasn't something I could exploit. Too bad. "While I lay captive by him for centuries, suffering the indignities of his experiments as he sought ways to properly utilize Diabolic essence in tandem with Fae magic, I eventually brokered a trust with him."

"How's that?" Carefully, I redirected essence into my fingernails, cautious and quiet.

"I showed him how proficiently I could take down my brethren, offering him more demons for experimentation all in some drive to control the very threads of the universe itself."

"And here I thought you loved us all. Guess it's okay to betray your own when you mean well."

That incited a reaction. Eligos' many limbs coiled round and round each other, muscles tightening and flexing.

I smiled, bright and bloody in his shadow realm, knowing my glistening teeth were the only light in the darkness since the comets had all but fizzled out. Their faded colors no longer reflected off Eligos' abandoned armor, but I kept my attention on the suit, awaiting any potential clank of metal.

He remained where he was, knotted in fury, too tense and unfocused to counter.

Now. Now was my opportunity to hit him where it hurt.

Unveiling my wings, I flapped them furiously, unyielding. I would beat Eligos. Before shifting my senses back to equal proportions, I caught Eligos unbinding his body, preparing to lunge for a strike.

Releasing my three tails, I bounced them against the shadowed floor, shifting my trajectory midway to colliding directly with Eligos, and went for my real target.

Eligos screamed, a pained, visceral, hateful sound as my claws met his suit of armor and sank into the metal. I shredded the stomach and hollowed out the back, brandishing a huge hole. I laced enough essence into that attack to know it'd take weeks, months, years for him to mend the wound. Hell, he'd be better off tossing the thing out with the trash. Host bodies, organic or not, didn't recover that well when ripped to bits by Diabolic attacks.

"That's for Mora, you cunt."

Eligos tackled me, the two of us entangled in the throes of chaotic combat, each slashing and hacking at the other. Too much of his essence had been redirected, aimed to fix his armor, his treasure, his most precious sentiment. I roared with laughter at his rage, ripping at his Diabolic flesh because he couldn't feel it without the suit, and didn't realize the deep level of damage I caused. Even in this Diabolic void, we were both outside of Hell, and sensation required possessing something from these lesser realms.

"You filthy—"

I reached out, plunging my claws into his jaw and ripping it off. The warmth of essence spilling from his gaping mouth fueled me, filled me. I continued attacking Eligos, gutting his meaty torso, hacking off limbs, taking deep bites of flesh and tearing it from him.

The shadows of his conjured world fell away, and we returned to the villa.

I stomped the few meaty chunks of his remains into the clay flooring.

"You lose." I relished the victory, taking delicious and sweet breaths before I'd seek out Mora to assist with her demon foes. Then we could enter the engine room together, where we'd save our Mythic and mortal companions.

Perhaps she'd won the battle. Despite amplifying my senses, I couldn't hear her rhythmic battle against the three demons Eligos had pitted against her.

I stared at the floor, the cracked tile flooring of a golem's hide. This wasn't the labyrinth.

Where was I?

I whirled around, studying the restored bars that had once held Wally. The cage that Novus used to trap Wally after tricking him into accepting a false offer of opportunity.

"It won't work," Eligos said.

I returned my gaze to the floor, where his broken remains had vanished. *Dammit.*

"Your measurements aren't precise enough to account for the glory of Diabolic essence," he continued; his voice came from the door leading out of this dungeon.

Eligos walked into the room adorned in his unblemished armor, aside from the single dent he kept for sentiment's sake, alongside the noble Fae whose head barely fit between the threshold, a literal representation of his arrogance. What was happening?

“You believe I underestimate your kind,” Novus said with a smile that consumed his bulbous head. “But I think you give far too much credit to Diabolics. For eternal entities possessing such veracity, you lot lack elegance and refinement, and honestly, it is only your base ability granted by devils that holds any value whatsoever.”

Eligos clenched his fists, golden eyes leering at the Fae, who waltzed toward the cage, strutting through me like a specter.

I was inside a memory. Fuck.

Eligos fed me his essence, pouring his consciousness into me, and I devoured it like an utter fool. This level of vulnerability was meant to be sacred. The most prying magics couldn’t peel away hidden truths without force, and I certainly didn’t attempt to delve into Eligos’ history. There was consent involved, even when I shared my mind, my truth with Wally, I knew more than anything I wanted him to see the sordid lies, frightened he’d reject me, and relieved beyond belief he had accepted me for all my flaws—no desire to fix or change them, but merely co-exist with a broken being that he hoped to grow with.

I loved Wally so much.

I missed him.

I needed to find him, which meant I had to escape this memory.

Novus stepped toward the cage, hand outstretched; his long snow-white fingers were bare without a single ring or jewel to accentuate his hand holding an orb. A Diabolic orb. I trembled in this memory.

Broken, bloody, beaten essence whirled toward the orb. I recoiled at the reminder of my own tattered flesh that’d peeled and fallen apart, sucked inside one of those awful artifacts once upon a time. All after I’d defeated a hateful magus who sought to lay siege on the Fae domain in an effort to strengthen the Collective’s hold. It took everything I had to slaughter him and his many mages, but it was the onslaught of Seattle's regiments striking at me under the guidance of the treacherous Abraham Remington who led them that had shocked me most that day.

This demon hadn't fallen to betrayal or lesser beings. No. I recognized the injuries. I currently carried them outside this memory. The demon funneled into the orb had been defeated by Eligos and lacked the resolve or ability to resist the overwhelming force of a Diabolic orb siphoning their very being into an orb twice the size of the one which contained me.

Their essence shuddered within the confines, discombobulated, and floating like the frost of a snow globe. Purple lightning crackled inside. I cocked my head. Not once in my time spent locked away in my orb had I found it possible to harness my essence to resist and fight back. Perhaps I hadn't tried enough, hadn't proven I didn't deserve life bound inside an orb.

I covered my ears, backing away, and unable to look at the demon fight for their freedom, a freedom Novus laughed at stealing.

"It worked." Novus spun around, joyous and vile, and suddenly I wanted to smash his skull in all over again. No. I wanted to go back and drag his death out longer, make it hurt more, make him beg and cry and barter before I shredded every trace of his existence. I had refrained on Wally's behalf, but a being as sadistic as Novus—one who used Diabolic orbs—deserved the pain only one taught in Hell could inflict.

"She's putting up more resistance than you said Diabolics could," Eligos said, his golden eyes studying the orb and flickering purple essence fighting against imprisonment.

"It doesn't matter; she's contained. We've successfully locked away our first demon," Novus said. "Soon, I'll create more of these, contain an army of Diabolics, and then we can capture the devil."

"The fake devil." Eligos held such venom in his words, more hatred acknowledging my impersonation than he ever had for the actual devil who punished all of us for our displeasing existence.

Novus wrapped his elongated fingers over the knight's plated shoulders, a gentle embrace bringing the two closer. "I allowed you to follow your fancy, send demons to taunt and test this *Beelzebub* roaming the mortal world. I can't be held accountable for your dreams not coming true."

"It's not that," Eligos said, practically spitting in his helmet. "I wasted resources, I deluded myself into believing I'd weakened a devil, and found a way to bring all of this carnage to an end."

"Not an end, dearest." Novus slid his hand up Eligos' neck, resting it atop the knight's head. "This is a beginning. A beginning for us. A beginning for the universe. A beginning for your dream. Soon, we'll defeat the false devil, and it won't matter what demons were lost seeking him out for a challenge."

What? I ground my teeth, recalling every demon that sought to challenge the devil Beelzebub in his mortal coil, believing him—*me*—weak and easy prey. It was difficult, but I slaughtered every foe and sent them to a true death, far out of the reach of their devil and home for resurrection. Still, I wondered too much, too long, if I carried a false bravado unbefitting of a devil. It turned out Eligos had learned the truth of my life and tested the limits of my power for the better part of a century. It wasn't until the 1800s Diabolics learned to avoid me. To think I resented Mora, believing it a part of her whispers and tests and manipulations.

I approached the memory of Eligos, seething and panting heavily against his untarnished armor, the armor I did well and true to ruin. "Fuck you. You sent five hundred demons to their deaths."

Give or take. Plus, I couldn't know if he was behind every demon who challenged me, seeking glory in their newfound freedom or retribution for their fallen devil at my hands—not my hands, but hands they believed were the cruelest devil. Hands that wrapped around their throats and choked the lives from their being, shattering their essence, devouring them entirely, and casting them into the oblivion of death.

"Yes, we created the orbs as a trap for you," Eligos said, turning his head while in his own memory. "But you haven't gotten to the best part yet."

I shuddered. How did he move within his own memory? I'd never experienced such a thing. It shouldn't be possible. He was self-aware while reexperiencing his own recollections? No. He should only be able to observe, not interact. Even the best mages couldn't handle both. And this type of memory exploration came more from their saturation magic than it did our essence.

The room swirled, twisting into an intoxicatingly painful surge of rage and anguish and destruction. I relished the high of the memory, lost in the blissful whirlwind of chaos until the room settled and everything stopped just in time for me to lock eyes with Magus Remington, only it wasn't Magus Remington. No, he was still young and sweet and filled with hopes and dreams and deceitful kindness. This was Abe, my friend, the one who believed Diabolics could co-exist with mages and Mythics.

I averted my gaze, even if he couldn't see me. Not really, since I was a phantom in this memory.

Still, his youthful face, his boyish expression, his haunting resemblance to Wally sent a shiver down my spine. How I hated the magus who lured me into love. Into what I deluded myself into believing love could be. It was a lie. I knew that now. Abe never accepted me. He teased me. He promised me things. He lied to me. All for his ambition.

Why was I seeing this memory? This was my memory, right? How did Eligos enter my memories?

Was that the purpose here? Eligos must've sought something buried in my past so he could exploit it—that was why he melded our minds and memories during the battle. I wouldn't allow it.

"You think he'll actually use it?" Eligos circled Abe, cloaked by a Diabolic shroud, so his presence remained hidden from the mage.

"But of course," Novus said, appearing out of thin air, revealing himself to Abe through a flicker of glittering lights.

Abe stared wide-eyed as Novus extended a hand holding a Diabolic orb. Not just any orb. The one which Magus Remington trapped me inside for nearly fifty years. The prison which removed me from the world. The Fae spoke to my mage captor in high-pitched tones, each piercing syllable something from the Sylvan language.

"How do you expect him to follow through on the plan?" Eligos scoffed, pulling Novus into the confines of his shroud, leaving Abe with the orb as his eyes curiously studied the symbols etched along the glass. "You gave him a message and washed away the memory in the same motion. Fae and their incessant need to remove all recollections of their presence."

"You Diabolics truly do lack finesse in every way." Novus tilted his head, whispering melodies to Remington. "We Fae make our moves delicately, precisely, and unbeknownst to lower beings. I've whispered inspiration, feeding his ego, fueling his passion, and sparking his curious desires. He'll trap the devil as his ambition dictates. He's already sought it, craved for a way to rid the world of the filth that is Beelzebub."

Eligos… Novus… Not only had they created the orbs and given my prison to Abe, but they had whispered the idea in his mind. I shook from the revelation. No. Abe was cruel and spiteful, taking glee in mocking me when alone together in the repository. Had that all come from the Fae whispers?

"My words will echo in his subconscious, fanning the flames of inspiration to his dream."

"It'd be easier if we took this false devil ourselves."

"No, it wouldn't," Novus said. "He possesses a lot of strength, more than we've been able to rightfully observe. We'll allow the mage and Collective to contain him. I predict betrayal of the heart is an easier thing to exploit than the shock of a Diabolic and Fae working together to bring this devil down."

I backed away, pressed against a wall, wishing to experience no more of this awful memory.

"In a few centuries, when our tests are fully completed, I'll retrieve the devil from wherever the Collective decides to store him," Novus explained. "In the meantime, we can relax knowing the mages have security no one but the Fae themselves can break through. And none of my fellow Court members have even a musing of curiosity for Diabolics like myself."

Centuries. They had planned to keep me locked away inside the repository, the vault, for centuries rotting inside that orb. But the coup against Magus Remington as Chancellor Alden and that misfit Ian conspired had led to my early release.

"When you got out ahead of schedule," Eligos said, breaking the mold of his memory and stomping toward me. "I convinced Novus it was necessary we collect you ourselves. You were once again being a loud tyrant, having decimated Seattle after some childish tantrum."

"That wasn't me." I snarled.

"You were also bound to a mortal with too many enemies for Novus or myself to account for, so he agreed it was best we keep you stored inside the villa until the right time to enact our plan came."

"And what is your plan?"

"To take that fragment of devil essence in your possession and create a weapon strong enough to pierce and kill devils." Eligos conjured an illusion of his golden lance—its transparent form indicated that much. "Adding it to the Diabolic essence I've already gathered and cultivated, I'll be able to enter Bael's realm and slaughter my first devil."

Of course, since Bael was one of the few devils who kept his Hell doorway open for any demon to come and go as they pleased. If I had to guess, he wanted to use my piece of devil essence to defeat and contain a full devil so he could finally pass through sealed Hell realms such as Beelzebub's.

"Precisely." Eligos' voice echoed, not from his armored helmet, but a rattling inside my head. His words beat against my skull, soft whispers slithering deep within my very being.

He'd gotten into my thoughts. I roared, resisting his intrusion.

Abe ripped loose from the strings holding him in place of this memory and approached me. This wasn't right. This was an illusion.

"No one could ever love you." His glare cut through me, almost as foul as it was on the battlefield when he encased me inside the orb so long ago. "You're unlovable, Beelzebub."

The symbols on the Diabolic orb glowed. No. I wouldn't allow it.

I raced out of the room, refusing to be locked away again. Never again.

"It's pointless, false devil," Abe and Eligos' voices chased me along the walls, following me at every turn. "You're worthless."

I'm not. I am loved. Wally loves me. He sees every flaw I possess and loves me still.

"Bez." Wally's beautiful voice cut through the taunting hatred. "Bez, help me!"

I flew through the empty Magus Estate, searching for Wally.

Each hall was empty, filled with haunting words from Abe and Eligos.

Finally, I caught Wally's scent and ran along the borders of this illusion.

He lay at the bottom of the stairs, bloody, lifeless. No. I shook my head until Wally's corpse vanished. This was a lie.

Wally screamed from afar. A sharp blade plunged into him, the sound of it gutted his insides, and he collapsed somewhere deep within the estate.

"It's not real. It's not real." I covered my ears. "This is an illusion."

Wally's bloodcurdling wail drained all the strength in my body. I collapsed to the floor, crawling ahead, compelled to chase the screams. To find him. Save him. I had to save him. Not here. Not in this lie. Outside this illusion.

Every second, every step, a new cry followed. Another death of Wally before I reached him before I saved him. A thousand times over, he died, leaving me searching the estate only to find corpses.

"You'll be alone forever," Eligos and Abe shouted in unison, an echoing horror only drowned out by Wally's dying screams.

Eligos hadn't shared his mind with me to unravel my secrets; he'd done so in order to lock me in a Diabolic nightmare of his making, forcing me to experience Wally's death again and again and again.

My essence was too weak to overpower this trap, my thoughts too fractured to navigate my own mind.

25

Walter

I had wriggled loose from the essence pouring free from the orbs and crawled away, but I couldn't catch my breath. Couldn't move anymore. I had to stand, fight, stop these newly freed demons from killing me or Kell. My eyelids drooped, heavy and exhausted. I pushed my hands off the ground, but my body collapsed, crumpling onto the floor, refusing to obey me. I closed my eyes…just for a second. All I needed was a second of rest, and then I'd figure out how to fix this problem.

Something slurped nearby.

I snapped my eyes open and shot up, panting. Essence had coiled around Kell's leg, wrapped around her calf like a giant slug.

"No," I shouted. Using the Demon's Demise, I sliced the spongy black tar until it fell back and flailed about.

I grabbed Kell's unconscious body, dragging her away from the essence before it regrouped and attacked us. It didn't, though. As I retreated, the essence slid away in the opposite direction.

It left a trail of slime as it wiggled away, reaching the glittery arm of the Fae, whose body had been scattered across the engine room. Once the essence reached the limb, it coiled around the arm, slurping it down like it had tried with Kell.

It wasn't the only released essence acting this way. All the pieces I saw slithered around aimlessly. There was something very off about these Diabolics who'd been released. None of them sought out me or Kell, not really. Yes, one latched onto her leg, but it should've attempted to possess her. Possess either of us in an effort to gain a host body and recover. Instead, all the essence did was lunge out, feeding on stray bits of magic, from the flesh of the Fae corpse to the magic of Kell's witch hat.

I ran over and kicked a chunk of essence before it had fully crawled inside Kell's hat. Picking it up, I chucked it farther away. Again, essence sniffed out the magic and moved at a snail's pace to reach the hat.

There was something very odd about this. Suddenly, it made sense why Eligos hadn't released these demons, only resurrecting the six in the orbs posted high up on the railing. Perhaps they'd been contained too long—but Bez had been locked away for nearly fifty years. How long would it take for a Diabolic to break down and lose their sense? I also had to take into account how the engine room drew upon their energy, tearing it apart and funneling it throughout the villa.

That was why Baron Novus continued collecting demons. However he'd merged them with Fae magics to break through Hell dimensions had caused the Diabolic essence to deteriorate, chiseling away at the consciousness of the demon, and probably burned the essence to nothing over time. Those six acted as the main source of transportation, and the other hundreds worked as secondary sources. Eligos sought to use a devil's essence because it would be infinite, never diminishing.

This essence also had a very different look about it. The black lacked the sheen metallic finish like others I'd seen. In fact, there was something necrotic about it, dying similar to the essence that belonged to the demon with sapphire eyes. There were faint flickers of color representing the aura of the unique demon, but like the blue lights that died out as Bez and Mora devoured the feathered demon.

If I had time to study them, observe them, I could figure out if this was a reversible effect or if they'd lost all form of sentience.

The portal above opened, shimmering a luminescent black light.

Eligos walked into the engine room with Bez at his side. I didn't understand. Bez's body looked a bit beaten, but there were no restraints, no reason he shouldn't fight back. Perhaps Eligos had convinced him I was in danger. Once he saw me, he'd realize there was no need to back down.

"Kneel." Eligos shoved Bez forward, toward his former body, currently impaled by the golden lance. "Now we can add the rest of the essence in your possession to my weapon."

Bez obeyed, dropping to his knees, his shoulders hunched, his posture sagging, and eyes vacant of essence—even the natural crimson irises and pink replacing the whites. Instead, he stared ahead with dull blue eyes and a fogged-over expression.

I'd witnessed Bez lock enough people in Diabolic nightmares to recognize the symptoms, but I didn't understand how Eligos had trapped Bez in one. Shouldn't Diabolics be immune to such things? No. Their elemental strikes were far more effective against each other than anything else. It would make sense they'd be equally susceptible to other Diabolic abilities. I struggled to stand, my body desperate for a break, but my mind unwilling to let Bez suffer another second. The horrors he must be enduring this second, something truly gruesome.

My thighs quaked, sending a tremble through my legs. Eligos had a plethora of nightmares to share with Bez, likely making him relive every awful thing he'd survived in Hell. The few things I'd seen, the handful he'd shared, and the endless eons of suffering he kept to himself.

"Let him go," I snapped, clenching my fists.

"If it isn't the little, worthless mage who holds no value without an ounce of essence coursing through your mortal coil." Eligos approached the railing, belting out his words with boastful diction.

I can play on that. Maybe.

"Worthless. Worthless Walter." Eligos mused, running his gloved hands along the metal rail. "That was his first true thought of you. You were always worthless to him, and seeing how much you have and how much you will fail him has left him lost in an eternal nightmare."

"Shut up." He was lying. The nightmare wasn't about me failing Bez, was it? The thought ate away at me because I had failed him. I should've moved faster, planned better, accounted for everything. Instead, I was worthless.

"I'll allow you to keep your life if you so wish. Not that it's much of one. Though, perhaps without a fake devil at your side, you can find a modicum of salvation."

Fake. I cocked my head. Fake. He knew Bez was a fraud. There was no anger in his tone, no sarcasm, no lilt of resentment for being deceived. He already knew. This wasn't some revelation he'd been tricked by a demon posing as a devil.

No.

I had replayed every single interaction with Ian and my mother for weeks after the carnage at the Magus Estate, attempting to figure out the subtle cues I'd missed of their deceit, their manipulation, their long con. I swore to myself I would never allow someone to make me a pawn in their game of powerplays again, and if I knew anything—I knew Eligos already realized Bez was a fake devil, which meant his goal, his trap, his intentions never involved capturing Beelzebub, but a lesser demon holding a piece of him.

I seethed with rage, pouring mana and saturating the area. It didn't matter what Eligos wanted, what he learned, or how he learned it. I'd fucking kill him all the same and rescue Bez from this bastard knight's clutches.

Nearby essence whipped about chaotically, closing in on my building magic. I needed to escape, to reach Bez, to stop Eligos. Aiming my palms at the saturated floor, I whirled the wind until it propelled me up to the railing. The breeze calmed my anxious mind, blissful, and for the few seconds I ascended, all the fear washed away, allowing me to plan.

There was no way I'd outmaneuver this demon, but he believed I was completely incompetent, unable to face true Diabolic strength. Worthless. Hopefully, he'd laugh off my attack the same way the last demon had when Kell retrieved her grenade launcher. I didn't have a weapon of that caliber or the essence to amplify, but I wouldn't need it.

Hovering in front of Eligos, I swung a fist. As expected, he didn't run, didn't even counter. He just let me bruise my knuckles against his helmet. I continued punching him with each hand, again and again, as the wind kept me afloat. It worked well until I enacted a glamour. I crashed on the metal grates and winced. Pushing upright, I punched Eligos in the torso, eyeing the gaping hole in his chest where dark blue, almost black like a night sky, limbs rolled around each other, coiling and knotting and weaving in a rhythmic pattern.

Just like with the first demon who chased me through the labyrinth, I used a glamour to hide my motives, cloaking the dagger I intended on stabbing Eligos with right in the break of his armor Bez must've provided for me. This demon's arrogance probably wouldn't even bother checking my glamour, analyzing it, believing it nothing more than a—

"Close." Eligos snatched my wrist and twisted it until I dropped the Demon's Demise. "I offer you an opportunity to leave with your life, unbound from a Diabolic, and this is what you do with your ephemeral existence? What a tragic thing you are."

I ground my teeth, tugging against his grip. While acting a fool, failing to release my wrist, I carefully cast saturation into the grates, trickling it toward Bez. If I could link to him, to his essence, I might be able to shake him loose from the nightmare.

SNAP.

"Ah," I screamed.

In one quick squeeze, Eligos broke my wrist. He didn't release my arm but maintained steady pressure, adding to the searing pain that sent a shudder through my aching body.

"You think I wouldn't notice you slinking toward your false devil with poorly cast magic?" He lifted me off the floor, holding me by my broken wrist. I clamped my teeth to bite back another scream as my arm burned. "I tire of you."

He threw me off over the railing, sending me plummeting to the lower reaches of the engine room. I cradled my broken arm, pushing the agony away and attempting to channel mana.

I barely cushioned my crash with the ground, bouncing back at the last second with a poorly worded repulsion incantation. I lay there, unable to think, plan—I couldn't even see straight.

Essence circulated around me, primal and base, lacking any real awareness as it lapped at my fleeting mana. It would do better possessing me, but it had no understanding of how given it lacked sentience.

I widened my eyes. That was it.

Bez refused to possess me after losing so much essence because he worried about the collision of consciousnesses, but these Diabolics no longer had a consciousness to collide with mine.

Still, this idea would probably kill me—a mortal or Mythic could only contain so much essence inside them at any given moment before it destroyed them. Bez took precise measurements when sharing his essence, very particular to offer enough to keep me safe, us connected, but not so much it devoured me from within. In order to stop Eligos, I'd need a lot. Enough to heal my injuries, to rescue Bez, to keep up with the knight's abilities. Enough to kill the demon who harmed my boyfriend.

I grabbed a shard of glass from a broken orb that stuck to the essence, which fed on the fading incantation I'd cast. Looking away, I sliced my palm. Sure, I'd already broken the wrist, but something about actually seeing the cut made it hurt more. Like a fucking shot. I shivered at the thought of a needle stabbing my bicep. The literal worst.

Shaking away my squeamishness, I blew air onto my broken bone, slowly mending it through a simple healing spell I'd learned from Sarai during our years at the academy and had now found a masterful hack for thanks to Kell and her wicked ways.

Craving the fresh mana, the essence crawled toward me. Pinpricks hit my skin as the black sludge slithered into my open wound. I bit my other hand, stifling a yelp. Alerting Eligos would make all this for nothing. Let him think I'd fallen and passed out. Let him think he'd won.

Once the essence made its way inside me, I took a deep breath, searching for its presence. It felt nothing like Bez's essence. There was no connection, no emotion, just raw energy. I needed more.

I slapped my broken hand onto the ground, summoning lightning until it crackled black, indicating a trace of Diabolic essence had truly rooted itself through my veins.

Essence sought me out, creeping toward me until a small horde surrounded me. Reeling back the tiny bit of essence inside me, I let the lightning burn bright and white with natural elemental casting that baited the mindless essence which stalked me. Each lumpy tendril plunged into my open wound, adding to my strength.

Inadvertently, my palm healed along with the joints in my wrist. I snatched the few remaining bits of essence that missed out on my magic due to my sealed skin and chomped down on them. Thick sludge slid against my tongue as they squirmed in my throat, latching onto my lips, reminding me of the horrid sight of Bez eating the live octopus he'd smooshed between a giant s'more. I gulped, swallowing the tarry energy.

My body buzzed. Mana and Diabolic essence hummed around me. This would work.

I balled a fist, staring at the literal aura radiating from my pores—I could see it all, nothing Diabolic hidden from my vision. Despite the presence, I didn't feel the faintest trace of anyone else inside me, not like how possession would work. Not even how it felt having a piece of Bez linking me to him. This was just pure Diabolic power coursing through my veins.

Willing the essence, it obeyed me with the same ease Bez's had over the last few months. I lunged, sending a torrent of telekinesis below me that sent me rocketing off the lower level of the engine room and back up to the railing beside Eligos.

I swung a fist, releasing all the pent-up rage and pain into a telekinetic punch. It landed, hitting the dent Eligos had kept on his suit of armor, sending cracks through the chest piece like splinters that added to the gaping hole in his stomach.

Maintaining the flow, I swiveled around, floating further behind the demon knight, ready to obliterate his armor altogether. Eligos caught my fist, squeezing tight until I released my telekinesis. *Dammit.*

"You think what you stole is enough to challenge a true Diabolic?" Eligos' golden irises leered. "These fragments you've gathered pale in comparison to the demons they once were."

Pulling his arm back and jerking me forward, he slammed my head into his helmet before flinging me back to the ground. I crashed hard, but it hadn't hurt. The essence protected me, shielded the pain, and helped me land a lucky shot. But I needed more if I wanted to stop him.

"Perhaps enough to snuff your mortal existence, but you won't have enough to challenge a real demon."

Racing to a pillar, I smashed all the orbs, releasing Diabolic essence that I quickly snatched and devoured, taking so much into my body, everything slowed. I smashed another pillar and another and another. If a dozen wouldn't stop Eligos, then perhaps a hundred would. My muscles rattled, flexing, strengthening. Every cell in my being pulsed like a billion independent warriors radiating power and demanding satisfaction for the anger consuming me—a fiery fury fueling my movements.

I shouted, throaty and feral as I commanded the essence to coat my hands in sheen black claws. The subtle hues of countless Diabolic auras bubbled and shimmered, creating a rainbow effect on my talons.

Using the same tactic as before, I studied Eligos' movements, hoping to land a few hits before he tossed me aside, learn his patterns, and come back a third time, then a fourth, a fifth—however many more times it'd take to kill this demon.

Only that didn't happen.

Eligos moved but so slowly that I landed a hit, darting around him, landing a second, and repeating this cycle again and again. I kept the strikes light, relying on the talons to nick his armor, repeating the process like the steady flow of erosion. I couldn't move faster than him and hit hard at the same time, so I went for tactically wearing him down. Eventually, he shifted his posture, pivoting away from me as shadows blossomed behind him, leading to his own private void world where he planned to hide and counter, make it impossible for me to track.

I eyed my discarded dagger, the Demon's Demise, which would kill him. Too far. Not enough time. My heartbeat pounded, thrumming in the back of my eardrums faster than the flutter of a hummingbird.

"Not happening." I snatched his armor, digging my talons into the hole and holding him here. I remembered how Bez snatched me when under Ian's control, preventing me from returning to Mora's void realm in Seattle.

It hit Eligos' armor like a cyclone: the shadows and I held the demon like a game of tug of war. And this particular rope—*his armor*—was precious to the demon.

His void closed as essence funneled out, prioritizing energy to fix his ripped suit. That'd be his downfall.

In a blink, I whirled behind Eligos, slashing deep into the back of the suit, claws tearing into the flesh of his Diabolic body coiled inside the armor.

When he swirled to strike, I circled him, everything moving in slow motion, then I'd hit Eligos heavy-handed, snap the world back into place, before zipping away and repeating it all over again from a different angle.

A quick blitz here, a deep gash there, and when the opportunity presented itself, a light nick to his actual body peering out to fix his beloved armor.

"Enough." Eligos bellowed, unleashing black flames in every direction.

I eyed Bez, who remained knelt and undisturbed. Having spent my entire life questioning my control over the Pentacles of Power, my ability, my comprehension of magic—I knew how to exploit his elemental attack. Taking a deep inhale, projecting essence into the air, I sucked in all the oxygen while using my Diabolic power to lightly stab at the essence Eligos didn't keep rooted to his core.

It smothered the fire, but Eligos didn't relent. Instead, he snapped his fingers, replacing the smolder with black lightning.

Wind wouldn't work. The air itself was too dry to siphon moisture from, and there were no large bodies of water in the engine room, so I traced a single symbolled low-level incantation for creating bubbles. Such a simple spell, it hardly cost an ounce of mana, and I managed to trace dozens of them in seconds thanks to the speed of a Diabolic.

Quite possibly the silliest spell I'd ever memorized, but the first one to pop into my head, allowing me to further dry out the air, amplifying the lightning Eligos had summoned. It moved faster than he'd planned, and when I waved the bubbles with telekinesis, pulling in stray strikes of static along the way, his high conductor of a suit sent all his electricity surging through him.

"I can do this all day." I ground my teeth, ignoring the swelling heat rising in my body. Bez's body always burned hot, but in all the months I'd shared in his essence, the sensation never struck like this. Sure, I'd feel the warmth of his presence, but this was like my blood boiled, scalding my insides.

I needed to expel essence and quickly. The longer it dwelled within me, the faster it'd liquify my organs. Darting ahead, I blurred around Eligos, shredding his armor with heavy-handed smacks. My claws tore the suit, my palms dented it, and the essence within me dulled the ache of hitting metal again and again.

"Wally, what have you done?" Bez stared at me in complete shock.

His crimson irises had returned, snapped free from the bounds of a Diabolic nightmare. Relief hit me until those beautiful eyes widened, evaluating the situation, comprehending the lengths I'd taken in his absence.

I must've looked savage, ruthless, maniacal—things I didn't have the time to worry about at the moment because this demon needed to die by any means. All in all, Bez didn't have to worry about my behavior. He could keep the bad boy cap in our relationship. I only did what was necessary. He hadn't discussed it, we hadn't found the time, but I understood Eligos meant something to him once upon a time. We would discuss it afterward; he could divulge what he wanted and keep quiet about what he didn't want until, hopefully, a day came when he wanted to share his feelings. What mattered was we'd have the time to figure it out after I ended this.

Metal collided with my jaw, cracking the bone and knocking me into the railing. I stretched my mouth wide, popping the many tiny bones until they all healed and clicked back into place.

In those few seconds, Eligos sprang forward, skirting past Bez and reaching for the golden lance embedded in Bez's former body. He ripped it from the corpse, spun around, and aimed the weapon at my devil, still on his knees and looking at me with the most perplexed expression.

Not happening. Not a chance. "You won't ever touch Bez again!"

I chased him, drawing the dagger to my hand with a telekinetic pull, and stabbed Eligos in the hole in his back.

Twisting the blade, I tore through his insides, hacking at limbs, ignoring the slaps of erratic tendrils, watching the golden glow of his essence fluctuate irregularly.

I expelled my essence, sending it forward and seeping into the cuts I'd created, allowing it to consume Eligos. This wasn't like when Bez and Mora devoured the sapphire-eyed demon. Eligos and the essence linked to me cannibalized one another until only droplets of black oozed out of the suit, attempting to flee. A golden shimmer of life.

I burned it away to nothingness, charred the last remnants of Eligos' existence from this world.

"Wally," Bez called out, eyes locked onto my shaky body, not even bothering to check for threats.

There were no threats for him to worry about. I'd actually done it. I'd killed Eligos.

My knees buckled. Instinctively, I cast telekinesis to steady my stance; the vestiges of what remained kept me upright until essence pooled out of my pores, stabbing my skin. I winced, holding back an aching scream as it peeled away layers before fluttering away with pieces of flesh. It hurt. Sores covered my arms. It was okay. I'd survived it.

My body convulsed, all equilibrium lost, and I tumbled over, unable to brace the impact.

Bez zipped so quickly, I lost sight of him before blinking and found him holding me when my eyes opened. I guess all the essence had finally faded away, meaning I couldn't keep up with Diabolic movements again.

It didn't matter. I'd won. I smiled at Bez's sweet embrace, gently holding me with one arm wrapped under my legs and the other around my back as he softly set me down.

Bez cried. Tears splashed my face, sizzling against my skin. Why was he crying?

I reached out to brush away his tears.

"I tried…tried to…stop…" I gasped between words, unable to pull any air into my lungs. "I wanted to help y—"

A surge of pain struck, coursing through my arm, spreading across my chest like a sudden ripple in the water and erupting throughout my entire body. Fiery explosions of pure agony. Each breath hit sharply, cutting my throat. Bez's gentle touch was sandpaper against my skin. Bez's cries pierced my ears until a dull hum replaced it, an incessant ringing. My vision blurred, and all the light stung my eyes, needles stabbing at my retinas making me tear up.

The last thing I saw as the darkness swept in was Bez shouting. Was he shouting? He had that adorable crinkle in his brow when he got pouty and grumpy, but the tears. Still couldn't make sense of those…

26

Beelzebub

Wally stopped moving, his body limp in my cradled clutches. Still, his grip hadn't released his dagger—valiant and vigilant to win this fight. A fight I should've shielded him from. Delicately, I unwrapped his fingers one by one until the blade clinked against the metal grates. Fatigue had washed over Wally's body, but he didn't have any injuries. Nothing external at least.

Every single cell in his body came to a halt, steam seeping from his pores releasing the final traces of Diabolic essence he had coursing through him. What was he doing with so much essence? What was he doing with essence to begin with? I clamped my jaw. This was my doing. My inability to stop Eligos.

Burying my doubt, I focused on what I could do *now*. I would fix this. Had to.

I channeled my own essence into my fingertips, piercing a tiny hole into Wally's chest and sending my essence to repair the damage. Closing my eyes, I fixated all my attention to the piece of essence swirling in Wally. There was so much damage. His heart had rips and tears, bits of muscle tissue floated around the organ, lost chum after it stopped beating. Blackened decay ran along the veins and arteries leading to liquified insides. Every part of Wally had been riddled with damage, from melted organs, shredded muscles, to rotted bones picked clean. In a matter of minutes, the essence he took had devoured what little mana he had and feasted upon what remained soaked into his mortal coil.

He had died.

Dead. Gone.

No. I shook him.

"Walter." My voice cracked. "Wake up."

Nothing.

I pressed my hands to his chest, forcing a beat to stir, to waken.

Nothing.

I struggled to breathe, calling out his name again.

Nothing.

I poured more essence into his body, commanding it to stitch together what remained, willing it to make the chunks of his heart beat again, and using it to create a flow of circulation as a way of accounting for the lack of blood he had left.

It didn't work.

His hazel eyes were glossy, hollow, and empty. There was nothing I could fix, nothing my essence could heal. He'd taken his final breath. All my essence did was stir a corpse.

"W-w-ally." I pulled him into a hug, crying inconsolably.

I'd failed him. I'd lost him. The nightmare Eligos locked me in was right—I would be alone forever.

"Where's that damn knight?" Mora's feet dragged as she shuffled into the engine room, subtle but there was a pained ache in her steps. "Way to leave me with those three demons. No worries, though. Naturally, I made a game of it before slaughtering—"

Mora silenced an almost audible reaction. The stiffening of her posture lessened, either too exhausted from her battle or no longer finding the need to present herself with poise.

"Bez, I'm…" Mora knelt beside me, blood seeped into the fabric of her clothes, and trickled out of deep slashes. Wounds that would heal given the host body she'd picked.

That's it.

"We can bring him back." Gently, I set Wally down onto the metal grate floor. "Give him your blood. He's not a Mythic and there's no essence so Maurice's blood will resurrect him."

"Bez, I can't. It won't work."

"You haven't even tried."

"Vampirism is a dice roll and requires a mortal to die with the blood in their system. Walter is… Wally's already dead."

"I might have a spell." Kell wheezed, dragging herself forward with each step.

Mora darted to her wife in a haze, wrapping an arm around Kell's back and steadying her shaky stance. "You don't have the magic to cast anything right now."

"Might need a little more essence, then I'll be right as rain." Kell had a weak smile, her somber eyes locked on Wally.

"No. Any more essence and you risk…" Mora swallowed hard. She wouldn't say it but all three of us knew what she'd stopped shy of warning. She wouldn't risk Kell being consumed and killed by ingesting too much Diabolic essence in one go. A failure I hadn't protected Wally from, a failure that killed him so I could live. Fact was, it was probably only the half-century of regularly sharing in Mora's essence that offered Kell such immunity to the effects when taking in larger doses like what she required after being set ablaze.

"I know necromancy spells, it'd be easy to reanimate his corpse, but I need magic now," Kell said, pleadingly. "The longer we wait, every second he lays there dead, memories are fading, falling away to the afterlife. It'll be impossible to restore them all if we wait."

"No." The word burned my throat, cascading sinking guilt through every fiber of my being.

Every second that ticked took away a memory. I'd witnessed a few zombie and revenant resurrections, they took hours under the best circumstances, most took days to enact. If we brought Wally back, he'd only be a shell of his former self, spending his eternity inside a rotting body and unable to remember half the things that brought him joy, mind lost in a fog. I couldn't do that to Wally. I couldn't punish him because I feared living without him.

"But I can't live without him, either." I caressed his damp blond curls.

Now that all the tension of pain had released from his body, Wally looked at peace.

With a telekinetic pull, I dragged the Demon's Desire dagger into my grip.

"Let's not get hasty, Bezzy." Mora approached, careful in her steps and words. "I could, perhaps, parlay with Bael. It's been centuries, but we parted on mostly good terms."

"That's right." I held the tip of the blade close to my chest. "A devil can do or undo anything at their whim."

"He never did quite comprehend the fragility of morality," Mora continued. "But he's a sentimental old fool."

"No." I swallowed hard, definitive. "Wally's body wouldn't survive the trip to Hell."

"He might," Kell chimed in. "I can figure out how to travel, maybe circumvent some stuff to account for the massive loss of Diabolic essence fueling transport. Give me some time and I'll have this villa front and center in Bael's Court."

"I'd advise against that, love," Mora said.

"If the only thing that can fully restore the dead is a devil, then a devil will bring Wally back." I plunged the dagger into my chest, grinding my teeth as demon essence raged against me—

instinctively protective when I carved upward and through my sternum. "I may be a fake, a fraud, but I have devil essence."

"Bez, ripping it out could kill you. For all you know that essence will fade the second its untangled from your body."

"It won't." I struggled, slicing tendrils of demon essence interwoven with threads of devil essence. Power that'd protected me for centuries. Power that'd guided my path. Power that'd kept me alive through difficult battles. "Devils are undying, refusing to accept defeat."

"You don't even know if throwing away those pieces will result in bringing back Wally." Mora stood in front of the pooling blood and essence pouring from me.

Scarlet and black whirled together, crimson sparks of light revealing how much of my essence spilled out during this endeavor.

"The piece of the devil I took lacks sentience, but it still has a will to live." I paused, ignoring the needled tar stabbing me from inside, attempting and failing to stitch together the large gash I'd crudely carved across my torso. "If I give Wally this essence, it'll restore him."

I hoped. I had to hope because otherwise he was gone forever.

"You don't exactly have a lot of your own essence to work with," Mora said.

"Got a whole slab of 'abandoned me' pieces over there." I nodded to the headless corpse Eligos kept propped as a trophy, a lure, something to bait me back to the engine room to steal the only part of me he wanted—the devil. "I'll regather it, collect my strength… After."

"Fine." Mora knelt beside me, further ruining her outfit as it soaked in the pool of carnage. "Let me at least help."

"Maurice is going to be pissed when he sees what you did to his clothes."

“He can eat me.” Mora took the dagger, and delicately cut between the threads of my essence; her touch held artistry, reminiscent of how she would handle a former lover.

As tendrils lunged from my chest cavity, whipping about and striking indiscriminately, Mora unleashed her own creating a black shield with an emerald hue.

“Thank you, Mora,” I said as warm blood spilled from my lips.

27

Walter

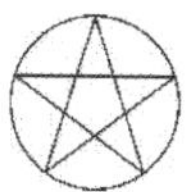

I floated through darkness, empty and silent. Bez's voice had been the last thing I'd heard before…nothing. Nothingness stretched long and infinitely no matter which direction my consciousness carried me. It must've been my thoughts alone in these shadows. I couldn't see my body, couldn't feel my limbs. I couldn't feel anything, not even my voice which I tried desperately to use and cry out for someone, something.

Would I float adrift in this emptiness forever? Was this where death led? I'd always heard…

"Well, well, well." Eligos' valiant arrogance clawed at the shadows, casting ripples in every direction. "Don't you have some mortal afterlife you should be wandering toward? How did you land in the serene embrace of oblivion? This comfort is reserved for Diabolics."

I whirled around until a shimmer of golden eyes stared back.

Again, I tried to call out. Curse him. Shout. Anything to express the disdain, the disgust I held for the dead demon knight.

"You worthless little thing." He chuckled. "Dying with so much essence in your body clearly dragged your mortal soul into the Diabolic afterlife, a place your feeble simplicity can't comprehend. Such inferiority, you can't even manifest a form to explore where you've stumbled."

Eligos stepped from the shadows, revealing a body of armor that tore through the darkness, brightening it with the silver suit.

So, this was where Diabolics went. But it was only the two of us. Shouldn't there be others?

"They're resting," Eligos answered. Could he hear me? Was I speaking without words? "Your thoughts stir loudly, silence them or I will silence them and you. I won't allow you to disturb the slumber of your betters."

I ground my teeth. The actual sensation of my locked jaw hit and while I couldn't see anything else from my body, I'd gotten one step closer to navigating this abyss. Not that I wanted to.

"Our eternal resting place is merely a quiet oblivion, a waiting room so to speak. If our devil so desires, they can pull us back from this infinite ocean," Eligos explained, a wicked grin echoed from his words. I couldn't see his expression beneath the helmet, but I felt it shifting in the shadows. "Something tells me Beelzebub, the real one, won't be resurrecting my lost essence. For the best. I think I'll enjoy the silence. A just reward, a calm slumber."

"It won't be all that calm or silent." A feminine voice slithered behind me. "Especially, not with what we have in store for you, Eligos."

Something sprang from the shadows, snapping off a piece of Eligos' armor. "What's the meaning of this?"

The metal sparked in the darkness as something shredded it like running a power saw through a pipe. That strike was merely the first of hundreds, each lashing out, taking a tiny piece of Eligos, illuminating the shadows with fireworks of electricity, devouring and destroying his precious armor. With his suit stripped and a blaze of rainbow lights in the darkness, all that remained of the demon knight was contorted limbs in the shape of his lost suit.

The array of lights faded, lost to the shadows once more, and Eligos went to unravel one of his limbs, pulling an arm from the bundled center of his form. But the darkness struck faster than the demon knight, ripping his limb off and dragging it behind the veil of shadows. This continued, something sprang from oblivion and snatched away a part of Eligos, then vanished to nothingness with the prized piece of the knight's body, his essence. Whoever, whatever did this moved so quickly I felt the breeze against my cheeks.

"Why?" Eligos cried out.

"You tortured us first. We thought it best to return the favor," the voice said behind me, but I was too enamored by what happened to Eligos to turn and face the speaker. And too frightened. Would I be next?

"No. You don't understand. I did all this for our demon brethren. I had a plan. I was going to release every demon from the devils. I was going to give us a choice. Something we haven't had in eons." Eligos fought back, a futile effort as the shadows beneath him opened and beings snatched away the many limbs bunched together creating his legs. "I only wanted Diabolics to be seen for our glory, our potential, our valiance."

"And where were we meant to be during this grand plan for all demon kind?" A woman's shape stepped from the darkness, the form merely a silhouette against the shadows with a purple aura lining the demon's representation. "You locked us in those orbs until our minds rotted away, trapped alive by your contraptions, unable to think or feel or rest. You sought to steal the slumber of oblivion from us, so now we'll ensure you find no peace here, Eligos."

The demon knight shrieked. Claws tore chunks out of him again and again until all that remained were golden eyes shimmering in the blackness of this void of death. The silhouetted demon plucked the eyes from the shadows and crushed them.

"I'd like to thank you, Walter," the demon said. "You released me, released so many of us."

I shivered as the silhouette approached. This demon along with all the others that leapt from the darkness—they were all from the pieces of Diabolic essence I consumed, the dozens of demons whose power I'd ingested to defeat Eligos. The power that ended this fight, ended me. But it saved Bez and… I choked back a sob. Dwelling on it hurt, thinking about it hurt, realizing I had nothing but haunting darkness in my future hurt.

"It's been far too long since I remembered myself, remembered who I was. It's a liberating, exhilarating sensation. I've missed myself so much."

"And who were you?" I asked, eyes widening at the sound of my own voice resonating in oblivion.

"I was called Agares."

Was. Because this demon had died. I had died. My eyes welled up.

"I'd like to thank you too, Agares." I forced a smile, realizing I needed to make the best of my new forever, and show gratitude for small kindnesses. "This wasn't how I expected spending my death. Not that I spent a lot of time planning for the afterlife. Still, pretty sure Eligos was going to make my death or my being dead gruesome."

I cringed at the silence that rippled beneath my feet, containing all traces of the demon knight consumed and destroyed and left in the clutches of those he'd trapped in orbs. There was no sensation, no sound, no anything, but I knew—*knew*—he was locked below me enduring unspeakable horrors.

"Not sure you'll be enjoying the freedom of death for long." Agares raised a silhouetted hand, caressing my face.

Admittedly, the act was gentle, kind, but the words were ominous, and I worried as a mortal soul I might find oblivion to be the most frightening place to end up trapped within.

"W-w-what do you mean?" I crept back, watchful of other demons that might lunge from the shadows and snatch me away. Not that I could stop them. I couldn't do anything here.

"Looks like there is still a spark of life in you," Agares said, purple irises shimmering as the darkness became replaced by white.

When the bright light finally faded, fuzzy colors came into place. Filmy sunlight cascaded across all the cloudy shapes and for half a second I thought I'd been dragged into the sky. My body was clammed up, little hands wrapped around each other to keep from fidgeting in my seat.

Why were my hands so small?

"You're probably quite proud of that magic you cast," Chancellor Alden's voice sent a spike of fear through my body.

Mother. What was she doing here?

The sharpness in her cold tone shaded away the blurry colors settling the concrete image of her home office, everything perfectly in place, cataloged and accounted for except a single tome she kept afloat beside me through several incantations.

I gulped. Well, I didn't do anything. This was like a dream—or since it involved my mother a nightmare—memory of the first time I'd accessed historical files on the Mythic Council. Only at seven years old, I didn't understand these particular files stored in the spelled text of pages she kept sealed were highly classified and not for musing curiosities.

"I'd be proud of you, too. The incantations used to seal this tome were quite intricate." She leaned closer, not a single hair out of place, not a single line on her unchanging expression as she hid her feelings, but I'd caught the faintest traces of anger from the lilt of her voice, which made me listen, anxious and attentive. "Except, you didn't crack these protective wards, did you Walter?"

I shook my head no, catching a glimpse of crimson drifting by the bookshelf, shimmering between the afternoon sunlight spilling light into the room.

"You made Alistair help you, trying to drag him into your snooping curiosities." This was the first of many conversations where my mother expressed her contempt for my obsessive researching and dreams of being lost in books all day, every day. "I find your desire to study, to learn, admirable. What I don't find admirable, Walter, is your laziness. Alistair has his own studies and shouldn't be distracted because you wish to lollygag."

"I'm sorry. I helped him figure out…" I bit my lip, keeping to myself how I'd deciphered her supposedly intricate incantations and found an easy workaround to the spell. Chancellor Alden wouldn't care how my knowledge bested her security, merely that I lacked the mana to unravel the seals on my own.

"I wish you'd apply this eagerness to practicing and mastering your control over the Pentacles of Power." She didn't hide the bitterness in her words, using them to cut me down during a scolding that'd last for the better part of an hour and would be revisited during a lecture at dinner in front of our entire family. "You haven't accessed any of your mana yet. Aldens do not rely on the kindness of others to cast on their behalf. We offer support. We master our own magics. We are the shield of the Collective, unbreakable. You are a chink in that shield."

She poked my forehead, ensuring I listened. My little hands squeezed around each other harder as I settled into this awful memory. Why was I reliving this memory of all memories? I wanted to see Bez, relive any of our encounters from the one-sided conversations in the repository, to the sweet nothings he'd whisper to me when he thought I'd dozed off. Hell, I'd settle for our first interaction when he attempted to murder me. That memory was less unsettling than any of the experiences I had with my mother.

"Psst. Psst." A hushed aside plucked me from reliving this memory. I turned my head, ignoring the reprimand from my mother, an act that went unnoticed by Chancellor Alden as she continued berating the empty chair I'd slid off of in search of whoever called out to me.

At the door of the office stood a small silhouette taking shape through shades of crimson. The red sparkled, illuminating four small, curled ram horns, three slender flicking tails, and a pair of tiny feathery wings. Bez. Only smaller but not like when he'd lost his essence. No, this version was childlike, same build and stature as myself at seven.

"Bez? What's happening?"

"Come with me." He extended a cloaked hand and outstretched claws.

I grabbed his hand, interlocking my fingers with his ghostly grip. We rushed out of the office and ended up in the Magus Estate. Only it looked different. Well, the doors at least. Each one was labeled with my name and an event. A moment, a memory, a fleeting thought I'd had during all the years I'd spent in this place whether for family functions, academy visits, or work.

"What is this?"

"Memories," Bez said, his voice light and squeaky with the faintest hint of rasp. "Gotta grab them all. Don't wanna leave any behind."

"Leave them where?"

"Oblivion," he answered. "Come on, we need to hurry."

We darted down the hallways, each doorway shimmered with crimson glitter before fading as we passed by it. When we reached the foyer, Bez paused and cocked his head back. At least I think so.

It was hard to tell from the lighting here and how it reflected off his silhouette.

Black sludge oozed down the stairs, a slow trickle then a gushing flood of essence consuming the entirety of the Magus Estate.

"What's happening?" I shivered.

Bez secured his hold on my hand; the fear washed away because I had nothing to worry about with him here. "Doesn't matter. Just the devil doing his thing. We got the memories here, let's go."

We stepped outside, but the front of the estate was replaced by the courtyard of the academy I'd attended.

"Are we here to grab more memories?"

"No. Got them all. You hadn't been lost in oblivion long, so they weren't that scattered," Bez explained.

"But why here?"

"You liked this place. I wanted us somewhere peaceful."

Right. I didn't talk about my time at the academy much, but like everything I shared with Bez over the years while he was locked inside the orb, he listened and remembered even my most random topics. He was simply sweet that way. I loved soaking in the sunshine and cool breeze of the academy courtyard, lost in my textbooks where no one bothered me. Not teachers, not classmates, and not my family.

"Now we just have to wait for the devil to do his job until you wake up."

"You said that before. What do you mean the devil?" I asked, quirking a brow. "We're waiting for you to finish healing me?"

"Looks like you can't do anything right, Little One." The hauntingly deep voice reverberated throughout the sunny courtyard, splintering the sky, and shattering the image of the academy in a billion shards of glass like snowflakes whisked away by a frigid gust.

Stone walls bound together by what looked like lava surrounded us. Bez's silhouette recoiled, turning my gaze from the looming shadow that approached.

"Don't look. Don't listen," Bez whispered. "It's just a broken memory. Not yours. You don't need it."

"Once again, I gift you an opportunity to prove your worth, and you fail."

"I'm sorry, Beelzebub," a young Bez said, his voice squeaky and scared. "I'll do better."

I turned to see him knelt on the floor, gray skin covered in blood and essence, deep slashes dug into his hunched back, and chunks of his stomach ripped away. The silhouette faced me toward the wall, making me stay very still as this memory unfolded.

"Wake up, Wally," Bez said, the voice of the grown demon, not the child. "I need to know you're okay."

"You shamed me in that tournament, allowing yourself to be bested by some damned demon from another realm," Beelzebub's voice sliced the air, creating a suffocating heat. "I am your god-king, and this is how you repay my tutelage? How you honor the life I grant you? You can't fight. You constantly fail to protect that which is assigned to you. You made for a terrible delegate, lacking any artistry for diplomacy, and I wouldn't waste the effort sending you to infiltrate another Hell. What can you offer the greatest devil of the best dominion? You can't even serve well. Why did I bring you back? I should've left you in oblivion to rot, you worthless thing."

"I'll do better."

"Perhaps you need a reminder of what happens to weak Diabolics."

A sizzle and pop of skin burning, bubbling, blistering rang in this room, only silenced by the loud wails Bez released. The snap of something whipping through flesh and meat, splattered essence with fizzling flickers of crimson onto the walls.

My heart pounded. My eyes watered. I tried to see the horrors inflicted but the silhouette held me tight, shielding me from the cruelty of Beelzebub.

Bones crunched. Bez's light voice cracked and went hoarse from screams of agony. His sobs trickled in and out as pure black essence seeped between the cracks of the walls, eating away the layers of the room, swallowing everything including the memory of horrors Bez endured.

Blackness swallowed the crimson silhouette, snuffing out the spark of demon essence that'd found me adrift in oblivion. This darkness wasn't a return to the nothingness. It was empty, pure power.

It all clicked together as the devil's violent presence slithered across my body, his primal base existence vibrating underneath my skin. It was undiluted devil essence coursing through my veins, so strong it pushed away Bez's Diabolic energy that guided me through the memories.

I opened my eyes and sprang forward. My head nearly butted Bez's as I sat up, taking deep breaths of life.

I was alive.

"Wally." Bez's face was splotchy but his expression lightened with a warm smile. Blood dripped down his chin. Slashes covered his chest and torso, deep and unhealing. I recoiled, pained by his suffering, suffering from the memories and what he endured to help me, save me. Beside him lay the discarded Demon's Demise which he must've used to hack through his essence, restoring me.

"I was… I was…"

"You're alive now, Wally. That's all that matters." Bez hugged me; a strong grip that pulled me in tight and should've hurt, should've something… I was too dazed, too lost to register the sensation of his embrace, but so grateful for it. Grateful for Bez. Grateful to have him in my life again because I was alive.

Alive. Bez saved me.

"You…you saved me by—"

Bez pulled away just enough to kiss me, silence my slow ramble. I was usually quicker with my words, quicker than his seductive tongue, but the haze of oblivion still lingered in my thoughts. So much was jumbled out of order. Memories piled on top of memories, mixed with the events in the darkness, and the cries of a young Diabolic who sought freedom from his cruel devil.

Bez's quivering lips were soft, delicate, frightened too much and I'd break. I didn't feel breakable though. In fact, quite the opposite. More than anything I wanted his passion, his fury, his love. I needed it. Craved it.

Sliding my tongue against his, I added a subtle surge of lightning. Inadvertently, perhaps, but the static buzz that passed between our locked lips amplified the intensity of this moment, making my entire body hum from the slightest graze of his fingers against my skin. I could finally feel him, feel his touch in the full electrical glory it offered.

"Wally." Bez broke away, forehead pressed to mine keeping the warmth and spark zipping between us.

He took careful breaths, practiced and forced by the look of it, for lungs he'd removed the receptors or need of air. Why? Was he reminding me to breathe? I didn't want to stop for air, and I didn't need it. My empty lungs didn't call out for oxygen. They, like every cell of my being, called out for Bez. For the flavor of his kiss, the touch of his lips, the sound of his rhythmic heart which worked to sync to mine.

Without his essence, the thrum of each of our hearts were off by a fraction of a beat.

I cocked my head. How'd I hear his heartbeat with such ease? Hear but not feel. I steadied my pulse, willing it, controlling it, forcing it to match the beat of the demon who held the entirety of it in his hands. Bez held every piece of me, and I'd gladly give him more.

Everything whirled, twisted, and my head dropped as grogginess hit me.

"Careful." Bez cradled me against his chest. "You're still healing. It'll take time before you can properly control your essence."

"Mine?"

"Don't overexert yourself. Rest. Let the devil heal your riddled flesh."

My eyelids grew too heavy to keep them open.

"Rest." Bez stroked my hair, probably fixing my knotted curls. "We'll talk soon."

"That's right. I was in oblivion, and you found me," I whispered. "I met another demon there, too. It was wild. Then I saw you and everything you…"

Bez lifted me off the ground, unveiling his wings and wrapping us together like he'd covered me in a blanket. The tickle of feathers was soothing as sleep took hold.

28

Beelzebub

I stepped into the library, approaching Antoninus' tank. He'd taken to hiding in the sand of his aquarium, resentful of the relocation, and clearly concerned for Wally's wellbeing. It'd been a week and a half since I tore the devil essence away, untethering it from my being, and using it to fuel my boyfriend's recovery. During that time, Wally slept, essence working to mend his many fatalities, and attacking any and everything that approached him. The devil essence considered all a threat, so I had no choice but to move the scorpion familiar someplace else.

"It's time for you to eat." I dropped a cricket into the enclosure.

Antoninus scuttled away, ignoring the feast I'd acquired for him.

"Do you realize how hard it is to find your particular dietary delights?" I asked. "We're in the middle of fucking nowhere surrounded by snow and ice."

I laid it on a little thick, and Antoninus probably knew I had no difficulty acquiring his meal since Wally had researched several stores not too far out of the way for someone like myself with Diabolic speed and flight. After Kell dropped us in the Alaskan wilderness, Wally did what he did best—research, plan, and prepare for everything. I ground my teeth, hoping none of that would be lost when he awoke.

When.

He would wake soon, recovered, and ready for whatever came next. I'd make sure of it.

In the meantime, I had to contend with the worst familiar ever. Using telekinesis, I lifted the scorpion back over to his prey. "Eat the damn bug or I'll eat you."

Antoninus hissed.

"Fine, you're right. Eating you is barbaric. I'll squish you, instead. Step on you until your cheap buggy armor cracks and breaks. Then I'll tell Walter one of the Diabolics must've stomped you to death." I grinned, menacingly and hiding all the sadness which came from speaking Wally's name. "Not a lie, either, because I will stomp you to death."

Antoninus clacked his claws, hissing as he snatched up the pathetic cricket who'd dropped his guard near the morose scorpion. Antoninus had not enjoyed a second of Wally's absence, and I could hardly blame him.

As the scorpion slowly slaughtered his meal, I trudged out of the library in search of my next distracting chore to fill my day.

Paws scratched at the bedroom door, and I zipped through the villa until I arrived beside a gloomy Sunny, a somber Cloudy, and a stoic Stormy. All three personas of the Cerberus pup had lost their spark without Wally, wishing to cuddle next to him as he slept.

"Let's go." I snapped my fingers.

Weather whimpered, giving me sappy wide eyes as the flames of his irises dimmed.

"That bullshit doesn't work on me, hound. If I've told you once, I've told you a thousand times—Wally cannot be disturbed." I conjured a small black flame in my palm. "And you are a bed hog that would get all three of your heads lopped off by essence if you took one clomping step into that room."

Stormy huffed; the fire in his eyes locked onto mine. Sunny perked up, cocking his head as I bounced the fireball between my hands. Even Cloudy blinked a few times, curiously studying the tasty treat of Diabolic flames.

"Sit."

Weather obeyed, tail wagging excitedly. I brought the fire close to Sunny's snout. Cloudy attempted to chomp down but I diminished the flames to crackling embers instantaneously, which he still licked off my palm, greedily indulging in the blistering crunchy snack. Little piggy.

"How many times have I warned you about that, Cloudy?" I recreated the flames, condensing them tight and small in my hands, adding a trickle of wind that would add to the buoyancy, giving it a real ball-like effect.

The one benefit of Wally's rest was it gave me a chance to properly train this untamed Mythic beast which Wally simply gave affection too freely, caving into the baby tyrants' demands, and refusing to scold his naughty behavior. Not in my home. I simply wouldn't allow it.

"Fetch." I hurled the ball down the hall, watching Weather race after it, working in tandem with his personas until he reached the first of many treats he'd get during our hike.

Stormy nipped Sunny's neck when the center head attempted to snap up the treat. Then, true to form, Cloudy whipped his head around, flipping the entire body the three shared as one over, and perfectly positioning himself to catch the fireball in his greedy gullet. Cloudy might have been mild mannered compared to the other two, but showed incredible tenacity when it came to food. A trait I completely understood. His appetite was better than the other two, as well, actually indulging in the time-consuming meals I'd made for myself as a distraction.

I walked over, tossing two more fireballs toward Weather. "A for effort, I suppose."

Sunny stuck out his tongue, clearly delighted by the sizzle of fire popping off it.

Stormy swallowed his fire, pouting, then glared at Cloudy and barked.

"All right, move out." I nodded toward the staircase and led the Cerberus out of the villa through the front doors of the foyer.

Since Kell had finally fixed the flaws in her tinkering, we could come and go from the villa as we pleased. No need to recite the former baron's dimensional traveling spell or rely on the singular entrance located in the helm where Kell hunkered down since we'd cleansed the place of Eligos and the other Diabolics.

I preferred the crunch of snow to the debris in the labyrinth. That was a chore on the checklist I'd mostly avoided working on. Too many spots there served as reminders of my failures.

Weather wiggled his body from heads to butt; the purple flames outshined the blue fire around his necks and grew into a sturdy mane that trickled flames down his spine, the tip of his tail, and around each of his ankles. Fire melted snow making Weather's plodding through the slush splash with boiling puddles.

I unveiled my wings, flying overhead and leading the hound on a trek across the barren wilderness for miles. When we looped back, I caught the faint, careful steps of a moose nearby. Hmm. I cracked my neck. Perhaps this was the perfect opportunity to train Weather in hunting for his meals since he'd spent his entire stay snacking on my food along with whatever fire we hurled his way.

A bell chimed, echoing loud in the open space and making all three heads of the Cerberus perk up, ears sticking straight up. Without a moment of hesitation, the hound bolted back to the villa.

"Stop," I shouted.

That vindictive old hag.

I flew after the pup, conjuring flames to lure his attention, which garnered nothing. He reached the front of the villa, nearly fumbling over his feet as he leapt for the raw steak Mora tossed in the air. Stormy and Cloudy clamped down on the meat, growling in a feud of tug-of-war over which would get to savor the filling flavor. Sunny took this adventitious opportunity to snap his jaw between the pair and swallow the perfectly seasoned meat he wouldn't have an ounce of respect for.

"I hate you." I glowered at the happy puppy who wagged his tail, then butted my knee with his center head, seeking praise and pets. "And I hate you more."

Mora smirked, ignoring my comment as she raked her fingers through her long, wavy curls. Now that we'd dealt with the Diabolic threats, she'd put Maurice back in storage and jumped into a different host body. A petite blonde, wearing a long-sleeved, low cut cocktail dress with a poofy bottom.

"That was my last steak."

"It can't be helped," she replied. "You've been feeding him scraps all week."

"And fire. More than the little bastard deserves."

Sunny frowned, the kind of judgy stare he must've learned from Wally. I turned my head. It wouldn't work on me.

"Magic doesn't have the necessary calories a growing baby like him needs." Mora extended her hands, petting Weather, deliberately avoiding Stormy's head since he wanted none of her affection or anyone else's.

"Oh, shut up."

"You can still go track your moose," Mora said, a coy smile which remained the same no matter what body she possessed with new features. Of course, she was listening in on our hike, probably evaluating the shift of my posture when I honed in on the nearby hunt. "You can get more steaks and I can make jerky. Yum."

"Now that Weather's satiated, no thanks to you, he won't want to go tracking." Which meant I'd have to attempt that training another day, another day without Wally.

"Well, since you're done with your chores, perhaps you can join me in the helm. I'd love to share some news on the progress Kell and I have made."

"What have you been doing to my home?"

"Mine too." Mora winked, letting out a devious and destructive giggle. "Squatter's rights."

I groaned, holding back a few profanities, then braced for whatever updates her and her paramour had added.

"I know you suspected I was plotting something when I arrived," Mora said.

I tsked. I knew she had something devious planned.

"And I did intend on telling you all about it once I'd settled how this magic functioned and arranged everything precisely after we found the perfect spot. But that Fae baron turned out to have created more obstacles than anticipated in the form of that tedious knight and the other Diabolics."

"Just spit it out."

"Oh, Bezzy. You know the best girls don't spit."

"What do you mean, perfect spot?" I raised my brows, eyeing the fields of snow in every direction.

"Well, remember when I said the Collective had no interest in this state. It also turns out—"

Wally coughed, tussling in the bed, in search of a glass of water that hadn't been waiting for him. Water I inconsiderately forgot to leave at his bedside. My eyes tightened on Mora who studied my face before I vanished in a blur.

"Guess I'll just tell Weather all about my intentions." The sound of Mora petting the pup faded once I reached the bedroom and swung the door open.

"Wally."

He sat up, observing the destruction of our bedroom. Devil essence had busted the dressers in half, stabbed holes through the walls and floor, broken the few portraits I left, shredded clothes hidden peacefully in the closet, and shattered the glass windows along with the planks I'd replaced them with twice to keep out the cold. Stone incantations turned out to be the best salve for this issue.

"What the…" Wally tilted his head, absorbing the destruction he didn't intend, and didn't have a part in.

"I might've celebrated Eligos' death a bit boastfully." I grinned. "Apologies. It started out playful, teasing you to wake up, then I went overboard as per usual."

"It's fine." He looked up at me, staring with pure black eyes. Not a trace of demonic energy—merely pure, undiluted devil essence.

"I guess there's no room in there for demon essence." I snickered. "Black eyes. Quite *becoming*, and you know I will be cu—"

"What?" Wally's eyes bulged with shock over the statement I'd failed to bury with humor.

He took heavy, confused breaths as the lovely hazel irises and whites of his eyes returned in true form, overpowering the essence inside him, which eased my fears. Wally was strong enough to handle anything, even housing devil essence and keeping it in check.

"What do you mean no room for a demon? What does that mean?" Wally asked, the desperate creak in his voice needed answers, explanations, things he could sort and study. That much I could give to him.

"When I devoured a piece of Beelzebub, I had to use the entirety of my demon essence to repress the single fraction of his." I approached, sitting on the bed beside him. "It was enough to overpower and subdue that tiny piece."

"Can you give me more?" Wally bit his lip, longer than usual as he fumbled for the right words. "More of your essence?"

"No. It would be destroyed on contact."

"What? Why?" Wally trembled as I kept strong in my explanation. "How?"

"Essence, like all things Diabolic, battles for dominance and control and territory. If I gave you my essence, that which resides in you would see my presence as a threat and obliterate it." I knew this because the bits of my essence that traveled inside of Wally when I poured the devil into him had all been snuffed out in a matter of seconds. The essence I'd poured into him every single day he'd slept and recovered was also eradicated instantly. "It wants to live, and now it's living inside of you, and in exchange it will ensure you live. It doesn't want to share, true to form for any devil. Even a piece of one."

"So, that means we won't be able to…"

"It means we'll never be able to bond again because the devil essence inside you won't allow it," I explained, running my hand against his thigh, testing the perimeters of his unconscious defenses. Nothing. It seemed the essence remained obedient so long as he remained aware. "This is good, though. You'll be safe from any and all demons. It's also not enough devil essence for sentience, so I don't have to fear for your mind."

Wally sniffled, cupping his hand around mine. It might've pained him more to lose our bond than it did me. And the idea of never truly, fully feeling him again cut more than any pain I'd suffered in Hell.

"But I'm sorry. If I'd done better our link wouldn't have been severed."

"Can you take back your devil essence?"

"It was never really mine." I shrugged, still adapting to the loss of power.

"It was. You earned it. I just died."

I caressed Wally's face, gently dabbing the welling tears. "I scavenged a bloody battlefield of demons against a devil. You fought. You fought the strongest demon I'd ever known in Hell, and unlike me, you won. You earned this."

"Well, guess I just have to hold out, wait until this essence fades away and hope there aren't any major complications in the meantime." Wally had an inquisitive expression, gears of his beehive mind grinding and whirling with thoughts.

"Devil essence, unlike demon's, doesn't fade," I said, gesturing to myself. "Otherwise, it would've been lost to me centuries back."

"Right. Duh." He huffed. "And you can't take it back?"

"Maybe one day, but you need it after all the Diabolic essence you consumed shredded your body."

"I'm so stupid. I knew not to do that, but I wasn't smart enough to figure out something better." He dropped his head in defeat of his own thoughts. "Anything better."

"You're the most brilliant, beautiful, methodic person I've ever known." I kissed his warm forehead, the heat of Diabolic essence changing the integrity of his mortal body in ways I had no idea how to comprehend yet. "I will note, the longer this essence is connected to you, the less likely it'll be that we can remove it."

"I'll be like this forever?"

"I wish I knew. You're the first mortal devil in existence," I explained. "I've known demons to live with a piece of their devil inside them for millennia, unable to detach from the essence unless killed by another Diabolic. Fun fact—because you love those—Lucifer was not as popular a devil as modern fiction would depict, and his demons slaughtered that beautiful bastard forever ago, marking him the first devil to die so-to-speak at the hands of rebellious Diabolics."

"We should run tests, form some type of case study. I don't like not having facts to rely on, texts to reference."

"We can do it all, but I imagine this will be a learn as we go kind of experience." I raised my eyebrows. "You know, your favorite thing: improvising."

He shuddered.

"I'll miss being connected to you, but I don't need the essence to feel connected to you," Wally said, skirting the subject until he had a course of action for his research. "I've felt our connection since the day we met."

"You mean when I tried to murder you and neither of us realized you'd stolen my essence?" I teased. "To be clear, we were connected that day."

"First off, I didn't steal." Wally held up a single finger, indicative this was an infallible fact, and he wouldn't hear otherwise. "I'm not a thief."

"I think a certain fairy at the Fae Divinity would disagree with that sentiment, seed stealer."

Wally rolled his eyes, ignoring my comment on the Fae Divinity—an event that likely soured all his wonder over the mysterious Fae. "I don't mean during the attack on the estate where we first spoke and had like the worst introduction in the history of introductions. I mean, the actual first time. The day I walked into the repository."

I swallowed hard, my throat constricted as my voice fell silent, unable to utter a response in the form of a quippy comment or clarifying question.

"You may not realize this, but I was fanboying over all the artifacts in the repository on my first day of work. First week. Month. Okay, year."

Oh, I realized. He gushed daily, hourly. I could clock it by the second on when his next delighted discovery would lead to an unnecessarily long tangent explaining the history of whatever trinket he'd been tasked with cataloging.

"On that first day, though, I was immediately entranced by the essence stirring in the Diabolic orb. Essence I wasn't allowed to ask about because, well, Remington never liked too many inquiries on the topic."

Burying my disdain and memories of Abe, simply grateful the prick had died, I reminisced on the doe-eyed boy fresh out of the academy, working in the repository after having failed his practitioner exam. I grinned, thoughts about all the mocking jokes I'd made of his longing gaze, the delicious puns Wally had never heard me make about his failures over the years.

I'm glad he never saw me like that. Not truly.

In the orb, I was my most jaded, bitter, and broken, believing everything I'd endured in Hell, in the mortal realm, had led to an unending sentence in that damned orb.

That hadn't turned out to be true though, thanks to Wally's intervention, I found my freedom from Abe's imprisonment, and an early reprieve from the foul intentions Eligos and Novus had in store for my future as they pulled the strings behind the curtain.

And now, I had the chance to continue growing with Wally, becoming whoever I wanted to be with him at my side.

"Besides, we both know I can have you inside me whenever I want." Wally smiled, goofy and embarrassed at his own terrible joke.

"Certainly, considering this dick doesn't quit." I leaned in close, savoring how his ears burned red and relishing the taste of his skin as I grazed my teeth along a blushing ear, making my way down his neck, nibbling, kissing, and letting the sensation envelop Wally. "If you're feeling well, perhaps we can test some of your new physical limitations."

His pulse thrummed faster, body warming, and I found myself in complete bliss.

"Like for research purposes?" he whispered, hands finding their way onto my body.

"Precisely."

He snickered as I went to kiss him. "Hi, Tony."

My face fell flat, and I gazed at the scorpion perched atop Wally's head, nestled between his curls like the worst adorned crown in history.

I sighed, realizing I shouldn't have hastily rushed to Wally's bedside without properly securing the door. The heavy plodding steps of Weather bolted up the steps, down the hall, and the Cerberus barreled into the room, lunging onto the bed. I prepared to catch the pup in a telekinetic hold, but Wally beat me to it.

Darting off the bed in blurred speed, he caught the rambunctious beast in his hands, holding the hound that easily weighed two-hundred pounds. He held the massive puppy above his head, his hands scooped under Weather's front legs, cupped across his chest while the back paws dangled, nails digging into Wally's bare chest as the Cerberus searched for his footing. Wally had gotten so strong thanks to the devil essence circulating inside him the nails didn't leave a single reddened mark on his pale flesh.

"Sorry, I tried to keep him entertained, but he sniffed out Wally's miraculous recovery and just had to say hello," Mora said, slinking into the bedroom.

"Yes, yes. I love all the kisses, Sunny." Wally lowered Weather to the floor, and the puppy rubbed against him, tail swatting Wally's thigh indicating he needed pets pronto.

"Cute undies." Mora eyed Wally whose face burned bright, almost turning the same shade of pink as his very revealing briefs. "Since you're awake, perhaps it's time we all discuss what Kell and I have done to the villa."

"Our villa," I said.

"You can keep it or what's left. I'm really only interested in one little piece of this prized palace."

I grumbled, while Wally rushed to dress himself.

29

Walter

"I think I'll meet you both in the helm." I held a shirt and pair of jeans in front of my chest and stomach as Mora kept her lingering gaze on me. "I'm going to take a shower."

"Care for company?" Bez asked, minxy as ever.

I grinned then grimaced. "I sort of just want to decompress for a minute. Also, I really need a thorough shower because I can smell myself, which is an indicator."

"I think you smell delicious," Bez said.

"Uh-huh. But you also think chocolate covered swordfish smells delicious."

"Truly divine taste, Bezzy." Mora sniffed the air like she was envisioning the meal only a Diabolic could enjoy, then rested her eyes back on me. "But he has a point. The Alden musk is a personal favorite."

I quirked a brow.

"Toodles." She waved her fingers back and forth. "Come along, Bezzy."

Bez reluctantly left without a word, giving me a moment to catch my breath. He whistled sharply, which was literally the worst type of flirty gesture. Weather's ears perked up, Sunny's expression softened with hesitation before my puppy trotted out of the room, following Bez and Mora without so much as a kiss or pet goodbye. Did Bez steal my Cerberus?

"You too, Tony. We'll catch up soon. So much to talk about." I lifted my familiar off my head, offering him a delicate breeze to carry him out of the room and reach the helm alongside the others.

The trickle of black lining the gust was unintended. I tensed. With Bez's essence, I had to focus, fixate on the entirety of the Diabolic essence that linked us together if I sought to cast demon abilities. The devil housed within me, didn't work the same way.

I was connected to Beelzebub, the literal devil locked away until the end of time. Thankfully, I couldn't feel him, but I remembered him. Somehow, pieces of Bez's memories had seeped into that devil essence which he'd held onto for centuries. There was so much of my boyfriend's past just beneath the surface of my memories, interwoven with the essence residing inside me, and as much as I wanted to explore my new powers, the lengths and capabilities I'd now be able to meet—I didn't want to unbox Bez's private history.

Stepping into the bathroom, I started the shower and allowed every thought to wash away. Okay. Not every thought. We'd need to have a conversation about Bez's memories laced within the essence now circulating through my body. In order to survive these changes, I needed to understand them, which meant I had to use these abilities. During my resurrection I glimpsed one of Bez's memories, and who knew how many more would surface in the future.

My body had changed. Nothing Diabolic in nature. I had to be honest, I wouldn't mind the tails. Not so much the wings. They seemed like a lot of work. No demony or devily appendages. I'd simply noticed my muscles had tightened. I wasn't sporting an eight-pack with the deepest V cut known to mankind like Bez, but for the first time in my life, I could see a bit of definition in my abs. The actual muscles began to appear slightly sculpted opposed to my soft, flat stomach.

Also as I stared at my reflection, I realized I was staring at my reflection. Crisp and clear, without my glasses. I snorted. Even the best incantations in the world couldn't permanently fix blurry vision or any senses, all of it temporary, reliant on constant recasting and maintaining fluid mana control. And contact lenses were the literal worst, whereas Lasik was roulette just asking for a bad outcome.

"Stop catastrophizing," I said, finally understanding the gist of the term.

I needed to stop fixating, dwelling on the worst possible consequence.

Point was, I liked my glasses and looked bizarre without them.

I hopped in the shower and scrubbed away the anxiety of a life I no longer led, ignoring the fact that someone had already washed away the blood and grime of battle while I rested unconscious. If Bez made one joke about sponge baths, I'd smack him.

Smiling, I focused on the life I had, one where Bez and I would bicker and joke and laugh and everything else. I tried not to dwell on what had happened… I'd died. I'd been resurrected. I was changed, presumably forever. Just enough devil essence to make me strong and immortal and Diabolic-esque, but not so much essence that it'd overtake me, burning through my flesh like before. This devil essence required a host, even without sentience, and as such would now work to keep me alive and well forever.

"Forever," I said. I repeated the word again and again until it left me with a semantic satiation, the experience when a word was uttered so many times that it seemingly lost all meaning. "What is forever?"

After I stepped out of the shower, I dried off and tossed on my clothes.

"You're planning to do what?" Bez shouted so loudly I heard him from the opposite end of the villa. "The fuck you are!"

"Hear me out, Bezzy," Mora whispered.

I cocked my head, drifting down the hall. Bez wasn't that loud. I mean, it was Bez—he was loud. But this came from enhanced senses. I focused on the grinding gears throughout the home, shifting, clicking, controlling all the magic weaved between every single speck of the foundation. Grimacing, I shook it all away. No. No, I did not like heightened hearing and suddenly understood why Bez preferred to dull his sensory extensions. That'd be the first thing I would ask him to teach me.

Whether curious for what infuriated Bez or eager to see him with his oh-so-trademarked scowl, I darted ahead in a blur arriving at the helm instantaneously. "What's going on?"

"Wally, you're all better!" Kell smiled, approvingly. "About time. Although, without your pestering I was finally able to finish all my lovely renovations."

I rolled my eyes. Of course, she'd taken advantage of my literal death to make changes she knew I'd oppose.

Kell had changed her hair, either through her recovery, a glamour, or possibly wig. In any case, the pink and black streaked pixie cut with a wavy top and short sides looked great on her.

She wore a sleeveless, backless white blouse indicating all her burns had healed in the time I'd been asleep.

"Well? What's the up and up?"

"Mora is gonna destroy the villa," Bez blurted.

"I'm not going to destroy it. I'm circumventing the magic to bigger and better uses."

"Okay," I asked, keeping my tone steady. "Please explain."

"Certainly," Mora ruffled her blonde locks. The new host didn't have any noticeable Mythic features, which seemed true to form on the parts of Mora I knew—she preferred a human body, no mana or magic, just a regular person. "If you recall, Wally, I lost my Diabolic void after allowing you the privilege of using it, exposing my weavings throughout Seattle to the entire Collective."

"Privilege," Bez snapped. "He paid you an ancient, one-of-a-kind artifact."

Agatha's Heart. Something Kell had never used to my knowledge. Then again, it could've been tucked away in the storage of her witch's hat which seemed infinite.

"Can I finish?" Mora asked, lips pursed in frustration in a way I surmised only Bez could cause. "Anyway, once I tore down my shadows, I considered relocating. Something I've had to do at least once a century no matter how cautious and careful and considerate I am around Collective and Mythic Council territories. So I asked myself, why am I tiptoeing around these fools, again and again?"

"Because they'd slaughter you," Bez said. "Band together and take you out, even if it costs a few thousand lives."

"Precisely. I have no interest in going to war. I very much prefer cultivating allies, opposed to making everyone my enemy." Mora locked her brown eyes, no hint of essence in them, onto Bez. "Unlike some Diabolics I know."

He scoffed.

"So, what exactly are you going to do?" I asked.

"Thanks to Kell's mastery of the unknown, along with what Bezzy learned from Eli-dead, and of course, the sweet nothings you muttered while asleep, I'll be able to finally create my very own kingdom in the mortal realm." Mora posed, possibly for flair, or merely satiating her ego and ambition which was clearly as big as Bez had warned—if not bigger.

"Excuse me?"

"Using the cloaking technology, I'm going to create a city, hidden here in Alaska. It's outside of Collective control, not on top of any Mythic lands, and won't intervene with mortal dwellings. It'll be a haven completely adjacent from the mortal realm but an easy hop, skip, and a jump away for anyone who wishes to come and go when traveling this quaint world."

"And who would be invited to this city?" Bez asked.

"Anyone who pledges fealty, of course. Besides, I've made a lot of friends over the centuries and I'm tired of keeping to the shadows when I play with them." Mora sauntered toward the navigation system. "I know plenty of people who'd kill for the privacy I'm offering. Hell, I know plenty who've killed simply to maintain their privacy."

"How would this work, exactly?" I asked.

Bez scowled at me, offended I'd even consider it when our magical house was apparently at stake. Truthfully, I planned to shoot down whatever Mora and Kell proposed, but it was best I understood the ins and outs of the plan before I disassembled Kell's tinkering. There were still Diabolics locked away in the engine room, trapped and fueling the magical cloaking.

"So glad you asked." Kell strutted, showmanship clearly important. "I'll be taking the magic that cuts through dimensions, weaves around realities, creates its own pathways, and altering it into a specific transfixed location. That'll expand and explode around the wilderness, careful not to disturb anything thanks to trans-dimensional frequencies."

"Yes, I know how pocket portals work," I said. "I did work at the Magus Estate and have clearance to the Dimensional Atrium there."

"Exactly," Mora said. "Who didn't have access? This will be unlike those Fae gifts. It'll be undetectable to anyone whatsoever thanks to the—"

"Diabolic essence," I finished. "What will happen to that once you create your cloaked kingdom?"

"That's the drawback." Mora gestured to Kell.

"It's sort of a one-shot. Which I'll have to get exactly right on the first go," she explained. "Releasing the energy to create a pocket realm will completely eradicate the Diabolic essence we currently have, cementing a perfect veil which will hide all forms of tracking and detection. Unfortunately, I couldn't figure out how to keep the essence intact. It apparently requires a more delicate, patient process or whatever. With the Diabolic essence obliterated, it'll prevent the traveling functions in the villa or the city, which I really wanted to keep."

"No. It's perfect." I smiled, grateful the locked away Diabolics would find the same peace in oblivion as Agares when the final pieces of their essence were destroyed along with the villa.

"Perfect?" Bez pulled me aside, talking in a hush. "This house is perfect. Perfect for us. We can see the world and no one can see us. All the resources you could ever ask for are connected by all the various layers of dimensional weaving throughout this home. You realize by stripping the villa of all its magic, all those divided sections will collide, completely crashing into each other and destroying this home. There'll be nothing left."

"I'm fine with that. I don't need this place. We can get our own place. Assuming there will be homes available."

"I've got the best architects and construction team money can buy," Mora said. "Besides, the two Diabolics ruling this kingdom will require very special manors, exuding our glory, not something as pedestrian as what the pretentious, former baron built."

"If it's something you want, I can try," Bez said to me, gruff and unenthused.

"Come on, Bezzy. You know I always get what I want." Mora stepped in close, raking her fingernails down his blazer and dress shirt. "And what I want is a kingdom for us: the Demon and her Wicked Witch, alongside the Devil and his Misfit Mage."

"I'm no longer a devil."

"Something I would really like to revisit because I feel late to the party and like the invitation I got said casual, then everyone showed up chic."

"Yes, yes, dearest." Mora waved her hand. "You can yell at me later."

"Oh, there will be more than yelling. We're talking spankings. Lots of reprimands about honesty."

I scrunched my face at Kell's comment and Mora's delighted smirk.

"Bezzy, nothing has to change. No one has to know."

"Fine. Whatever. You all do what you want." Bez zipped away.

"I'm gonna go talk to him." I nodded toward his fading blur. "You two do whatever you two have planned. Just promise not to destroy the place while we're all still inside it. Especially with Tony and Weather."

Tony clacked his claws and Sunny yapped.

"I'd never do something so reckless." Kell winked. "You should know me better than that by now."

I chased after Bez, reaching the bedroom where he sat and sulked.

"What's wrong?"

"Nothing."

"It's something." I sat close to Bez, my thigh pressed against his.

"It's a lot to consider, all changing so quickly." He furrowed his brow. "And I knew she was up to something, which I should've paid attention to. Instead, I was distracted."

"Because of me. Because I died."

He lay his hand on my shaky knee, a knee I hadn't even realized nervously bounced. "No. Never. Focusing on your recovery was the only thing keeping me afloat or grounded from thoughts that spiraled in every possible direction."

"Like?"

"When I told you the truth… Since sharing my secret, it was a weight lifted from centuries of fear. Fear of what would happen if someone learned the lies I'd cultivated guising myself as Beelzebub. Then the worst did happen. I confessed to Eligos so he'd spare you—realizing his plot wouldn't work—which he responded to crudely, because it turned out he knew all along."

I listened as Bez explained it all, Eligos' plan for his piece of devil essence, how he and Novus created the orbs, the influence and guidance they whispered to Magus Remington.

"You're worried what happens if the rest of the world finds out?"

"Yes. No. Maybe. I don't know. I just liked the idea of being here in the villa, hidden away for none to see. However long we needed. You could learn and grow and adapt. I could, I don't know."

"It seems like the city, the kingdom, Mora wants will offer that too."

"Doubtful. She likes busy places, meeting plenty of new and malleable people."

"We could kick her out. Change the locks, put up a sign that says no girls allowed in the demon boys' clubhouse." I nudged his shoulder with mine, watching his face light up with a smirk. "We'll post Weather at the front door, guarding our little oasis. Tony, too. He's small but far more ferocious."

"No. I just want to make sure you're okay with it. Losing this place."

"Bez, as long as I'm with you, I'm happy wherever we go." I interlocked my fingers with his, resting my head on his shoulder.

"Your hair smells inviting." Bez moved his thumb, massaging the skin between my thumb and index finger. "Perhaps we can table this conversation and discuss more important matters?"

"Such as?" I played coy, turning my head to meet his gaze.

Bez kissed me. Gentle like he wanted to test my reaction, the delicacy of my resurrected body. I invited his tongue with my own, playing with the tongue ring he'd glamoured—or possibly pierced in his new host body, one that resembled Bez so completely I'd forgotten what this person looked like before the composite took hold.

Bez broke his lips away from mine, continuing his kisses along my neck and shoulder.

He ran his hands under my shirt, lifting it, and licking my chest, my nipple, covering my face with the fabric as he gave up helping me undress and kissed my abdomen. Clawed fingers gently brushed and tickled my skin, wet lips kissed my stomach, sending a blissful jolt of static. Buried beneath this shirt was suffocating in the most exhilarating sense. I fumbled to free myself, knowing full well I'd done this to Bez on more than one occasion when seeking to tease his cock before he freed himself. He'd stripped my pants off and I still hadn't wriggled loose from the tangled tee.

Dammit. At least Bez had the excuse of horns getting in his way.

I flexed my biceps, shredding the cotton holding me back, and sucked in a deep breath as Bez's warm mouth swallowed my tip, running his tongue along every nerve ending. I checked for horns. Nothing. Duh.

Bez had a minxy expression, running his tongue ring down my shaft.

I panted, enticed.

"Take off your clothes," I demanded.

"I'm busy." He swallowed my cock, rubbing his fingertips—not claws—against my hips, sending sparks that made me thrust into him again and again, lost in pleasure.

I pushed him off, knocking him onto the floor, lying on his back. Carefully, I unraveled the loose knot of his tie and yanked it off, simultaneously ripping the buttons off his dress shirt with my other hand.

Straddling his hips, I grinded against them as I held his shoulders down and leaned forward, kissing him. Indulging in the taste of his lips, I released my grip. Big mistake.

Bez spun me off him with my face pressed against the floor, positioning my knees and adjusting my hips. He trailed his tongue up my spine, one column at a time, patiently, then zipped across the room—each step a slow-moving act where the world itself stilled as my eyes locked onto the blurred actions with precision—retrieving a small bottle from the drawer. He returned, continuing to kiss my back as he stroked himself, lubing his cock.

"I love you, Wally."

"I love you, too." I bit my lip as he entered me.

"Say my name." He held my hips, taking slow strokes easing his full length inside me. "I need to hear you say it. Please, Wally."

"I love you, Bez."

He thrusted all the way in.

"Bez," I moaned.

Again.

"Bez." I quivered.

Each time I uttered his name, he pumped faster and harder into me, eliciting the deepest pleasure. Every muffled grunt and satisfied groan, unable to utter his name further only enticed him to pound with more furious passion. Even lacking the link, the bond which intertwined our sensations hadn't dulled this moment. If anything, I felt more connected to Bez now. I wanted more than anything to feel his satisfaction, his pleasure, exciting me to work harder to understand every aspect of his body. Something we spent the last six months mastering of one another.

He stroked my cock, rubbing the precum along the head. It brought me so close I thought I'd explode until his touch stopped leaving me pulsating a breath away from cumming, edged right to the precipice of orgasming—something very unlike Bez who'd always preferred to make me cum first, watch me twitch in ecstasy before continuing only to make me convulse all over again, demanding I satisfy his delights by having my own.

"I'm sorry. I just…" He paused, putting all his weight onto my back and resting his head on the back of mine. "Do you still see me as Bez? When you learned the truth, you were fine. But am I still Bez without the devil? Was I ever?"

I grabbed his hand, pulling it close to my mouth. He'd balled a fist, not desiring or perhaps fearing affection and comfort. I stared at his tight knuckles.

"You are whoever you see yourself as. I've seen you as Bez, the wicked, mean devil." I kissed a knuckle. "I've seen you as Bez, the gentle, caring devil." I kissed his next knuckle. "I've seen you as Bez, the brave, unrelenting demon who's saved me more times than I can count." I kissed a third knuckle. "You are the man I love. Devil. Demon. Diabolic. You hold my heart, and you always will."

"Really?"

"Yes." I turned, catching a glimpse of his watery crimson eyes. "Are you worried what others will think, seeing you as a demon, not a devil?"

"Fuck everyone else." He playfully popped his hips against my ass, and I gasped at the sudden, heavy thrust. "Sorry."

"I'm fine." I moved my hands, bracing for any playful excitement.

"I suppose that's what I hate, worrying what you… Not you." Bez kissed my nape. "You're powerful, brave, unrelenting—a real annoying quality—"

"Hey!"

"I mean that in the best way. You make me considerate of more than myself. Something I've struggled with for too long." Bez moved, gentle, but at a steady pace. "I spent too long in Hell, serving the needs and attention of others, so much so I forgot myself. Lost myself. Dreamed up a demon knight friend who in the end didn't remember a damn thing about me, not really. Even so, when I arrived here—all I wanted was to become someone who'd be remembered, worshiped, feared."

"Loved?"

"No." His lips quivered against my nape. "I'd never understood it. Thought it a mortal daydream. A fantasy Mora lived in."

"Bez." I ran my fingertips along his slow-moving hips. "Do you want to talk about it? I mean, without your cock inside me?"

We both snickered.

"Yes, I do. I want to talk to you about everything, ever, always, Wally."

I turned to kiss him, but Bez wrapped his arms under mine, then around the back of my head, pinning me as his teeth grazed my neck. "But right now, I want to fuck you."

He waited, running his fingers through my damp curls.

"Yes," I moaned.

He thrusted quickly, excitingly, pounding into me for at least the next fifteen minutes from what the clock indicated when I glanced up in a haze of ecstasy. Each minute passing made my body tighten, ready and unable to hold back. I came, clawing my fingers along the floor as I erupted with fiery passion. Literally.

Black flames trailed the floor, inadvertently cast by the spark of my nails against the hardwood.

"Bez," I said, biting back a whimper as he continued thrusting. "Bez…"

"Don't worry about it." He readjusted, releasing his hold, and turned my head—all while still taking steady strokes—pressing his cheek against mine so we could watch the fire trickle toward the wall, engulfing it. "I've got it under control."

And he did. His essence kept the fire I'd cast in check as he continued. I lost myself in the dance of the flames, the heat licking my skin, and the arousing grunts Bez made. Slick sweat coated each of us from the ongoing passion, the fire, the desire. Savoring every second, my body shuddered in sync with Bez's as he took twitchy thrusts when he came. He growled, feral and unwilling to stop. Resting on top of me, he kissed my shoulders, taking easy thrusts.

He stopped, leaving himself buried in me, continuing to kiss, lick, and nibble my skin.

We lay there, silently staring into the fire that slowly consumed the bedroom wall. Each flick of the flames held in the careful control Bez possessed, and I couldn't wait to fully understand this side of myself. A side I could share and learn from with him. A side that'd be ours and my own all at once. It was a paradox of feelings, feelings I couldn't wait to discover with Bez.

"I love you, Bez." The fire ate away the self-portrait of Baron Novus, the one Bez had punched a hole through. "We should probably put out the flames before they reach the closet. We might be destroying the villa, but I'd rather not trash everything inside. You know there are thousands of one-of-a-kind artifacts in here, ancient tomes, collectible…"

"Shush." He hugged me tightly, sweaty and strong. "Let's just enjoy the bedside fire and the quiet crackle. No need for lectures."

"I wasn't lecturing."

Bez pulled his hips back a smidge, bumping them into me, making our skin slap. "This counts as cock warming, for your information."

"It does not, and everyone just says FYI. They've even got a store."

"Which flopped, like the malls I told Mora would fail. But does anyone listen to me? No."

“You’re insufferable.” I stifled a giggle, arching instinctively as Bez pressed himself closer.

“I know.” He lay on top of me, nuzzling my hair. “Sorry.”

“Never be sorry. Be annoying. Talk to me. Talk it out until we figure it out. Annoy me. Did I mention you’re annoying?”

“Dick.”

“You love it,” I said. “And so do I.”

“I love you, Wally.”

30

Beelzebub

I spent the past two weeks really considering Wally's words, his curiosity, and who I wanted to be seen as moving forward. Thankfully, since setting up Mora's private city required blowing the villa to hell, I kept busy packing away everything deemed worthy of preserving. According to Walter, that included just about everything he could pry from the walls and floor. It was actually surprising he didn't attempt taking the walls and floors—especially the ones crafted from golem hides.

Flying outside, I carried a stack of overstuffed boxes bound together by telekinesis and dropped them into a cramped storage unit. A gorgon's eyes rested on the flick of my tails, slithering through the snow in a similar pattern with theirs. Carefully, I locked my gaze with his, watching his scales shiver at the mere presence of a Diabolic, likely intimidated by my crimson eyes. It could be the cold, yet the incantations thrown about by mages to offer pockets of warmth made me doubt the chill got to the serpent. A pair of harpies whispered to each other, commenting on the added depth of gray to my contour feathers and at the length of the flight feathers. If they only knew the flight feathers weren't the largest appendage I had to show off. I winked, showing zero hesitation.

Thanks to Mora's highly specialized construction team, the Alaskan wilderness now swarmed with Mythics of all kinds and misfit mages looking for reprieves from Collective oversight. She'd assembled quite a mass of willing souls to offer assistance in the creation of this city. All the same, I didn't want any of them getting ideas over the belongings from the villa. I used a tail to pull down the rolling door, then lay one of Wally's premade incantations to seal it.

Soon, they'd know the truth of things. My heart thumped and my hands shook. This wasn't anxiety swallowing me, but elation creating a buzz at all the possible reactions, hopeful for something good and okay if it wasn't. I was okay because I had Wally for each step, each choice, each new experience in figuring out who I was again. Who I ever was.

Weather trudged through the snow, playing and sniffing everyone who crossed his path all while investigating the trailers set up for lodging. He yapped at the goblins posted by the trucks packed with supplies. Stormy growled at a few werewolves on a smoke break, proudly asserting himself as he should. With Antoninus perched atop Sunny's head, the young Cerberus wouldn't have anything to fret. That fiendish familiar had become quite protective—and bossy, using the hound as personal transportation through the snow.

A minotaur took heavy breaths, the fiery coals in his chest burning hot, and turning the snow his hooves stepped through into sloshy muck. He directed golems of stone and steel to lay the foundation for Kell's contraption, the one which would redirect the villa's energy. Mages kept our presence glamoured from any passersby, which seemed unnecessary, but apparently satellites had become quite popular. Nymphs frolicked through the snow, whispering to the wildlife, encouraging them to explore further out, at least until the cloak was up and the land would return to them as the city remained hidden behind a veil.

Mora snapped her fingers, proudly displaying her Diabolic abilities as she zipped about continuing to issue directives for all those in attendance.

I didn't know if I wanted to live in a city of magical beings escaping the oversight of the Collective or Mythic Council, but I liked the idea of a private world to share with Wally. One where he could study to his heart's content, learning anything, meeting anyone, and mastering the essence I'd gifted him without fear of jealous demons, hateful mages, or curious Fae like the dead baron.

These were all thoughts I could contend with another day, for now I'd gladly stay on task. I returned to the villa to gather more boxes.

"Kell, I saw you drop that book into your hat," Wally said, carrying a box down the stairs.

"Come on, you won't miss one silly book about plant life, will you?"

"Was it actually about plant life?" Wally raised his brows.

Kell adjusted her witch's hat. "Would I lie to you?"

Yes. Yes, she would.

"Just make sure to give me the title of your plant book so I can properly log it as borrowed in the inventory list."

"Borrowed? Wait. You made an inventory list?" Kell pursed her lips, somewhere between a frown and surprise. "For everything here?"

"Of course." Wally beamed.

He'd hardly slept since recovering, his body buzzing with essence, and showing great strides early on in these many changes.

"Can't have you taking what we properly pillaged and plundered," I teased.

"Exactly." Wally winked, playful, light-hearted, and for the first time in a long while without the weight of the world or its many demanding pressures pressing down on him.

We finished packing everything from the library and moving it into storage, to which Kell attempted to slip another artifact in her hat unseen. I used a tail to pry it from her hands. She'd gotten better about lifting things, something undoubtedly learned from Mora's influence, but as the best thief among these fools, I wouldn't let anyone deprive Wally of his wants. Once the pocket dimension had been created, he'd nominate himself to account for everything, creating the perfect cataloging system, which Kell would definitely tweak. Mora wouldn't care because she clearly had bigger goals in mind, and I could enjoy the humor of their bickering.

Speaking of bickering, Kell had begun to call Wally's inventory system into question, so I took the opportunity of a deserved break and drifted toward Mora who instructed witches to set up preparations on conduits that'd funnel and disperse the Four Corners.

"Why the witch magics?" I asked. "Thought this was Fae and Diabolic workings."

"Had to make alterations on Kell's behalf," Mora said, flipping the blonde bangs from her face. "Plus, the Diabolic essence will end up eradicated. It's merely the match to spark the creation. Fae magic from the villa and witch magic will remain the kindling that keeps this place safe and empowered."

"And how will that work?"

Mora sauntered toward a case, unfazed by the knee-deep snow around her host's exposed skin in a short skirt. Opening the case, she revealed Agatha's Heart. A stone artifact strong enough to magnify any beings power to challenge an army if they so foolishly sought, such as the arrogant Ian who used it and myself to challenge the Collective.

“That’s the artifact Wally gave you back in Seattle.”

“Quite astute,” Mora said, delicately centering it in the freshly laid foundation.

“How long have you been planning this?”

“A few centuries.” She shooed the working golems. “The world’s a big place but everyone seems to have already laid their claim. Fighting over limited territory seems wasteful, so I thought I’d make my own. I could visit the splendors I enjoy and have someplace lovely to lay my head.”

“Hence why you needed this particular artifact.”

Mora crinkled her brow, almost confused by the accusation. “I’ve collected a lot of wonders over the years, knowing any one of them might be the key to giving me the kingdom I always wanted. It’s mere happenstance the artifact you and Wally retrieved is the one I’m using.”

“We ready to flip the switch?” Kell asked, delighted, and approaching with Wally at her side.

“I thought you said it was a button?” he asked.

“It’s a figure of speech.”

“With you, you never know.” Wally stared at the switch that’d ignite the secret city Mora dreamed up for a kingdom all her own. “So, this is the button? The one that’ll blow up the villa and set everything into motion?”

“Yes,” Kell said, adjusting her hat.

“And everything’s ready?” he asked, almost hiding that perfect minxy expression.

“Just about, but—”

I smirked at the glint in Wally’s lovely hazel eyes and the joy on his face as he jabbed the big red button reserved for Kell.

"What the fuck, Walter?" Kell snapped. "You didn't even let me finish what I was saying."

Agatha's Heart thumped.

"I thought you were done." He shrugged. "Your explanations are usually quicker."

Kell glared, visibly infuriated; her pulse beating almost as loudly as the slow drum of Agatha's Heart.

"Sorry." Wally had the cutest, coyest, fakest apologetic expression. "I thought this was one of those 'we do it together' things like with the lever."

"Lever?" Kell's expression twisted, probably unable to recall her own chaos of throwing the villa from gods-only-know-where to this secluded wilderness. "It wasn't. And we didn't."

"My bad. Guess I got excited."

"This was my big moment. A once in a lifetime opportunity and you pushed the button. My button to push. Without me."

"You should've joined in then, instead of rambling about all the rules and steps and precautions."

"When, Walter? You pushed the button and didn't even give me a chance to—"

The villa exploded, bright and beautiful. Black flames engulfed the snowy tundra, replacing it with blades of grass, gravel, and fresh soil all around for miles. The night sky above lit up, replaced by comets burning in every color of the rainbow. The icy wind was replaced by a perfect autumn breeze. The crunch of snow beneath our feet vanished because we no longer stood in the Alaskan wilderness. We were now in a private dimension, cloaked from all prying eyes, a single step away from the mortal world but a thousand hidden dimensional layers from it.

Black tendrils of essence stretched high overhead, alongside us, and deep in the earth below, weaving all over like tangling spiderwebs pulled tight. Colors of every kind illuminated from the essence, not reflective from the flurry of comets, but representative of the lingering traces of demons that dwelled, fractured and broken, still existing despite total loss of awareness.

Kell knelt in the grass, holding Agatha's Heart and muttering a spell. The sorcery spilled from her lips in waves, calling out to the tendrils. Essence latched to the heart. It beat, slow and steady like a drum announcing a great change.

And change it did. Every trace of Diabolic essence withered and faded, vanishing entirely, yet leaving behind a power tethered to the artifact and held in check by the vast amount of Mythic residue in the air.

Every breath held the taste of magic in it.

Wally held wonder in his expression, eyes curiously studying the trees sprouting all around, fields of flowers blossoming, hills and valleys stretching tall and wide, and riverbeds burrowing into pathways almost as intricate as the Diabolic webs. Finally, Wally rested his gaze on the essence, watching the spark of life fizzle away as every thread vanished. His smile lit up his entire face when the demons died, truly fading away to oblivion. Wally had explained how lost and trapped they'd all been thanks to Baron Novus' experiments. Even if we could've released them all, killed them all, I doubted Wally would want to keep the tainted villa. Admittedly, I enjoyed the serene sight of the home burning to rubble ash among the flourishing forest around it.

"This is the city you wanted to create?" I asked.

"First steps," Mora said. "That's why I've assembled a quality team to knock down this default Fae setting and make room for the growing kingdom we'll have."

"Deforestation on day one?" Wally shook his head. "Seriously?"

"Don't worry. As the kingdom expands, so will the life." Mora grabbed Kell's hand, leading her witch toward a gaggle of Mythics. "Come along, love."

“She seems really at home here.” Wally leaned on my shoulder, watching Mora usher orders.

“You know what they say, you can take the demon out of the monarchy but not the monarch out of the demon.”

“They also say you can take the researcher out of the repository but not the…” Wally furrowed his brow, pensive and confused. “Okay, sort of lost myself in the pun on that. Whatever. Let’s go check things out.”

Wally dragged me deep into the forest exploring, pausing to examine every single thing we crossed, while I spent the time studying him and the eagerness he had.

“The plant life here is amazing,” Wally said, leading us further down a trail. “It must be a Fae preservation tactic. You know they keep every form of life preserved in their realms, even extinct life. I should probably make a list of off-limit areas for Mora’s construction.”

“Why?”

“This place is huge; I’d hate for her to bulldoze everything, even if the dimension expands, we can’t be certain that means the same unique vegetation will return.”

“Well, that can wait.” I grabbed his arm, pulling him close. “Why don’t we explore for the time being, find the perfect place with the perfect view to plant our flags?”

Mora might’ve laid out where and what this city would look like, but if I planned on making it a home for Wally and myself, then I wanted to ensure we had the best spot to lay our heads each night.

“I can think of one flag you can plant and where you can plant it.”

“That’s a terrible pun.”

“You’re a terrible pun.” Wally turned, leaning in close.

"That doesn't even make—"

Wally kissed me, rough and with teeth and tongue, trailing his fingertips between the waist of my slacks. I savored the bite on my lower lip, the graze of his knuckles against my abdomen.

I went to grab him by the hips, but he zipped away.

"If you want to plant your flag," he said, hidden by the trees. "Then you'll have to catch me first."

I grinned, noticing his voice echoed from one direction but the light giggle that escaped his mouth came from a different one. "Gladly."

I chased Wally, unable to track his mana hidden by the essence, unable to track his essence hidden by the magic of this dimension, leaving me to rely purely on my senses. It didn't take long to locate him, even with the coverage of the forest. He lacked finesse in his movements, his feet pattering a bit too loudly against the soil, the "oomph" he let out when he bumped into a tree, and the instinctive scratch of his claws slashing bark defensively.

Still, I relished the delight in his giddy breaths—air he didn't require, yet craved out of habit or perhaps some uniqueness to being a living mortal fueled by true devil essence. We had time to figure it out, all of it.

We had forever.

Always.

Him and me.

And as such, I wanted to enjoy this game, take my time.

"There's a chance I'm too fast for Bez now, and I should—" He bit his lower lip to cover his whisper aloud, but it was too late. If his words hadn't been enough, the harder press of his teeth against his lip released a single blood drop before essence mended the wound. Even so, I tasted it in the air above every other lush aroma in the forest.

"Too fast for me?" I asked, having weaved in between the foliage, appearing behind a startled Wally.

I wrapped my arms around his waist, scooping him up before he could flee, and spinning him in circles. The laughter he released and the reddening of his ears made me smile.

"Guess I get to plant my flag now." I released him, only momentarily, before pinning him against a tree.

"Looks like it." Wally eyed the obvious bulge in my slacks.

My skin vibrated, preparing to vanish in a blur. "But perhaps you should have to catch me first."

"Come on, Bez." Wally grabbed me by the wrist, yanking me toward him, putting up far more resistance than I realized as I pulled free of his clasp.

Or attempted, anyway.

My footing wavered and I stumbled backward when trying to balance the weight of his incoming body, the buzz of darting away playfully, and the need to catch him. We spun into each other, crashing onto the ground.

"You said something about coming?" I smirked at him, laying atop me.

He huffed. "I hope that thud on your ass hurt."

"That's not very nice," I whispered, licking his ear.

As expected, Wally leaned closer nuzzling my neck. He bit my tie and pulled it, tugging me forward as he rose, and arched his back, straddling my hips.

"Yanking everything of mine but the one thing I want you to." I slapped his ass with both hands, squeezing them tight.

"Securing your cake?" he asked with a mouth full of fabric, which gave me a hundred different ideas for the evening.

"Always." I kissed his neck and ran my hands up his back, under his shirt to feel the full warmth of his body.

It didn't burn as hot as mine, but the magnitude of power radiating inside him sweltered in comparison to the mage I'd met.

He dropped the tie, preparing to kiss me.

Using one of my tails, I unknotted my tie and stuffed it back into his mouth. "Not yet."

He grumbled, playful, but glaring.

"You've got to earn it." I rolled on top of him, full of zeal and control, until something wrapped around my throat and pulled me back.

I lay flat on the ground; Wally slipped off my slacks in a single motion. My body tingled at the rush his assertive yearning created. He spit out my tie, then repositioned himself on top of my hips, grinding against my throbbing erection as he kissed me deep and passionately. His eyes were wide and fully black, a matching, slender forked tail waved behind him.

"My misfit mage has grown so much." I caressed his face.

"Huh?" His expression turned quizzical. "I was never really a misfit mage."

"You were mine. You always will be my misfit mage, no matter what the future brings."

"And you'll be my darling demon." He bit his lower lip, nervous hazel eyes returning to full form. "I mean, if of course, you want to be known as a demon. I'm still not sure how you feel about that. I know what you've said, what you've skirted around saying, what you've said without saying—and sure you think I don't realize that, but I totally catch the unsaid subtext you give off. Especially with deflective humor or horny antics—"

I planted a heavy, wet kiss on his lips. "I want to be known as a demon. The demon Bez, a trickster who fooled a billion beings into believing he was a devil."

"The demon who bested the devil, too." Wally rubbed my shoulders.

"I wouldn't go that far."

"I would. And hoping you can best one more right now."

I released all my tails.

"Question, though," Wally stated, completely lost from the moment and in one of his trains of thought. "Why the demon Bez and not, well I never asked because you never seemed interested in divulging, and it was really none of my business…"

He rambled on, in the cutest little way searching for the polite way to understand why I wanted a name of a devil who so cruelly taunted and terrorized and destroyed me for eons.

"I'm no longer that demon from Hell," I said. "I'm not sure I ever was. The name never fit me. I hated it, hated him, and I wanted to become someone new. I have. I've earned the name Bez. It's who I am. It's who I love to be. It's the name I relish making you scream as I plow you."

"Bez," Wally whined.

"Not quite the pitch I'm going for, but we've got time." I coiled one of my tails around Wally's, and wrapped the other two around his wrists, pulling his hands close to my chest.

His face was close enough to lick and so I did, tasting the sweet mortal man I loved seeped in essence.

A gust whirled around us.

"They're cute." I tilted my head past Wally's frazzled expression, staring at the small, black feathered wings that sprang out of his back. "Not very big, though. Doubt they'd carry a cherub."

He tried to catch a glimpse, unable to crane his neck that far.

"Trust me, they're adorable."

"Wasn't it you who said size doesn't matter?" He pushed forward.

The two of us rolled on the ground; I unveiled my gray-feathered wings, wrapping us each tight in the embrace, as I lost myself in Wally's lips, his touch, the quiver of his body as I stripped his clothes off. He moaned, aching for more, and I gladly delivered, thrusting into him.

THE END

ACKNOWLEDGMENTS

Thank you so much for returning for the second installment of Wally and Bez's adventures. I truly hoped you enjoyed the direction their journey went. It was an absolute blast to continue exploring Wally and Bez's relationship, their dynamic, and the love they have for each other. Something else I really enjoyed about this book was exploring more on Mora—including the introduction to Kell, the sweetest wicked witch you're likely to meet. Those two were an absolute delight and their dynamic is electric.

This book focused less on the Mythic world, less on the mage society, and allowed us to delve into the Fae world—well, in a sense—which is part of the Mythic world, but the Fae really do stand on their own among the elite Mythics. I also got to dive into more of Bez's past. Did anyone catch the references of Eligos before his evil knightly ways were revealed? I actually introduced him very briefly in book one. I wouldn't expect many to recall him since he had one scene which was quite chaotic and filled with revelations on Bez who wasn't actually Beelzebub. Anyway, if you love solving the mystery in a story, or like to have an idea of the foreshadowing for future installments, be sure to keep an eye on those innocuous minor characters. You never know what drama they could stir up in future installments.

I'd like to give a huge thank you to everyone who gave this book a chance. I hope you had as much fun reading about Wally and Bez's adventure as I had writing it. If you could be so kind, I'd greatly appreciate an honest rating and/or review for *The Misfit Mage and His Darling Demon*. Ratings and reviews really do help introduce books to potential readers.

AUTHOR BIO

MN Bennet is a high school teacher, writer, and reader. He lives in the Midwest, still adjusting to the cold after being born and raised in the South.

He enjoys writing paranormal and fantasy stories with huge worlds (sometimes too big), loveable romances (with so much angst and banter), and Happily Ever Afters (once he's dragged his characters through some emotional turmoil).

When he's not balancing classes, writing, or reading, he can be found binge watching anime or replaying Dragon Age II for the millionth time.

Author website: https://www.mnbennet.com

Amazon page:
https://www.amazon.com/stores/MN-Bennet/author/B0BLJJK5NF

Goodreads page
https://www.goodreads.com/author/show/23017668.M_N_Bennet

Made in the USA
Columbia, SC
06 February 2025

53138473R00214